KU-060-898

FRIENDS TO FOREVER

BY
NIKKI LOGAN

Nikki Logan lives next to a string of protected wetlands in Western Australia, with her long-suffering partner and a menagerie of furred, feathered and scaly friends. She studied film and theatre at university, and worked for years in advertising and film distribution before finally settling down in the wildlife industry. Her romance with nature goes way back, and she considers her life charmed, given she works with wildlife by day and writes fiction by night—the perfect way to combine her two loves. Nikki believes that the passion and risk of falling in love are perfectly mirrored in the danger and beauty of wild places. Every romance she writes contains an element of nature, and if readers catch a waft of rich earth or the spray of wild ocean between the pages she knows her job is done.

Visit Nikki at her website: www.nikkilogan.com.au.

For the Garvey clan (two-legged and four).
Thank you for your years of friendship
and your tolerance of my weird writerly ways.

To Liz for setting the bar so inspirationally high.

And to Rachel for keeping me sane
and on the right path with this one.

PROLOGUE

Ten years ago, Perth, Western Australia

'MARC, have you got a minute?'

Beth Hughes caught up with her best friend between classes and steered him away from the teenage throng doing a fast book change between fourth period and fifth. The rock that had taken up residence in her gut since she'd spoken to his mother seemed to swell in size.

Marc looked at her in surprise. Understandable, given the past few weeks of slow retreat on her part. If he'd refused point-blank to go with her she would have understood. A weak part of her wished he would. That would be easier all round.

'Three minutes, Duncannon.' Tasmin Major swanned past, a friendly smile on her Nordic face, tapping her watch. 'Geography waits for no one.'

'I'll be there,' Marc threw after her, trailing Beth around behind the water fountains, tension rich in his deep voice. She ducked between the back wall of the library complex and some badly pruned shrubs into a rubble-filled clearing she'd never visited before. The place others came to do their smoking. Their deep-and-meaningful conversations. Their making-out.

The location got Marc's attention completely. His steps slowed.

'Beth?'

Her pulse beat thick and fast, high in her throat, reducing even further the space for her breath. She sucked in a few mouthfuls of air and forced them down as she turned to face him in the privacy of the little space.

'What are we doing, Beth?' His face was cautious. Closed. She curled her fingers into a ball behind her. 'Does your boyfriend know you're here?'

She stared at him, forcing air past her lips, hating how he'd taken to saying the word *boyfriend.* 'Damien's in fifth period.'

'Where we should be. Or do grades mean less to you now that you hang with the beautiful people?'

Her eyes fell to the dirt he scuffed at his feet, heat invading her cheeks. 'I needed to see you.'

'You see me every day.'

In passing. 'I needed to speak with you.' She lifted her focus. 'In private.'

A grey tinge came over him. His body straightened even more. Not for the first time, Beth noticed how broad he was getting. Those shoulders that had made the swim team captain seek him out a few months back. The way his jaw was squaring off. As if a switch had flipped on his sixteenth birthday and a man had started breaking out of the scrawny exoskeleton she knew as Marc. Maybe she'd left this too late…

Her stomach tightened.

'You have to hide out to talk to me these days?'

She could have pretended to misunderstand but Marc knew her too well. 'I don't want to make trouble with you and Damien.'

'I'm pretty sure McKinley's already aware that we're friends, Beth. I've known you since fourth grade.'

'I don't want… He might read into it.'

'Then you might want to choose another location for this conversation. You do know what The Pit gets used for, right?'

Beth swallowed hard, her eyes dropping to his lips for a second. She forced them up. 'I just wanted privacy.'

The second bell rang and urgent footsteps sprinting into classrooms petered out. Everything around them fell silent. Marc widened his feet and crossed his arms across his chest. 'You got it. Every other student at Pyrmont High is now in class.'

'I'm changing streams,' she blurted before she lost her nerve. 'I'm switching to B.'

Marc stared at her, his nostrils flaring. 'You're changing out of the classes we've been taking all year? Into McKinley's stream?'

'Not because of Damien—'

'Right.'

'I want less science. More arts.'

'Since when?'

'Since now.'

'B-stream is soft, Beth.'

'It has Literature and Philosophy in it. They're uni entrance subjects.'

'You're switching to avoid me.'

The rock in her gut doubled in size. 'No.'

Yes.

'Why?'

A throbbing started up behind her eyes. 'This has nothing to do with you—'

'Bull. You've been backing off from me since term

started. What's going on? No room for a mate in your busy new social schedule, Ms Popularity?'

'Marc—'

'I may not be as smart as you, Beth, but I can see which way the wind is blowing. Is McKinley threatened by me?'

She shook her head. Damien's field of vision was far too narrow for him to notice how Marc was filling out, growing up. He had way too much going on in his life, in his world, to worry about what some science geek was up to. It never occurred to him that Beth would see Marc as anything other than a buddy. An *old* buddy. The expendable buddy she'd had until *he* came along.

And now Damien just expected that she'd switch camps. Just like she switched streams. But since that fed right into what she knew she had to do…

'So that's it, huh? That's what you wanted to tell me—that you're switching classes?'

Beth struggled to take in a breath. He made it sound so minor. But still so ugly. Her words grew tight. 'It means we're only going to have one class together.'

'I know. The best thing about B is that it means only seeing McKinley once a week.' He glared at her. 'You're that desperate to get away from me?'

She would like nothing more than to have Marc Duncannon in her life for ever. But, as it turned out, that wasn't going to work. Guilt tore at her insides and thick shields shot up into place. 'The world revolves around the sun, Marc, not you.'

His face paled and the guilt turned inward, digging into the flesh around her heart. The truth was Marc Duncannon revolved around Beth Hughes and always had. Or, more rightly, the two of them rotated in a complicated, connected orbit. Something both their parents felt was unhealthy.

For him.

If it was just his nut-job mother who thought it, Beth wouldn't have given it another thought. But her own mother agreed and so did her father. And Russell Hughes was never, ever wrong. After a long and tearful conversation, Beth gave him her word that she'd cool things down with Marc for a while. See what happened. And she'd never broken her word yet.

'If you're not doing it to be closer to McKinley and you're not doing it to be away from me then why are you doing it?'

'Why can't I just be doing it for me? Because I want to?'

'Because you don't make decisions like that, Beth. You never have. You plan stuff. You commit.'

'So I've changed my mind. It happens.'

Not to you. It was written loud and clear all over his face. Could he tell she was lying?

'What about uni? Biology?'

A fist squeezed deep in her chest. Damn him for not just letting her go. Why was he pushing this so hard? Forcing her to hurt him more. 'That was your dream, not mine.'

He blinked, then stared. 'After all this time? You've been on board with that for three years.'

She shrugged, faking ambivalence she absolutely did not feel. 'Seemed like a good enough idea at the time.'

'Until something better came along? Or should I say someone?'

'This is not about Damien. I told you.' He stepped

closer and Beth retreated towards the library wall. When had he grown that big?

'I know what you told me. I just don't believe it.' He towered over her. 'We've been friends for eight years, Beth. Half our lifetimes. And you just disappear the moment a popular guy comes sniffing? Are you truly that desperate for affection?'

The library wall pressed into her back. She knew he'd be hurt, and she knew he lashed out when he was hurt. She'd seen him do it with his mother. 'People change, Marc. We all grow up. Maybe we've just grown apart?'

'I know you're changing, Beth. I've watched you.' His eyes glazed over, a deep russet brown, and skimmed her, head to toe. She'd never been more aware of the changing shape of her body. Then he sneered, 'I just never expected you'd change into such a cliché.'

'I'm just… I just need some space. We've lived in each other's pockets for so long we don't even know how to be around anyone else. Or who we are if we're not together.'

Lies, lies…

His snort was ugly. 'Don't dress this up as self-discovery. This is about the school jock making a play for the school tomboy. And you're falling for it hook, line and sinker.' He slammed two hands either side of her face and leaned into her.

She flinched and her heart raced at his closeness. *No, this is about your mother asking me to cut you loose. Begging me to.* She wanted to scream it into the face that she knew as well as her own. But she couldn't. It would kill him to discover what his only surviving parent thought he was worth.

'You could be anything you want, Marc. You don't

need me to be it with you. There's a whole world for us to discover.'

He leaned in further. The tightening in her body where he touched it wasn't fear. Marc was the only person on the planet she trusted implicitly never to hurt her.

'What's wrong with us discovering that together?' he ground, his chest heaving with restraint. 'We have history. A bond. What does McKinley have that I don't have?'

No rock-tight bond. No complicated history. No parents pressuring her to put some distance between them.

'I'm only asking for space, Marc. What's wrong with that?'

His face twisted and he swore. 'I've been giving you space for two years, Beth. Maybe if I'd done *this* back then I wouldn't be standing here now getting the brush-off from my best friend.'

And then suddenly his mouth was crushing down on hers, his body pressing her into the hard limestone of the library wall behind her. Shock stiffened her against the hardness of his chest as his hands slipped down to tangle in her hair and hold her face still for the assault of his lips. She swam in his scent, in his angry heat, in his perfect, practised kiss. The unfamiliar slide of a blazing hot mouth over her own and the furious press of his body. And then the dizzying sensation of their flesh melding into one, his enormous hands sliding around to protect her head from the lumpy wall behind her, his mouth shifting and softening on hers.

And then—somehow—she was kissing him back. Her own mouth moved tentatively against his and her body pressed forward. A choked whimper cracked deep in her throat and Marc worked his tongue past her uncertain lips coaxing them open. His furnace-hot tongue twisted and danced around hers, intensity pooling around her, engulfing all. Her body *whoofed* to flaming life, hormones tangling and exploding like kindling around them.

Overwhelming and unfamiliar, something she'd never allowed herself to dream. To want.

Marc.

Suddenly Beth was free and Marc staggered back against the force of her desperate shove. She held up a shaking hand to stop him coming closer. His face darkened as he looked at her.

'Does McKinley know you kiss like that?' His chest heaved.

How could he know? They'd never kissed. She'd never kissed anyone. Until today.

She dragged her fist across her lips. 'Don't ever—' *do that again, make me feel that again* '—touch me again.' Her voice was husky and low and appallingly unfamiliar.

'Beth…'

A world of emotions surged up and spilled over. 'Don't *speak* to me…again.'

His frown doubled. 'You don't mean—'

She lifted tortured eyes to him. 'Why does it have to be all or nothing with you? I just wanted some space, Marc. Room for us both to discover who we are. That's all. Did you think you could keep me all to yourself for ever?'

'I know who I am. And I thought I knew who you were. But I guess not.' He crossed the little clearing in two steps. 'You want space, Elizabeth? Fine. Take as much as you need. If you're that desperate, then have a good life with McKinley.'

And then he was gone.

Her best friend.

Like a kite in a wild wind, she'd tried to give him some rope, some height, but instead he'd ripped completely free and was gone. Her fingers trembled as they touched her swollen lips and she slid down the rough library wall until she huddled in a tearless, emotionless, empty heap.

CHAPTER ONE

Ten years later, south coast, Western Australia

WHO knew silence came in so many shades?

There was the deep, black silence late at night, under the West Australian stars, miles from anywhere. The earthy green silence of Beth's shambolic warehouse studio, only broken by the splashes of colour from her latest artworks. There was the newly discovered, beige-coloured silence inside her head, where voices and thoughts used to clamour but had now all eased into a comfortable hum.

And there was this one…

The simmering red silence of a man who was not particularly pleased to see her. Not that Beth had imagined he would be. It was why she'd put this off for so long. The awful sound of nothing echoed through the heartbeat thumping past her eardrums. She cleared her throat.

'Marc.'

He may have been half a house larger than the boy she remembered, but Marc Duncannon had two trademark giveaways and one was the way he stood when he was on guard, legs apart as if readying himself for a physical assault.

Muscular arms stole up to cross in front of a broad chest as he continued to stare wordlessly at her. Twisted humour raced in to fill the aching void inside where she wasn't letting herself feel. While he'd grown a kick-butt chest in ten years, she was no bigger in that department than when he'd last seen her. Yet another disappointment for him.

Coming here suddenly seemed like a spectacularly bad idea. 'Are you not even going to say hello?'

He nodded briskly, his lips tight, resenting opening at all. 'Beth.'

One stony word, but loaded with meaning and breath-stealing in its timbre. More than she'd had from him in over a decade. A total contrast to the way he used to say her name. Beth. Betho. Bethlehem. They'd had their short lifetimes to come up with stupid nicknames for each other. He'd only called her *Elizabeth* once. The day he'd kissed her.

The day she'd ripped out his heart.

She swallowed past the lump threatening her air supply. Past the welling excitement that she was here—with Marc—again. 'How are you?'

'On my way out.'

Okay... She'd prepared herself to be unwelcome but it still felt so foreign radiating from him. 'I just needed... I'd like a couple of minutes. Please?'

His hazel eyes darted away briefly but the miracle of any part of him moving seemed to thaw the rest of him out. His whole body twisted and he resumed loading equipment into his four-wheel drive. Beth risked closing the gap, but her breath got shorter with her distance from him, until she either stopped advancing on him or took her last living gasp.

Seeing him again would almost be worth it.

He threw words out like a shark net to entangle her before she got nearer. 'You could stand there gawping or you could help me load the Cruiser.'

Beth scrambled to help, stunned by the gift of so many words in a row. It wasn't friendly. But it wasn't silence. And, given it was possibly the only chance she was going to get, she took it.

'I went to your old house. Your neighbours told me where you were,' she started to jabber. 'I heard about your mum. What happened? You two were so close…'

Oh-so-familiar eyes lifted below hooded lids and glared at her. Intense and intensely…adult. 'That's what you've come all this way to ask?'

Her heart lurched. Marc didn't do sarcasm when they were kids but it seemed he'd perfected the fine art in the years since she'd seen him.

'No. I'm sorry…' It was lame but what else could she say?

He turned to face her and straightened, frustrated. 'What for, Beth? For turning up unannounced or for dropping off the face of the earth for a decade?'

How could she have forgotten what a straight shooter he was? She took a shaky breath. 'That's why I've come. I wanted to explain—'

He moved off again. 'You'll have to explain some other time. Like I said, I'm on my way out.'

She watched as he tossed a few final items into his dusty black Land Cruiser. A satellite phone. A first aid kit. A wetsuit. She frowned. 'Where are you going?'

The hard glare he shot her from under the broad ridge of his brow should have had her quailing, if not for the fact that she'd developed immunity long ago, from exposure to much worse. Courtesy of her husband.

'We've had a report of a stranding out at Holly's Bay. I'm going to check it out.'

'Stranding?'

'A whale, Beth. It needs help. I don't have time to entertain you.'

She fought the bristle his unkind words inspired. She was here to help her healing process, not to pass the time. Would she have put herself through this otherwise? 'I just need a minute…'

He ignored her and moved around to the driver's side door and yanked it open. 'The whale may not have a minute. You've already slowed me down.'

She made her decision in a blink. It had cost her too much to come here today; she couldn't let him just walk away from her. Who knew if she'd find the courage to try again? She sprinted around to the passenger side of the four-wheel drive and leaped in as he started it. Up close and in the confines of a cabin, he was bigger even than he'd seemed at a distance.

'Get out, Beth.'

His voice certainly fitted the new him. Deep, rough. But still essentially Marc. That part tugged at her. 'I need to talk to you. If I have to do that on the move, I will. Whatever it takes.'

He practically growled, 'You're wasting time.'

Anger finally broke through her carefully constructed veneer. 'No, *you* are, Marc. Drive!'

Marc Duncannon concentrated on keeping his hands glued to the steering wheel, cemented there harder than clams on a reef. The tighter he held them, the less likely they were to shake, to give him away. He didn't want her getting the slightest clue about how thrown he was.

Beth Hughes.

She was still the same lean, athletic build she'd been as a kid. It still suited her, even if it made him wonder how long ago she'd had her last meal. Same high brows, straight nose. Full coral lips. He would have recognised her even if she hadn't spoken and he hadn't heard again the soft tones he'd given up as a memory, but there was something very worn out about the way she held herself. The way her long dark hair hung, defeated, from a dead straight parting. As if she was doing her best not to stand out. Very un-Beth. She'd always been such a show pony.

Now she looked a little too much like his mother's tormented appearance the last time he'd seen her. He clenched his jaw and leaned on the accelerator harder, flying down the long track leading from the homestead to the coastal highway.

His vehicle now reeked of Beth's particular scent. That skin cream that, clearly, she still used after all these years. Coconut something. Chemical free. Cruelty free. The scent he associated with summer and beaches and bikinis…and Beth. The scent that would take weeks to fade from his upholstery.

The way it had taken months to finally force her from his mind. Or not, he realised as every bit of him tightened. Seemed it had only lain dormant. Buried deep. Two seconds in her presence and half a childhood of memories came flooding back.

So much for moving on.

He concentrated on the road ahead.

From the corner of his vision, he saw her twisted mouth, teeth chewing on her full lips. The old habit socked him in the guts. She used to do that when she was problem-solving or trying to outfox him. But back then she couldn't sustain it and they'd break apart into one of her heart-stopping smiles. Not today. Her lips opened and she took a deep breath, ready to hit him with whatever it was she wanted.

'Since when did you become a whale rescuer?'

Not what he was expecting. And why did she sound as rattled as he was? She had the upper hand here. It surprised him enough to answer. 'It's part of life on the south coast. And I'm the closest trained landholder.'

'You train for this?'

'Through experience.'

'How many times have you done it?'

'Five. Two last year. This stretch of coast is notorious for it.'

'Why here, particularly?'

Small talk killed him. Especially with the one person he'd never needed it with. This was what they were now? Maybe never seeing her again was the better option. He shrugged. 'No one knows.'

Silence fell, thick and muddy. He slowed the vehicle and yanked the steering wheel hard to the right. They bumped off the asphalt onto a badly graded limestone track and headed towards the massive expanse of ocean. The crescent bay opened out before them like an electric-blue half-moon.

'How long before we get there?' she asked, voice tight.

He could practically feel her brain turning over. Her heart thumping. It vibrated off her and slammed straight into the waves of tension coming off him. 'About one minute longer than you said you needed.'

She saw his sideways glance. Interpreted it correctly. 'I needed to see you. To explain.' She cleared her throat. 'To apologise.'

Apologise? 'For what?'

Her mouth thinned. 'Marc…'

'Friendships end, Beth. It happens.' He used the casual shrug to shake free some of his tension.

Her eyes flared with confusion but then they hardened and blazed with determination he'd never seen from her. Adult Beth had some balls, then. 'Nonetheless, I've come a long way to see you. I'd like to say what I need to say…'

The Land Cruiser bumped up off the track onto the small dunes and Marc manoeuvred them as close to the edge as he safely could. The white crescent shore stretched out before them, meeting the blue of the Southern Ocean. Next stop, Antarctica. Down on the sand, about twenty feet apart, two large, dark shapes rolled and buffeted in the shallows.

Two whales. Marc swore under his breath.

'Your explanations will have to wait, Beth. I have work to do.'

CHAPTER TWO

BETH took one look at the scene unfolding on the beach and pushed herself into gear. It had been two years; her needs could wait a little longer. Those animals couldn't.

Marc grabbed his satellite phone and started dialling even as he ran to the back of his vehicle, peeling off his clothes as he went. By the time he had his T-shirt and jeans off, he'd communicated their location and the number of stranded whales to someone at the Shire and asked them to rally assistance.

Beth did her best to get busy lifting items out of the car to avoid staring at him, open-mouthed. Once-gangly Marc Duncannon had spent some time in the gym, apparently. The weights section. Her belly flipped on itself in a most unfamiliar way.

He tossed the disconnected phone into the back of the vehicle and stepped into his wetsuit, hauling it up over muscular legs and then flexing his broad back as he shrugged it up over his shoulders and arms. As soon as it was secure, he snared up the first aid kit and a small bag of supplies and thrust the phone into it. He shoved a snatch-strap, rope and every ockie-strap he could rummage up in behind it. Then he threw his T-shirt, a hooded trainer and an old towel at Beth, saying, 'You're going to need this,' and was off, down the dunes, racing towards the water.

Beth did her best to keep up. She stumbled several times in the thick sand and paused to kick off her unsuitable shoes, losing more ground on Marc. But she didn't need to be near him to know what was going on; his stiff body language was as clear as a neon sign as he ran down the shore, close to the first whale.

The sleek, marble-skinned animal was already dead.

An awful sorrow washed over her: that she might have delayed Marc for the precious minutes that counted. That this enormous creature was already gull-food because of her.

Marc paused briefly, those magnificent shoulders drooping slightly, but then he kicked on, further down the beach to where the second body rolled in time with the surf. As he got closer, he slowed and took a wide approach, lifting his hands high in the air in warning. Beth instantly slowed.

It was alive.

By the time she caught up with him, he was on his second wide pass of the beleaguered mammal. It lay partially submerged in the quicksand where earth met ocean, every second wave high enough to wash gently over its lower half. But exposed parts of its upper body were already dangerously dry. Compared to the liquid mercury-looking surface of wet whale skin, the dry parts looked like the handbag she'd left in her hire car at Marc's farm.

That couldn't be good.

'Put the sweatshirt on, Beth.' He didn't bother with a please and she didn't expect niceties right now. But it didn't mean she was prepared to be dictated to. Not any more.

'It's thirty-three degrees. I'll boil.'

'Better that than burn to a crisp. We're going to be out here for some time.' He moved to her side and relieved her of his T-shirt and the towel. Then he zipped up the wetsuit more fully over his chest, fastened the neck strap and tugged a cap down hard over his shaggy hair. 'And you're about to get wet. You'll thank me in two hours.'

'Two hours?' They'd be out in the water for a couple of hours, with an injured dinosaur? Alone? But Marc wasn't worried; he ran headlong into the water between the dead whale and the live one and soaked the towel and his shirt.

His five-times experience certainly showed.

By the time Beth had wriggled herself into Marc's sweatshirt and pulled up the hood for some shade, he was already beside the dangerous giant. A false killer whale, Marc told her. The fact it was not a true killer whale didn't fill her with any confidence. It was still big enough to send them both flying with a toss of its wishbone tail, which bore an arrow-head-shaped scar. One enormous dark eye rolled wildly at his approach. Marc slowed and started speaking softly. Steadily. Random words that meant nothing.

The eye wasn't fooled for a minute.

But when Marc gently laid the saturated towel onto its parched skin, the eye rolled fully shut and the beast let off a mighty groan that vibrated the sand beneath Beth's feet. Her heart squeezed. It wasn't pain, it was sheer relief. She sprinted forward and met Marc in the water, hoping that he'd think the tears in her eyes were from the glare coming off the ocean.

'Around the other side,' he ordered brusquely, glancing up as she wiped a stray one away. 'Stay up-beach from that ventral fin; it's pure muscle.'

'The *what* fin…?'

'Underneath.' He threw the sodden T-shirt her way and she just caught it. 'The fin closest to her belly.'

The whale barely moved as they took it in turns draping the wet fabric over its parched skin. Within fifteen minutes, Beth's wrists ached from wringing out the water to run down the whale's hide and she moved to a slosh-and-drag technique instead. Brutal on the back, but the most effective way of keeping the poor animal wet. A fierce concentration blazed in Marc's eyes, a flush of exertion highlighting the familiar ridge of his cheekbone. Familiar yet unfamiliar.

Her mind bubbled with memories of a younger Marc studying. Or whipping her butt at chess. Or listening to her dramas. That same focus. That same intensity. No question that some parts of him hadn't changed.

Even if the rest had.

Neither of them spoke, their focus centred on the whale. Beth's reason for coming to the south coast flitted entirely out of her head, dwarfed in significance compared to the life and death battle going on in the shallows of Holly's Bay.

'You need a break.' Marc's voice was reluctant enough and firm enough to cut through the hypnotic routine of *slosh-and-drag…slosh-and-drag*. But it was also dictatorial enough to get Beth's hackles up.

'I'm fine.'

'You're parched. Your lips are like prunes. Stop and rehydrate. You're no use to either of us if you collapse.'

Either of us. Him or the whale. Beth didn't want to see the sense in that but he was right; if his focus was on rescuing her, the whale could die. She straightened and used the sleeve of his sweatshirt to wipe at the sweat streaming into her eyes.

'I could use a swig of water myself,' he said, clearly hoping she'd fall for the incredibly juvenile ploy, but she barely heard him, focusing only on four little letters.

Swig.

Her body immediately picked up and ran with the evocative image: an icy bottle straight from the cooler, the hissing sound the cap made twisting off. The clink of the cap hitting the sink. Her near favourite sound in the world. Second only to the breathy sigh of a cork coming out of a good bottle of Chenin Blanc.

A sound she hadn't heard for two years. Since she'd stopped drinking.

Her mouth would have watered if it hadn't been so dry. Like Pavlov's dog, just the thought of a particular spirit could still make her saliva flow. Despite everything she'd done to put it behind her, her body still compromised her from time to time. When she least expected it. It sure was not going to be happy with what was about to cross its lips.

She moved up the beach and hauled a two-litre bottle of still water out of one of Marc's supply bags and then cracked the cap. She suddenly realised how thirsty she was, but she was determined not to let Marc see that. She stood and jogged back to his side of the whale and passed him the bottle first. He glared at her meaningfully, but took it and helped himself to a deep, long draw of purified water. His Adam's apple bobbed thirstily with each long swallow.

'Once this is gone we can use the bottle to help wet the whale,' she said.

Marc shook his head. 'We're going to have to make this last. I only have one more.'

Four litres of water. Between two people, on a blistering Australian day, with reflected light bouncing up off the surface of the salty, salty water.

Oh, joy.

He finished drinking and passed the bottle straight back to her. Beth's pride had limits and watching the way the clean water had leaked down his throat had stretched it way too far. Every fibre of her being wanted to feel liquid crossing her tongue.

If that had to be water, so be it.

She didn't guzzle, though she well could have. At least AA had taught her something about restraint. Greedily sculling their precious water supply was not something she wanted Marc to witness. And a small part of her was afraid that once she started she might not stop.

She made herself lower the bottle after a few restorative swallows and, buoyed by the wetness coursing into her body, she jogged lightly back through the beach sand and knelt to slide the bottle into the shade of Marc's supply bag. As she did, she dislodged the other occupants. The satellite phone. First aid kit. A clutch of muesli and chocolate bars, a small hand-wound torch. The second container of water. And a—

Beth leapt back as if burned.

A large seventies-era silver hip flask tumbled out onto the sand. Ornate, neatly stoppered and probably his father's before it was Marc's, one of the few remembrances he might have of the man who had died when Marc was nine. The sort you kept whisky in, or vodka, or just about any liquor you didn't care to advertise. Beth didn't need to pick it up to know it was full of something bad. He wouldn't have thrown it in the emergency pack for nothing.

She shoved it back into the bag and rose to her feet, shaking. She hadn't worked this hard for two years to blow it now. She glanced at Marc to see if he'd noticed, but he was too busy gently rubbing the wet towel over the whale's bulbous face to notice.

She'd finally hardened herself against facing her demons on every street corner in the city. Every billboard. Every radio commercial. To encounter liquor on a remote beach in the middle of nowhere. In front of Marc… What kind of a sick karmic joke was this?

She stumbled as her feet sank back into the loose shore sand and water rushed into the twin voids around her ankles. As she went down onto one knee, a wave came in and soaked her to her middle, her pale blue jeans staining instantly darker with salt water, the cold assault shocking her mind off the hip flask and what it held.

But her sunken perspective was how she noticed something else. The whale's ventral fin was partly underwater, even after the wave washed back out. The one that had been high and dry a couple of hours ago when they'd arrived.

She scrambled to her feet, nearly falling across the whale in her haste.

'Marc…'

He looked up at her, fatigue in his face, and something else. Fierce determination. This whale was not going to die while he breathed.

'Marc…the tide's coming in.'

He turned his eyes heavenward and closed them briefly in salute. His lips moved briefly.

'Is that good?'

Hazel eyes lowered back to hers, clear and honest, as if they'd forgotten she was an unwelcome blast from the past. 'That's very good. Maybe we can refloat her.'

'It's a her?'

'You can tell by her short, curved dorsal fin.' His head jerked in the direction of the other whale. 'I think that one might have been her calf.'

The unfamiliar stab of grief slid in under her ribs and washed over her with another shove of the waves. This mum had followed her baby in to shore. Maybe she'd stranded herself trying to save her little one. Was that why her eyes kept rolling around—was she trying to find her calf? Empathy for the animal's loss nearly overwhelmed her, stealing the breath she desperately needed to keep her muscles working. But she embraced the pain and almost celebrated it. Two years ago, she wouldn't have felt such sorrow. Two years ago, she wouldn't have felt much of anything.

Her eyes fell back on the suffering whale. Her ire—and her voice—lifted. 'Where are they?'

He kept up the rhythmic sloshing. 'Who?'

'The rescuers. Shouldn't they be here by now?'

The sloshing stopped. He stared. 'We *are* the rescuers, Beth. What do you think we've been doing for the past three hours?'

'I meant others. People with boats. Shovels. Whale-rescue devices.'

The sun must have been causing a mirage… That almost looked like a smile. The one she'd never imagined she'd see today.

'Oh, right, the whale-rescue devices.' Then he

sobered. 'A big group of volunteers is about fifty clicks to the west, helping with another stranding. As soon as they have that situation stabilised they'll be out to help us. Our solo whale doesn't stack up against their entire pod, unfortunately.'

'A whole pod stranded?' Beth cried. 'What is wrong with these creatures?'

If not for the tender way she ran the dripping T-shirt across the whale's skin, taking unnecessary care to avoid its eyes, Marc would have read that as petulance. But he squinted against the lowering sun and really looked at her strained face. Much paler than when they'd started. Despite the blazing sun. Back to the colour it had been when she'd first climbed out of her rental car back at his property.

Beth was tired. Emotionally and physically spent already, and they'd only been out here a couple of hours. She looked as wretched as his mother when she was coming off a particularly bad bender. The bleached cheeks and shadowed eyes had the same impact on him that his mother's had.

Used to. Before he shut down that part of him.

Beth had much worse to get through yet. The rescue was only just beginning. Maybe he should have shoved her out back at the homestead. Done her a favour and sent her packing. If he'd left just five minutes earlier he would have been out here alone, anyway, so what was the difference if she left now? He had enough supplies to get him through the night.

Water for life. Food for strength. Potassium for cramps. Whisky and wetsuit for warmth. Enough for a day, anyway. Hopefully by then backup would have arrived.

'It often happens this way,' he said, taking pity on her

confusion. 'There's nearly forty volunteers at the other stranding, apparently.'

Beth stared at him between refreshing her whale-washer in the ocean and leaning towards him over the animal as the water ran down over it. 'Forty! Couldn't they spare us a couple of people?'

'Anyone spare is already on their way to other isolated strandings that the aerial boys identify along this stretch of coast. They know we've got this one in hand.'

Beth laughed a little too much and waved her paltry, dripping T-shirt around. 'This doesn't feel very in hand.' Marc dived forward and covered the whale's blowhole to protect it from the cascading water. The whale feebly blew out at the same time. At least she could still do that much.

He found himself suddenly possessed of very little tolerance. 'Hey, if you want to go, knock yourself out. I'll do better without your negativity anyway.'

Beth lifted her head and glared, the first sign of fire in those bleak eyes since they'd got out of his Land Cruiser. 'I'm not negative; I'm terrified. I don't know what I'm doing.'

The raw honesty spoke to some part of him a decade old. It triggered all kinds of unwelcome protective instincts in him. This really was more than she'd bargained for when she came cruising down his drive, looking all intense.

He sighed. 'You're doing fine. Just keep her body wet and her blowhole dry. It's all we can do.'

They fell to silence and into a hypnotic rhythm in time with the wash of the ocean, the groans of the whale and the *slosh…slosh* of their wet fabric. Marc did his best to ignore her, but his eyes kept finding their way back to her. To features drawn tight that had once shone with zest. Trying to work out why she'd come. Part of him was curious—the part that had always wondered what the heck had happened all those years ago. But the other part of him wasn't into lifting lids off unknown boxes any more. And he'd done far too good a job of driving Beth Hughes clear out of his memory. Until today.

'Do you need to contact Damien? Tell him where you are?'

Frosty eyes lifted to his. 'I'm not required to report in.'

'I didn't say that. But I figured he'd be concerned about you.' She looked as if a stiff breeze would send her tumbling. *I'd be worried if you were mine to worry about.*

Whoa. Thank God for inner monologue. Imagine if that little baby had slipped out. A blast well and truly from the past.

Beth dipped her head so the hood shielded her face from his view. 'He won't be.'

There was something in the way she said it. So final. So cold. He couldn't help himself, although he really didn't want to have any interest in her life 'Why not?'

Slosh…slosh. Silence.

'Beth?'

Even the whale seemed to flinch at the sudden outburst of skinny arms to its right. 'We're not together any more, okay? I no longer answer to anyone.'

Her marriage was over? The King and Queen of Pyrmont High were no more? A nasty imp deep inside him badly wanted to smile. But there was nothing satisfying about the pain on her face.

'I'm sorry, Beth.'

'Don't be,' she mumbled from down the tail end of the whale. 'I'm not.'

She moved like a car wash up and down the three metres of the whale's body, sloshing as she went. The animal was relaxed and trusting enough now to let her do it without fussing. Her hand trailed along the marbled mercury of its skin as she went and every now and again it shuddered as though ticklish. He empathised completely. There was a time he would have given just about anything to have her hands touch him like that.

He slammed a door on that memory.

So she'd married McKinley young but now she was single again. And hot on the trail of her old pal Marc. A light bulb suddenly came on in his mind. 'I hope you're not expecting to pick up where we left off, Beth?'

She froze and looked up at him. 'Excuse me?'

Ooh. He hadn't forgotten that arctic look. The ice princess. There was a masochistic kind of pleasure in having it levelled on him again after so long. 'Because as far as I'm concerned we were done that day behind the library.'

Even under the hood of her oversized sweatshirt he could see her nostrils flaring. About as wildly as the whale's blowhole. 'You think I'm here to come on to you?'

'I'm still waiting to find out why you're here. You came a long way for something. Go ahead and say what you wanted to say.'

Permission seemed to paralyse her. Her mouth opened and closed wordlessly several times. Whatever she was going to say, it wasn't easy.

Her hands stilled on the whale. 'I hurt you back in school and I wanted you to know I'm very sorry,' her soft voice began.

Every part of him stretched sling-shot taut. He cast her a sideways glance. 'You didn't hurt me.'

Her pretty face folded. 'That can't be true. I was there, I remember…'

'What do you remember?'

She blew air out of full lips. 'How you looked. How we left things.'

How badly he'd handled himself? He shrugged. 'Like I said. Friendships end.'

'Not usually like that. You kissed me, Marc.'

Right on cue, he got a flash of the wide-eyed awakening on her face. The coconut taste on his tongue as her mouth had parted with surprise. As he'd sunk into the heaven of her lips. He clenched his teeth against the bittersweet memory. Forced it back down deep where it belonged. His muscles clamped up again. He calmed himself for the whale's sake. It was stressed enough for all of them.

'That wasn't a kiss, Beth. I was trying to make a point.'

Confusion marred her pale skin. 'What point?'

A lip-searing, unforgettable point. A friendship ending point. 'That you would have kissed anyone offering at that point.' *That you didn't need McKinley for that.*

She disguised her sharp intake of breath behind loudly dumping her whale-washer in the drink and then she bought herself some recovery time by wringing the life out of his old T-shirt. For one second he felt like a heel for hurting her. But he pushed that away too. Best course now—like back when he was a kid—was not to let himself feel anything at all for Beth Hughes. Time had passed. They'd both moved on. In a couple of hours she'd be gone.

'It's been ten years. It's not like I've been sitting around obsessing about it.' *At least not for more than a few months.* 'What else is there to say?'

Slosh...slosh. Her eyes glittered as she measured what he'd said. 'Other than "Good to see you, Beth".'

Her tight words cracked and his stomach flipped fully over. He was still a sucker for those big brown eyes if they were awash. Either she was a master manipulator or this really was a big deal for her. But it was for him too, after years of not letting himself think about her. *Good to see her?*

'We never lied to each other before.'

Her face grew pale beneath his hoodie and he turned his attention back to the whale, unable to stomach her expression.

They worked silently for another twenty minutes until Marc couldn't stand the quiet. 'If you want to take the Cruiser back to my place, that's fine. I'll get a lift back when reinforcements come.'

She lifted tired eyes. 'No, thank you.'

No? 'Why are you still here? You've said what you came for. You're sorry for the hurt you imagine you caused.' He made his shrug much more casual than he felt. 'Doesn't that mean we're done?'

It should. If it was the real reason. He could see in her eyes it wasn't.

They flicked away and back in a blink. 'You haven't accepted my apology yet.'

That stopped his hands and he slowed his bend to re-wet his towel. 'Is that a requirement?'

Her eyes held his. 'I'd like you to.'

Which meant the apology was more about her than him. *Why does that surprise you? Just acknowledge the woman's apology and get her the hell off this beach!*

Yet something in him couldn't do it. 'I don't see you for ten years and then you turn up looking for absolution?' Uncertainty filled her eyes. 'Why would you expect it?'

'Because…' Her pale face scrunched up, confused. As if she hadn't thought about that until now. 'Because you're Marc.'

He had to take two steps back from the whale for that one. In case it felt his surging anger through his touch. 'That might have been our dynamic as kids, Beth, but a lot has changed in the years you've been gone. I'm not a gutless boy any more.'

She seemed shocked. 'You were never gutless, Marc. You always went straight for what you wanted.'

Not always. He struggled to get his temper under control, his hands back on the whale. 'Bully for me.'

'You don't believe me?'

'I don't believe that's why you thought I'd fall for your apology.'

Her colour started to rise. 'I just want to know that you forgive me for what I did.'

And here we go… 'Ah, now we're getting to it. So, in addition to accepting your apology, you want forgiveness? What is this, some kind of twelve-step programme?' He'd studied up on those back when he was researching his mother's condition. Back when he still gave a damn. 'Make good for all the people you've burned in life?'

It was Beth's turn to sway away from the whale. He crashed onwards, too worked up to give much care for her enormous eyes. 'Where did I fall on the list, Beth? How did I fare against your other screw-ups in life? I hope I was at least in the top half.'

Her eyes blazed and it was beautiful and awful at the

same time. Now that he was faced with opportunity, hurting her was not quite as satisfying as he'd imagined back when he was seventeen and holding all those feelings close to him.

She stood and stared, her head tilted, her eyes glittering magnificently. 'Thank you, Marc. This actually makes it easier.'

He was already frowning into the sun too much to do it further. 'What?'

'In my head you were still the old Marc—gentle and concerned about people. I was really anxious about facing that man. But the new Marc is just a sarcastic pig and much easier not to give a stuff about.'

He snorted. 'Story of my life.'

She shook her head, disgust all over her face. 'Oh, boo hoo…'

Only one person on this planet had ever spoken to him like this—cut-throat honest. Getting straight down to the bones of an issue. And here she was again.

He gave as good as he got. 'Last time I saw you, Beth, the only thing you wanted from me was a goodbye. Well, you got it. Don't kid yourself that I've been mooching over that all these years. It was a good lesson to learn so early in life. It toughened me up for the real world. It drove me to succeed at school and in life."

She forced her tiring body to scoop up more water and sloshed it all over the whale, but never took her eyes off him. 'Fine. Here it is, Marc. I'm sorry that I hurt you back in high school. I made the wrong decision and I've come to regret that in my life. I'm sorry that I bailed on our plans for uni, too, and that I might have contributed to you not going—'

Pain lanced through him. 'Don't flatter yourself.'

She persevered. 'But most of all I'm really sorry that

I came to find you today. Because, up until now, you were the person I held in my heart as the symbol of everything I wanted to be. Clever, loyal, generous. I've spent years wishing I was more like you and—finally—I see the truth. Beneath all those new muscles you're just an angry, bitter, *small* man, Marcus Duncannon. And I've been wasting my energy feeling so bad about what I did.'

She stood up straighter and looked around her. This was where she should have stormed off. He could see she was dying to—making that kind of spectacular scene just wasn't complete without a flounce-off. But she had nowhere to go and a whale to save.

He blinked at her. There was absolutely nothing he could say to an outburst like that, which was fine because he was having a hard time getting past one small part of the significant mouthful she'd just spewed. It clanged in his mind like a chime.

You were the person I held in my heart... Every part of him rebelled against the impact of those words on his pulse rate. His mouth dried up and he could feel his heart beating in his throat.

Ridiculous. Unacceptable. She didn't even know she'd said it.

But it burned like a brand into his mind.

They stood staring at each other, chests heaving equally. Then all the fight drained out of him. 'Don't dress it up, Beth. Tell me what you really think.'

She glared at him but couldn't sustain it. The tiniest of smiles crept through. 'It's taken me a decade, but I've learned to say what I think. I don't pull any punches these days.'

'You never had any trouble with confidence as far as

I remember. You were always brash, always willing to go headlong into something with me. With anyone.'

But particularly with me... Those days were some of the best in his life. Back when Marc Duncannon and Beth Hughes were interchangeable in people's minds. There was nothing she wasn't willing to try once.

Fearless.

Marc frowned on the realisation. No, she hadn't been fearless. There were things that had definitely scared the pants off her, but she'd done them. With him by her side.

She looked up at him earnestly. Pained. 'That is not something I count under my virtues, Marc. Being an enthusiastic follower is not the same as thinking for yourself.'

He snorted. 'You're not trying to tell me you were an innocent accomplice?' He wasn't ready for another woman in his life blaming everyone around for her problems.

'I was a completely willing accomplice. I lived to follow you into trouble. I was fully up for any crazy idea you had.'

'Then what...?'

'I hadn't learned yet to ask for what I wanted. To put myself first.'

His stomach sank. *McKinley.* 'Don't tell me... You developed that sense right around the final year of school.'

She stared at him. Hard. 'On the contrary. It took me nearly a decade.'

Somewhere in there was some hidden meaning he should probably have been seeing. He felt like he always used to with Beth, as if he was operating on seven second delay. Always the last to get it. Always needing things spelled out. He'd forgotten what that felt like. He used to think that he was just not bright enough for her but now, with adult eyes, he wondered if it wasn't just that she tended to be cryptic.

He blew out a breath. 'Okay, as much as I'm enjoying our little trip down memory lane, it's not helping this whale. I want you to take over on the wetting; I'm going to try something.'

'Wait! What?'

'You'll see.'

Beth shifted nervously. 'No, I… Will it take long?'

'Probably. Why?'

'I need to…' She looked around. 'Despite the heat…'

Understanding hit him. 'Oh. Well, you're in the ocean. Go here.'

The look she gave him was hysterical. 'I'm not going to pee in the water while you're standing in it. And while a whale's lying in it.'

'What do you reckon the whale does, Beth?'

'I'm not a whale!'

True enough. She was slight enough to be the krill that whales liked to feast on. 'Look, the tide's running diagonally from the south, so if you go over there—' he pointed to a spot about ten metres away '—then the whale and I will be safely upstream.' He grinned. 'As it were.'

Beth turned and looked at the spot, then back at him. 'I can't.'

'Bashful bladder?'

'You're not helping, Marc.' She started to search around the shore for another alternative.

'Before you even suggest it, the dunes are not safe. Tiger snakes. Up beach might be okay but it's a lot more exposed and it's probably safer if we stay fairly close together.' *If you stay close to me.* 'Besides, a swim first will cool you off.'

'Oh, my God…' She looked around one more time, desperately, as if a Portaloo might materialise on the beach if she willed it hard enough.

It was difficult not to find that panicked expression endearing. Despite everything. He tightened his jaw. 'Come on, Princess. When did you get so precious? The quicker you get out there the quicker it'll be over.'

'Are you laughing at me?'

He forced his face into a more neutral expression. 'I wouldn't dream of it.'

'I'm sure you'd have the same concern if you were in my situation.'

'I was in your situation, Beth. About an hour ago. I just didn't make a fuss about it.'

It took her about two seconds to realise he hadn't left the water. Or his wetsuit. She lurched away from the whale—and him—and waded hastily away. 'Oh, my God. Men are so disgusting!'

He just grinned at her, the years falling away. 'It's human,' he cried after her as she kept striding up-beach, slowly into deeper water. He kept poking, in the painfully reasonable tone he knew she hated the most, calling after her fleeing shape. 'We all do it.'

Her cheeks had flamed from a heap more than windburn. Watching the mighty fall should have brought him more satisfaction. But Beth's prudishness only served to remind him of the vast gulf that lay between them. That always had. In school, she'd always had an aura about her, a subtle kind of quality that set her apart from everyone else. Definitely from him. Her brains certainly had. She was by far the brightest person he'd known, but she didn't hang out with the brains. Or the geeks.

Or the beautiful people—until the end—though it was where she and her luminescence had truly belonged.

She'd pretty much hung out with him. Rain, hail or shine. And he'd pretty much lived for that back then.

When he was younger, he hadn't thought to wonder about it. It wasn't until he was about fourteen and some helpful jackass had pointed out the social differences between poor Marcus Duncannon and rich girl Elizabeth Hughes that it had started to niggle. But she'd been unwavering in her friendship, uncaring about the condition of his mum's ancient car, the shabby hems on T-shirts he'd been wearing for two years. Or the fact that she had to ride buses to hang out with him. Some deep part of him had feared she might bail on him like everyone else when his father's life insurance money had run out. But she hadn't.

Not for three years. On the other side of *that* day, it had all looked more sinister. Maybe slumming with the poor fatherless kid gave her some kind of weird social cachet, some intrigue. Maybe he propped up her ego daily with his sycophantic interest. Maybe she was just biding her time until someone better came along.

Or maybe she just outgrew him. She'd said as much. He just never would have picked McKinley as the sort of chump she'd grow towards.

At seventeen he'd thought about ditching school immediately. Lord knew his mother needed the extra income back then. And he certainly could have done without the daily taunts of the beautiful people that his Beth was now one of them. McKinley's Beth, in fact, but always *his Beth* deep in his heart.

And now the Princess of Pyrmont High was peeing in the ocean. In public.

There was a certain satisfaction in that. No matter

how belated. He hadn't let himself go over these memories for years. Call it a self-preservation thing. He didn't like the person he'd become in those final months of school.

Beth's discomfort at being so debased only birthed a raw, shining affection deep in his gut—a feeling he hadn't allowed for a long, long time. He laughed to dislodge the glow deep within, to sever the golden filaments that threatened to re-establish between them.

He laughed to save himself from himself.

Then he locked his jaw and forced his attention back onto the only female out here who deserved his sympathy.

The ocean was full of water. What were a few drops more? And Beth was incredibly overheated. The idea of taking a quick swim before… Well, it wasn't the worst idea in the world.

She waded out into the deeper water, waist height, and peeled off Marc's oversized fleecy sweatshirt before bundling it high above her head to keep it dry. Then she slowly lowered her body up to her neck in the cold Southern Ocean. The frigid kiss of liquid on parched skin made her shiver. Cool ocean water rinsed away dried sweat. She tipped her head all the way back until cold water washed around her ears.

Bliss.

'Turn around!' she shouted back to Marc, onshore. Yes, it was pointless but it felt very necessary. He complied, busying himself with the whale, but she was sure his whole body was lurching with laughter.

Sure, laugh at the spectacle. Nice. Her humiliation was probably a gift to him.

She swapped the sweater into a raised hand, carefully

unfastened her jeans with the other and tugged them down single-handed, muttering the whole time. There was no way she was going to repeat Marc's wetsuit trick. She may have done some low things in her life but there were some barrel bottoms even *she* wouldn't scrape.

Getting her jeans down single-handed was one thing but getting them back on when she was finished, wet and underwater…

'Oh, no.' Beth looked urgently between Marc and the great expanse of nothing around them and realised there was no way—nowhere—she was going to be able to get out of this water with dignity.

'Come on, Beth. I'm doing all the work here,' Marc complained from his side of the whale.

For crying out loud! She wriggled left and then right and eventually stepped free of her adhesive jeans, trapping them on the ocean floor between her feet and standing fully up. Then she slid Marc's enormous hoodie back on over her cotton blouse. Its thickness cut out some of the sun's glare and pressed her wet blouse more tightly to her, cooling her even more. With one hand, she held the sweater high of the waterline and then she hooked her jeans up out of the water with a foot, into her free hand.

Then she started wading back to shore, barelegged. Her underwear was no worse than a bikini bottom, after all. Just because it was flouncy…

Just because it was Marc…

Her heart fluttered wildly, imagining his reaction to her stick-thin legs. The last decade and the abuses she'd put her body through really hadn't done her any favours. She stiffened her spine and trod ashore as though this had been her plan all along, letting his sweater slip back down to mid-thigh, and then laid her wrecked jeans out to dry on the sand high above the tide mark next to their bag of supplies. Her eyes instinctively fell on it, knowing what lay within, pulsing like a dark heart. And what lay *within* what lay within.

Walk away.

The thickness of the sand hid the unsteadiness of her gait. Not that Marc would have noticed; he was looking everywhere *but* at her long bare legs. The whale. The horizon. The sky. The extra delay probably irritated him if he couldn't even meet her eyes.

That didn't help her mood any. 'Okay. I'm back. What was so urgent?'

He waited until she got behind the whale before letting his eyes rest back on her. Then he cleared his throat. 'I'm going to try and dig a trench around her,' he said, indicating the now dangerously still whale. 'If I can get my snatch-strap around her, maybe we can drag her out a bit further.'

'Will it hold?'

'It pulls my Land Cruiser; it should tow a small whale.'

Beth frowned. 'Is digging under her safe?'

'I'll trench in front, then we'll try and saw the strap through the sand beneath her.' His hands mimicked the action, the cords in his wrists and forearms flexing with the motion. It briefly flitted through her mind that those bulging muscles could probably tow the whale to sea all by themselves.

Beth shook her head. 'No way. She must weigh half a ton. That sand will be too compressed.'

For a tiny moment he looked at her with a hint of admiration. Pleasing him had always pleased her. Even now. The slightest of glows leached out from somewhere deep inside her. But then he dropped heavy lids down over his eyes and the connection was lost.

'I've been thinking about that. If we can time it with the suck of the wash back out to sea it might loosen the sand just enough. It's worth a try. But we need to be ready for high tide.'

'What happens then?'

'We try and refloat her.'

'By ourselves?' Her voice sounded like a squeak, even to her.

'If we get lucky, the cavalry will arrive with a boat to tow her back out.'

'And if we don't?'

Steady eyes regarded her. 'If we don't, I hope you're stronger than you look.'

CHAPTER THREE

SHE wasn't. Not nearly. But she was getting better.

It had been a long, uphill road recovering from being Mrs Damien McKinley, but she'd found the strength to try. And it appeared that strength begat more strength, because she'd found extra to come here today. To face Marc. Even though ninety per cent of her whispered not to bother. Not to risk it. The ten per cent of her that disagreed was noisy and shovey and refused to be ignored. It remembered Marc. It trusted him.

Looked as if it had just learned a powerful lesson.

Marc Duncannon was not the man she remembered. He'd grown up in so many ways and while his physical changes were an unarguable enhancement, she couldn't say the same for his personality. Then again, after the decade she'd endured, she was no prize either. Maybe losing his father so young had damaged him irreparably. So close to losing his best friend. And apparently then his mother.

She frowned. 'So, you didn't tell me what happened with your mum. You two were so close.' Each was all the other had left. Even if Beth had really struggled to like Janice by the end.

Marc's whole body straightened and turned to stone, halting his digging. His mouth set. His eyes darkened dangerously. 'Did you imagine I'd still be living at home with my mother at this age?'

Scorn like that would have hurt a lot more once, before she calloused up at Damien's hands. Still, the fact that it still managed to slice down into her gut said a lot about how she still felt about Marc. She took a controlling breath. 'Obviously I expected you to have moved out of home but I never expected you to have moved out of her life.'

The blizzard in his eyes reached out and lashed at her. 'You still like to research before you travel, obviously.'

The one trip they'd taken together, when Marc had got his driving licence at the start of their final year in school, had been an exercise in military precision, thanks to Beth's aptitude for planning. Anything to take her mind off the fact that she and Marc were going to be camping. Out in the sticks. Alone. Right about then, her awareness of him as anything other than her best mate had crashed headlong into adolescent awareness of him as *a* mate. As in biological. That had been an awkward, confusing feeling that had never quite diminished.

'I had to start somewhere to find you. Your neighbour remembered me.' The woman had been very kind and given Beth the information she needed to track Marc down. Albeit with a slight lift to one eyebrow. She tried again. 'I thought…because Janice was all you had…'

Marc resumed his powerful digging, the chop and slide of his body adding emphasis to his curt words. 'I hope you're not trying to convince me that you had warm feelings for my mother. I remember how fast you used to like to get in and out of my house.'

Beth flushed. She hadn't realised how poorly she'd been covering her dislike of Marc's mum back then. It hadn't always been that way. It was just that as Marc grew older, Mrs Duncannon seemed to grow more hostile. Almost jealous. Until that last day…

Marc stood in his trench and eyed her. 'After school I spent some time up north on the trawlers. When I got back, I thought it was time to get my own space,' he said. 'She liked the city, I wanted the country. It's as simple as that.'

Right. And this whale was made of Jell-O. But if he didn't want to talk about it…

On a non-committal *uh-huh*, she let her focus drop back to where her hands continued to slosh the whale with a T-shirt that was now mostly shredded fabric. Ten years was a long time. One-third of their lives. What else could have injured him in that time? A woman? He didn't have a ring—not even a tan mark; she'd checked that out while he was choking the life out of his steering wheel earlier. But there was no doubt he was harbouring some wounds.

The thought brought her a physical pain that somehow rose above the ache in her lower back. That anyone would have hurt him like that. Bad enough what she'd done…

She dragged a deep breath in and concentrated on what her hands were doing. But silence wasn't an option either. 'Ask me a question.'

'About what?'

'Anything other than Damien or that day at school.' *Or what I've been doing for the past ten years.*

He waved his whale-washer in the air and then complied, plucking a question from nowhere. 'Favourite colour?'

'Still green. Moss-green, nothing too limey. My whole studio is painted that colour.'

'You have a studio?'

'Sounds more glamorous than it is. It's a partially restored old warehouse belonging to my father. I suspect I'm not supposed to be living in it. Council rules.'

'What do you do there?'

'I paint. Oils. My work is all around me.' For better or worse. The images from her abyss period were dark and dismal. But powerful. Lately, new brighter themes had started emerging. 'When I changed to B-stream it gave me an art double and I discovered I loved it. And I'm good at it.'

Two confused lines folded across his brow. 'That's good. I'd like to—'

...see them? The way he cut himself off made her wonder. They fell to silence. 'Ask me about my first car,' she eventually said.

Cars. The great equaliser. He smiled slightly and shook his head. 'What was your first car, Beth?'

'Toyota. Right after school. God, I loved that beat-up piece of junk. First thing I bought and paid for myself.' Until she'd stopped driving it because of the drinking.

'First kiss?'

She shook her head. 'Nope. Not talking about that day.'

Marc's eyes flared. 'Hold on, sidebar for just one second. That was your *first* kiss?'

She stared at him. 'You were my best friend. You don't think I would have told you the second someone kissed me?'

His eyebrows rose in apparent disbelief. 'No one ever tried?'

Beth shrugged; the hurts that had meant so much when she was younger were insignificant in the light of everything that had happened since. 'Guess I wasn't all that sought-after in school.'

He opened his mouth to say something, thought better of it and then changed tack. 'Until McKinley.'

'Right. But that topic's off-limits too.' Then something occurred to her. 'Wait—it wasn't *your* first kiss?' Marc dropped thick lashes down between them. Her mouth fell open. 'Seriously? Who was it?'

He had to know she was going to keep nagging until he told her.

'Tasmin Major.'

'Olympic Tasmin?' Her voice rose an octave.

'She was only state level then.'

But a twice Olympic freestyle diver since then. Tasmin was one of the classmates Beth thought of when she was counting her own many failings. Pretty. Gentle. Athletic. *Olympic.* And now she'd been Marc's first kiss, too. Maybe more? That thought bit deep down inside. Right down deep where she always considered their kiss behind the library to be special. Even if it had led to the end of their friendship.

Her throat tightened up. 'Why didn't you tell me?' More importantly, how could she have not noticed? She'd been so attuned to Marc's every breath.

He sidestepped her outrage. 'Why would I tell you? It was just a kiss.' Beth gave him her most penetrating stare, straight out of childhood. 'Okay, a bunch of kisses, but it's not like we were dating or anything.'

'I hope not, because that would mean I really was oblivious to everything going on around me.' Curiosity got the better of her. 'Why were you kissing Tasmin if you weren't dating?'

Marc dragged his eyes off to the horizon. Back to the whale. Anywhere but on hers.

'Marc?'

He hissed and tossed his hands up. 'She volunteered.'

Beth blinked. Several times. 'Tasmin Major volunteered to kiss you? Did I miss some kind of recruitment process?'

Cautious eyes met hers briefly. 'Actually, we volunteered with each other.'

Beth's stomach compressed into a hard ball. An insane jealousy surged through her as she realised what that meant. They wouldn't have been the first kids in school to do it. 'You went to her for *kissing practice*? Why?'

The look he gave her took her back a decade, too.

'Okay, other than *practice*, obviously. I can't believe you went to Tasmin. I mean she's nice and all, but… What was wrong with me?' And why on earth was this hurting so much?

That brought his head up instantly. Hazel eyes blazed sincerity. 'Nothing was wrong with you, Beth. But we were friends.'

She thought of all the girls at school who turned their snooty noses up at Marc because of the way he lived and dressed. As if they would ever find a finer person. Her estimation of Tasmin rose a notch because she wasn't one of them, even if it also meant that she'd spent half their childhood with Marc's tongue down her Olympic throat.

Then something else hit her. 'Who were you practising for?'

He tipped his face back down to the whale, sloshed harder. Resolutely ignored the question. Beth waited. Silently. Her heart pounded. How far had she truly come if she was this frightened of finding out?

'It's old news, Beth. Hardly important now.'

Her frown threatened to leave permanent grooves between her eyes, encrusted in the salt. 'I thought I knew everything about you back then, Marc. It's thrown me.'

He waved his shredded towel. 'I just wanted to get the whole first kiss thing out of the way, Beth. Can we just leave it at that?'

She looked at the tightness of his lips, the shadow in his gaze. She softened her tone. 'That library kiss was pretty accomplished. You guys must have practised *a lot*.'

The corner of his mouth lifted. 'Good times.' Then he looked back up at Beth, his eyes guarded. 'Anyway, I thought that day was off-limits. Moving on...'

Right. Moving forward... The past was in the past... 'Next question.'

It took Marc nearly two hours to hand-dig a deep enough trench a metre on-shore of the whale and reinforce it with driftwood to hold back the collapsing sand. In that time, the blazing afternoon sun dipped its toes into the ocean on the horizon and the most magnificent orange light coated everything around them. Her artist's eye memorised the colour for future use. Beth sighed as much as the whale did as the scorching heat suddenly eased.

In the dying light of dusk, Marc laid the strap out and then asked Beth to take one eyeleted end. She mimicked his bent stance, her prune-skin hands pressed down to the shallow ocean floor and her back screaming its protest. Then they started sawing the strap under the sand, towards the whale.

Push...pull. Push...pull. A slow, agonising rhythm.

Beth felt the moment they got close to her because, exactly as she'd suspected, the sand compressed into a rock-hard mass under the whale's weight. But Marc's idea worked, though slowly. With every wave that ran in, the suck of the water rushing back out between every one of a million grains of sand loosened it just a tiny bit and they were able to saw the strap, inch by agonising inch, beneath the giant mammal. The tide had crept in so much and they bent over so far that Beth's lowered face was practically touching the rising water. Her muscles trembled with exhaustion, screamed with frustration, but she wasn't about to complain to Marc, even though every part of her felt as if she'd been hit by a truck.

Her back. Her skin. Her feet. Her arms. Even her head thumped worse than any hangover she'd ever earned.

Marc grunted as loud as she did. The whale did nothing but blow the occasional protest out of its parched blowhole. Finally, just when tears of utter exhaustion pricked, he called a halt.

Standing upright nearly crippled Beth after the abuses of the day and she cried out as her muscles went into full cramp, stumbling back onto her knees in the rising water, wetting the bottom half of Marc's fleecy sweatshirt. It galled her to go down in front of him, but how much did he expect she could take? She caught herself before she sank completely down onto her bottom but she was incapable of getting back up. She froze in an odd kind of rigor where she was. Her hands shook as if they were palsied. Her head drooped.

Marc was with her in seconds, his strong arms sliding around her middle to keep her up out of the water. 'Beth, grab on to me...'

Tears came then. Angry. Embarrassed. Relieved. It had been so long since she'd last felt any part of Marc against her and it felt so right now. Safe and strong. Welcome and long-missed. Where she was bone and long hollow muscles, he was solid and smooth and rooted to the earth. Even in the water.

And he was her friend. At least he had been. Once.

He might have been stronger but he was just as tired as she was, it seemed. He needed her cooperation to get her back on her feet. Hours ago, he could have lifted her single-handed. 'Come on, Beth, pull yourself up,' he said, low against her ear.

If she turned her head just a bit she could breathe in his intoxicating scent. 'I'm sorry…' Her vision blurred.

His strong fingers tucked around her waist, burned there.

'Don't be. You did well. We got the strap around her.' His voice was tight as he steadied her back onto her feet but she let herself lean into him until the last possible second. He smelled of salt and sweat; an erotic, earthy kind of scent that elicited all kinds of tingling in her. Nothing like the over-applied, cheap colognes Damien liked to mask himself with.

She turned her face more closely into Marc and breathed in deep.

He pulled her out of the water, supported her long enough that they got up on the beach to where the supplies were. She collapsed down onto the sand, knowing she might never get back up but knowing she couldn't keep standing.

Even for him.

'Take a break, Beth. We've been at this for seven hours. No wonder you're exhausted.'

He didn't join her on the sand. Instead, he snagged up the supply bag and fished around in it until he retrieved two muesli bars, a chocolate bar, a banana and an unfamiliar packet of powdered mix. He offered her a choice. As hungry and tired as she was, the thought of putting food in her stomach did not appeal. There was only one thing in that supply kit that had her name on it. And she wasn't letting herself have that, either. She pushed his hand away.

'You have to pick one, Beth.'

She shook her head.

'Fine.' He tossed the chocolate bar at her. 'This will give you immediate energy and potassium for the cramping, but in one hour I want you to have this.' He waved the pouch of powder.

'What is it?'

'Sports mix. Endurance athletes use it. Just mix it with water. You need the fats and carbs if you're going to last.'

Was that a comment about her weight? 'I thought men liked women skinny?'

He looked at her, appalled.

Mortification soaked through her. *Oh, God, Beth. Don't speak.* Clearly, she was too tired to think straight. She shook her head again, incapable of an apology that wouldn't make things worse. Her mind's eye slipped to what was left in the supply bag. How had she dealt with this sort of moment before? She couldn't remember. Excruciating comments didn't feel so bad when you were blind drunk and so was everyone around you. You sure had less to regret that way.

Had she forgotten even how to feel shame?

'The powder's slow release energy, Beth. It'll get you through the next few hours.'

If she could just get through the next few minutes she'd be happy.

Marc crammed a muesli bar into his mouth on a healthy bite. Where Beth nibbled, he practically inhaled. Then he took one of the endurance pouches and filled it with water, shook and consumed it in a drawn-out swallow. Beth was too tired to drag her eyes off the long length of his tanned throat. How could even a throat be manly? But here she was, ogling it for the second time today.

She forced her eyes down to the half-melted bar in her hands. Chocolate was one of those foods she tried to avoid. Something she liked a little bit too much. Something that challenged her hard won willpower. But Marc was ordering her to eat it, and she was feeling so weak, so…what to do…?

She took a small bite.

She forced herself to go slow, not to wolf it down, although her blood and her brain screamed at her to. It was part of her process. If she gave in on something small, then what chance did she have over something big?

This was where the downward slide began. Her eyes went to the pack of supplies.

'Okay, come on.' Marc stretched out his hand to her, mumbling around the last crumbs of his muesli bar. 'If you don't get up again, you'll seize up and be here all night.'

The thought of rising was horrible. She groaned and stared at his extended hand. 'I can't…'

'She needs us, Beth.' His gentle words pushed every guilt button she had. Beth looked over to the dark mass half-submerged in the even darker waters of dusk. It may be cooler now that the sun had set—significantly cooler—but the whale wasn't in a position to wet her own skin. Or drag herself back out to sea.

And maybe *taking a break* was actually the start of the slide—insidiously disguised?

Beth forced herself over onto her side and then pushed painfully to her knees. It was the least elegant thing she could remember doing. Marc took her hand in his callused, strong one and pulled her the rest of the way to her feet. She stumbled against his neoprene hardness before steadying herself and pointlessly shaking the worst of the beach sand off her soggy sweatshirt.

His hands were high on her bare thighs, brushing more sand off before either of them realised what he was doing.

A rush of heat raged up her skin where his fingers touched and she leapt back with a speed she couldn't have found if he'd begged her. Marc stiffened and a pink flush showed itself above the collar of his wetsuit. God, that was one hundred per cent habit from the good old days. The days before gender was an issue. Now, having his hot hands on her icy skin was *absolutely* an issue. For both of them.

It had to be.

'Okay,' he said, clearing his throat and straightening to his full height. 'Back in the water.'

Beth willed her legs to follow him back down to the surf. How many hours had passed since she'd stumbled down the dunes this morning? As bad as she felt—and she couldn't remember a time she'd felt worse, even in the depths of her withdrawal—they'd achieved a lot. The whale was still alive, its skin was in reasonable shape, and they had implemented the first part of Marc's plan to refloat her.

Sure, tensions were high between them and, yes, maybe she'd rather be curled up by an open fire right now watching reruns of *Pride and Prejudice*, but she was hanging in there. She felt vaguely hydrated now that the scorching sun had eased off and the chocolate was doing its job and feeding energy directly into her cells. Their conditions could be much, much worse. That thought gave Beth's spine the tiniest of reinforcement.

And then the sun set.

CHAPTER FOUR

THE moon was high in the bitter night sky by the time Beth risked further conversation. She poured the last mouthful of the fresh water into the endurance powder Marc had nagged her to have and shook the pouch thoroughly, knowing he was monitoring her from the water to make sure she drank it. She managed not to gag—just—as she chugged the chalky banana-flavoured mix. Then she turned to look at Marc, still sloshing the whale.

That little moment on the beach had been a major slip. For both of them. She'd had two hours of dark silence in which to go over—and over—the events of the day, looking for the moment when something had shifted between them. The moment when time had unwound just a tiny bit and taken them both back to a place that meant Marc could make a mistake like touching her. A woman he barely knew any more. He barely liked.

It was the peeing thing. As though seeing her so reduced in front of him had gone some way to settling old hurts. Maybe the loss of dignity had won her a measure of forgiveness?

Lord, if that were all it took, she'd be in serious credit by the time the night was out. Embarrassment over a bodily function was just a patch on the hits her dignity had taken in the years since she'd last seen him. He'd be delighted if he knew.

She chewed her lip. Maybe that was what he needed to hear—that she'd suffered? Impossible to know—he was as mysterious to her these days as the darkening ocean all around.

She stumbled back to the water. 'That was quite possibly the most disgusting thing I've ever tasted.'

Marc answered as though it hadn't been hours since she'd last spoken. His twisted smile was reluctant. 'You get used to it. It'll keep you going.'

'I can see why they call it survival food. You'd really want to be lost at sea before you cracked open supplies.' She turned her eyes to the dark, still shadow further down the beach. 'Do you really think that was her calf?'

'Yeah, probably.'

'Did it die because it was so young?'

'It's not that much smaller than Mum. It wasn't a new calf, I'd say. Some whales last days, others only hold out for hours. Just like people, some are tougher than others.'

A deep sadness snaked out and tangled around her heart. She could identify with an animal that turned out not to be as tough as it might have thought. 'Poor baby.'

Slosh…slosh…

'You never had kids? You and McKinley?'

Beth was unprepared for the bolt of pain that question brought her. She turned her face away from him and busied herself around the whale's small parched eyes. It had finally occurred to her that a marine animal wouldn't object to having salt water around its eyes.

Marc's question hung unanswered in the night silence. He patiently watched her.

'No. No kids,' she whipped out.

'You didn't want them?'

I didn't deserve them. And they sure as heck didn't deserve to be born into a life as wrong as hers and Damien's. 'Not particularly, no.'

Let him think whatever he liked.

'Funny.'

That was it. Just that one word. She sloshed away for a bit longer, but then curiosity got the better of her. She straightened. 'What's funny?'

'I always pictured you as a mother. Deep down, I thought that might have been the attraction with McKinley. He seemed like he was raring to get straight into the family and kids thing.'

Beth snorted softly. He was raring to get into one part of it, at least, like most teenage boys. If he struck strangers as family oriented, it could only be because he'd grown proficient at maintaining the same illusion as his own parents.

'No. Damien didn't really have any drive regarding family.' Any drive at all. Except for drinking. When things had first started going wrong in their marriage, she'd briefly considered children, something to bring them together. But, as it got worse, she'd secretly made sure that was never possible. Even when she was in the deepest reaches of the abyss, she'd somehow managed to remember to protect herself against pregnancy. Not that the issue arose very often by that point.

Slosh...slosh.

'What did you end up doing?' Marc asked casually. 'For a career.'

Her shoulders tightened up immediately, which made

the sloshing even more uncomfortable. Embarrassment surged through her. Not because she hadn't had a perfectly legitimate job but because it wasn't even close to the glittering career he was probably imagining her having.

'I worked in retail.' She cringed at the blush she could feel forming and struggled to make working in a dry cleaners sound more impressive. 'Customer service.'

He frowned. 'You didn't go to uni?'

Just one of the many lifetime goals she'd poured down her throat. She bit back a testy response. 'No.'

He stopped sloshing to stare at her. Was that satisfaction in his eyes—or confusion?

'Damien didn't want me to start a career.' Lord, how bad had her life become that admitting *that* was easier than admitting she'd soaked her professional future in alcohol before it began?

'But he let you work in retail?'

Let. She tightened her lips. 'I chose to work. I wanted something that was mine. Something that didn't come from Damien or his family.' And she'd had it…as long as she could keep a job.

He shook his head.

'What?'

'You were so gung-ho about going to uni.'

For three years it had been their shared goal, one of the things that kept them so close together, kept them in the same classes. In the same lunch timeslot. Until the conversation with his mother that had changed all of that.

You're sucking him into your dreams, Beth, Mrs Duncannon had whispered urgently one time she'd visited the Duncannon household, her grip hard on sixteen-year-old Beth's forearm. Her voice harsh. *He's not bright like you, he's not suited to further study. He needs to get a job and start making his way.*

That had struck Beth as an odd thing to say about the boy who was already flipping burgers after school to help out financially. Who'd done all the research on the best universities. Picked up all the pamphlets, looked into all the courses. Was making the grades. Who had a plan for where he wanted his life to go and his compass set to get there. But Mrs Duncannon hadn't bought a word of Beth's nervous reassurance.

As long as he's with you, he'll never go for what he wants in life. He's not a pet to be trained and instructed. He'd walk through fire if you asked him to, Beth Hughes. And some days I think you really would ask, just to see if he'd do it.

She'd never visited Marc at home after that. The ugly picture his mother painted of their friendship filled her with shame and echoed in every event, every activity that followed. It made her question their relationship. Marc. Herself. She'd tentatively asked her own mother about it and Carol Hughes's careful answer and sad expression had told Beth everything she needed to know.

Both women thought she was dragging Marc along with her. *Both women* wanted her to pull back from their intense friendship. For his sake. She looked at the capable grown man standing before her and struggled to see how anyone could have worried about his ability to speak up for himself. Even as a teenager.

The irony was that Mrs Duncannon and her own mother had it all back to front. Beth would have followed Marc into the pits of hell if he'd asked her. Because she trusted him. Because he was like another part of her. A braver, more daring part. The idea of studying biology had never entered her one-track mind until he'd mentioned it, but separating after school never had either. And so she'd thrown herself willingly into Marc's dream. Adopting his had made up for having no direction of her own. Until the day she'd cut Marc loose and was forced to face her lack of ambition.

Her shoulders tightened another notch. 'Goals change.' She shrugged. 'You went up north after school, you said.'

His eyes shadowed over. 'I lost my…enthusiasm… for further study.'

'Because of me?' *Or did Janice get in your head, too?*

He glared at her. 'Responsibility for your own actions is fine; stop taking responsibility for mine.'

'If your goals shifted, then why are you surprised that mine did?' she asked.

'Because…' Marc's eyes narrowed. 'Because it was *you*. You could have done anything in the world that you wanted.'

Silence fell. Sloshing dominated. When he did speak again, it was so soft he might have been one of the night sounds going on all around them. 'So, what *was* the attraction, Beth—with McKinley?'

He still thought this was about Damien. Why not—it was what she'd wanted him to believe at the time. She had to find a way to cool their friendship off and Damien had been her weapon of choice. She'd used him to put distance between herself and Marc.

Used with a capital U.

'Damien was harmless enough…' *At the beginning.* 'We were kids.'

Okay, it was a hedge. Maybe her courage was as dried out as the rest of her. Her heart hammered hard in her chest. The anticipation of where this conversation might lead physically hurt. What he might think. What he might say. She just wasn't good at any of it. She licked dry, salty lips and wished for some tequila to complement it. Then she shuddered at where her thoughts were taking her.

After all this time.

You wanted forgiveness. Maybe that started with a little understanding.

He shook his head. 'You weren't like other teens, Beth. You were sharper, wiser. You were never a thoughtless person.'

The use of the past tense didn't escape her. How could a tense hold so much meaning? She sighed. 'I was overwhelmed, Marc. Damien made such a public, thorough job of pursuing me, it turned my head.' *And I was desperately trying to recreate what I'd had with you. What I'd lost.*

Marc was silent. Thinking.

She beat him to the punch that was inevitably coming. 'That day behind the library. When I told you… When you kissed me. You accused me then of selling out to the popular crowd.'

A flash of memory. Marc's hard young body pressing hers to the wall. His hot, desperate mouth crushing down on hers. Terrifying. Heaven-sent.

He assessed her squarely. 'I was an ass. I accused you of being desperate for affection.'

Surprise brought her head up. 'You were angry. I knew that.' *Eventually.*

He studied her, his mind ticking over. 'That explains why you dated McKinley. Not why you married him.'

The very thing she'd asked herself for a decade. Even before times got really tough. She frowned into the darkness. 'Damien was like two people. At school he was a champion, a prefect. His parents rushed him into growing up.' The specialised tutors, the pressure to achieve at sports, the wine with dinner. 'But he was still just a teenage boy with the emotional maturity to match. Once I agreed to date him, he seemed to expect me to cave automatically in…other areas.'

And *expect* was the operative word. She'd never met another person with the same kind of sense of entitlement as her ex-husband. She swallowed past a parched tongue and remembered how desperately she'd tried to wipe the blazing memory of Marc's kiss from her mind. How she'd thrown herself headlong into things with Damien to prove that all kisses were like Marc's. Only to discover they weren't. How much leeway she'd given Damien because she knew she had used him and feared she'd done him some kind of wrong by kissing Marc. By liking Marc's kiss. How Damien had taken that and run with it.

How she'd just let him.

She shrugged. 'I married him because I slept with him.'

Marc's lips tightened and his hands scrunched harder in the wet towel that was becoming as ragged as her own whale-washer.

'And because he asked.' She let out a frayed breath. 'And because there was no reason not to, by then.'

And because she'd had no inkling about the kind of man he was about to become.

Beth held what little air she had frozen in her lungs. Marc had honoured her request that he not speak to her again after the day behind the library. His absence had ached, every day, but it made it easier for her to bury what she'd done. Both hurting him and kissing him. And to forget how that kiss had made her feel. The awareness doorway it had opened.

Knowing she'd done it for Marc had never really helped. Having the approval of both their parents had never really helped. But physical separation combined with a sixteen-year-old's natural talent for selective memory had made it possible to move on.

After a while.

The whites of Marc's eyes glowed in the moonlight. 'You didn't have to marry him just because you slept with him.'

She knew he'd see the truth in the sadness of her smile. 'I've always accepted the consequences of my actions. Regardless of what else you think of me, that hasn't changed. I chose to do something contrary to the values my parents taught me. My church.'

Marc shook his head. 'McKinley was a jerk. It always surprised me that he married you at all. That he didn't stop chasing you once he…'

His words dried up and Beth swallowed the hurt. 'Once he had what he wanted? Go ahead, say it. Everyone else did.' Marc frowned. She straightened her shoulders. 'I hadn't planned to sleep with him but once I did, turns out I was a…natural student.'

The irony wasn't lost on her. She'd spent all year trying to come to terms with the blossoming feelings that Marc was beginning to inspire in her, yet she'd barely touched him. But she'd slept with the boy she was physically immune to.

Or maybe that was why?

'And he was naive enough to make that kind of life decision based on one girl?' Marc asked.

She swallowed around the large lump in her chest. 'We both were. Except that Damien grew up a lot in the following few years,' she went on. 'Discovered that other women could be good in bed, too. Extremely good, if you knew where to look. And my one piece of power vanished.'

And hadn't he let her know it.

'So you left him?'

Beth stared. 'No. I didn't. Not until two years ago.'

He gaped. 'You cannot be serious.'

Heat chased up her icy skin. 'My *vows* were serious. I was determined to make a go of it, certain he'd grow out of his...phase and maybe we could turn things around.' Determined not to lose any more face with her family. Her few remaining friends. Having screwed up so much in her life. 'Then, somehow, years went by. Empty, pointless—' *passionless* '—years.'

Only it wasn't *somehow*. She knew exactly how, but she wasn't about to go there. Not with Marc. Telling a room full of strangers was one thing. Telling the man who'd been your closest friend...

He growled, his eyes darkened. 'Hell, Beth.'

Her laugh was bitter. 'I thought you'd be thrilled I reaped what I sowed.'

He blew air out from between his lips in a fair imitation of their whale. 'Look, Beth. Yes, at the time I was pretty much gutted that you chose that moron over our friendship. But I never would have wished that on you. No matter how angry I was. I...' His eyes flitted away. 'I cared for you. You deserved better.'

She straightened up, not ready to hear him defend her. Not ready to hear how short a time he'd been impacted. Not ready for all her angst to be for nothing. 'I think I got exactly what I deserved. Like I said, I always was prepared to accept the consequences of my actions.'

'For years? Wasn't that a little extreme?'

She stared at him warily. Better he thought her a martyr. 'Some lessons take longer to learn than others.'

She shrugged off the comment and the conversation. 'So…what did you do after we went our separate ways?'

Marc made busy with the sloshing. 'Kept a low profile.'

Super-low. He might as well not have existed. Which was pretty much what she'd asked of him.

He'd walk through fire if you asked him to…

'The national skills shortage hit during my summer job up north, right after graduation, and suddenly I was pulling in a small fortune for an eighteen-year-old. It set me up beautifully to buy an old charter boat the next year and refurbish it during the off-season. Now I have three.'

'So it worked out okay, then—even though you didn't make it to uni?' Relief washed through her.

His smile wasn't kind. 'Trying to decide how high up the list you need to put me?'

Her make-good list. If she was going to finish the job she'd come for, she had to be thorough. Confession time. She found his eyes and held them, took a deep breath. 'Top half.'

'Sorry?'

She cleared her thick throat. 'You asked earlier which half of my list you were in. I just wanted you to know you were in the top half.' She clenched her hands. 'High in the top half…'

His next words were cautious. Almost unwillingly voiced. 'You seriously have a list?'

She nodded.

His brows dropped. 'Why?'

Panic surged through her. What a stupid question

not to have anticipated. She swallowed hard. 'Self improvement.'

His frown looked like doubt. But he let it pass. 'How high was I?'

Somewhere off in the dunes, a bird of prey shrieked out across the night. Her voice, when it came, was hushed. Quiet enough that he'd have to hear her heart pounding. 'The top. Number one.'

It took a lot to shock Marc Duncannon. But she managed to pull it off. He had a few goes at answering before coherent words came out of his gaping mouth. 'I'm the first person you've come to find?'

Shaking her head made thick cords of salty dark hair, still a tiny bit damp from her dunking earlier, swing around her face. It had to suffice as a screen. 'Actually, you're the last.'

'But did you just say—'

'Top of my list, yes, but the hardest. I left you till last.'

God. Would he realise what that meant? It was screamingly obvious, surely? The silence was almost material. Even the whale seemed to hold her breath. Emotion surged through his eyes like the waves battering them both. Hope, hurt, anger… Then, finally, nothing. A vacant, careful void.

'You've held onto those memories all this time?'

Her stomach sank. 'Haven't you?'

He looked away and when his eyes returned to hers they were kindly. Too kindly. 'No.'

No? Beth blinked.

'Give yourself a break, Beth. We were kids.'

His unconcerned words struck like a sea snake. Bad enough to have sabotaged for nothing the only relationship of her life that meant something to her. Now she'd wasted years of angst, endured a mountain of guilt… and it had barely registered on his emotional radar.

'Losing our friendship meant nothing?'

He sighed. 'What do you want me to say, Beth? It cut deep at the time but everything worked out. Life goes on.'

Mortification streaked through her. She stared at his carefully neutral face. Maybe Janice had been right? Cut free of her, Marc had gone on to make a success of his life—not what he'd always told her he would do but then how many of her school mates had ever actually grown up to do what they imagined they'd do for the rest of their lives? She certainly hadn't. While she was literally drowning in her regrets, Marc had rebounded and done a fine job of getting by without her.

Everything she'd been through… For nothing?

'Beth?'

She shot her hand up and turned away from his indifference. She tossed her tattered whale-washer ashore and turned to wade out into the deep, dark water. The only place she could go. To let her heart weep in private. She pushed her legs angrily through the water for a few steps and let the angry ache fill her focus.

'Beth!'

She wanted to keep walking, to show him he meant as little to her as, apparently, she did to him. But she just wasn't that good a liar. She turned when the water was thigh high.

'Not in the water,' he urged. 'Not at night. Go up on the beach.'

Screw you. 'Why not?'

'Sharks will be drawn by the dead calf. They're more active at night. We shouldn't go in deeper than our knees.'

She practically flew back to the shallows. Survival before dignity. Marc didn't say anything further. It took her several minutes walking down the beach to reach a place she felt was sufficiently dark and safe. Safe from the dune snakes. Safe from the whale-eating sharks. Safe from Marc Duncannon and his awful neutrality.

She sank down onto the sand and let the tremors come.

Her life had changed direction that day behind the library and it had changed again eight years later and this man was central to both. A man who was so entirely unaffected by what had happened to them back at school.

Deep breathing helped. Plunging her bare toes into sand that was still warm from the day helped. Closing her eyes and imagining she was anywhere else but here helped.

Whatever it took to fool her body into thinking it wasn't facing an unbearable amount of pressure. Something she wasn't really used to having to face. As a rule, a drunk body didn't care what was going on around it. And she'd been drunk for the better part of eight years. Even when she wasn't.

In the early months of her marriage, she'd walked a careful line with Damien and his rapidly developing fondness for the bottle, keeping him just shy of the point where he liked to express his drunken feelings with his fists. But that line quickly got too hard to predict and so it was just easier to give in. To tumble behind him into the abyss where he was happiest and she was safest. The help she might have had evaporated. Friends. Her parents. They'd all stopped trying after her repeated assurances she was fine.

Why wouldn't they? She was Beth. Beth didn't make

mistakes. But Beth—as it turned out—was a gifted and convincing liar.

By the time they'd realised she wasn't fine, she was well and truly sunk. After a while, she didn't even hate it. The abyss was a pleasantly blur-edged place to lose your youth. And she'd learned how possible it was to function in normal society while artificially numb.

And then one day she'd woken up and looked around at the empty half of her bed, the total strangers dossed down in her living room and she'd seen, with awful clarity, the faces of all the normal people she'd thought she was cleverly keeping her drunkenness from. Their averted eyes. Worse—their pity.

For no real reason, she'd thought about Marc that morning. About the boy who'd had such faith in her. The boy she'd lived her life for as a teen. The boy she'd finally forced from her dreams—her marriage—after his memory had steadfastly refused to leave. And she'd realised she hadn't thought about him in years.

She'd sat crying in the shower long after the hot water ran icy cold.

Those convulsive shivers had been nothing on what was to come. The spasmodic wretchedness of weaning herself off the liquor, alone in her father's old warehouse, surrounded by the tormented images she'd painted in her darkest days. The destructive try-and-fail spiral that had made her feel increasingly bad about herself. Increasingly desperate for the unconditional acceptance a bottle offered. The only thing that had kept her going was painting.

Then one night she'd stumbled—drunk, to her eternal shame—into an AA meeting and found a room full of survivors who'd given her compassion and empathy and a path out of the abyss, not judgement.

Those strangers had saved her life.

Long before any make-good list, she held onto Marc's name as a ward against ever again forgetting someone who had represented such goodness in her life. She'd scrawled his name down on a scrap of paper that day she'd tumbled from the shower and she'd carried it in her wallet ever since, in lieu of the photos she'd thrown out years before in a fit of drunken heartbreak because looking at him had hurt too much.

She'd known that facing him today wouldn't be easy. But it had never—ever—occurred to her that he simply wouldn't care any more. If he ever actually had.

'Beth? Are you done?' His voice called her back from the darkness, just as it had two years ago that morning in the shower. 'I need you.'

There was urgency in his voice she couldn't ignore. And, in the face of what the whale needed, her decade-old issues could wait a few hours more. She quickly did what she'd come to do and then staggered, too sore and tired to run, back down the beach towards him.

The whale was thrashing violently in the water, the nasty arrow-head gash on its tail sawing back and forth, its whole body twisting.

'Is she having a seizure?' she cried as she neared.

'She can feel the tide,' Marc called. 'She's trying to move herself. We have to do it now.'

'You can't be serious?' He wanted to get into the water with a crazed half-ton animal? Immobile with exhaustion was one thing…

'She's too far on-beach. She won't be able to pull herself out. We have to help her.'

He had a loop of rope laid over his forearm and he was making darting efforts in between the wild thrashes of the whale, trying to snag the eyelet of the strap they'd managed to drag beneath her hours ago. But every time he got close, the insensible sea-mammoth twisted in his direction and he had to leap away, stumbling into the water.

With one mighty lurch, Marc plunged his arm into the water on the whale's offside and jumped back, bringing the strap with him. It took only a moment to push the rope through the eyelet like a sewing needle. Then he pulled half of it through and tossed it high over the whale to splash into the water next to Beth.

She knew what he needed her to do.

The whale had slowed its frantic efforts now, perhaps realising that it wasn't going to be able to do this alone. Beth made three attempts, feeling blindly along the sand in the dark shallows for her end of the strap, squinting against the salt water that splashed up into her eyes. Her careless groping meant Marc's entire sweatshirt was soaked in cold water, but she didn't care. She wouldn't be needing it for long now that they were going to free the whale, and her own temporary discomfort wasn't a patch on what this animal was going through.

On her fourth attempt, she emerged victorious. She clutched the strap tightly in one hand and felt around for Marc's rope. When she found it, not yet soaked, still floating on the surface, she shoved it with trembling hands through the eyelet and then walked backwards away from the whale, pulling the rope taut. Marc did the same.

The strap slowly emerged and rose, flexing and dripping, above the water line as it tightened around the whale's rounded belly.

'We need to walk behind her, Beth. It'll pull the ends together and tighten around her flank.'

Behind her? But that meant… She lifted wide eyes to him.

He was silent for long seconds. 'I know. But, sharks are survivors, too. We'll have to hope they're more interested in the dead calf than in its dangerously thrashing mother.'

Was that likely? Beth's skin burst into terrified gooseflesh all over.

His loud voice carried over the sound of the whale's writhing. 'I don't see that we have much choice, Beth.'

'There's always a choice, Marc!' she yelled back. AA had taught her that. They could both walk away from this animal and leave her to nature. Maybe it was meant to be.

He knew which way her mind was going. 'Is that a choice you could make, Beth? Because I couldn't.'

No. When it came down to it, neither could she.

He called out again. 'We'll try and twist her your way so you're pulling in the shallows. I'll take the deep end.'

'Oh, great, so I'll get to watch you be eaten by sharks instead. That'll be nice!'

She gritted her teeth and plunged into the deeper water. The adrenalin did its job and fed her a steady stream of power. They didn't waste any time, pulling their ropes hard and closing in until they stood side by side—mountain by waif—up to Beth's waist in water. It was a lot by her standards but not much for a whale. Hopefully, it would be enough. The manoeuvre pulled the snatch strap tight around the whale's bulging midsection. Marc moved them slightly to one side so that their rope wouldn't impede the thrust of her powerful tail.

'Ready, Beth?'

She wasn't. She never would be. But it seemed life was determined to plunge her back into the real world with a vengeance. She found his eyes, drew strength from them and nodded.

'Pull!'

She put her entire, insignificant weight behind her and leaned back hard on her rope. Marc immediately made more progress, his side of the rope vibrating above the waterline enough to give off a dripping, high-pitched whine. The whale groaned in harmony.

Beth's already damaged hands screamed as her end of the rope bit into them and she stumbled forward at the pain, losing purchase and crying out.

'Wait!'

Marc let his rope loosen and the whale heaved a sigh. Beth quickly stripped off Marc's drenched sweatshirt and wrapped it around her hands to protect them and then pulled her rope tight again. The salt water sluiced into open blisters, stinging badly.

'Okay…go!'

They heaved again and the whale slid slightly sideways, adding her remaining strength to their far less significant pulling power. But it was movement. And, after thirteen hours in the sand, that was not a small achievement.

'She's moving!' Beth squeezed out unnecessarily. No way would Marc not have noticed. 'Keep going!'

Adrenalin roared now through her body, warming her and giving her a capacity she never would have believed she had. She leaned hard on the rope and pulled with all her remaining strength, twisting her body and virtually walking—inch by inch—out into deeper water, up around her armpits, towing the enormous beast.

Marc was right there beside her, his neoprene muscles

bulging with the force of every pull. Neither of them was suffering quietly and their roars of effort merged with the whale's to disturb sleeping creatures for a kilometre. The whale suddenly twisted so that she was side-on to the beach, her tail now fully submerged, her body more torpedo-shaped in the water than it had been on the sand. Still rounded where the strap held her firmly. Beth and Marc changed their positions, widened out so that they could contribute to the whale's slow sideways thrash into deeper water. If the sharks wanted either of them they'd be easy pickings right now. The water lapped at Beth's breasts.

The whale battered her tail violently, slamming on the water for added purchase. But the miracle of buoyancy meant it was easier to tow half a ton of whale flesh. They did—slowly, painfully. And then—

'Beth, run!'

Marc dropped his rope and surged away from the manic animal. Beth stumbled and went under as her rope suddenly went slack and Marc hauled her up after him, her throbbing legs pushing against the pressure of the deep water.

The whale twisted and surged and turned the quiet shallows into a spa of froth and bubbles. The rope zinged out of its eyelets with an audible crack and the snatch strap dropped harmlessly away. In the time it took Beth to suck in a painful breath, the whale was free, half submerged, then fully submerged. And then—finally—it sank like an exuberant submarine, surfaced once to grab a euphoric lungful of air and then disappeared silently under the deep, dark surface.

Beth screamed her joy as she ploughed through the water, and then she lurched sideways as something harder and warmer than the whale slammed into her.

Marc swung her in a full three-sixty, hoisting her up in his arms and hauling her backwards out of the waist-deep water, whooping his elation. But their momentum and fatigued legs couldn't hold them and they stumbled down together into the shallows, Marc sinking to his knees and bringing Beth with him.

Tears of pain and exhaustion streamed freely down her face and she pushed uselessly against his body to right herself. But the natural chemicals fuelling her body drained as fast as they had come and left her shattered and shaking. The strength she'd miraculously found just moments ago fled. She sagged back against Marc's strength, useless.

He collapsed unceremoniously onto his bottom in the ankle-high surf and he dragged an insensible Beth between his wetsuit-clad legs. His hands pulled her more tightly against him. She crawled up into his rubbery shoulder.

'We did it,' he repeated hypnotically, as though reassuring a child, stroking her dripping hair and pressing her hard into him. As though she belonged there. Beth squeezed her streaming eyes shut and soaked up the gorgeous feeling of being this close to him. After so many years. She nuzzled in closer. A bad idea, no doubt, but impossible not to. Every accidental touch they'd shared as kids flashed through her mind and she saw, clear as day, how she had evolved from comfortable touching to flirtatious touching and finally experimental touching. Stretching boundaries. Testing boundaries. Testing him.

Their gasping breath was the only thing now disrupting the silence. Marc's murmurs softened further and started up a senseless whisper against her ear. Not even real words, just sounds. But they did their job; she sagged harder against him and let the trembles come. Elation this time instead of fear or anxiety or—worse—the DTs. A much better kind of tremor.

But they transported her exhausted mind immediately back to a perfect spring day behind the library when Marc had kissed her for the first and only time. His body wasn't this hard then, or his shoulders this broad, but he'd been on the verge of filling out to the potential she'd always known he had. She'd clung to him then just like this; as if he was saving her life with the hard press of his mouth on hers. The touch of his tongue against hers. And she'd shaken afterwards exactly the same. Except that time she'd been completely alone. The kiss was the last time they'd so much as looked at each other.

The cold water soaking into her body offered a splash of reality. That was a lifetime ago. Before the alcohol. Before she'd abandoned him.

He doesn't care, she reminded herself. She straightened slightly and went to pull away.

He resisted her pull. 'God, I've missed you, Beth.'

The words were so simple, so brutally whispered hard up against her ear, she wondered if he'd even meant to say them aloud. But he had, and his words screamed for acknowledgement. She let her body sag back into him and wriggled up until her face rested in the crook of his neck, her arm slung around his neck.

He wrapped his arms more firmly around her and just held her, cold and shaking, against his body. Rocking in the icy surf.

It didn't matter that she'd never been with him like this before—that she'd never let herself be vulnerable like this with anyone—it felt very, very right.

'I'm so glad you were here,' she said. 'I couldn't have even begun to manage this alone.'

He chuckled but even that seemed to hurt his aching body. It morphed into an amused groan. 'If it weren't for me, you wouldn't have been here in the first place.'

She lifted her head and looked at him seriously. Eye to eye. Their faces so close. Water still dripped down her skin. 'I could say the same.'

If not for her treatment of him in that all important final year of school, would he have gone on to study at uni like they'd planned? Would he have been living somewhere other than the remote south coast of the state running a charter company?

'It is what it is, Beth. You can't control everything.'

'Why not?' she sighed against the warm skin of his throat. Too tired to move and not particularly inclined to. 'Whose great idea was that? That we have no say in our destiny?'

'I didn't say that. Just that sometimes things just… happen. You can't hold yourself responsible for everything that occurs.'

She crawled in more comfortably. He took her full weight. 'That sounds an awful lot like you're accepting my apology,' she whispered.

His broad chest rose and fell beneath her torn-up hands. She held her breath.

'We were both kids,' he mumbled against her wet hair. 'We both did things we regret.'

She lifted her head to stare quizzically at him. 'What do you regret?'

His eyes darkened. Then blanked carefully over. 'I regret a lot of things.'

Stop talking, Beth. Now! That voice in her head seemed to know exactly where she was going next. She ignored its excellent advice. Her saturated chest heaved. 'Do you regret kissing me?'

Marc sucked in a breath, and she was too close to him to miss it. She wished she could see his eyes to gauge his reaction. 'I regret the manner in which I did it,' he said simply.

Pushing her hard up against the library wall and forcing her lips apart with his? She could see why he might regret that. If not for the fact that she'd been waiting years for him to take the initiative. She just didn't know it.

The sixteen-year-old tomboy deep inside asked the same honest questions she always had. 'How do you wish you'd done it?'

His thick voice was strained and it drew her eyes up to his. 'That's not a question you can ask me, Beth.'

She lifted her head. But the move cost her. She winced as her over-taxed muscles reacted sharply to the move. 'Why not?'

'Because of what you said afterwards. What you made me promise as you pushed me away.'

Don't ever touch me again. Don't speak to me again.

She closed her eyes. 'I was angry. And confused. It never occurred to me that you would actually honour that.' But he had. All damned year.

'Confused how?' His tired eyes took on a sharper edge.

'Because I...' Lord, how to get out of this one. 'Because it was *us*. Kissing. It threw me.'

He straightened. 'Because you hated it? Or because you liked it?'

For all her faults, she'd never been a liar. Not to Marc. But she was proficient at hedging. 'Are you seriously asking me to rate your kissing prowess?'

'Do I look like I have any doubts about that?'

Her mouth twisted. 'No. You always were infuriatingly confident.'

His expression changed in a blink and then was gone. Maybe the moonlight was playing tricks on her, making her see vulnerability that couldn't possibly be there. Not in that body. Not in this man.

'It matters to me, Beth. Whether you hated it. Whether I actually damaged our friendship, too.'

Too. Misery came surging back in at the reminder that she'd said the words that destroyed their friendship. Even if she hadn't set out to. She was only going to ask him to back off for a while. But he'd kissed her and she'd panicked. Those soft lips pressing against hers, forcing hers wider. The hands that had plunged into her hair to hold her captive sent electric sparks through her body and threw her into confusion. The press of his eager body into hers had made her want things she shouldn't want. The desperate, intense pain in his eyes echoing hers. The thick smoke-like energy he'd been pumping out all around them.

Did she like it?

Enough to rip his heart out with her reflexive overreaction. She took a breath. Held his eyes. Held her breath. 'I didn't hate it.'

This was where he'd kiss her in a movie. The water. The cold. The intimacy. The moonlight. And her admission practically cried out for his mouth on hers.

Instead, he nudged her head back down to his shoulder and rested his cheek against her wet hair. She felt his low words against her ear, vibrating in his throat. 'Thank you, Beth. Deep down, I worried I'd struck the death blow.'

No. That honour remains with me. Snapping on the heels of that thought came another. He'd wondered about his part in that kiss? That wasn't the admission of a man who'd never given it another thought…

Beth lifted her face to study his. A particularly full wave washed over them and buffeted Beth against him with its chilly brush. Waiting for a kiss was stupidly naive and impossibly romantic. Her heart squeezed hard. Had she been so starved for affection in her loveless marriage that she was finding it now in impossible places? Marc was just moved by their circumstance and harking back to better times. That was all.

Since there was to be no kissing, she needed, really badly, to get off him. But her body had practically seized up in the foetal position and straightening her limbs was a new kind of agony. Just when she thought she'd already met all the cousins in the Pain family.

'Easy, Beth. You need to walk off the ache. Your muscles will be eating themselves.'

Pretty apt, really. Starting with the giant thumping one in her chest cavity. Crawling into Marc's lap had not been part of her plan as she drove up the coastal highway this morning, but now that she had it was hard to imagine ever getting the sensation out of her mind. Her heart.

But she had to.

Her back screamed as she pushed against Marc's chest and twisted up onto her knees, between his. She gave herself a moment to adjust.

'Just one more thing…' he said before she could rise much further.

Those powerful abdominal muscles she'd spied back at the car did their job and pulled his torso up out of the splash and hard into hers. His lips slid warmly, firmly against her mouth and he took advantage of her shocked gasp to work them open, hot and blazing against her numb flesh. Her lips drank heat from him and came tingling back to life, startled and wary. His hands forked up into her wet hair and held her face while he teased and taunted her blissfully with his tongue, letting her breathe his air as though he were giving her the kiss of life.

Which, in a way, he was.

Relief and a decade of desire surged through her. Forgiveness tasted an awful lot like this.

He lifted his face and stared into her glassy eyes. 'This is how I would do it if I had my time over,' he said softly and then lowered his mouth again.

Whether he was making a point or making good on a ghost from his past, Beth didn't care. His mouth on hers felt as if it belonged there. Her nipples, already beaded from the icy ocean, suddenly remembered they had nerve endings and they sang out in two-part harmony from the pleasure of being crushed against solid granite. Heat soaked out from the contact even through his wetsuit.

Marc seemed to notice too, because he groaned against her mouth and let one hand slide down to where small waves lapped against her underwear, worked under her blouse and then surged back up, scorching against her frozen spine.

It was the only other place that her skin met his. Other than his amazing, soft, talented mouth. Maybe she just hadn't kissed enough men, but she couldn't imagine how a kiss could possibly be better. Or more right. It was every bit as confronting as their last one.

Only this time she was equal to it.

It was a weird kind of rush, kissing a total stranger and your oldest friend. The man who knew everything about you. And nothing at all. Exactly as that unwelcome thought shoved its way to the front of her mind, she felt Marc stiffen beneath her. He ripped his lips away and turned his head. Disbelief painted his features.

'Stop…'

A rock lodged in Beth's chest. He tugged his hand out from under her shirt and resolutely pressed her away from him. She twisted sideways against the pain of his rejection and found herself on hands and knees in the shallows, undignified and lost. How must she look to him?

But he wasn't looking at her as he scrambled to his feet.

Beth followed the direction of his eyes up the beach, where a dark mass lurched and twisted on the shore near the calf.

'She's re-stranded,' he said, stumbling away a few steps, his voice thick from their kissing. Or from the agony of having failed to save the whale.

When he turned and reached out his hand, she waved him off. 'I can't, Marc. I hurt too much. You go. I'm going to need a second.'

It was a measure of their past friendship that he didn't falter and worry about helping her up. If anyone had ever respected her independence, it was Marc. Just another way he used to show his belief in her.

Pain came in all shapes and sizes. As Marc found the strength to run up the beach towards the beleaguered whale, stooping to grab his whale-washer from the shore, Beth knew she'd have to too.

They were in this together. Ready or not. And she was not about to let him down for a second time. Not when he was the only man she'd ever known who had ever believed in her.

She cried out as she straightened her tortured spine,

an anguished mix of pain and frustration and self-recrimination. Then she lurched up the beach after him, the golden glow of his kiss feeding her the necessary strength.

Just.

CHAPTER FIVE

THEY hadn't spoken in an hour.

Not because they were angry with each other, Marc knew. Not because there was weirdness after their kiss, which had happened so naturally. And not only because their spirits were broken by the return of the whale they'd worked so hard to save. It was just that they were both putting all their energy into the endless drag-and-slosh—slower, shorter, choppier. Eternal. At least there was no blazing sun to contest with now.

The whale could see her calf from her new beach position and Marc wondered if the stillness of her body meant she knew it had died. Attributing human qualities to it was as pointless as it was hard not to. Beth's eyes followed his to the whale's small round ones.

'Why do they do it—strand themselves?'

Marc shook his head. 'No one knows for sure.'

She blinked her fatigue. 'Do they want to die?'

'I don't think so.'

'Can't they see the land?'

'Some blame our electromagnetic technologies which throw their guidance systems out of whack. Others say their inner ears are damaged by under-sea quakes which mess with their ability to navigate.'

'What do you think?'

'I don't know. I just know what it does to them.'

Beth stroked the whale's cool skin. 'I think she came back for her baby.'

Marc nodded. 'Could be. I've seen mothers and calves together in the deep water creches, the bond is definitely strong enough.'

'Maybe she just wanted closure.'

Beth's dark head tipped back, rolling gently on her shoulders to ease the ache. His eyes followed hers upwards. It seemed bizarre to notice, through the death and the pain and the blistering cold, how pretty the night was. It truly was a beautiful Australian night. More stars than he'd ever seen in his life—that was what he'd thought when he'd first moved to the deep south of the state. The Milky Way in all its blanketing glory. It was kind of nice to see someone else appreciate it.

Beth arched her head back so far she almost stumbled. He twitched to race to her—even knowing he'd never get there—but caught himself just as she did.

'We're so small,' she murmured, regaining balance, her face still turned heavenward. 'Do you think that there's a Marc and a Beth and a whale somewhere out there fighting for life, just like we are?'

Marc followed her glance up to the sky. 'I guess… statistically. Could be.'

Her thoughts were as far away as those stars.

'It seems impossible that life could only exist on one planet out of a million twinkling lights.'

'You aren't seeing the planets. Only the suns in solar systems full of other planets.'

She turned cold-drugged eyes on him and considered what he'd said for an age. Marc frowned. Her speech was getting slurred, her lids heavy. He'd have to get her out of the icy water soon. She was turning hypothermic. And talking about space.

'We're such an insignificant part of an insignificant part of something so big,' she murmured. 'Why do we even worry about things that go wrong? Or things that go right. Our whole drama-filled lives are barely a blink of the universe's eye. We make no difference.'

Marc stopped sloshing. 'It makes a difference here and now. And life is not about how long it is. It's about how full it is.'

'Full?'

'Full of love. Joy.' He looked back at the whale. 'Compassion.'

She lowered her face to look at him. 'Even if it's only a blink?'

'I'd rather have a moment of utter beauty than a hundred years of blandness. Wouldn't you?'

Her eyes blinked heavily. 'You would have made a good astronaut,' she mumbled.

Marc frowned.

'Fourth grade. You wanted to be a space-man. You thought there was a space princess you were supposed to save.' Her teeth chattered.

A numb smile dawned. 'I haven't thought about that for years. I can't believe you remember it.'

She returned her focus to him. 'I remember everything.'

She'd driven him crazy in the playground, insisting on being the astronaut and refusing to be the princess. Was that the beginning of her tomboy ways? An insane glow birthed deep inside him that she'd held on to those memories. It suggested she hadn't stopped caring when she'd pulled the pin on their friendship. She'd just stopped being there.

His smile withered.

'So tell me about your mum,' she murmured.

His gut instantly tightened as she forced her eyes to focus on him.

'What happened between the two of you?'

His heart started to thump. Hard. 'Didn't we already cover this?'

'Nope. I asked, you hedged.'

'Doesn't that tell you anything?'

'It tells me you don't want to talk about it.'

'Bingo.' He glared at her. 'But I'm sure that's no deterrent to you.'

The more defensive he got, the more interested she got. It seemed to slap her out of her growing stupor. 'Not particularly.'

He threw his shoulders back and shot her his best glare. Subtlety was wasted on Beth. 'If you give me a few minutes I'll see if I can find a stick for you to poke around in that open wound.'

Her face was a wreck. Grey beneath the windburn, shadows beneath her eyes. But she still found energy to fight him on this. 'I'm more interested in why you have an open wound in the first place.'

Because my mother is a nightmare.

'Family stuff happens, Beth. I'm sure your relationship with your parents isn't perfect.'

She got that haunted look from earlier. 'Far from it. I've disappointed them in a hundred different ways. But I still see them. What happened with Janice?'

'You don't remember? How she could be?'

She tilted her head in that hard to resist way. He'd never felt less like indulging her. He didn't discuss his mother. Period.

So why was he?

'I always assumed it was because she lost your father,' she said. 'That it kind of…ruined her.'

He stared. 'That's actually a fairly apt description.'

Beth frowned, stopped sloshing. Her teeth chattered spasmodically between sentences. 'I remember how hard she was on you. And on me. I remember how hard you worked at school and at the café to do well for her. But she barely noticed.'

His heart beat hard enough to feel through his wetsuit. He crossed his arms to help disguise it. 'What do you remember about her personally? Physically?'

Beth's frown intensified. 'Um… She was tall, slim… Too slim, actually. Kind of…' Her eyes widened and her words dried up momentarily. When she started again she had a tremor in her voice that seemed like a whole lot more than temperature-related. 'Kind of hollow. I always felt she was a bit empty.'

Marc stared. She'd just nailed Janice. And those were still the early years.

'I'm sorry,' she whispered, as if finally realising she was stomping through his most fragile feelings.

'Don't be. That's pretty astute. After we…went our separate ways, she got worse. Harder. Angrier. The more I tried to please her, the less pleased she seemed. She'd swing between explosions of emotion and this empty nothing. A vacant stare.'

Beth swallowed hard enough to see from clear across the whale. She'd completely stopped sloshing. Her pale skin was tinged with green.

'She'd always been present-absent. Since my dad died. But it got worse. To the point she'd forget to eat, to lock the house up, to feed the cat. He moved in with the over-the-road neighbours.'

A tight shame curled itself into his throat.

'It took me another two years before I discovered she was hooked on her depression medication,' he said, swiping his towel in the ocean ferociously. 'And that she had been since my dad died.'

The earth shifted violently under Beth's feet and it had nothing to do with the lurching roll of the whale. A high-pitched whooshing sound started up in her ears.

'Your mum was addicted to painkillers?'

'*Is*. Present tense.'

Oh, God. The unveiled disgust on his face might as well have been for her. The description of Janice ten years ago might as well be her two years before. Beth's voice shook and she forced herself to resume sloshing to cover it up. 'And that's why you don't see her?'

'I have no interest in seeing her.' He dropped his stiff posture and almost sagged against the whale as he bent to soak his towel again. 'Working on the trawlers was more than a financial godsend; it gave me space to breathe. Perspective. And an education. I watched some of those blokes popping all manner of pills to stay awake. Improve the haul. I saw what it did to them over a season. When I got back and saw through educated eyes how she was, I was horrified.' Those eyes grew haunted. 'She was my mum, you know?'

Beth nodded, her fear-frozen tongue incapable of speech.

'All Dad's insurance money, all the money I'd been sending home from up north… She blew most of it on pills. She was no further ahead financially than when I left.'

Beth wanted to empathise. She wanted to comfort. But it was so hard when he might as well have been describing her. Suddenly Janice's desperate taloned grip on Beth's forearm all those years ago made a sickening sense. 'What did you do?'

His sad eyes shadowed further. 'I tried for three years. I gave her money, she swallowed it. I signed her up to support groups and she left them. I hid her Xexal and she'd tear the house up looking for it. Or magically find some more. I threatened to leave…' he shook his head '…and she threw my belongings into the street. One day I just didn't take them back inside.'

'You moved out.'

'It was all I had left to fight back with. She was hell-bent on self-destruction and I wasn't going to watch that.' He shuddered. 'I thought losing me might have been enough…'

But it wasn't.

'Do you see her at all?' Beth whispered.

'Not for four years. The one useful thing I did do was buy out her mortgage. She can't sell the house without me so I know she has somewhere to sleep, at least. And I get meals delivered to her now instead of sending her cash, so I know she has food. For the rest…' His shrug was pure agony.

Compassion and misery filled Beth at once. For Marc, who loved his mother no matter how difficult she'd been. For Janice, who lost the love of her life when Bruce Duncannon had a cardiac arrest and who had never truly coped as a single parent. And for herself, whose path wouldn't have been so very different if not for the blazing memory one Sunday morning of a young boy who'd always believed in her.

A powerful love.

'Would you ever try again?' She felt compelled to ask. Knowing if she was in Janice's shoes she'd want *someone* not to give up on her. Deep down inside. No matter how much she protested. The way her parents had hung in there for her. Despite everything.

Marc lifted his gaze. His brows folded. His eyes darkened. 'Too much would have to change. I've accepted that the only time I'll see my mother again is if she's in hospital, in a psych ward or in the ground.'

The gaping void in his heart suddenly made shattering sense. She remembered what it was like living with Damien in the early days, before she'd succumbed to the bottle. She could only imagine what it must have been like for a child living with that. Then the man, watching someone he loved self-destruct.

But she herself was that hollow. An addict. Never truly recovered, always working at it. As if Marc didn't already have enough reasons to hate her, this would be too much.

'Go ahead and say it, Beth. I can see your mind working.'

Startled, her eyes shot up. She couldn't say what she truly wanted to say. But she found something. 'What about yourself—did you ever seek help for yourself?'

The frown came back. 'I don't need help.'

'You're her son. There's—' She caught herself just before she gave away too much. 'I'm sure there's assistance out there for you, too.' She knew there was. Her parents had accessed it.

The frown grew muddled. 'To help me do what?'

Beth lifted her shoulders and let them slump. 'Understand her.'

His expression grew thunderous. 'You think I lack understanding? Having lived with this situation since I was nine years old?'

Beth wanted to beg him to reconsider. To be there for his mother, since no one else was. But she burned for the little boy he must have been too. 'If not understanding, then…objectivity? You had it briefly when you returned from up north and look how clearly it helped you to see.'

'Objectivity did nothing more than make me realise what a junkie my mother had become.'

Beth winced at the derogatory term. She'd had similar words ascribed to her over the years. Five years ago, they struck her shielded centre and were absorbed into a soggy mass of indifference. These days they cut.

Disappointment stained his eyes. 'I really thought you'd have understood, Beth. I wasn't oblivious back in school. I know you stopped coming around because of her.'

I stopped a heck of a lot more because of her. She'd started pulling back from their friendship because Janice had begged her to. And that withdrawal led to everything else that followed.

'I just… She's your mother, Marc, and all you have left. I know it's hard but I just don't want to see you throw it away—'

'Throw it away?' he thundered. 'I *bled* over that decision, Beth, even worse than when you—' He stopped short and snapped his mouth shut, glaring at her through the darkness. 'She's an addict. You have no idea what it is like to live with someone who is controlled by their compulsion. The kind of damage it does to everyone around them. How the poison spreads.'

Tears pricked dangerously in Beth's eyes, welling and meeting the salt that still clung to her lashes. It dissolved and filled her eyes with a stinging mix that she had to blink to displace. He was talking about her. He just didn't know it. She turned her face away on the pretext of re-wetting her shredded rag. Behind her, pain saturated every word.

'I have no interest in ever putting myself in that position again,' Marc vowed.

She knew plenty about being an addict but what *did* she understand about living with one? Her response to Damien's addiction had been to cave in and join him. Hardly a battle. Walking away from Janice must have been brutal for Marc—on all fronts—but it meant he kept his sanity. He survived. He controlled the spread of the poison.

Misery washed through her.

She lifted damp eyes back to his. Nodded. 'I understand, Marc. I do understand.' Only too well. Her eyelids dipped heavily. 'I'm sorry I wasn't there for you,' she risked after a long silence, forcing her lids open.

Marc was silent for the longest time but finally spoke. 'I'm sorry you weren't too. I could have used a friend.'

Did he not even have one to turn to? 'When did you walk out?'

'Christmas Eve four years ago.'

She'd spent most Christmas Eves trying to act straight while her over-protective parents threw anxious glances between her and Damien, who'd done his best to appear attentive. Meanwhile Marc had been carrying suitcases away from his mother's house. Lord, what a contrast. 'Who did you… Were you alone—at the time?'

'Are you asking whether I was single?'

She was so tired she could have been asking anything. 'I'm asking whether you were alone.' Worrying he'd had no one only made it worse.

He nodded. 'I was.'

No father. No extended family in Australia. No friends. No girlfriend. Just a long-time addict mother.

She closed her eyes for the pain she could hear in his voice all these years later. As a boy, Marc's defence of his mother was legendary. He held on to love for a long time.

'I went back out onto the trawlers for another couple of seasons. More than they recommend, but I felt I had nothing to hang around the city for. That decision turned my life around.'

'You're still such a glass half-full person, aren't you?' She'd clung to the concept when things were at their lowest ebb. 'I remember that about you.'

He paused the sloshing. 'We're responsible for our happiness just as much as our actions. No one else is going to do that for you.'

True enough. She was a walking example. If she hadn't dragged herself back from the abyss… An exhausted yawn split her thought.

'I have to move faster,' she said to herself as much as him. 'If I keep slowing down, I'll stop for good.'

'You can stop any time you need to, you know that.'

If only life were that simple. That simply wasn't true sometimes. As she and his mother knew only too well. 'I'll be here as long as you are.'

'Still competitive?'

There was no way she was going to abandon him another time he needed her. But there was no way she was going to tell him that either. She forced her body to double its pace.

'You got me.'

CHAPTER SIX

BETH had long given up trying to control the violent shaking of her frozen body, but the advancing ice-age finally showed in the loud chattering of her teeth. Not surprising, given she'd lost Marc's fleecy sweatshirt to the dark depths of the ocean during the refloating. It meant she only had her flimsy blouse to keep her top half warm. And nothing on the bottom.

Marc had eventually accepted she wasn't going to go back to the car and leave him alone with the dying whale, but he didn't like it. Exhaustion had even wiped the frown off his face. But her loudly clattering teeth seemed to break the last of his tolerance.

'Beth, you're freezing.'

Both their bodies were well into survival mode now, her own barely conscious of what was going on around it. Neither of them could do more than lean on the whale for support and drag arm-after-painful-arm from the water to slosh onto the animal to keep it wet.

'You have to get out of the water,' he said. 'You need to warm up.'

Her chill caused her voice to vibrate. It hurt even to speak, so tight was her chest. 'It's warmer in the water than out of it. And I'm not leaving you, Marc. You'd have to work twice as hard and you have nearly nothing left now.'

'I'll feel better knowing you're safe and dry.'

'I'm not leaving.'

She couldn't see his glare in the darkness but she could feel it.

'Fine,' he finally growled. 'Give me a second.'

He spread his dripping towel out on the whale's hide and splashed slowly ashore. Beth lost him in the darkness after he passed her. It seemed like a lifetime, alone in the dark with the whale, but he finally returned.

'Take this,' he said bluntly, thrusting the last muesli bar at her.

Too exhausted to eat, she tucked it into the hip of her knickers. Too exhausted to protest, he just watched her do it.

'Now this,' he said, and thrust something else at her.

Beth reeled back and almost lost her footing, catching herself at the last second against the whale's cold body. Her mind lurched out a preventative *no!* a split second before her body hummed an eager *yessss!*

'It's whisky. Dry, but it will warm you up a bit.' He raised the silver flask right in her face and it glinted in the moonlight.

Her stomach roiled. Her blood raced. Her body screamed with excitement.

'Get it away from me.' She didn't mean to shove him so roughly, didn't even know where she found the energy, but the flask fell from his hands into the salt water. He scrabbled to pick it up, frowning in the moonlight.

'Take it, Beth. You need to have something.'

'I've been drinking water.'

'That'll keep you alive but it won't stop you getting hypothermia. If you won't get out of the water, then it has to be this.'

'I don't drink.'

Her ridiculously weak protest actually made him laugh. 'Well, you're going to have to make an exception, Princess. Survival comes first.'

He shook the water off the flask and held it out to her again.

Her chest heaved and her eyes locked on it. She could just reach out and—

'I can't, Marc…' *I can't break down in front of you.*

'It won't kill you.' He unstoppered the flask and took a healthy swallow, wiping his hand across his sticky lips when he finished to make his point. Beth had never felt more like a vampire. She wanted to hurl herself at those lips and suck and suck…

Shamed tears sprang into her eyes. 'Please, Marc. I can't.'

I can't show you what I really am…

His eyes narrowed but he was relentless. 'It's this or the car, Beth. Your choice.'

What was a bit more salt on her already crusty face? She ignored the two tears that raced each other down her cheeks. 'Do you want to see me beg, Marc?'

His frown practically bisected his face. 'I want you to be warm, Beth. I want you to drink.'

She forced her back straighter. 'And I won't.'

'For crying out loud, woman! Why are you so difficult?'

Old Beth and new Beth struggled violently inside her. Old Beth just wanted to throw her alcoholism in his face to punish him for forcing her hand like this. For putting her in the position of having to defend herself. To expose herself. To *him*, of all people. The man she'd already let down in a hundred ways. The man whose good opinion seemed to matter to her more than anyone else did. *New* Beth understood that using it as a weapon would only hurt him horribly and, ultimately, disappoint him more.

She knew she couldn't say nothing, either. But saying something didn't have to mean she was beaten. She could trust him with the information. Like she'd trusted her AA sponsor with all her deepest secrets. Couldn't she? Never mind the fact that he'd just told her his mother was an addict and made it painfully clear how much that disgusted him. This was Marc… He'd see she had her addiction under control. He'd see how hard she was working. He'd understand. He always had.

She laughed, low and pained. God, now she was lying to herself! Who was she kidding? This was *Marc.* She deserved his disgust for what she'd done and how she'd been.

She stared at the determination in his face. He meant it when he said drink or car. A numb kind of fatalism came over her. Whatever he did—however he reacted—it couldn't be worse than the wondering. Than fearing what might happen if she was revealed to the world. To him.

But her heart still hammered and it pounded into the miserable ache that filled her chest. Why was it easier to trust a total stranger with the truth than the man who'd been her closest friend?

It was hard to tell where the cold-trembles stopped and the terror-trembles started, but she thrust out her violently shaking hand towards him and raised defiant eyes and said the words aloud she'd been saying twice a week for two years.

'Hi. I'm Elizabeth and I'm an alcoholic.'

* * *

Marc's stomach tightened right before it dropped into a forty-storey free fall. His breath seized up and his skin prickled cold all over. He dropped his towel on the whale and turned away from Beth without so much as looking at her trembling outstretched hand. He marched off into the darkness, ignoring the shocked mortification on her face. He couldn't trust himself not to.

I'm Elizabeth and I'm an alcoholic.

His heart hammered. People made those jokes all the time, but the degraded, pained tone in her voice and the bleached courage in her eyes told him she wasn't kidding.

Beth was an alcoholic.

His Beth.

He kept walking, ignoring the fact he couldn't see what was two feet in front of him in the sand and his feet were dangerously bare. A deep, savage ache drove him forwards. That Beth—*Beth*—could be afflicted like his mother. That it could happen to two people he loved. What was he—some kind of jinx? All the people he cared about ended up dead or…

The living dead.

He clutched the flask—a piece of his father—close to him. Beth's eyes had shifted back and forth on it as if it were made of excrement one moment and pure ambrosia the next. He knew that look only too well. It was the way his mother used to look when she hurried past a pharmacy all stiff and tall. Just before her body caved in on itself and she'd turn back for the entrance with a hard mouth and dark eyes, dragging him along into hell.

Beth wanted this whisky. Badly.

His fingers flexed more tightly around it. Growing up, she'd been his role model. Sensible. Smart. Courageous.

Everything he valued most in a friend. Everything he'd searched for in himself. Yet sensible, smart, brave Beth had ended up addicted to alcohol. If she could succumb…

But she was fighting it. Some deep, honest part of him shouted that through the darkness. She wanted it but said no. His chest ached for the pain that had contorted her face. For the extra agony that this night must be for her. As if the cold and pain weren't bad enough.

He recognised it, even if he didn't understand it.

That thought brought him up short. Maybe she could explain. Help him understand. He owed her the chance, surely? He pivoted on his bare feet and followed the silver moonlight trail back to where he could vaguely see the shadow of a whale and a slender woman silhouetted against the rising moon.

Beth lifted bleak eyes to him. It hurt that he'd put that look there. He bent to re-drench his towel and took several deep breaths before trusting himself to speak.

'How long?'

There were probably more intelligent, sensitive questions to ask right at that moment but, more than anything, he needed to know how long she'd been struggling. Half of him hated it. The other half hated that she'd gone through it without him. She glanced away at the moon and then didn't quite find his eyes again. She was terrified. But hiding it. Something deep and painful welled up inside him, cut into the already sensitive flesh around his heart. He was hurting her.

Just like she'd hurt him. Except this didn't feel like justice.

Wide, stricken eyes returned to his. 'Eight years drunk. Two years sober. I'm recovering.'

Was there even such a state? Wasn't someone

alcoholic for ever—just a sober alcoholic? Her focus kept returning to the flask. Shifty, sideways glances. He wanted to empty the contents into the sea but, the way she was looking, she might just plunge into the water and try to guzzle the salt water. A deep hunger blazed in her eyes. It elbowed its way in amongst the self-disgust. It reminded him of the look in her eyes that day behind the library.

'Did you start at school?' he asked.

She shook her dank locks. 'About a year after I got married.'

Marc winced. Did she start the moment she hit legal age? 'Why?'

Her eyes widened and tears grew in them. 'Things got…hard.'

'Life gets hard for everyone.' Not everyone turned to the bottle. Alcohol. Pills. It was all the same—a cop-out.

'I know. I'm not special. But I made that choice and now I'm living with the consequences.'

At least Beth accepted that she was at fault. He'd heard every excuse under the sun from his mother. She had headaches, she wasn't sleeping, one medication made her crave another… It was never truly *her* fault.

His mouth tightened. Beth's eyes kept flicking back to the flask he held down at his side. She lifted a hand and pressed it to her sternum as though a ball of pain resided there and crushing it helped. Something old and long-buried made him turn and hurl the flask as far out to sea as he could. Its shape and weight gave it a heap of extra flight.

'What the hell are you doing?' Beth cried out and lurched towards its airborne arc.

Christ. Did she want a drink that badly? 'I'm removing temptation.'

'That was your father's!'

Surprise socked him between the ribs. That she cared at all. To think of that. His mother never would have thought of him through her haze. She'd have been braving the sharks to retrieve her pills. Not like the old days when he was the centre of her world. The dual centre, shared with his father. His frown doubled. 'It's just a thing, Beth. It's not him.'

'You could have just put it back in your bag!'

'Would it have been safe there?'

Her back straightened up hard, even though it must have hurt her to do it. Raw hurt saturated her voice. 'It's been safe in there all day.'

What could he say to that? He should have known an addict would sniff out the nearest fix.

Beth's breathing returned in big heaves, punctuated by bursts of compulsive shaking that rattled her bones. 'Now *you'll* freeze,' she accused.

'I'll get by. I have more insulation than you.' He folded his arms, spread his legs. Classic Marc. 'But we aren't talking about me. We're talking about you.'

'Oh, I must have missed the point where your inquisition turned into a conversation.'

His mouth tightened. But her words had an effect. He forced himself to take a step back, to ease his body language. This was clearly hard enough for her. 'I'd like to hear about it, Beth. To understand it.' Though he had to force himself to say so calmly.

'So you can decide how disgusted you should be? Or how much like your mother I am?'

He stiffened. 'We're going to be out here a long time yet, Beth. Did you really expect to drop a bombshell like that and then just go back to talking about the weather?'

No, she didn't. Then again, she hadn't planned to mention it at all—not to him—and, as it turned out, her instincts were spot on. She stared at him warily where once she would have blazed unconditional trust up at him. 'It took me six months from the day I closed the door of Damien's house behind me until the day I could stand up in AA and announce I'd been sober for a month.' She sloshed his side of the whale because he'd frozen in position. 'Then two. Then five. Then ten.' She shuddered in a breath. 'Two years of my life trying to undo what I've done. I've judged myself enough for everyone in that time.'

I really don't need it from you.

He flushed, which was a miracle enough, given the temperature. Then he cleared his throat. 'Please, Beth. No judgement.'

Uh-huh, sure. She drowned in his steady, silent regard but finally sighed, 'What would you like to know?'

His pause was eternity. 'All of it.'

Fair enough. She'd opened this door with her dramatic declaration. She might as well fling it wide and see what rumbled out. It couldn't be any worse than the raw disgust he'd failed to hide. She took a moment gathering her thoughts. Her aching exterior merged with her interior perfectly. She couldn't tell him all of it but there was still plenty left.

'I hurt my family when I married Damien so young,' she began, mostly a whisper but close enough that he could hear. 'I hurt you. Turns out I hurt myself too. But at the time he was everything I thought I wanted—a holy grail, like some kind of hall pass of credibility.

People treated me differently when I was with him and I…liked it. I'd been a pariah for so long…'

'Because of me?'

The monotonous sound of the ocean began to mesmerize her. 'No. Because of me. I chose you over all of them and their money.' She pushed the words out through a critically tight chest. Between the cold and the anxiety, it was amazing she could breathe at all. 'He found out pretty quickly that he didn't like much about married life. The responsibility. The expectation. And I was so young and trying so hard to be what I thought a good wife would be. When he insisted on a drink, what else could I do?' She took a deep breath. 'I'd ask him what he wanted and bring a second.'

'Misery loves company.'

So true in Damien's case. 'But then that point passed and it got so much worse.'

Marc stopped sloshing, his whole body wired. 'Worse how? Did he hurt you?'

She straightened up, took a moment working out how to answer. 'Sometimes.' Shame washed through her. 'I just blamed the drink. The more he drank the angrier he got, but the more I drank the less I cared.'

'So your drinking was Damien's fault?'

Her clumped hair screened her face as she shook her head. She'd never blamed her problems on anyone but herself and she wasn't about to start now. No matter how tempting. 'I made my own choices. It took me a long time to realise that, though.'

'So what finally made you stop?' The deepness of his voice rumbled in the night.

'I realised I was halfway through my twenties and I'd done nothing with it. I had a job but not a career. I had a marriage but not a family. I had a husband I didn't like and friends who only came over if I was buying. I had no interests.' She shook her head. 'I was a drunken bore with no achievements to my name, married to a man I didn't love. So I packed an overnight bag and I left.'

That made her sound stronger than she'd actually been, cowering in the shower, sobbing, but the last thing she wanted from Marc was more pity. Or to lose any more face.

For long minutes the only sounds were the repetitive sloshing of water on the whale's hide and the heaving of their lungs. And the *tick-tick* of Marc's brain as he got his head around her speech.

'What happened with McKinley?'

'Nothing. He didn't even try to stop me leaving. I wasn't the only one that was miserable. We both made the mistake.'

'You've cut all ties?'

'He signed the divorce papers without even getting in touch. I haven't seen him since.' Although she did hear about him from time to time. Those stories were always peppered with sadness for the man he should have been and relief for the woman she'd so nearly become.

'How hard was it—getting through the recovery?'

Was that more than just curiosity in his voice? Beth immediately thought of Janice. Sugar-coating wouldn't help him. She straightened her tortured back and met his eyes. 'You slog your guts out getting through the physical addiction and then you're left with the emotional dependence.' As hard as that was to admit. 'But you can get through it. I did. Until, one day, you've been stronger than it for longer than you were addicted.'

Until curve-balls like today swing into your life.

'You did it alone?'

'My parents wanted to help, of course, but I… It was

something I'd done to myself. I felt like I needed to undo it myself. To prove I could.'

'So what got you through?'

You did. The memory of Marc. The idea of Marc. She chose her words carefully. 'A dream of what I wanted to be.' *Who I wanted to be like.* 'And a strong AA sponsor.'

Marc was silent for a long time. He shook his head. 'I feel like I should have been there for you. So you didn't have to turn to a stranger. I should have been strong for you.'

Her heart split a little more for the loyalty he *still* couldn't mask. Despite everything. 'No, I had to be strong for me. Besides, it wouldn't work if Tony was a friend. The emotional detachment is important.'

'We've been pretty detached this past decade.'

It only took a few hours in his company for that to all dissolve. She lifted her eyes back to his and held them fast. 'Do you feel detached now?'

His silence spoke volumes.

'Will you be someone's sponsor one day?'

That was a no-brainer. 'Yes. When I'm strong enough.'

'You seem pretty strong now. The way you speak of it. Like a survivor.'

Warmth spilled out from deep inside at his praise. She was still a sucker for it. 'I have survived. But every day presents new challenges and I'm only just beginning to realise how sheltered I've been.'

Confusion stained his voice. 'As a child?'

'My parents shielded me from unpleasantness for the first half of my life and my drinking numbed me to it for the second. I've never really had to make a difficult decision or face a stressful situation. They were there for me. Or you were. I've always followed instructions or someone else's lead. Or avoided painful situations completely. I still have a lot to learn about life.'

He regarded her steadily. Was he remembering all those years where she'd tagged along with him, his partner in crime? Or the way she'd cut him from her life when things got too tough behind the library? *When the going gets tough, the tough go drinking.*

'You sought me out. That can't have been easy.'

'No. It wasn't.' But she had an unspoken and barely acknowledged incentive—seeing him again. He'd come to mean as much to her as alcohol. A yin to its powerful yang. That scrap of paper in her wallet a talisman. The painful ball in her chest made its presence felt. 'But I'd chew my leg off to have a drink right now. Do you call that coping?'

He flinched at her raw honesty. Pain washed into his eyes. But hiding who she was wasn't sustainable. He might as well see her, warts and all. For richer or poorer. In sickness and in health. Presently, sickness. But one day…

'It's been a rough night…'

The understatement of the century.

'If the flask washed up at your feet right now, would you open it?'

Her chest started heaving at the image. As though his words magicked up the little vessel, filled to overflowing with the liquid escapism she'd relied on for years.

No pain. No shame. No past.

No future.

Sadness flooded through her. 'Would you believe me if I said no?'

His deep silence brought their discussion to a natural close. She'd run out of story and courage. Her attention drifted back to how cold and how wet she was and she sagged against the whale as the after-effects of her monumental confession hit her body.

Marc frowned at her. 'I'll ask you one more time. Will you go back to the car?'

It hurt her to say no, but she'd promised herself she wouldn't leave him down here alone. And if she gave in on just one thing… She shook her head. A particularly icy shock of wind chose that moment to surge across the beach. She gasped at the savage, frigid gust and her skin prickled up into sharp gooseflesh.

Marc swore and glared at her. 'Don't say I didn't give you a choice…' He grabbed up his decrepit towel and ploughed out of the water and around to her side of the whale. Then he stepped in behind her and wrapped his whole body around her like a living, breathing windbreaker. Her body sang at the close, hard contact, the port in this storm his strong arms represented. A moment later, the slight warmth bleeding through his wetsuit also registered.

She sighed and convulsively shivered.

Marc swore and pulled away for an icy instant. She heard the zip of his wetsuit opening, the gentle brush of his fingers pulling her wet hair to the side, and then the blissful brand of his hot chest straight against her barely covered back. Skin on skin. Fire on ice. It soaked in like a top shelf brandy.

'Christ, Beth. You're glacial.'

He took her hands in his and crossed his arms around her, closing her more fully against his warmth. Her numbness leached away like ice melting and exposed a shelf of complicated emotions she'd been doing her best to muffle. She stiffened immediately.

'Don't argue, Beth. You had your chance. Let's get back to it.'

Their two bodies formed a hypnotic rhythm—bend, scoop, slosh…bend, scoop, slosh—half the speed they'd been going before the sun had set. His towel dripped on Beth's arms as she bent to refill the two-litre water bottle she was now using to wet the re-stranded whale. If not for the awful truths she'd just shared, their position would have been downright sexy. A half-naked man glued to a half-naked woman. As it was, it was just plain uncomfortable. For both of them.

And it went on for an eternity.

Despite the warmth seeping in from behind, Beth's teeth started chattering again. Marc convinced her to pull her barely dry jeans on again as some protection from the wind and she took the brief on-shore break to wolf down the muesli bar she'd had tucked away. Her body immediately started converting the grain into desperately needed energy and warmed her briefly from the inside. It wasn't a patch on the blazing warmth of Marc's skin.

She was too cold to worry about pride as she slipped back into the surf and then tucked herself shamelessly back into his body. He received her with the practice of years, not hours.

As if it was her rightful place.

Skin rubbed against skin periodically as Marc's body followed hers down and back up. His breath was warm against her bare neck. The sensations she'd been numb to for several hours came roaring back—making her tingle, making her remember. Making her—for once—ache for something more than a drink. A neglected part of her longed to peel his wetsuit right down to his waist, to see in detail and up close just how much of a man Marc Duncannon had grown into.

But she'd have to settle for feeling the topography of his body against her back instead.

'Does it feel good?' Marc said, low and almost unwilling against her ear.

She gasped and half turned in his hold. 'What?'

'Addiction.' She could feel his tension against her back, she didn't need to hear it in his voice. 'I figure it must for so many people to do it.'

Beth thought long and hard about that. About the rush, about how it felt when it was gone. Or denied. About why he wanted to know. She twisted back around in his arms and continued sloshing. 'It's not a choice you make. For me, it wasn't about how good it felt when I was drinking. It was about how bad it felt when I wasn't.'

'Describe it to me. Both feelings.'

She swallowed the lump of tears that suddenly threatened. Even though she knew this was more about his mother. *There* was the Marc she remembered. He wanted to understand.

'Were you ever infatuated with someone?' She forced the words out. Between the cold and the strong arms cocooning her, it was amazing she could speak at all.

'Like love?'

'No, not love. Obsession. Did you ever have a massive crush on someone inappropriate when you were younger—someone you could never be with?'

Marc stopped sloshing. 'Maybe.'

Tasmin? Except that he'd finally prevailed with her. They'd started dating in the final months of school.

'Do you remember how it possessed you? How it took over your days, your nights, your thoughts? You can't remember it starting but then it just…is. It's everything. It's everywhere. Like it's always existed. Like it could never not exist.' She stopped sloshing in his hold. 'Have you ever felt something like that?'

The tightness of his voice rumbled against her back and birthed goose bumps in its wake. 'Go on.'

'It's how it was with me and my addiction. I didn't recognise how it consumed me when I was deep inside it. I arranged my day around it. I made allowances for it. It became so normal. I learned to function around the compulsion. Just like the most concentrated of adolescent infatuations. And every bit as irrational.'

She felt him shake his head and she tensed. 'Is that no, you don't remember how it feels,' she asked, half turning back towards him, 'or no, you don't understand?'

His lips were enticingly close to her face. His breath was hot against her cheek. He swallowed hard. 'I remember.'

'Then you know how it can take you by stealth. The passion. The fixation. The feeling that you'll die if you don't have it in your life. And you don't even feel like it's a problem.'

Those arms tightened. 'It feels that good?'

'It feels great because you're love-sick. And all those endorphins feed your obsession. And it's hurting you but you don't notice. You don't care. Nothing matters as much as the feeling. As the subject of your passion. It's like a parasite. Built to survive. The first things it attacks are the things that threaten its survival. Judgement. Willpower. Self-awareness.'

Marc's silent breathing began to mesmerize her, his warmth sucking her in. She couldn't tell whether her words were having any impact on him. 'And being denied it physically hurts. It aches. You become irrational with the pain inside and out and you lash out at people you care about. And the more they intervene, the more you begin to imagine they're working to keep you away from the thing that sustains you. And that's when you start making choices that impact on everyone around you.'

She felt him stiffen behind her and knew he was thinking about his mother.

'But adolescents learn to deal with infatuation,' he said. 'Or they grow out of it.'

Or they give in to it. She wasn't surprised to hear condemnation in his voice, but it still saddened her. How many people saw addiction as a sign of moral weakness. A character flaw. 'Mostly because life forces them out of it. Classes. Structure. Discipline. Financial constraints. Exposure to new people. Cold reality has a way of making obsession hard to indulge.'

She turned back towards Marc again. The unexpected move brought her frigid jaw line perilously close to his lips as he leaned in for a slosh. The hairs on her neck woke and paid attention. 'But imagine that you're of legal age with ready cash, no particular structure to your day,' she whispered, 'no restraints on whether or not you indulge it. A husband who makes drinking a regular part of his day.' *And all the reason in the world to want to numb the pain.* 'No reason at all not to allow the great fascination to continue. Why wouldn't you?'

Steel band arms circled around her and held her still. Close. Her eyes fluttered shut. He spoke close to her ear. 'Because it's killing you?'

'By then, you are so hooked on the feeling you just… don't…care.'

He turned her in his hold and looked down on her, a

pained frown marring his face. 'You didn't care about dying?'

She shook her head. Hating herself. Hating the incredulous look on his face. Not that she couldn't understand why, after everything he'd been through with Janice. She could feel it in the tension in every part of his body.

'Because you truly fear you'll die without it,' she said.

His frown trebled and he pulled her towards him. Into his warmth. The kind of moment she'd lived for back in school. It was old Marc and old Beth from a time that the two of them could have conquered the world. From inside the crush of his arms, she could feel his chest rising and falling roughly. He was struggling with everything she'd just told him. And why not? It had taken her two years to finally recognise where her addiction seeded. And when.

Emotional and physical exhaustion hovered around her. She struggled to keep her eyes open, leaning her entire upper body into his. So tired, the only thought she had about the two perfect pectoral muscles facing her was what a comfortable pillow they'd make. His hand slipped around her back to better support her.

'I don't know what to say,' he said, voice rough.

'There's nothing you can say,' she murmured thickly. 'It's enough that you know.'

'Thank you for explaining.'

'I'm glad you understand now.' Her words slurred. Her eyes surrendered to the weight on them and closed. She leaned more heavily into him.

His voice was only a murmur but it echoed through the chest she pressed against. 'You want my understanding? I thought it was forgiveness you wanted?'

Nodding only rubbed her cheek against his chest. It was perfect friction. She did it twice. 'Both. I don't want you to hate me.'

Marc's thumping heart beat hard against her ear. Five times. Six times. 'I accept your apology, Beth.'

Something indefinable shifted in her world. Like the last barrel of a lock clunking into place releasing a door to fling open. And out rushed all her remaining energy like heat from a room, finally freed from her determination to win his forgiveness. Marc was the last of her list. She'd focused on those names for so long she'd never really given much thought to what lay beyond them. A dreadful unknown spread out before her. Something she had to brave without help.

Later. When she wasn't so warm and tired.

She found her voice. 'Thank you.'

He took her face in his hands and tipped it up to his. She forced her lids to lift. Hazel eyes blazed down onto her. 'I think I've been angry at you for a really long time.'

She blinked up at him, barely able to drag her lids open after each close. Knowing these words came straight from his soul. 'I know. I'm sorry.' She laid her face back against the pillow of warm muscle and sighed as the heat soaked into her cold cheeks.

'Why couldn't I let it go?' he murmured.

I don't know. The words came out as an insensible mumble as her lips moved against his skin. His arms tightened around her, held her up.

'Why couldn't I let you go?'

His voice swam in and out with the lapping tide and, ultimately, washed clear through her head and out again as she slipped into sleep, quite literally, on her feet.

CHAPTER SEVEN

A HIGH-pitched shriek dragged Beth from a deep, uncomfortable slumber. A musty smell filled her nose and she shifted around uncomfortable rocks that had somehow found their way into her bed.

Her eyes cracked open. Not a bed…the back of a car. And the shriek was a Wedge-tailed Eagle that, even now, circled the dim skies in search of breakfast. The rocks were the detritus that littered the back of Marc's four-wheel drive, cutting into her back and thighs where she lay on them. And the mustiness was a mix of the skanky old blanket that wrapped tortilla-like around her and the salty moisture of her clothes, her hair. Dry yet damp.

God damn it, Marc!

Fury forced her upright and every seized muscle in her body protested violently. She should have kept moving. She should have kept helping. Not sleeping comfortably—or even uncomfortably—while Marc froze his butt off alone with the whale.

She lurched like a caterpillar towards the rear doors of the wagon and used her bare feet to activate the internal handle. Icy-cold air streamed in as she pushed the doors with her legs and her skin prickled all over with gooseflesh.

It took longer than it should have, but she eventually scrambled out of the car and tucked the dirty blanket more securely around her against the chill wind. Up here, exposed above the dunes, it was almost worse than down on the shore. The world around her was still muted but tiny fingers of light tickled at the horizon.

'How long have I been out?' She didn't waste any time with pleasantries as she got back to the shoreline. Marc was up to his knees in the rapidly retreating ocean, practically sagging on the whale for strength. 'Why did you let me sleep?'

He turned his face her way. Haggard but still beautiful. To her. 'You passed out in my arms, Beth. You were exhausted.'

'So are you.'

'I wasn't the one asleep on my feet.' Frost rose from his lips with every word.

Beth's whole face tightened on a frown. Anxiety flowed through her. 'How are you?'

'Freezing. Thanks for asking.'

'What can I do?'

'You can not give me grief for putting an unconscious woman into my car.'

She bit back her frustration. 'I'm sorry to be ungracious. I just… You were alone.'

'I've done this before, on my own, Beth.'

'You shouldn't be alone.'

Well…! That was a mouthful and a half straight from her sleepy subconscious. The moment the words left her, she knew she meant more than just today. This man deserved the right woman by his side, for ever. A bit of happiness. He'd earned it.

Not that she was the right woman. Beth frowned at

the instant denial her mind tossed up. It was a little too fervent.

'Why are you single?'

He lifted one eyebrow. 'Why are you asking?'

'Because you'd be a catch, I would have thought. Even in the country.' Where men outnumbered women ten to one.

'Thanks for the confidence.'

All the time that had passed might not have existed. They fitted instantly back together. Back into the gentle jibes only friends could make.

'I've had girlfriends.'

Olympic Tasmin for one. 'Anything special?'

His eyes studied the lightening horizon. 'Nothing lasting, if that's what you're asking. But all nice women.'

'So what went wrong?'

He glared at her. 'I hope you're not warming up to offer relationship advice?'

Despite herself, she laughed. 'No. I may be a lot of things, but a hypocrite is not one of them.' Her eyes went to the whale. She looked ominously still. 'How is she?'

'Worse than either of us. But hanging in there.' His words were full of staged optimism. As though the giant animal could understand him.

'You're not going to give up on her, are you?'

'Nope.' He turned to the whale and spoke directly to her. Beth got the feeling there had been several man-to-whale conversations while she was out like a light. 'I'm not going to let you go.'

She frowned, those words striking a chord she couldn't name deep inside. They seemed somehow important but she couldn't place why. The eagle called again, high up in the part of the sky that was still a deep, dark disguise.

'It says a lot about you.'

His look upward was a question.

'How hard you're fighting for this whale. To give her a chance. You really haven't changed that much after all.'

Marc bit down on whatever he'd been about to say and clenched his jaw shut. Hard. She practically felt the atmosphere shift. Maybe he wasn't in the mood for conversation after her revelations in the small hours of morning. She fought the heat of shame that rose on that thought and the sinking surge of self-doubt that followed. Then she braced herself against the cold, tossed back the blanket and bundled it into her arms. Before her body could convince her not to, she plunged back up to her knees in the icy wash and sank the blanket under the water; its frigid kiss shocked her into full awakening. She dragged its weighty thickness up and over the whale, shrouding its skin in dampness. The nasty arrowhead scar on its tail was exposed again.

That couldn't be good. It meant the tide was retreating. If it went much further out it would mean the whale would be high and dry.

As soon as the blanket was secured, she moved, aching, up the beach and collected the empty two-litre container and commenced the bend-fill-slosh ritual all over again. Her body didn't even bother protesting this time. It knew when it was licked.

Marc watched every move.

'How are *you* doing?' he finally asked. Tension tinged his voice, but it was concern etched in his face. And caution.

Oh.

She stumbled slightly when she realised he was talking about drinking. Or *not drinking* in the case of this very difficult eighteen hours. And he wasn't particularly happy to be asking.

The thought of alcohol had not even crossed her mind since she'd woken. That had to be a first. Although it shot back with a vengeance now. Hunger. Thirst. Craving. Needing. They all mixed together into an uncomfortable obsession for just about everything you could put in your mouth.

She feigned misunderstanding. 'I'm ready for a big plate of bacon and eggs, a big mug of hot tea and a Bloody Mary.'

Hazel eyes snapped to her. 'You joke about it?'

She sighed. Pushed her shoulders back. 'Keeping it bound and gagged gives it too much power. Maybe it's time I started to lighten up about it all.' *Take some of the control back.* 'Get back to a normal life.'

'Fair enough. What will you do now?' he asked. 'To make a living? To have that normal life?'

It was a good question. Her dark years were behind her. Her list was done. She had the rest of her future to think about. She blew out the residual tension from their previous question. 'I have no idea… The past two years has been all about recovery. It's been a day by day kind of thing.' She stared at him, blank. 'I suppose running a bottle shop is out of the question?'

His glare was colder than the water.

'Sorry. Bad joke.' Bleakness filled her. 'I feel like all I've done is drink and then not drink.'

'You have a decade to catch up on.' He looked hard at her. 'What about uni? It's never too late.'

Beth frowned. 'I don't think so.'

'Mature aged students are perfectly common now.'

Taverns, parties, temptation. 'I don't think I'd be a good fit on campus.'

His mouth tightened as he realised. 'Online, then?'

Something she could study in the comfort of her own cavernous warehouse. In the silence of her own lonely hours. 'What would I study?'

'What do you enjoy?'

She blinked at him.

'What about your painting?'

She shook her head. 'That's something I do for therapy. It won't earn me a living.'

'Why not? Maybe you could help others like you helped yourself. Give back.'

Her head came up. Giving back rang all kinds of karmic bells. Art therapy. She hadn't known such a thing existed until she'd needed it. But it did. And it worked.

Marc shrugged. 'There'd be no shortage of people needing assistance.'

Purpose suddenly glowed, bright and promising on her horizon. She *could* give back. Lord knew she'd had her fair share of assistance from others who gave their time. She chewed her lip. 'I could. That could work. Something simple that will help people.'

His eyes narrowed. 'You don't want to rule the country any more?'

Alcoholism had taken more from her than just years. 'If I can just rule *me* I'll be happy.'

He stared at her long and hard. Compassion filled his eyes. His voice was low and sad. 'You'll get there, Beth. I believe in you.'

A deep sorrow washed through her. 'You always did.'

Silence fell. Beth shook her head to chase off the blues she could feel settling.

'What would you change?' Marc's voice came out of the dim morning light, tossing her earlier words back at her. 'If you had the opportunity to do ten years ago over again. What would you do differently?'

Ah. This one she'd pondered plenty and she'd refined it during some of their long silences in the water. She bent to re-soak the blanket and thanked God that she had no sleeve on which to be displaying her heart. 'I wouldn't have put so much importance on what others said. I definitely wouldn't have encouraged Damien's advances.'

She kept her eyes away from his as she stretched the blanket out across the whale's back. 'I wouldn't have listened to…' *Your mother.* But now, more than ever, she couldn't say that. There was already so much lost between them. Vindicating herself would condemn them. 'I wouldn't have shut you out of my life.'

'You didn't.'

She looked up. 'I did.'

He shook his head. 'I mean you didn't succeed. I kept a low profile but that didn't mean I wasn't aware of everything you did. Where you went. Right up until school ended and I lost you, I was watching.'

Watching. Beth stared. She bled for the near-man who'd been so hurt but still so very loyal. Maybe despite himself. Her voice was tiny. 'I thought you were gone.' Present-absent in the way only a teen could be.

'No. I was still there.'

Her chest tightened. 'Why?'

He considered her from under lashes crusted with salt. 'We were friends. Friends don't abandon each other.'

Beth's cheeks flamed.

'I wasn't having a dig, Beth.'

She shook her head. 'I know. But it doesn't change what happened.' She stared at him. 'You deserved better.'

You still do. Her tight heart pushed rich pulses of blood around her body and they throbbed past her ears. Her eyes stuck fast to his. She made her decision.

'I need to tell you something. About my last days drinking.' She took a second to gather courage by trailing down to the whale's exposed tail and draping the soaked blanket over it. Water cascaded over the vicious arrow-head wound.

She took a deep breath and then met his eyes again. 'I forgot you, Marc. When I was deep in the hands of my addiction, I kind of…blocked you out. For years.'

His nostrils flared. His hands stilled.

'After graduation I thought about you every day. Wondered how you were. What you were doing. Thought about what I had done. I thought about the connection we used to have, the stories we had in common. Every day I tried to recreate with my husband what I'd had with you, and it just wasn't working. As I slipped further and further into numbness I think I just…' She swallowed and took a shuddery breath. 'Remembering you hurt. So I just stopped.'

Those beautiful hands tightened on his towel. Just as they'd tightened in her hair while he'd kissed her. Last night. All those years ago.

'I can understand that.' Hurt thickened his already gravelly voice.

She shook her head. Forced herself to continue. 'One day I woke up and there you were, blazing and persistent at the front of my mind. Like a ghost with a mission. Except I was the ghost. And I realised I'd been…non-existent for so long. I remembered how you used to believe in me no matter what but, this time, instead of that making me sad, hurting, it made me determined.'

She turned her eyes back to his. 'You gave me strength, Marc. I stopped drinking because of the memory of the boy who had so much belief in me. More than I'd ever had in myself. And because of the goodness in you that I'd always wished was mine. The strength of character.'

His eyes dropped away, which meant she could breathe.

'I just wanted you to understand the part you played in pulling me out of the morass. I can't thank you because you didn't even know it was happening. But I can acknowledge it. And I think I understand it now. What it meant.'

She clamped nervous hands together. 'Drinking helped me forget how I'd treated someone I loved. How the choices I made snowballed into a lousy life with a lousy husband and a lousy future. That I'd done that to myself. But the memory of my feelings for you saved me when everything was lost. When I was.'

His frown folded his handsome face and his jaw twitched with tension.

She drew in a massive breath for strength. 'You filled my heart in high school, Marc, and I think you filled it right through my marriage, except I couldn't bear to acknowledge it. One day I just...forced you out of my heart to protect myself.' She laid a hand on the whale. 'But then I crashed into the water with you yesterday and discovered you were still the same loyal, generous, brave person who I loved back then. You haven't changed.' She dipped her eyes, then forced them back up. Took a deep, deep breath. 'My feelings haven't changed.'

His silence screamed.

Mortification waited greedily in the wings but she held it back. 'I don't expect anything in return—' *much as she wished for it* '—I just wanted you to know. That you'd changed my life. That you'd *saved* my life. That our stories are connected.'

His neoprene chest heaved up and down, his eyes blazed hot and hard into hers. The hundred variations of things he might say whispered through her head. Then he finally spoke and it was laced with agony.

'I'm not a crutch, Beth.'

Her stomach plummeted. *What?* 'No, I—'

Sudden shouting from the direction of Marc's car split the quiet of the pre-morning. A dozen figures appeared at the dune tops, silhouetted against the dawning sun. They carried coils of rope slung over their shoulders and more blankets. Beth should have cried with relief that the cavalry had finally arrived but she wanted to scream at them for *just five more minutes*. It felt vitally important that she have just a bit more time alone with Marc.

She swung her eyes back to him.

His voice was hard. Hurried. 'I can't be the thing that sustains you, Beth. You can't swap one fixation for another, put that kind of responsibility on me. I lived with that for years.'

His mother... She opened her mouth to try and explain again as people started streaming down the dunes towards them. Euphoria that assistance had finally arrived crashed headlong into the sudden shot of urgent adrenalin surging through her body. In that moment she felt the best she had all night.

And the absolute worst.

Marc lay his shredded, saturated towel along the whale's broad back for one last time. Then he pinned her with his gaze. 'Me accepting that you're sorry for what happened a lifetime ago… Are you expecting that it will change anything? Other than for you?'

'I…' *Was she?* What did it really change, other than to mark the completion of her list? One more step in her road to healing.

'Because it doesn't change anything for me, Beth.' He cast her one final tired look and then dragged his exhausted legs out of the water.

The earth shifted under her feet. In all her imaginings, it had never occurred to her that Marc would accept her apology but that he might not truly forgive her. Realise the depth of her feelings but not value it. Each was meaningless without the other.

Her heart pounded. 'I thought, maybe if you understood…'

'I understand more than you know.' His tired eyes rested on her. 'It's been ten years, Beth. Any feelings we had are nothing but a memory. We're both different people now. If I helped you to get over—'

Could he still not say the word?

'—everything, I'm glad.' His eyes lifted. 'But I'm not some kind of lucky charm to keep you sober. And telling me you were alcoholic doesn't go any way to restoring the lost trust between us. Did you honestly expect it would?'

An awful realisation dawned with the sun that suddenly peeked its warmth above the sand dunes. She *had* expected that, yes. That her cosmic reward for finding him and confessing her shame—her many shames—would be a beginning as blazing and new as the sun climbing over the horizon. That the man who had played such an important role in her recovery would be given back to her and they could have a fresh start.

Strange hands were suddenly all over her, pulling her gently back from the water as two wetsuit-clad bodies slid into her place and plunged fresh blankets into the water. Beth ignored them and reached out to urgently snare Marc's hand as he left the water, desperate not to become separated even for a moment. Something in her knew that if that happened she'd never find him again.

His eyes dropped to where her fingers twisted amongst his with white-knuckled urgency. When they lifted, they were tragic. 'I can see that you've done it really tough since we parted, Beth, and that brings me no joy at all. But drunk Beth wasn't the one who tore our friendship apart that day behind the library. Dumping me for someone better was a choice that you made stone cold sober.'

The awful, sinking reality hit her. No matter what her motivation, how honourable, she *had* ripped apart their friendship in cold blood. She'd *let* his mother drive a wedge between them, and then she'd *let* Damien exploit the gap. She'd done nothing to stop any of it. Then and now. She still couldn't bring herself to tell him why she'd really let him walk away that day.

'But you accepted my apology…'

'I believe that you're sorry.' His words grew harder. Shorter.

'But our friendship…?'

His eyes were flat and pained. And as unmovable as granite. 'I've lived without it this long…'

Pain ripped through her as the first shards of light speared across the sky. Why had she expected more? Every part of her wanted to shut up tighter than a clam. Protect herself. But that had got her nowhere so far in life.

'Wait!' Her desperate voice broke, drawing him back as he turned towards two approaching men in Department of Conservation uniforms. 'What happens now?'

Marc's face was haggard, tragic as he shrugged. She loved every line. 'I go home. You go home. I appreciate your help with the whale but, as far as I'm concerned, we're not connected any more. Our story's over.'

Not connected?

'But…you kissed me.'

His eyes were tragic. 'Yeah.' He stared long and hard at his oldest friend. 'You'd think I'd learn, huh?'

Beth stumbled backwards in the sand as he walked away.

A gentle female voice murmured near her ear—buzzing in her throbbing head—and supported her up the beach as others draped thick blankets around her shoulders. Her eyes streamed from the sudden onset of morning light after so many hours of darkness. Dawn should have brought a bright new beginning for their friendship, not this awful gaping chasm. This was like losing him all over again. The impossibility that he could literally not want her back in his life in any form. That he could forgive her past but not her present…

She sank down into the sand as someone thrust an energy bar and Thermos of tea at her. Voices throbbed in her spinning head and she let herself be tended to like a child as they tut-tutted over the open blisters on her hands and the sunburn on her tight skin. Her head cranked around to follow Marc's progress as he dragged his feet up the beach with the wildlife officials, deep in conversation.

Someone was asking her where she was staying and she felt her lips responding, identifying her motel. Then capable hands lifted her to her feet and supported her as they moved up the beach, up a different track to the one leading to Marc's car. Her head cranked around to catch sight of him as he disappeared up the far dune.

He didn't even say goodbye. To her or the whale.

A hollow, awful emptiness filled her.

That was exactly as he'd left her ten years ago.

CHAPTER EIGHT

BETH'S grungy warehouse had never been so packed. Nor so popular.

She'd opened her doors four months ago to offer art classes to women in need of some beauty in their lives. An outlet. It was full six days a week with women recovering from addiction, abuse and trauma. They fiddled with pigment, they dabbed on canvases, but, more importantly, they talked about their lives. Opened up about their troubles, in person and on canvas. Sometimes they created something extraordinary.

It was the most natural kind of therapy in the safety of a group who had all experienced loss. Discovering how many kinds there were helped Beth put her own into perspective. She'd sacrificed a decade of her life to shame; she wasn't about to let that continue. She may have lost Marc again but she knew now that she was made of more than just those events that happened *to* her.

But success led to attention and, before long, the council had been on her doorstep to discuss the running of an unauthorised home business. Which was how she came to be standing here tonight, proudly wearing a dress made by one of her students from fabric screen-printed by another, a glass of sparkling water in hand, watching forty complete strangers dissect her paintings.

Running art classes from home was a no-no, according to council bylaws. Running them in an approved art space was fine. And Beth's father's rundown old warehouse was just inside the arts precinct boundary. Two weeks of hasty framing and hanging later and—*voilà*—*Our Stories* was born: an art exhibition featuring the best student work arising from four months of therapeutic art classes backed up with her own works from the past decade.

Not paintings she'd ever imagined she'd be displaying—in a million years—but necessary to pad out the collection and, in a strange kind of way, therapeutic in itself. No one assembled knew what had driven her to paint the darkest and most harrowing images—that was true of all the exhibited works—but they knew what the theme of *Our Stories* was. Their imaginations were surely filling in the blanks.

Exhibiting the works so she could keep offering classes was the goal; selling them was pure bonus. Not for great fortunes but, in the case of Kate Harrison—a mother of two who'd crawled away from a lifetime of violent abuse—selling four paintings inspired by her gorgeous, shuttered children was the first five hundred dollars she'd ever earned herself. By her own hand.

It might as well have had six more zeroes after it.

Two of her own paintings had already sold. Enough to pay for all the framing. It was surprisingly validating to have someone willing to buy her darkest moments, and deeply healing to know that the paintings would be leaving here at the end of the exhibition. Although why anyone would want to put her greatest moments of sorrow on their wall, she couldn't imagine. The enthusiastic buyers called them bold and brave. To Beth they were time capsules. Something that belonged for ever in the past.

There were more recent works of hers exhibited too. An Impressionistic acrylic number of a man's hand, slender-fingered and stroking the curve of a woman's jaw. Another one simply entitled *Duck!* was a comical close-up of a wood duck perched in a man's lap. As she watched, someone slapped a fat red 'Sold' sticker on it.

There was only one work in the whole place that had a hasty *'Not for Sale'* Post-it note affixed to it. It was where the bulk of the strangers were crowding right now—the painting that had generated some interest from the local newspaper. The enormous canvas piece she called *Holly's Bay.* Painted from under the sea, looking back to shore, where two sets of feet braced on either side of a half-submerged whale in the shallows. She'd painted it in her first fortnight after getting home from her trip to the south coast, working day and night until she'd finally exorcised the wash of pained feelings she'd brought home with her.

Better that than what she would have done two years ago to ease the pain. Which wasn't to say she didn't still feel the emotion when her guard slipped, but the worst of the feelings were forever suspended in the thick paint, like tiny creatures trapped for eternity in primordial bog.

The crowd speculated about what was above the waterline. Only Beth really knew. And Marc.

'Tell me that's our new life model.' One of her students sat up straighter next to Beth, her eyes fixed on the warehouse entrance. Their first and only life model had been a seventy-eight-year-old man with nicotine-stained fingers who was a little too eager to take off his clothing for a room full of women. Particularly since they were only drawing hands that week.

Beth twisted to see what had grabbed the student's attention. She practically tripped in her haste to get off the sofa and behind something to obscure her. The instinct to hide was immediate and all-consuming. She ignored the curious looks of her guests as she shuffled herself resolutely behind the small cluster of people, out of view of the man who had just walked in the door.

Marc.

He's here... He's here...

Between the bodies of her human shield, her eyes locked onto him and held fast. His own moved slowly over the artworks on the far side of the building. He moved quickly past her students' unlabelled work and onto her next one, accurately scenting which had come from Beth's particular soul. There he stopped. Studied. Considered.

It gave her ample time to rediscover him from the safety of her hide. He didn't seem comfortable in his suit jacket although it fitted him perfectly. He kept rolling his shoulders and tugging at his tie. Beth's heart kicked up. Why was he here? Would he recognise aspects of himself in several of the exhibited works?

He shifted sideways again as he moved on to the next work, then stopped and stared long and hard at it—a stylised acrylic of a house, not one of her own. She shifted in opposition, keeping him in view between the bodies. Keeping herself out of view. She knew her student was glancing between them with interest and she cursed herself for being a coward. This was ridiculous, hiding out behind guests.

She straightened her shoulders on a deep breath and

stepped out from behind the gaggle of art appreciators as Marc's roaming gaze brought him to the piece called *Duck!* He stepped closer, his long fingers tracing the fine acrylic ridges in the work. His eyes trailed over every element in the painting. Shielded. Protected. Then he turned unexpectedly and his gaze collided with her own unprepared one.

She tried to suppress the excited chorus of her subconscious, but he must have seen something of it in her face because his lips thinned. He stepped towards her tightly. She couldn't help mirroring him.

'Beth.'

Potentially avid ears were all around and the last thing she wanted at her students' first exhibition was any kind of scene. Beth took his arm and turned him back to the framed work, peered up at the colourful representation of a fat little duck perched happily on a pair of blue jeans and pretended to study it. Discussing the painting was a far safer option than whatever he was here for.

'Do you know where this is?' she murmured, her mind screaming all the while—*Why are you here?*

Marc dragged his eyes off her and back onto the painting. Eventually. His words were careful. 'That's our stowaway.'

They'd been on their way home from their first and only camping trip. They'd swapped seats so learner driver Beth could clock up some obligatory training hours at the wheel. It wasn't until they were underway that the duck chose to pop its sleek little head up from the back seat, where it had presumably spent the night.

'You screamed like a banshee,' Marc said on a twist of lips.

Thinking about the past was so much easier than worrying what was about to happen in the present. He'd spent the rest of the year ribbing her and she'd defended herself till the last. Like now.

'I didn't know it had chosen to make itself at home in my mother's back seat back at the campsite. I was tense enough remembering how to drive with you watching me, without the added surprise of a little blue beak and a pair of beady eyes staring at me in my rear-vision mirror.'

Beth's high-pitched holler had sent the duck into a frenzy of terrified flapping in the small cabin of the car and it had been all she could do to keep the vehicle on the road. Marc had twisted from his front seat position to try and shoo the manic duck back out through the hastily lowered window, but had only succeeded in agitating it into a flurry of wings and webbed feet.

Eventually it had plopped, half exhausted, into his lap and sat there blinking at both of them. He'd spent a minute pressed frozen into the back of the passenger seat before realising the duck was quite at home on his lap and, by the time they pulled into a national park wetland fifty kilometres off the highway, he even had a gentle hold on its rotund little body—as though it were a football he was holding on his lap and not a hitch-hiking wood duck.

That had been the beginning of the end for Beth. Seeing him holding the bird so gently, hearing him chatting to it in improvised duck language and watching its little head twisting and perking up in response. Her heart had turned in on itself right then and there. If she had to name the moment her heart shifted…

'I'm not sure who was sorrier when we released him onto that lake, you or the duck,' Marc joked now, smiling at the bird in the painting. 'You really captured the little guy.'

But, before she could answer, he shifted and his eyes fell on *Holly's Bay*, mounted high to his right. His smile froze. Blood drained from his face. Beth stared, captive, as his eyes locked on the powerful reminder of their time in the water.

'Why are you here?' she whispered. No point making any more small talk. Not when the question clamoured in her mind like pealing bells. She locked her eyes firmly onto the feet in her painting.

He faked it as well as she did, staring up at the painting as though casually discussing its composition. 'The exhibition made the *South Coast Examiner* because of the whale. Because of our story.'

Our story is over…

'I was up in Perth anyway and…' He paused, staring at the giant painted feet pressed into the ocean floor in front of him. He cleared his throat. 'That's not true. I needed to come. I needed to see you.'

'Me?' Longer words simply would not come.

He looked down at her sideways. 'Do you want me to go?'

He'd walk through fire if you asked him to.

'No. But I need a second.' She took a steadying breath, conscious of curious eyes all around them. Mostly her students. Her heart thumped like a sonic pulse. Lucky there were no whales this far inland or she'd be throwing out their guidance systems with the waves coming off her. She sheltered in something safer.

'What happened to the whale? Did she make it?'

Marc took a second to refocus. 'They got her back out to sea.'

'Did she stay there?'

'Impossible to know. The second refloating seemed to be a success.'

Beth nodded. 'Maybe she knew she had nothing to stay for.' More fitting words had never been spoken.

'Maybe.' His voice caressed her, even though his eyes stayed carefully fixed to the painting.

'She made a new beginning for herself. I hope so. She deserves her second chance.'

Beth didn't mean for it to be loaded. But too much had happened between them for it to stay an innocent comment. Marc glanced around at the milling crowd. Then back to her. 'Is there somewhere we can speak?'

Not inside. Every inch of her warehouse held either buyers, exhibits or their artists. The only off-limits place was her bedroom and he was categorically not invited there. Not outside of her turbulent dreams, anyway.

She nodded and forced her feet to cooperate as she stepped away from him and led the way to the garden door. 'Garden' was a little too generous for the tiny courtyard space she'd filled with potted green. But it offered privacy and quiet, both of which she figured they'd be needing. She closed the door behind Marc and then turned to lean on it. He roamed the tiny space and kept his back to her.

Contradictory feelings raged through her. Excitement. Dread. Curiosity. Anxiety. Lucky she had a blank canvas in her store room. She was going to need to exorcise this lot.

'Why are you here, Marc?' She faked the same bravado she'd had to employ once when an abusive ex-husband tracked down one of her students during class. It worked then, but she wasn't convinced she was pulling it off now.

He turned. 'I wanted to speak with you.'

'Go ahead.'

Marc propped himself against a concrete bird-bath and rested both hands on its ornate edge, fingers curling around it tightly. Then he lifted shuttered eyes back up to her. 'I…regret…how I left things between us back at the Bay.'

There was nothing between them. He'd made that abundantly clear. Beth stared silently.

'I've had weeks to think about everything we talked about that day in the water and how I reacted. And to track you down.'

Thump, thump, thump… 'You've been trying to find me?'

'Your parents wouldn't give me your address.'

'They knew—' *how I was after getting back from seeing you.* She swallowed. Changed tack. 'They're protective of me these days.'

He took in her pensive body language. Stiff straight limbs, hands clenched in front of her. 'Will you sit, Beth?'

'No, thank you.' Not on your life.

He just nodded. Then he met her eyes with his serious hazel ones. 'I wanted to apologise. I didn't handle myself well that morning at Holly's Bay…'

Just the morning? Letting her hurt feelings show wouldn't help anyone. She smiled tightly.

'…I felt that I owe you more of an explanation.'

'Is there more? You seemed very sure of your feelings.'

His eyes dropped away from hers. 'Those haven't changed. But there's more to it than I…' Breath hissed out of him. 'Please, will you sit?'

This was hard for him. Every protective part of her wanted to reach out. Help him. But she did the only thing her self-respect would allow. She nodded and moved to one of the outdoor chairs. He pulled one up opposite. She fought the urge to automatically fill the silence like sea water rushing into footprints on the shore.

'I'm ashamed of myself for letting you walk away from that beach doubting yourself. Your worth. You were brave and honest with me that day and I handled everything badly. You were a friend, Beth, and that should have earned you more from me.'

Were. 'You said you weren't interested in my friendship.'

'I wasn't. I'm not.' Beth sucked in a breath and he winced. 'But not for the reason you think. I owe you an explanation.'

He took her hands. 'I can see you've done it really tough over the years, Beth. I only have to look at the images hanging on your walls to realise you've been in a dark, miserable place. How hard it must have been for you to get through it alone.'

She just nodded. Months with her students had taught her to acknowledge her own strengths rather than apologising endlessly for the weaknesses. 'Pity doesn't help me.'

His brows met in a frown. 'No. I can see that. Even more now. These past few months have obviously been good for you.'

She smiled sadly. 'Someone told me that we were responsible for our own happiness. I chose to go out and find some.'

His stare was fathoms deep. His voice flat. 'You've met someone?'

What? That would require forcing Marc out of her heart and, given how long his memory had endured her horrific marriage, that wasn't likely to happen for some time. 'I meant I've found it in me. I'm in a good place.' His frown intensified. He looked undecided. Was he regretting coming? Was he having second thoughts? 'Go ahead, Marc. Finish what you came to say.'

'I wanted to… When I indicated that your friendship was not of interest to me, that might have suggested that I thought you were not worthy…'

Her laugh was hard. 'In a manner of speaking.'

His eyes closed briefly. 'I regret my choice of words. That you might have thought I meant… That it might have set you back.'

Frost snapped along her veins. Would she always be an addict first with him? 'You're worried you might have sent me back to the bottle?' A hint of colour crept above his collar. Her lips set hard. 'You think you have that much power?'

His gaze was resolute. 'You told me you loved me.'

Beth's stomach dropped and her breath caught. But, before she could speak, he continued. 'In school, you had feelings for me. Then, later in your marriage, those feelings…complicated things. Was that true?'

Beth stiffened in her seat. She should just say no. All of this would go away. 'I'm not in the habit of making things up to suit the moment.'

He glared at her.

She hissed. 'Yes, it was true.' He opened his mouth to speak and she rushed on. 'But I've dealt with those feelings as part of my healing process and I know they were based on a memory. A teenage memory. Not real life. You don't have to worry.'

He let out a stream of repressed air and stared at her, a tight expression on his face. 'I'm not worried, Beth. You honour me.'

The stark pain in his eyes hit her between the breasts. Stole her breath.

'Why did you tell me?' he barrelled on. 'What did you hope to achieve?'

'I… Nothing. It wasn't a planned thing. I just felt you deserved to know. I felt close enough to you to tell you.' Until you sliced my heart out with a few lazy words. 'At the time.'

'You regret it?'

The harsh laugh bubbled back up. 'Wouldn't you?'

'That's partly why I'm here. It…wasn't easy to hear, Beth.'

Compounding the awkwardness of what had been a stunningly miserable twenty-four hours? She set her shoulders back. 'I'm sure it wasn't.'

His hand went up. 'You misunderstand me. It wasn't easy to hear because there was a time I would have given anything to hear those words on your lips.'

Beth wasn't speechless often, but this was what it felt like.

'You gave me the gift of your feelings. So that I would understand you better. I'd like to repay that.'

Beth frowned. 'What don't I understand?'

'Why I can't stay friends with you.'

A sick awareness rolled over her. He wasn't here to make up.

Marc filled his not insubstantial chest. 'I worshipped you for nine years, Beth. From fourth grade through to the end of school. You were…everything to me. My partner-in-crime. My confidante. My inspiration. Those feelings grew as we did. Us being separated was never an option in my mind.'

Mine neither, she wanted to say. But words couldn't squeeze out past the growing lump in her chest. Blind panic started to take her. She gripped the edges of the chair for strength.

'I felt the very moment when you finally realised you were a female and I was a male. When you started to look at me differently. Like a man. I started planning from that moment. Studying biology was all about you, Beth. A way to stay together. Tasmin Major was all about you. I had our first kiss all planned out in my mind. Where. When. What it would mean.' Recrimination saturated his quiet voice. 'I had our whole lives planned out in my mind.'

Too late, too late, her soul whispered. That cast her betrayal of him in a very different light. She thought back to that kiss. Marc's pain. Bad enough that she'd hurt herself so much.

She forced herself to speak. 'You never said…'

Would it truly have changed anything? She couldn't imagine how two kids could be any more interconnected than she and Marc were, anyway. His mother and her parents still would have begged her to release him from her influence. Had they seen which way the wind was blowing?

'I wanted everything to be just right. I should have told you sooner.'

'Why are you telling me now?'

Marc's eyes practically bled pain. 'If I thought there was any chance that I could put you away from me, perhaps we could stay friends.' He stared down on her, words thick with sorrow. 'But I can't. You're buried too deep in me.' His fingers pressed hard to the left side of his chest. He dropped his eyes to his outstretched feet, then lifted them again. His face hardened. 'My mother's weakness controlled her and spilled over into my life until it controlled me too. I can't let that touch me again. For anyone.'

His deep voice broke on those final words and his Adam's apple lurched up and down beneath his button-up collar. He was twenty-eight and eight years old at the same time. Beth's heart broke for the young, confused boy who'd endured a life with someone struggling with compulsion. And then it wept for her; knowing she couldn't willingly put Marc through pain any more than she could simply will alcohol out of her mind for ever.

If he cared less about her, her choices wouldn't affect him and they could stay friends. And if she cared less about him, she wouldn't fear hurting him and they could stay friends.

Caring so much forced them apart.

A bone-deep ache started up at the base of her spine. 'Irony is a bitch.'

Marc stared at her sadly.

'When we were younger, I used to think that we were two halves of the same person,' she said. 'We thought so much alike, we enjoyed the same things, we practically breathed in synch. Tearing our two halves apart was the hardest thing I'd ever done in my life but I did it because I believed it was the right thing to do.' *For you.* She ignored his frown and kept on. 'And then for years I beat myself up, fearing I'd made the wrong decision.

'But here I am, a decade on, back in exactly the same position.' Her laugh was bleak. 'Boy, the universe is really trying to spell something out for me, huh?'

'Don't take this on, Beth. This is about me, not you.'

Oh, please. 'I've spent a long time re-training myself to believe I'm about more than my addiction. But apparently that's not true.'

He flinched. 'Beth, don't…'

He'd have more luck stopping a freight train. She stared up at him, angry, hurt and confused. 'You see the addiction first, Marc. And the person second.'

His eyes blazed down on her. 'That's not true.'

'Can you honestly say—hand on heart—that you wouldn't feel differently about me if I wasn't recovering from alcoholism? If I was just a normal woman who'd been away travelling for years? That you wouldn't be back to planning our lives together? That you wouldn't be thinking about kisses and long lazy days in the bedroom and how many kids you might want to fill that big, empty, south coast homestead with?' She sure had been. In those vulnerable half asleep moments between dream and reality.

'Beth…'

He didn't have a prayer of disguising the leap of wishful thinking in his expression and Beth knew that was exactly what he wanted. He wanted normal. And she wasn't.

It hurt enough that she pushed, like pressing a toothache. 'What if I'm as good as it gets, Marc? It's been years and you're still alone. What if we are meant to be together and there's no one else out there for you? And you're tossing me aside without so much as a chance to prove myself.'

She didn't believe for one second that a man like Marc wouldn't find someone to share his life with. What did it say about her that she hoped he would and wouldn't in the same breath?

His face tightened. Colour streaked along the ridge of his angular cheekbone. 'This is about me not wanting to repeat the errors of the past. I spent half a lifetime suffering life with an addict, Beth. I'm really not in a hurry to do that again.'

Her gasp was like a horrible, pained punctuation mark. *Suffering?* That was how he'd view being with her. She ignored the splitting torture of her heart as it ripped away from her chest. Her voice shook with the force of not saying what she really wanted to.

Why can't you believe in me?

He saw her face and cursed. 'Bad choice of words. I'm sorry—'

She shot up a hand. 'Don't apologise. *I'm* sorry that it's taken me this long to catch on to how people see me.' She dropped her head and took several deep breaths. The pain welling inside her *begged* to spill out as blistering sarcasm, but she forced it down. She pressed her hand to her breast and found the courage to meet his eyes. 'I'm still in here, Marc. Your Beth is still here, trying her damnedest to get back to a place that is healthy and happy. But you can't see her, can you?'

In the dreadful silence that followed, the sounds of the art exhibition washed anxiously around her, as though trying to buffer her from the pain of what had just passed between them.

She forged ahead. 'I understand about living with someone who is controlled by a substance. I remember how that felt. What that did to me. How hard it was to fight. And I was an adult by then…'

Marc looked away.

'I've spent the last two and a half years rebuilding myself. I've spent the last four months convincing twenty women that it's okay to put themselves first, to do what they need to survive. Not to accept anything less than what is healthy for them. How can I possibly wish anything less for you?'

Or for myself.

She swallowed hard past the deep abiding sadness as a sinking wave of realisation broke around her. 'You and I are bad for each other, Marc. Maybe we always were, despite all the friendship. Maybe our parents saw that and that's why they…' She took a long breath. 'I'm dry now. *I* did that. On my own.'

'I know…'

It's not enough. His lowered eyes spelled it out. Even though it had cost her so much, her best effort still wasn't enough. The tragedy of that pricked in her eyes. But letting herself cry was not an option.

'You will always fear your mother in me,' she whispered. 'And I will always fear suspicion in you. And that's not good for me. I need to surround myself with support and strength. Not doubt and judgement.'

Raw pain soaked his words. 'I'm so sorry.'

'Don't be. Imagine if we'd both just gone with our instincts and ended up hating each other.'

Imagine if we'd ended up blissfully happy, a tiny, tiny voice taunted. She ignored it.

His hand lifted towards her and then dropped. 'So what happens now?'

She shrugged. 'I don't know. I've never—' Beth stopped cold. She'd been about to say that she'd never ended a friendship before. But that wasn't true. She blinked up at him. 'I guess our story really is over.'

Marc stared at her. Long, hard. As if memorising every detail of her face. Then he cleared his throat. 'I should go.'

'Yes. I think so.'

He didn't move. He just stared. 'Is it wrong that I want to hold you so much?'

Her struggling heart gave a final, fatal lurch. Her

throat closed right over and her words struggled to get out. 'It's wrong to tell me.'

He just nodded. Then—finally—he turned for the door. When his fingers were on the handle, he turned back. 'Be happy, Beth. You deserve…everything.'

But not you, apparently.

Her essential goodness forced her to speak. Quickly, before she lost him. 'I'm sorry about what I said. You won't be alone for ever. There is someone out there for you.' *Someone better.* It was hard not to hear the demon doubts.

'I hope so.'

She saw the scepticism in his eyes and grabbed his arm. 'You have to go out and find her, Marc. She's not going to just appear at your door one morning.'

Thinking it was agony. Saying it killed her.

His smile was tragic. He nodded. 'No. That only happens once in a lifetime.'

The memory of walking up to him in his driveway suddenly filled her mind. The heat. The nerves. The secret anticipation. It seemed like lifetimes ago.

He turned and opened the door and she followed him back into the noisy hum. The lively animation of her guests seemed cartoonesque compared to the numbness of her dulled senses. Even the anxious glances of a few of her students didn't manage to penetrate the growing fog.

This feeling was frighteningly familiar. She fought it.

'You're not selling the whale?' Marc nodded his head to *Holly's Bay* as they passed. It broke her heart anew that the last words between them would be small talk. She wouldn't let that happen.

'She represents a turning point in my life. I'll never part with her.'

Not if I have to part with you. Beth walked him through the crowd to the door. Deep, thumping pain accompanied every step. Dead woman walking.

Just before the door, he turned to the painting of the house, the one he'd been drawn to when he'd arrived. His eyes were dangerously neutral. 'This one. Is it for sale?'

'They all are.' Except for one.

Marc frowned. 'It speaks to me. I can't explain it. The colours. The empty house. Like it sums up everything we've…' He paused, blew out a breath. 'Everything that's happened.'

The pain. The loss. The waste.

Beth swallowed hard. 'It's yours.' He looked at her and reached for his back pocket. She shook her head. 'Take it as a gift.'

'But the artist—'

Beth's chest tightened at everything they weren't saying. 'The artist would want you to have it.'

He stared at her long and hard and every sound in the room seemed to drop away until her throbbing heartbeat was the only sound at all. And Marc's voice. She leaned in and gently lifted the artwork off the wall and held it straight out to him.

His eyes fell on the emotional image painted in acrylics as he spoke. 'Thank you. I'll treasure it.'

Beth glanced at the two words scrawled on the back of the canvas. Pain speared through her. For everything she'd lost. He'd lost.

Even Janice Duncannon, whose name he would eventually find on the back of his painting. 'You should. It was meant to be yours.'

It seemed impossible that the two of them could be further apart now than ever. That nothing she'd done had brought any of them closer. That so much suffering would continue. She held the door for Marc as he exited and feasted greedily on the sight of his broad shoulders and back one last time.

'Goodbye, Marc,' she whispered as he stepped through.

The shoulders shifted as he started to turn and she pulled the heavy door quickly closed before she had to endure the tragedy of looking into his eyes one final time. She turned and sagged back against the door, her eyes grabbing and holding the image of *Holly's Bay* as though it were a lifeline.

Then she pushed her heavy body away and stumbled, blind and deaf, towards the only sanctuary in her world. Her bedroom.

The place she'd done all her grieving. All her hiding. All her healing.

And knew the latter would be a long time coming.

CHAPTER NINE

BETH dashed at the salty tickle of sweat suspended on her brow and stood back to examine the painting, wedging the brush between satisfied teeth. Even a spring day could reach the high thirties on this side of Australia and today was one of them. But she'd begun this particular work outdoors and—*sunstroke be damned!*—she was going to finish here.

She'd woken in the quiet hours of the morning, exploding with inspiration, and dragged her sketchpad onto her bed. She'd started blind, no concept of what might flow from her charcoal as she sketched out the initial shape of two skydivers freefalling but, as dawn broke, she'd found herself mixing up the deepest indigos, bold silvers, the rich acrylic colours and striking contrasts of a fantastical setting, not an earthly one.

She set up her easel in her cramped courtyard as soon as the sun had risen and set to work on the acrylic incarnation of her idea.

She skipped breakfast, perfectly sustained on adrenalin and creative surge, her hand flying over the canvas until her subconscious started to make its direction known. Colours merged, images resolved. The gentle morning light bathed her inner eye with a soft glow that translated beautifully on the canvas. The scene she painted bubbled up from the depths of her imagination—her soul—and for the first time in months an immense peace flowed through her.

She changed brushes and better defined a stylised spaceship in an imaginary universe far from her little courtyard. A place where a well built astronaut protected in layers of silver spacesuit floated and stretched forward to hold something. Or someone.

Lunch was a few hastily downed crackers and a cup of tea before Beth tackled the mystery of what—or who—he was reaching for. A skydiver, according to her initial sketch. But the flowing white dress and zero gravity that flowed from her brush suggested an angel.

But no, she realised as she instinctively mixed up a bronze colour and fashioned a crooked crown on her head. *Not an angel—a princess.*

Her breath caught. Marc's space princess. With long platinum hair that flowed all the way down to a green planet that glowed beyond the spaceship. Almost like a pathway home.

Warmth surged through her.

She switched brushes again and detailed the princess's hand, stretched urgently out and barely snagging the gloved index finger of the astronaut. It didn't take a genius to recognise the desperate, tenuous hold of the fallen princess with the tragically crooked crown. Beth had held on just like that to the memory of Marc throughout her marriage, no matter how deep down she shoved it. It had sustained her like that astronaut's air supply.

She returned to the canvas. In minutes she'd outlined the astronaut's other hand, the creases in his space glove showing how tightly his fingers encircled the princess's fragile wrist. But the more Beth fiddled with her painting, the more she discovered. Like the fact that the astronaut wasn't tethered to his spaceship. But the princess's long flowing hair anchored her to her planet.

Beth gasped. At first glance, it looked as if the astronaut's grip on the princess's wrist was the only thing stopping her from drifting off into deepest, darkest space. But the strong determination with which she'd captured his finger...the way she strained against the anchor of her hair on the green planet to reach him...

Was she saving him?

Or were they trying to save each other? Even if it meant they might cartwheel off into airless space, somehow she knew that they would be fine just as long as they held on to each other.

Beth swiped at her forehead and stared wide-eyed at the image still only partly emerged from the blank canvas even after a full day of non-stop painting. She'd have to go back and repair parts, let it dry overnight, prepare it for layering tomorrow. But she'd been powerless to stop until the whole image was purged from her mind. Sketched out on canvas. Captured for ever.

Until she knew what it meant.

A cloak of deep satisfaction settled on her. She'd scratched and screamed against the necessity of forcing Marc from her thoughts, and failed abysmally. She'd cursed and professed her outrage to the universe, uselessly. But, as she stared at the painting, she realised that the promise she'd made herself only prevented her from acting on her feelings.

Not having them.

Marc may not choose to be her friend, but she could still be *his*. Wasn't that what friends did? He may not be able to love her but she could love him. She could maintain that tenuous finger-hold on their relationship. Stop them drifting apart for ever. She'd waited this long to find her way back to him. What was a decade more?

On that thought, she slipped into a tranquil, gentle kind of acceptance. She took all those torturous feelings, all those loving feelings, all those desperate feelings and rolled them into a tight ball and bundled them away deep. Somewhere safe. Somewhere reinforced. Somewhere just for her.

The somewhere this painting had come from.

Her demons thoroughly exorcised, Beth stretched aching shoulders and flexed her cramped back and realised how hungry she was. And thirsty.

And how late it was getting. Janice would be waiting for her.

She propped her new canvas onto a shelf to dry overnight and sprinted for the shower.

Beth passed Marc's mother a steaming coffee with a reassuring smile.

Janice Duncannon looked even more nervous tonight than the last few meetings she'd been to. And they'd been to a lot together in the eight weeks since the exhibition. Accompanying Beth to AA was one step closer—one step easier—than going to Narcotics Anonymous. But the older woman knew that was where she needed to be. She was just building up the courage. With Beth's help. This woman's son was the reason Beth had been able to claw her way out of the abyss; the least she could do was return the favour.

If not to him, then to someone close to him.

Beth had seen the ravages of addiction clearly on Janice's face the first time she'd come to her warehouse classes, but she'd also seen the signs of someone struggling to overcome it. Janice had been doing it alone, too proud to call on her only son for help. She lived under his roof and ate the food he supplied but couldn't face the man she'd thrown out on the street in a chemical-induced fog.

The two of them had built up a strange kind of friendship since Beth had first invited her to art classes. They were decades apart in life experience, but dependence had a way of stripping back the years like old wallpaper. And, of course, they were sisters in heartbreak. Loving—and losing—a brilliant, complicated man. It just happened to be the same one.

Janice's hands pressed tightly to her coffee cup and she glanced around anxiously.

Beth frowned. 'You okay, Janice?'

Life-worn eyes looked at her but, as Beth watched, determination pushed the uncertainty from them. 'Yes, Beth. Thank you. I just…' Janice bit her lip. 'Perhaps I should have told you…'

A familiar voice sounded near the doorway. She'd been hearing it in her dreams so often these past weeks she'd become immune and it took a few seconds—and the lifted heads of a few of the people around her—for her to realise Marc's voice was real this time, excusing himself through the people packed into the meeting room. Heading towards them.

Her heart contracted like bellows.

She tore her eyes back to the woman at her side, who looked both guilty and eager at the same time. 'Oh, Janice, this was not a good idea.'

Did the woman not know her son at all? He hated being ambushed. As the whole room was about to find out.

'He called me when he found my name on the painting,' she whispered fiercely. 'After four years, I was *not* going to miss this chance.'

Beth couldn't blame her. Not really. Her judgement, perhaps, but not her intent. And she couldn't know the recent history between her son and Beth.

The powerful shoulders she'd never thought she'd see again pushed through the gathered throng towards his mother, setting her active imagination whirring, remembering how they'd given him the strength to hold her in his arms in the water one frigid night. But, three metres away, his focus shifted slightly to the left and his feet froze instantly. The colour leached from his eyes.

Too late for her to flee now.

He seemed to pull energy from the people pressing against him and buttress it up around him. Then he pushed himself forward again. Her heart pounded in time with his steps.

He stopped in front of her. It was a miserable replay of the day she'd walked up his driveway. Except this time they were both on the back foot. And this time his eyes barely stopped on hers as he spoke.

'Beth.'

Words simply would not come past the sudden dryness of her mouth. But she managed to squeeze out a nod and a breathy, loaded word, humiliating in its timbre. 'Marc.'

Guarded eyes darted between the two women. Beth couldn't tell which of them he was more pained to see, but being confronted by both of them in a room full of addicts had to be more than the strongest of men could take.

He turned to his mother with accusation in his eyes.

And not an insignificant amount of pain. 'Tell me you didn't plan this.'

Janice Duncannon's hands shook, but that was the case whether she was facing her son or not. The withdrawal tremors gave her a very human kind of frailty and Beth saw its effect on Marc. She ached for the confusion and vulnerability in his face. She desperately wanted to step by his side.

'Would you have come if I'd told you?' Janice asked. Immensely brave words, given they were the first she'd spoken to him in years.

Probably not, his face said. 'I thought I was here to meet with your support group. Why are you in a room full of alcoholics?' He dropped his voice as though the term would offend those around them. As though they weren't already blindingly aware of their condition. Then his voice got tighter and he zeroed in on the real problem. 'Why are you with Beth?'

He still hadn't looked at her properly and her throat ached at being dismissed so.

'Elizabeth and I are friends,' Janice said simply.

He did look at her then. Hard. Inscrutable. It told Beth exactly how much he was hurting right now. What was wrong with her that she wanted to protect him more than herself—even when he was looking at her like that?

'How nice for the two of you. Comparing habits?'

Beth sucked back a gasp.

Janice hadn't forgotten so many of her mothering skills that she was prepared to tolerate lip from her son. Even a fully grown tree-sized one. 'It turns out she and I have more in common than just love for you.'

Beth had walked these linoleum floors too long to believe they might actually open up and swallow her but she prayed for it anyway. Marc shot her another glare, this one a tiny bit uncertain. But his words were for Janice. 'I wasn't aware that anything outside of a capsule motivated you these days, Mother.'

Janice paled, her face a tragic mix of pride, hurt and hope, but she stayed upright. Beth had seen her sag at less. Her compassion for the troubled woman rose another notch. Lots of work to be done there, but she had faith in her son. And, these days, Janice believed in herself again.

'Be that as it may,' his mother said, 'it was concern for you that saw me ask you here tonight. You and Beth need to talk.'

'I'm not sure what she's told you—'

'Beth's told me nothing,' Janice chastised. 'She's very loyal to you. But the fact she never speaks about you speaks for itself.'

Beth groaned. 'Janice—'

'I should have known it wouldn't be any kind of genuine plea for my help with your sickness,' Marc said, eyes bleak. Beth threaded her fingers together to stop her from reaching out to him. *But he came tonight*, a tiny voice whispered. That wasn't the action of a man who truly could not forgive.

But to then find he'd been set up…

'My *sickness* and I are getting along just fine, thank you.' Marc hadn't heard strength in his mother's voice for a long time, judging by the way his eyes flared wide. Janice barrelled onwards. 'At the very least, you owe your oldest friend some closure.'

Oh, God… She glanced around desperately for Tony. She was going to need a sponsor pep talk tonight…

Marc glanced at her. 'We've had our closure. Two months ago.'

Janice frowned. 'Marc… You were friends for so long.'

His grin was arctic, but he faked it for the close pressed crowd. 'I think when years spent not being friends overtakes the number of years of friendship, then it rather cancels itself out.'

Ouch. All that time so easily wiped from his mind.

'Really?' Janice straightened to her full height and a decade tumbled off her. 'Is that how you feel about your father? He's been gone for many more years than you had him.'

Marc looked thunderous.

Beth took her chance. 'If you'll excuse me, I'm just going to—'

'Stay!' both Duncannons barked at once.

Marc pinned Beth with his turbulent gaze. 'I thought we'd said everything that needed to be said, Beth. What happened to your commitment to stay away, if you'd go to these lengths—to buddy up to a sick old woman?'

Beth hissed at exactly the same moment Janice roared in outrage. 'I am fifty-two, Marcus Duncannon! Hardly old.'

'You look fifteen years older,' he shot back.

'Yes, well, drug addiction will do that to a body!'

Janice's raised voice and her confident, startling admission silenced the whole room. Beth stepped forward into the awful tension to end the rapidly deteriorating scene. She turned to Janice and wrapped her cool hand around the older woman's unsteady one.

'Janice, I recognise you mean well, but please don't get involved. I've stuffed up enough relationships without adding yours and Marc's to my list. You guys have a real chance here. Do not jeopardise that for me.'

She turned next to Marc. Just smelling him weakened

her resolve and broke her heart anew. But she found his eyes. 'I am *not* trying to keep you in my life by proxy. You made yourself perfectly clear and—surprising as it might seem to you, given the past years of my life—I actually do have enough dignity not to beg for something you're not interested in giving. And I have honoured my promise to stay away.'

Even if it's killing me. Even if it was still robbing her of sleep.

'So have I,' he snarled.

Everything about him called to her. The way his hair fell across his forehead. The breadth of his shoulders. That defensive splayed-leg stance. It had been a tough few weeks, but she'd survived. She'd just have to start purging him from her mind and heart all over again.

Thanks, Janice.

Marc's permanent absence had left a huge gaping hole in her world. It hadn't been there even when they were apart for a decade because that part of her had still belonged to him. Now it was owned by no one.

She took another breath and held his focus. 'I get that there are some actions that can't be undone. That I broke something irreplaceable back when we were kids. I'll never be able to convince you of exactly how much I regret the choices I made back then but—you know what, Marc?—I was sixteen. I was virtually a child. I made mistakes and I'm sorry for them. But I've paid for them one hundred times over. I can't keep paying for ever. Not even for you.'

There was a world more she wanted to say but the thickening of her throat cut her short. There was no way she would allow herself to cry in front of Marc ever again. 'Janice, I'll see you next week. You should stay—'

'Don't leave, Beth.' The simple words caused a hard ball of pain in her chest and her pulse kicked up. She turned cautious eyes to him, her breath suspended. But then his eyes glittered. 'These are your people, after all. I should be the one to go.'

A hundred knives sliced through her. Just when she thought he didn't have the power to hurt her any more…

Her people. Addicts. Losers.

He would never, ever see past his prejudice.

He turned to go and Janice grabbed his sleeve urgently. 'Marc, don't do this. You've been in love with that girl since fifth grade. I could see it back then and I can still see it.' She appealed up to her towering son. 'Life is so brief. I know what it is to exist without joy. The gift of love is not something that you should walk away from twice.'

He looked set to do just that but Janice stopped him with a stunning proclamation. 'It's my fault she left you.'

Beth snapped her head around, not prepared to have another sacrifice be for nothing. 'Janice, no—!'

'I told Beth to cut you loose, son.' Janice's fingers bit into his arm like they'd dug into hers when she was sixteen. Deceptively strong. 'Actually, I begged her. I couldn't watch you fall more and more in love with her, making all those plans to go to university, to leave.' She took a deep breath. 'To leave me. You were all I had.'

Marc paled and stared at Janice. She went on, relentless. 'Without you, I had no one. I was terrified. That was a terrible crushing responsibility to put on a boy—' she glanced at Beth with stark regret in her eyes '—and an awful pressure to put on a young girl. But I was desperate.'

Marc's nostrils flared. He turned to Beth. 'You did it for her? Not for McKinley?'

Beth's heart pounded. 'I did what I thought was best—'

His head reared back at that. 'In what universe was tearing out my heart *best*?'

Heat rushed up her throat and collided headlong into the blood draining from her face. *I didn't know.* The words trembled on her lips, wanting so eagerly to tumble off into the fray. But, in her heart, Beth knew it wasn't quite true. On some level she'd known just how important she was to Marc.

She reached to the nearby chairs for her purse. 'I'm sorry that I wasn't stronger. I'm sorry that I'm still not strong enough for you. I made that choice, not in cold blood, as you accused, but in hot, confused desperation. But it *was* my choice and I *will* live with the repercussions.'

She pushed without grace through the meeting attendees, who were all desperately trying to pretend they weren't there. Every one of them would have had the same or worse in their own troubled lives. She'd given up worrying about her dignity when she first stood up in front of this group and introduced herself as someone controlled by alcohol. AA wasn't the place or the time for blushes.

When she hit the stairs, she made her choice in a split second. Anyone else would bolt for the street but she wanted to hide, not run. So her choice was easy. She took the roof stairs two at a time for four floors and burst out into the cold night air, her lungs aching. Downtown unfolded in front of her in a glittery, anonymous mass of lights. A half-hearted rain shower misted down on her. She tucked herself into the lee of a ventilation duct.

When the door opened quietly behind her a few minutes later, she cursed her choice. Marc knew her too well. He stepped out onto the rooftop and scanned the dark corners.

'How did you know where to find me?' she murmured.

He turned towards her voice but didn't step closer. 'I just thought about where I'd go in the same situation. I knew you wouldn't want to drive while you were upset.'

They stood silently, together in the half dark, a light sheen of moisture forming on their hair. Beth didn't care and Marc didn't notice.

'I'm sorry for exploding in there.' He genuinely seemed at a loss to explain himself.

'You never did like surprises.'

His laugh wasn't amused. Words dried up between them again. 'I just wasn't prepared. Both of you at the same time. It was…' He looked around at her rooftop hideout. 'Are you okay?'

Part of her burned to stay angry with him. But another part vibrated at an inaudible frequency just to be standing this close to him again. 'I just wanted some privacy.'

'You got it. It's nice up here.'

'I come a lot.' After most AA sessions, at least. 'Where I can think.'

'You can see most of the city.'

'More on a clear night.'

That finally drew his attention to the fine wet mist drifting down on them. And Beth's lack of a coat. 'You're getting wet.'

She laughed. 'I think I'll survive.'

'Here…' Anyone else would have stripped off their

jacket and given it to her. Not Marc. He stepped closer, almost looming over her, shrugged his jacket up and half off and held it over them both like an odd-shaped umbrella. It was surprisingly effective against the very light rain. But it brought them into dangerously close contact and forced their respective scents to swirl under the impromptu canopy. Coconut mingled with something indefinably spicy in a heady, seductive alchemy.

Oh, dear… Beth could practically feel all her good intentions dissolving as his scent chased around her. She blurted the first words that came to her by way of restoring her equilibrium.

'I didn't know, I swear. I wouldn't have come.'

Marc stared down at her in the inky darkness of their homemade shelter and flicked wry eyebrows. 'I know. I can see my mother's fingerprints all over this.'

'She meant well.'

'Strangely enough, I actually believe that's true.' He sighed, stiff and unsure in the dim light. 'Look, Beth—'

She wasn't up to another confession. Or a rehashing of all the reasons he couldn't be her friend. Or a declaration of ancient feelings hastily followed up with a *but…* She struck pre-emptively.

'I can't do the once-every-couple-of-months thing, Marc.'

His answer was too fast. Too defensive. 'I didn't expect to see you here—'

She could be flippant. She could be hostile. Either one would keep her safe. But both were a cop out. 'But you've been checking up on me. Staying just in the periphery of my awareness. Making it impossible to put you out of my thoughts.'

He seemed lost for words for once. Caught out. Beth

barreled on before she lost the nerve. 'It was what *you* wanted, Marc. For us to have nothing more to do with each other. And I understand why now. It hurts too much.' Her voice cracked on the last word.

His eyes fell shut 'I didn't want to hurt you.'

The urgent need to protect him washed through her. *Ugh—still?* When would her heart get back to prioritising itself? 'But you keep reopening that door. Every time you check up on my classes. Or talk to my parents. Or buy my paintings through an agent. You're hovering just out of sight. I can't do it any more.'

It was exactly what he'd just accused her and Janice of. Finding ways of staying connected. No wonder he'd been so angry about it.

We despise most in others what we fear in ourselves.

'You weren't supposed to know.' Heat surged off him. Enough to feel. His head dropped and, when it rose again, his gaze was intense. 'I find myself thinking of you more and more, until the only way I can shift it is to see you or see someone who has some connection to you. I know it's ridiculous but my mind doesn't seem to care about that.'

A deep pain screwed tighter in her gut. 'Fight it harder.'

His laugh was dark. 'You're underestimating its strength.' He touched his forehead. 'In here I know it's wrong, but I find myself picking up the phone anyway. It's a miracle I can hang it up before you answer. It's like I'm compelled…'

Her heart flip-flopped. To hear these words… But they didn't undo the reality. She stared at him intently. 'Welcome to my world.'

He snapped his mouth shut with jaw-jarring force as

the penny dropped. His blush speared higher, angrier. 'This is not the same.'

'Your mind tells you one thing but your body wants another. You know you should stay away but you can't. How is that different?'

'It's totally different. What I'm doing can't…' Marc's nostrils flared and he frowned deeply.

'Can't hurt anyone? Is that what you were going to say?' Her tight voice softened with compassion. 'I think we both know that's not true.'

Confusion chased across his features. And not a small amount of anxiety. Was this the first time he'd ever seen the potential in himself?

'But you're right. There is one difference.' She gently peeled his fingers from around hers. 'I'm not judging you for it. I'm just asking you to honour the promise you asked me to make. I understand why you asked for it and now I want it too.' A deep, infinite sorrow filled her as she moved past him to the roof door. She paused there. 'One day I hope you'll remember the woman before the addict,' she whispered. 'Then ask yourself why you kept coming back to me.'

Be happy.

Marc wondered if she'd said the words or if he'd just imagined the pained whisper as she closed the door on their friendship.

Now I want it, too. Beth wanted him gone. And why not? He'd done a bang-up job of making sure she wouldn't want to stay. Laying out landmines between them. Flaying her with his words. She seemed strong but so had his mother, once. How long would it be before she slipped back into old habits when things got tough?

Never mind that she hadn't in all this challenging time.

As far as you're aware. He'd not known with his

mother. For years. His sickening fury on finding out about her addiction was as much about the many years he'd been oblivious as anything else. Anger at himself. How could a son not have noticed? If he'd twigged earlier, could he have done something? It would have to be easier quitting earlier in the addiction, surely? And with his support…

His eyes drifted to the stairwell.

It was why he was keeping tabs on her. To see if she was staying healthy or whether she'd weaken and—

His own thoughts brought him up short.

Beth was right. He did see her first as an addict. He had since the moment she'd told him about her dependence. He'd scratched the word 'recovering' from his vocab and just focused on the 'alcoholic' part. The part that said she was weak.

The part he feared in himself.

Who was he to judge her strength? He couldn't even be in the same room as Beth without wanting to touch her. He *was* the infatuated teenager she'd spoken of that day on the beach. Except he'd never grown out of his obsession. He'd gone years cold turkey and after only one day back in her influence she was back to haunting his nights. She wasn't the one who kept drifting back into the sphere of *his* life. She wasn't the one scratching around for plausible excuses to see him again. She'd been as good as her word and stayed away when he'd asked her to.

What kind of a hypocrite did it make him?

He'd judged Beth for being human. For not being able to deny herself something she craved on a cellular level. But she was fighting it. She'd gone through so much these past months and hadn't had a drink. The clarity of her skin, her eyes, the softness of her hair told him that. Her body was rebounding from the abuses of its past. Ripening.

And his was responding accordingly.

All these years later, even after a decade of alcohol abuse, she was still the better human being. Nothing had changed. She was demonstrating every day the kind of strength he'd lacked all his life. He couldn't even do something as simple as stay the hell away from her.

Addict is as addict does.

That made his decision clearer but not easier. He would make himself keep completely away. Not just because she'd asked him to and because he knew it was the moral thing to do. But because he needed to see if he could. He needed to prove that he was stronger than it was.

Dependence. Compulsion.

He was not his mother.

He would deny himself his Beth fix, next time it burned its way into his psyche and refused to be ignored. The next time it set up an infuriating clanging in his head and filled his thoughts with memories of her. He'd dig around in his soul and see if he could find the strength to do what was right for *her*, not for him.

If he couldn't beat it, how could he ever judge anyone else for failing?

The difficulty he had staying away from her was directly proportional to the importance of managing it. If it was easier it wouldn't matter.

And Beth mattered.

CHAPTER TEN

STAYING away lasted all of four weeks. But Beth could hardly blame Marc when she'd all too readily replied to his email inviting her out on this charter today, convincing herself it was important to get closure.

Again.

A third set.

Masochist.

'I don't know how you do this, day in, day out.' The shade of her skin had to be reflected in the sickly tone of her voice as the *Libertine* pitched and rolled on the southern swell. She kept her eyes firmly on the golden contours of the distant shore as a way of holding off the seasickness.

Breathe in, breathe out...

'You get used to it,' Marc said from his spot at the vessel's wheel.

'Can't imagine how,' a portly red-headed American man clutching a seasickness bag said tightly from right next to her. He and Beth had both climbed up to the bridge to escape the nauseating blowback as the diesel fuel motored them slowly through the outer reaches of Holly's Bay. Nothing short of the threat of vomit would have got her this close to Marc Duncannon. Just hearing his voice still hurt.

So why in heaven was she here?

The American picked his way to the far side of the fly bridge to peer down on his wife and the nine other passengers on the lower deck, their eyes peeled to the brightly reflecting water in search of their prey.

'Thank you for coming,' Marc said quietly, still looking out to the horizon. Dark sunglasses hid his soul from her.

Gulls squawked overhead as they followed the boat in anticipation of a snack. One of the tourists below obliged with a piece of something that sent the birds into a squabbling, diving frenzy. The ugly sound grated on Beth's already tortured nerves.

'I almost didn't. I thought we'd said everything there was to say a month ago.'

'We did.' His reply was almost lost on the breeze. Beth stepped closer to hear. 'But it wasn't quite complete. There's one more loose end to tie up.'

Ouch. 'Now we're a loose end?'

The breeze cut into her skinny frame. No sleep and no appetite would do that. She could hold it together during daylight hours but there was no one to fake it for at night alone in her studio. She wrapped her arms around her diminishing torso.

Marc frowned. 'Are you doing okay, Beth?'

'You shouldn't care.' Frustration and pain lifted her voice. 'How I am or whether we have unfinished business shouldn't be on your radar. We're not a part of each other's lives any more.' Beth pointed to shore. 'You made the call not to be friends that day on the beach last year. Then you drove all the way to Perth to tell me again a few months later. Then you followed me onto a rooftop to remind me. Now...what? We're about to cover it a fourth time?' She glared at him. 'For a man who isn't interested in friendship, you sure do a good job of keeping in touch.'

He swept the horizon in a broad arc, then those sexy sunglasses fixed right back on her. 'Yet here you are.'

She stared at him. Knew he was absolutely right. Her interest in him—her desire to see him—hadn't waned one little bit. When he wrote and asked to see her, it was a short internal battle. 'More fool me. Are you going to tell me why I'm here?'

'When I took this charter I knew I'd be calling you.'

'Why?'

His twisted smile wouldn't reach his eyes. She didn't need to see them to know that. Marc killed the motor and turned to watch her. 'Wait for it...'

Over his shoulder, a sudden jet spray of water made her leap. The tourists on the lower deck screamed with delight and tilted the boat as they shifted as one body to the starboard side. Their cameras started chattering like the seagulls overhead. Not far out, a whale breached long enough to evacuate its blowhole and suck in a giant lungful of air. Then it sank out of view again and it was as though it had never existed.

Beth forgot her anxiety instantly. Whales still got her blood racing, even smaller ones. She brushed Marc's arm with her shoulder as she crossed to the side. He seemed to lean into her touch but it had to be the lurching of the boat on the swell. Out of the corner of her eye, she saw him move to the ladder leading down to the deck and snap a barrier rope across behind the leaving American, effectively making the bridge off-limits to everyone else.

Over to the right, another whale breached, and then another, and another and Beth realised Marc had stopped the boat in the middle of a pod of the enormous dark mammals. False killer whales. Her thoughts immediately turned to *their* whale and how she had gone after the rescuers finally got her back out to sea. She'd been so tired, so dehydrated, and with that nasty arrow-head gash on her tail. Beth had convinced herself their whale would be fine but there was no way they'd ever really know.

'How did you know where to find the pod?'

Marc stepped up close behind her and draped a jacket around her angular, chilled shoulders. Her mind instantly went back to that night on the beach. Today's cold breeze was nothing compared to that night. She'd never been so critically numb again.

Not on the outside, at least.

'I came across the pod two weeks ago. They've been coming here daily. Enjoying the calm shallows of the bay.'

She twisted around and up to look at him with one brow arched. 'Shallows being relative, of course.'

And *calm*, as her stomach lurched on a particularly large pitch of the boat. She lost count of who was who. There had to be a dozen whales down there. They breached the surface in pairs, solo, spread out and close. The occasional one leaped clear of the surface with such power and gusto it made Beth wonder just how deep the whales' underwater domain really was.

'The hull of your boat must look like a small solitary cloud in a massive dark blue sky to them.' Like that night on the beach when she'd looked up into the limitless sky, again now she felt small and irrelevant.

Marc braced himself with an arm immediately next to hers, his hard body leaning into her from behind. More reminders of that night. Beth didn't care that it was inappropriate for both of them. She let his strength leach into her. Just one more time.

'Their curiosity draws them to the boat. All I had to do was get us in roughly the right part of the bay and they did the rest.'

The water show went on and Beth's breath caught and tumbled across the laughter that she couldn't hold back. This was such a gift. Finally, one whale rolled, belly up, close to their boat and its giant eye breached the water for seconds. It seemed to look right at the two humans standing together on the top deck in a way that was inexplicably moving. Then it completed the slow roll and disappeared under the surface.

Or back above it, from the whales' perspective.

Beth turned to Marc on an exclamation but he gently guided her chin back to the waves. 'Wait…'

And then it happened. The giant spinal arch of the same whale as it curled up out of the water propelled by its mammoth tail, and then the stunning salute of the tail fins standing up tall in the water. Elegant, barnacle crusted and with only a triangular scar to mar it—

Beth's breath froze in her throat. Not a triangle… an arrow-head. She half twisted in the circle of Marc's arms, unable to tear her gaze away. 'It's our whale.'

He pressed his chin to the top of her head and let his other arm reach around her to grip the gunnel. His silence said he was just as moved as she was. They watched the beautiful, strong tail sink silently down into the dark depths with the kind of splashless entry Tasmin Major would have killed for.

Beth's voice trembled. 'Oh, my God…'

'One more surprise. Wait…'

She followed his pointed finger and stared, unblinking, at the glistening ocean. Nothing…nothing… And then—

'Marc!' she practically squealed, before clamping her lips shut.

A whale calf, no bigger than Mum's tail, breached the surface in a playful splash. Its body followed the exact arc and trajectory as its mother.

'I figure she must have been pregnant when we rescued her.' His voice was breathlessly close to her ear. Somewhere deep down that bothered her. But her eyes were glued to the calf. 'It's not uncommon for whales to have an older calf with them while gestating a new one.'

Her voice thickened dangerously. 'This is a creche?' She'd heard that whales liked to spend their calf's first months in a sheltered, food-rich bay.

'I think so.'

Marc kept her safe in the circle of his arms while she cried. Too much had happened between them to make her ashamed of the tears that streamed down her face. Joy. Relief. And sadness for the final farewell that she knew this was.

Maybe it really was closure she'd been waiting for.

After all, they didn't hate each other. They just couldn't be together. They were like humans and whales—drawn to each other by instinct but, ultimately, too dangerous for each other.

The sun had its toes well and truly in the water on the horizon by the time Marc finally pulled the pin on their private whale watch. The downstairs tourists were too worn out to keep up more than the occasional quiet conversation and one by one they moved inside the comfortable cabin.

'You should get below deck,' Marc hinted reluctantly, stroking her wind-blown hair back into some order and then stepping back, as though—finally—realising the impropriety of his earlier proximity. 'It's going to get real cold real fast.'

Beth dragged her eyes off the still frolicking beasts and turned towards the ladder, knowing this was it. Before her common sense could stop her, she curled an arm up around his neck and pulled Marc's head down to hers. Her lips pressed for an eternity against the corner of his.

'Thank you,' she whispered against his mouth. Against the pounding of her own pulse. *I love you.* 'I'll miss you.'

His hand snaked out and arched around her wrist, gently preventing her from leaving. His thumb circled her skin. He didn't bother hiding the pain on his face. 'This goodbye feels final.'

No more games. She nodded out to the frolicking whales. 'Maybe we just needed to see her for it to truly be over?'

Some distant, optimistic part of her thought maybe a bit of healing time might have worked miracles. Might have changed his heart. *Might have made her more acceptable.* Marc was so damaged by his mother's addiction that he couldn't see his way to caring for someone living with one. End of story.

'Is that still what you want?' he whispered. 'For it to be truly over?'

Her head came up. 'Marc, don't do this. Nothing's changed…'

'I've changed, Beth. I stood in a room with two dozen alcoholics a month ago and listened to their stories, imagined they were you. After you left me on that miserable rooftop, I spoke to some of them about their battles. The triumphs and the impact of the defeats. How they felt about the people they'd lost in life.'

Her heart hammered.

He shook his head. 'I spoke to my mother, which was the greatest miracle. We're now having a weekly lunch. That has all changed me, Beth.' He took a deep breath. 'I thought addiction was something that happened to weak people.'

Her eyes flared wide and he rushed on. 'I wasn't particularly disposed to view it logically and fairly because I've been on the receiving end of the effects of addiction for half my life. What are the odds that both of the significant women in my world would be fighting addiction?'

'Actually, pretty high—' she started.

He raised a hand. *Okay. Rhetorical question...*

'Beth, you showed me that addiction is every bit as illogical and damaging as the most fanatical of teenage love affairs. And, having been a teenager who loved passionately, if secretly—' those hazel eyes blazed '—I now have a bit more understanding of what it means to be addicted. How it consumes everything in its path. Warps everything. And how much courage it takes to fight that kind of compulsion, every single day.'

A whale crashed into the sea behind them but Beth couldn't drag her eyes off Marc for a moment.

His eyes dropped to the deck and then dragged back to hers. 'Turns out I don't have that courage. I don't have the strength of character I used to think I do. It took six months of desperately trying to stay away from something I craved down to my very cells. Trying and failing. Wanting it every...single...day.'

Her mouth dried up completely.

'Beth, you have demonstrated more courage in climbing out of addiction than I ever have in my entire life. I worshipped you for your fearlessness back when we were kids and, later, when we were teens and you gave the social expectations of the whole school the finger.' The small smile he conjured carried genuine warmth. 'I realised halfway through our icy adventure with the whale that nothing about your courage has changed. You just lost your way for a bit.'

He stepped closer. 'Ten years ago when you walked away from me—from us—I considered that a weakness. Something lacking in you. I closed my mind to you and to my heart. It suited me to blame someone for the pain I suffered. But I was blaming the wrong person.'

He took a deep breath. 'It killed me how cleanly you were able to excise me from your life. I thought it meant you didn't care, but I was wrong. For better or for worse, you did that for me. And at considerable cost to yourself. I can see that now. It takes infinitely more strength to walk away from something like that than to endure being walked away from.'

Heated shivers prickled through her whole body.

'Even these past months, while I've been torturing myself with the intensity of wanting to see you more and more every day, you cut the ties and left them where they lay. It burned me that you could walk away from me apparently so easily while I couldn't even honour my own promise to stay away. That I had so little strength.

'I chose to interpret weakness in you because it's easier than admitting the weakness is really in myself. Up on that rooftop you told me to fight harder, and I realised that I've fought *alongside* you saving whales, I've fought *with* you against the establishment more times than I can remember. But I have never once fought *for* you, Beth.' His eyes blazed. 'If I had, you might have stayed all those years ago. Or that day at Holly's Bay or on that rooftop.'

His voice cracked on that last word and Beth found her hands tangling in his. She felt his pain in her own body, sharp and aching. And so familiar.

'When you left with McKinley I rebuilt my life. When I walked away from Mum, I rebuilt again. I've been patting myself on the back for having the strength and courage to start over repeatedly. But it dawned on me after that meeting that I let you walk away rather than fight for what I wanted. I walked away from my only remaining family when things got too hard. I let you drive away from that beach doubting yourself because it was easier than admitting that *I'm* the one who lacks strength. In the way it counts most.'

Her eyes blurred over and she had to swipe away at both of them with their linked hands to keep him in focus. 'Marc, don't…'

'Beth, my running from you, from how I feel when I'm with you, was not just about me not wanting to repeat the errors of the past. It was about me protecting myself when I should have been protecting you. And that shames me.'

Pain lanced from him to her and his eyes darkened. 'I have my priorities straightened out now. If staying away from you is the thing I can do to help you stay strong, then I give you my solemn oath I will do it, if it's what you want.' His face and his words spoke of resilience and determination. 'But know that you are now officially on the top of *my* make-good list, and I'm a patient man. I hope that one day I have the opportunity to mark you off it.'

She shuddered. 'It hasn't been easy for me to walk

away from you. I've bled as much as you have. But I guess I've just had more practice.'

Hazel eyes blazed at her, filled almost to overflowing with blind faith. Only this time she felt as if she'd earned it. 'You do not lack strength, Beth Hughes.'

She stared at him steadily. Amazing, considering her galloping heart. 'And you are not a crutch…'

'I know.'

'…I just love you.'

His eyes glittered. His chest heaved. 'I know.'

She took a steadying breath and held his eyes. 'But I'm still an addict. That's for ever. Can you forget that?'

'Would you want me to?'

Ten years of her life. Her hardest battle fought and won. A huge part of the woman she'd become. 'No.'

'But I can understand it. If you'll let me.'

What was he offering? For all his fine speech-making, he hadn't made any promises. He was just offering understanding. Or to leave her life if that was what she wanted.

Pfff… As if that was an option now…

'What do you see first when you look at me?' she risked. But it was important that she knew where she stood. 'Addict, friend or…woman?'

She felt the impact of the intensity she'd decided she'd never see again. It washed over her like waves hitting the shore. His chest rose and fell in choppy lurches.

'Honestly?' Marc shook his head. 'All of those things. Plus I see the mother of my children.'

Beth's breath faltered completely. *Children…?*

Moments after he'd lauded her courage was not the time to have it dissolve. In the silence that followed she became aware of the tightness of every part of her, the avid fixation of hazel eyes in front of her. The time it had been since she last took a breath.

'I'd like to stay on your list,' she croaked, stepping forward into the possible abyss. 'Maybe we can start with friends...'

'I can't promise you how long that will last. I'm not feeling very friendly.'

The barely repressed hunger in his eyes told its own story. She drew herself close, smiling. Not afraid with a woman's eyes. 'For as long as it lasts, then.'

Then, as she went to circle her arms around him in a hug, he pulled her to her toes and pressed his mouth to her hungry, thirsty lips.

'Do friends do that with each other?' She wobbled as he released her for air a moment later.

He tipped his face towards her again and said, 'Okay, so we're good friends.' Then he took her chin in his hand and met her lips more fully with his hot, blistering ones. The kiss went on for eternity, deep and blazing and as comfortable as a roaring fire on a cold coastal night. He folded her into the protection of his arms and kissed her back. Hot, hard and so...*so*...much better than a decade before.

'Shortest friendship in history,' he mumbled as he finally lifted his head. Love and admiration and desire and wonder all shone from his hazel eyes.

'That's fine with me,' Beth murmured against his jaw. 'I never really wanted to be your friend, anyway.'

'Brat...' Marc swatted her behind.

Beth pulled herself free. 'Wait...' Marc stroked her hair away from her flushed face and waited. 'What took you so long? It's been a month.'

'I've spent the past four weeks trying to prove I was stronger than my feelings.'

'And did you?'

He shrugged. 'I've proven it's taxing and exhausting and exasperating to deny yourself something you want so badly. But I did it.'

She laughed. 'Not for very long.'

He kissed her again. Then slid his lips around to the side of her throat. 'Long enough to know,' he murmured against her ear.

Her head tipped back as her knees sagged in response to his marauding lips. *Oh, God...* But she managed to murmur, 'Know what?'

'That I love you because of you. Not because of me.'

Her legs buckled and Marc caught her weight against his body. She swallowed back a choke of tears. 'You've only seen me four times in seven months.'

'And that's about to change.' But he must have felt her tension because he lifted his lips and looked at her, intense and loving. 'There's never been anyone in my heart but you, Beth. Even when you weren't in my life. You said at your exhibition that I'd be alone without you and you were spot on. No one could compete with what you'd become in my heart, even while I was in denial about the place you held.'

His pedestal.

'I'm just human, Marc. The higher you place me, the further I'll fall.'

Determination and caring glowed on his face. 'No more falling. Not while I'm there with you.'

He pulled her close into a strong, protective hug. Beth's eyes washed with tears. When had anyone in her entire life made her feel so safe?

'So, what now?' she murmured against his cheek. 'Where do we go from here?'

'I'd like to take you to dinner. We've never been on a date.'

A date—when he was standing here with her body pressed so intimately into his? Beth laughed. 'I think we've skipped the dating stage, don't you?'

Marc chuckled against her ear, warm and intoxicating. 'After that, I need to get you some sea legs. You're going to spend a lot of time on my boats. You'll be my first mate.'

She pushed back to look at him. 'Oh, will I? All the way from the city? What about my students?'

His smile was as seductive as it was bashful. 'They can come down on retreat. You know…when you move into the homestead with me.'

She pushed back to look at him. 'Wow, we're moving quickly. Is that where this is leading?'

'Ultimately. Raising kids isn't going to work if we're two hundred clicks apart.' Serious, unashamed eyes held hers. 'But dinner first. You look like you haven't eaten in weeks.'

She wrapped her arms more tightly around him. 'I feel like I haven't eaten in years.'

He tipped his head down to hers and murmured against her lips, 'Then let me feed you. It would give me the greatest of pleasure to watch you eat. The rest can wait.'

Her mouth found his again in a perfect fit and her blood thrilled at the taste. But a thought pulled her back again. 'Wait…your *first* mate? I was hoping to be your only mate.'

The sexy smile he gave her then made up for half a lifetime of loss. He slid his hands down her arms until their fingers entwined and he pinned them gently behind Beth's back, pressing her more firmly against him.

His lids dropped as his lips did.

'Deal.'

SECOND CHANCE WITH THE REBEL

BY

CARA COLTER

Cara Colter lives in British Columbia with her partner, Rob, and eleven horses. She has three grown children and a grandson. She is a recent recipient of an RT Book Reviews Career Achievement Award in the 'Love and Laughter' category. Cara loves to hear from readers, and you can contact her or learn more about her through her website: www.cara-colter.com.

For Linda, with much love. And Queenscliff.
The combination that made this story a joy
I will never forget.

CHAPTER ONE

"HUDSON GROUP, HOW may I direct your call?"

"Macintyre Hudson, please."

Could silence be disapproving? Lucy Lindstrom asked herself. As in, you didn't just cold-call a multi-million-dollar company and ask to speak to their CEO?

"Mr. Hudson is not available right now. I'd be happy to take a message."

Lucy recognized the voice on the other end of the phone. It was that same uppity-accented receptionist who had taken her name and number thirteen times this week.

Mac was not going to talk to her unless he wanted to. And clearly, he did not want to. She had to fight with herself to stay on the line. It would have been so much easier just to hang up the phone. She reminded herself she had no choice. She had to change tack.

"It's an urgent family matter."

"He's not in his office. I'll have to see if he's in the building. And I'll have to tell him who is calling."

Lucy was certain she heard faint suspicion there, as if her voice was beginning to be recognized also, and was on the blocked-caller list.

"You could tell him it's Harriet Freda calling." She picked a fleck of lavender paint off her thumbnail.

"I'll take your number and have him call you back when I locate him."

"It's okay. I'll hold," Lucy said with as much firmness as she could muster.

As she waited, she looked down at the paper in her purple-paint-stained hand. It showed a neat list of names, all of them crossed off save for one.

The remaining name stood out as if it was written in neon tubing.

The boy who ruined my life.

Macintyre W. Hudson. A voice whispered from her past, *Everybody just calls me Mac.*

Just like that, seven years slipped away, and she could see him, Mac Hudson, the most handsome boy ever born, with those dark, laughing eyes, that crooked smile, the silky chocolate hair, too long, falling down over his brow.

Just like that, the shiver ran up and down her spine, and Lucy remembered exactly why that boy had ruined her life.

Only, now he wasn't a boy any longer, but a man.

And she was a woman.

"Macintyre Hudson did not ruin your life," Lucy told herself sternly. "At best he stole a few moments of it."

But what moments those were, a voice inside her insisted.

"Rubbish," Lucy said firmly, but her confidence, not in great supply these days anyway, dwindled. It felt as if she had failed at everything she'd set her hand to, and failed spectacularly.

She had never gone to university as her parents had hoped, but had become a clerk in a bookstore in the neighboring city of Glen Oak, instead.

She had worked up to running her own store, Books and Beans, with her fiancé, but she had eagerly divested herself of the coffee shop and storefront part of the business after their humiliatingly public breakup.

Now, licking her wounds, she was back in her hometown of Lindstrom Beach in her old family home on the shores of Sunshine Lake.

The deeding of the house was charity, plain and simple. Her widowed mother had given it to Lucy before remarrying and moving to California. She said it had been in the Lindstrom family for generations and it needed to stay there.

And even though that was logical, and the timing couldn't have been more perfect, Lucy had the ugly feeling that what her mother really thought was that Lucy wouldn't make it without her help.

"But I have a dream," she reminded herself firmly, shoring herself up with that before Mac came on the line.

Despite her failures, over the past year Lucy had developed a sense of purpose. And more important, she felt *needed* for the first time in a long time.

It bothered Lucy that she had to remind herself of that as she drummed her fingers and listened to the music on the other end of the phone.

The song, she realized when she caught herself humming along, was one about a rebel and had always been the song she had associated with Mac. It was about a boy who was willing to risk all but his heart.

That was Macintyre Hudson to a *T*, so who could imagine the former Lindstrom Beach renegade and unapologetic bad boy at the helm of a multimillion-dollar company that produced the amazingly popular Wild Side outdoor products?

Unexpectedly, the music stopped.

"Mama?"

Mac's voice was urgent and worried. It had deepened, Lucy was sure, since the days of their youth, but it had that same gravelly, sensuous edge to it that had always sent tingles up and down her spine.

Now, when she most needed to be confident, was not the time to think of the picture of him on his website, the one that had dashed her hopes that maybe he had gotten heavy or lost all his hair in the years that had passed.

But think of it she did. No boring head-and-shoulders shot in a nice Brooks Brothers suit for the CEO of Hudson Group.

No, the caption stated the founder of the Wild Side line was demonstrating the company's new kayak, Wild Ride. He was on a raging wedge of white water that funneled between rocks. Through flecks of foam, frozen by the camera, Macintyre Hudson had been captured in all his considerable masculine glory.

He'd been wearing a life jacket, a Wild Side product that showed off the amazing broadness of his shoulders, the powerful muscle of sun-bronzed arms gleaming with water. More handsome than ever, obviously in his element, he'd had a look in his devil-dark eyes, a cast to his mouth and a set to his jaw that was one of fierce concentration and formidable determination.

Maybe he didn't have any hair. He'd been wearing a helmet in the photo.

"Mama?" he said again. "What's wrong? Why didn't you call on my private line?"

Lucy had steeled herself for this. Rehearsed it. In her mind she had controlled every facet of this conversation.

But she had not planned for the image that materialized out of her memory file, that superimposed itself above the image of him in the kayak.

A younger Mac Hudson pausing as he lifted himself out of the lake onto the dock, his body sun-browned and perfect, water sluicing off the rippling smooth lines of his muscles, looking up at her, with laughter tilting the edges of his ultra-sexy eyes.

Do you love me, Lucy Lin?

Never *I love you* from him.

The memory hardened her resolve not to be in any way vulnerable to him. He was an extraordinarily handsome man, and he used his good looks in dastardly ways, as very handsome men were well-known to do.

On the other hand, her fiancé, James Kennedy, had been homely and bookish and had still behaved in a completely dastardly manner.

All of which explained why romance played no part in her brand-new dreams for herself.

Fortified with that, Lucy ordered herself not to stammer. "No, I'm sorry, it isn't Mama Freda."

There was a long silence. In the background she could hear a lot of noise as if a raucous party was going on.

When Mac spoke, she took it as a positive sign. At least he hadn't hung up.

"Well, well," he said. "Little Lucy Lindstrom. I hope this is good. I'm standing here soaking wet."

"At work?" she said, surprised into curiosity.

"I was in the hot tub with my assistant, Celeste." His tone was dry. "What can I do for you?"

Don't pursue it, she begged herself, but she couldn't help it.

"You don't have a hot tub at work!"

"You're right, I don't. And no Celeste, either. What we have is a test tank for kayaks where we can simulate a white-water chute."

Lucy had peeked at their website on and off over the years.

The business had started appropriately enough, with Mac's line of outdoor gear. He was behind the name brand that outdoor enthusiasts coveted: Wild Side. First it had been his canoes. It had expanded quickly into kayaks and then accessories, and now, famously, into clothing.

All the reckless abandon of his youth channeled into huge success, and he was still having fun. Who tested kayaks at work?

But Mac had always been about having fun. Some things just didn't change.

Though he didn't sound very good-humored right now. "I'm wet, and the kayak didn't test out very well, so this had better be good."

"This is important," she said.

"What I was doing was important, too." He sighed, the sigh edged with irritation. "Some things just don't change, do they? The pampered doctor's daughter, the head of student council, the captain of the cheerleading squad, used to having her own way."

That girl, dressed in her designer jeans, with hundred-dollar highlights glowing in her hair, looked at her from her past, a little sadly.

Mac's assessment was so unfair! For the past few years she had been anything but pampered. And now she was trying to turn the Books part of Books and Beans into an internet business while renting canoes off her dock.

She was painting her own house and living on macaroni and cheese. She hadn't bought a new outfit for over a year, socking away every extra nickel in the hope that she could make her dream a reality.

And that didn't even cover all the things she was running next door to Mama Freda's to do!

She would have protested except for the inescapable if annoying truth: she *had* told a small lie to get her own way.

"It was imperative that I speak to you," she said firmly.

"Hmmm. Imperative. That has a rather regal sound to it. A princess giving a royal command."

He was insisting on remembering who she had been before he'd ruined her life: a confident, popular honor student who had never known trouble and never done a single thing wrong. Or daring. Or adventurous.

The young Lucy Lindstrom's idea of a good time, pre-Mac, had been getting the perfect gown for prom, and spending lazy summer afternoons on the deck with her friends, painting each other's toenails pink. Her idea of a great evening had been sitting around a roaring bonfire, especially if a sing-along started.

Pre-Mac, the most exciting thing that had ever happened to her was getting the acceptance letter from the university of her choice.

"Pampered, yes," Mac went on. "Deceitful, no. You are the last person I would have ever thought would lower yourself to deceit."

But that's where he was dead wrong. He had brought out the deceitful side in her before.

The day she had said goodbye to him.

Hurt and angry that he had not asked her to go with him, to hide her sense of inconsolable loss, she had tossed her head and said, "I could never fall for a boy like you."

When the truth was she already had. She had been so crazy in love with Mac that it had felt as though the fire that burned within her would melt her and everything around her until there was nothing left of her world but a small, dark smudge.

"I needed to talk to you," she said, stripping any memory of that summer and those long, heated days from her voice.

"Yes. You said. Imperative."

Apparently he had honed sarcasm to an art.

"I'm sorry I insinuated I was Mama Freda."

"Insinuated," he said silkily. "So much more palatable than lying."

"I had to get by the guard dog who answers your phone!"

"No, you didn't. I got your messages."

"Except the one about needing to speak to you personally?"

"Nothing to talk about." His voice was chilly. "I've got all the information you gave. A Mother's Day Gala in celebration of Mama Freda's lifetime of good work. A combination of her eightieth birthday and Mother's Day. Fund-raiser for all her good causes. She knows about the gala and the fund-raiser but has no idea it's honoring her. Under no circumstances is she to find out."

Lucy wondered if she should be pleased that he had obviously paid very close attention to the content of those messages.

Actually, the fund-raiser was for Lucy's good cause, but Mama Freda was at the very heart of her dream.

At the worst point of her life, she had gone to Mama Freda, and those strong arms had folded around her.

"When your pain feels too great to bear, *liebling,* then you must stop thinking of yourself and think of another."

Mama had carried the dream with Lucy, encouraging her, keeping the fire going when it had flickered to a tiny ember and nearly gone out.

Now, wasn't it the loveliest of ironies that Mama was one of the ones who would benefit from her own advice?

"Second Sunday of May," he said, his tone bored, dismissive, "black-tie dinner at the Lindstrom Beach Yacht Club."

She heard disdain in his voice and guessed the reason. "Oh, so that's the sticking point. I've already had a hundred people confirm, and I'm expecting a few more to trickle in over the next week. It's the only place big enough to handle that kind of a crowd."

"I remember when I wasn't good enough to get a job busing tables there."

"Get real. You never applied for a job busing tables at the yacht club."

Even in his youth, Mac, in his secondhand jeans, one of a string of foster children who had found refuge at Mama's, had carried himself like a king, bristling with pride and an ingrained sense of himself. He took offense at the slightest provocation.

And then hid it behind that charming smile.

"After graduation you had a job with the town, digging ditches for the new sewer system."

"Not the most noble work, but honest," he said. "And real."

So, who are you to be telling me to get real? He didn't say it, but he could have.

Noble or not, she could remember the ridged edges of the sleek muscles, how she had loved to touch him, feel his wiry strength underneath her fingertips.

He mistook her silence for judgment. "It runs in my family. My dad was a ditchdigger, too. They had a nickname for him. Digger Dan."

She felt the shock of that. She had known Mac since he had come to live in the house next door. He was fourteen, a year older than she was. When their paths crossed, he had tormented and teased her, interpreting the fact she was always tongue-tied in his presence as an example of her family's snobbery, rather than seeing it for what it was.

Intrigue. Awe. Temptation. She had never met anyone like Mac. Not before or since. Ruggedly independent. Bold. Unfettered by convention. Fearless. She remembered seeing him glide by her house, only fourteen, solo in a canoe heavily laden with camping gear.

She would see his campfire burning bright against the night on the other side of the lake. It was called the wild side of the lake because it was undeveloped crown land, thickly forested.

Sometimes Mac would spend the whole weekend over there. Alone.

She couldn't even imagine that. Being alone over there with the bears.

The week she had won the spelling bee he had been kicked out of school for swearing.

She got a little Ford compact for her sixteenth birthday, while he bought an old convertible and stripped the engine in the driveway, then stood down her father when he complained. While she was painting her toenails, he was painstakingly building his own cedar-strip canoe in Mama's yard.

But never once, even in that summer when she had loved him, right after her own graduation from high school, had Mac revealed a single detail about his life before he had arrived in foster care in Lindstrom Beach.

Was it the fact that he had so obviously risen above those roots that made him reveal that his father had been nicknamed Digger Dan? Or had he changed?

She squashed that thing inside her that felt ridiculously and horribly like hope by saying, proudly, "I don't really care if you come to the gala or not."

She told herself she was becoming hardened to rejection. All the people who really mattered to Mama—except him—had said they would come. But her own mother had said she would be in Africa on safari at that time and many people from Lucy's "old" life, her high-school days, had not answered yet. Those who had, had answered no.

There was silence from Mac, and Lucy allowed herself pleasure that she had caught him off guard.

"And I am sorry about messing up *your* Mother's Day."

"What do you mean, *my* Mother's Day?" His voice was guarded.

That had always been the problem with Mac. The insurmountable flaw. He wouldn't let anyone touch the part of him that *felt*.

"I chose Mother's Day because it was symbolic. Even though Mama Freda has never been a biological mother, she has been a mother to so many. She epitomizes what motherhood is."

That was not the full truth. The full truth was that Lucy found Mother's Day to be unbearably painful. And she was following Mama Freda's own recipe for dealing with pain.

"I don't care what day you chose!"

"Yes, you do."

"It's all coming back now," he said sardonically. "Having a conversation with you is like crossing a minefield."

"You feel as if Mother's Day belongs to you and Mama Freda. And I've stolen it."

"That's an interesting theory," he said, a chill in his voice warning her to stop, but she wasn't going to. Lucy was getting to him and part of her liked it, because it had always been hard to get to Mac Hudson. It might seem as if you were, but then that devil-may-care grin materialized, saying *Gotcha, because I don't really care.*

"Every Mother's Day," she reminded him quietly, "you outdo yourself. A stretch limo picks her up. She flies somewhere to meet you. Last year Engelbert Humperdinck in concert in New York. She wore the corsage until it turned brown. She talked about it for days after. Where you took her. What you ate. Don't tell me it's not your day. And that you're not annoyed that I chose it."

"Whatever."

"Oh! I recognize that tone of voice! Even after all this time! Mr. Don't-Even-Think-You-Know-Me."

"You don't. I'll put a check in the mail for whatever cause she has taken up. I think you'll find it very generous."

"I'm sure Mama will be pleased by the check. She probably will hardly even notice your absence, since all the others are coming. Every single one. Mama Freda has fostered twenty-three kids over the years. Ross Chillington is clearing his filming schedule. Michael Boylston works in Thailand and he's coming. Reed Patterson is leaving football training camp in Florida to be here."

"All those wayward boys saved by Mama Freda." His voice was silky and unimpressed.

"She's made a difference in the world!"

"Lucy—"

She hated it that her name on his lips made her feel more frazzled, hated it that she could remember leaning toward him, quivering with wanting.

"I'm not interested in being part of Lindstrom Beach's version of a TV reality show. What are you planning after your black-tie dinner? No, wait. Let me guess. Each of Mama's foster children will stand up and give a testimonial about being redeemed by her love."

Ouch. That was a little too close to what she did have planned. Did he have to make it sound cheap and smarmy instead of uplifting and inspirational?

"Mac—"

"Nobody calls me Mac anymore," he said, a little harshly.

"What do they call you?" She couldn't imagine him being called anything else.

"Mr. Hudson," he said coolly.

She doubted that very much since, she could still hear a raucous partylike atmosphere unfolding behind him.

It occurred to her she would like to hang up on him. And she was going to, very shortly.

"Okay, then, Mr. Hudson," she snapped, "I've already told you I don't care if you don't come. I know it's way too much to ask of you to take a break from your important and busy schedule to honor the woman who took you in and pulled you back from the brink of disaster. Way too much."

Silence.

"Still, I know how deeply you care about her. I know it's you who has been paying some of her bills."

He sucked in his breath, annoyed that she knew that.

She pushed on. "Aside from your Mother's Day tradition, I know you took her to Paris for her seventy-fifth birthday."

"Lucy, I'm dripping water on the floor and shivering, so if you could hurry this along."

She really had thought she could get through her life

without seeing him again. It had been a blessing that he came back to Lindstrom Beach rarely, and when he had, she had been away.

Because how could she look at him without remembering? But then hadn't she discovered you could remember, regardless?

Once, a long, long time ago, she had tried, with a desperation so keen she could almost taste its bitterness on her tongue, to pry his secrets from him. Lying on the sand in the dark, the lake's night-blackened waters lapping quietly, the embers of their fire burning down, she had asked him to tell her how he had ended up in foster care at Mama Freda's.

"I killed a man," he whispered, and then into her shocked silence, he had laughed that laugh that was so charming and distracting and sensual, that laugh that hid everything he really was, and added, "With my bare hands."

And then he had tried to divert her with his kisses that burned hotter than the fire.

But he had been unable to give her the gift she needed most: his trust in her.

And that was the real reason she had told him she could never love a boy like him. Because, even in her youth, she had recognized that he held back something essential of himself from her, when she had held back nothing.

If he had chosen to think she was a snob looking down her nose at the likes of him, after all the time they had spent together that summer, then that was his problem.

Still, just thinking of those forbidden kisses of so

many years ago sent an unwanted shiver down her spine. The truth was nobody wanted Mac to come back here less than she did.

"I didn't phone about Mama's party. I guess I thought I would tell you this when you came. But since you're not going to—"

"Tell me what?"

She had to keep on track, or she would be swamped by these memories.

"Mac—" she remembered, too late, he didn't want to be called that and plunged on "—something's wrong."

"What do you mean?"

"You knew Mama Freda lost her driver's license, didn't you?"

"No."

"She had a little accident in the winter. Nothing serious. She slid through a stop sign and took out Mary-Beth McQueen's fence and rose bed."

"Ha. I doubt if that was an accident. She aimed."

For a moment, something was shared between them. The rivalry between Mama and Mary-Beth when it came to roses was legendary. But the moment was a flicker, nothing more.

All business again, he said, "But you said it wasn't serious?"

"Nonetheless, she had to see a doctor and be retested. They revoked her license."

"I'll set her up an account at Ferdinand's Taxi."

"I don't mind driving her. I like it actually. My concern was that before the retesting I don't think she'd been to a doctor in twenty years."

"Thirty," he said. "She had her 'elixir.'"

Lucy was sure she heard him shudder. It was funny to think of him being petrified of a little homemade potion. The Mac of her memory had been devil-may-care and terrifyingly fearless. From the picture on his website, that much had not changed.

"I guess the elixir isn't working for her anymore," Lucy said carefully. "I drive her now. She's had three doctors' appointments in the last month."

"What's wrong?"

"According to her, nothing."

Silence. She understood the silence. He was wondering why Mama Freda hadn't told him about the driver's license, the doctor's appointments. He was guessing, correctly, that she would not want him to worry.

"It probably *is* nothing," he said, but his voice was uneasy.

"I told myself that, too. I don't want to believe she's eighty, either."

"There's something you aren't telling me."

Scary, that after all these years, and over the phone, he could do that. Read her. So, why hadn't he seen through her the only time it really mattered?

I could never fall for a boy like you.

Lucy hesitated, looked out the open doors to gather her composure. "I saw a funeral-planning kit on her kitchen table. When she noticed it was out, she shoved it in a drawer. I think she was hoping I hadn't seen it."

What she didn't tell him was that before Mama had shoved the kit away she had been looking out her window, her expression uncharacteristically pensive.

"Will my boy ever come home?" she had whispered.

All those children, and only one was truly her boy.

Lucy listened as Mac drew in a startled breath, and then he swore. Was it a terrible thing to love it when someone swore? But it made him the *old* Mac. And it meant she had penetrated his guard.

“That’s part of what motivated me to plan the celebration to honor her. I want her to know—” She choked. “I want her to know how much she has meant to people before it’s too late. I don’t want to wait for a funeral to bring to light all the good things she’s done and been.”

The silence was long. And then he sighed.

“I’ll be there as soon as I can.”

“No! Wait—

But Mac was gone, leaving the deep buzz of the dial tone in Lucy’s ear.

CHAPTER TWO

"WELL, THAT WENT well," Lucy muttered as she set down the phone.

Still, there was no denying a certain relief. She had been carrying the burden of worrying about Mama Freda's health alone, and now she shared it.

But with Mac? He'd always represented the loss of control, a visit to the wild side, and now it seemed nothing had changed.

If he had just come to the gala, Lucy could have maintained her sense of control. She had been watching Mama Freda like a hawk since the day she'd heard, *Will my boy ever come home?*

Aside from a nap in the afternoon, Mama seemed as energetic and alert as always. If Mama had received bad news on the health front, Lucy's observations of her had convinced her that the prognosis was an illness of the slow-moving variety.

Not the variety that required Mac to drop everything and come now!

The Mother's Day celebration was still two weeks away. Two weeks would have given Lucy time.

"Time to what?" she asked herself sternly.

Brace herself. Prepare. Be ready for him. But she already knew the uncomfortable truth about Macintyre Hudson. There was no preparing for him. There was no getting ready. He was a force unto himself, and that force was like a tornado hitting.

Lucy looked around her world. A year back home, and she had a sense of things finally falling into place. She was taking the initial steps toward her dream.

On the dining-room table that she had not eaten at since her return, there were donated items that she was collecting for the silent auction at the Mother's Day Gala.

There were the mountains of paperwork it had taken to register as a charity. Also, there was a photocopy of the application she had just submitted for rezoning, so that she could have Caleb's House here, and share this beautiful, ridiculously large house on the lake with young women who needed its sanctuary.

One of her three cats snoozed in a beam of sunlight that painted the wooden floor in front of the old river-rock fireplace golden. A vase of tulips brought in from the yard, their heavy heads drooping gracefully on their slender stems, brightened the barn-plank coffee table. A book was open on its spine on the arm of her favorite chair.

There was not a hint of catastrophe in this well-ordered scene, but it hadn't just happened. You had to work on this kind of a life.

In fact, it seemed the scene reflected that she had finally gotten through picking up the pieces from the last time.

And somehow, *last time* did not mean her ended engagement to James Kennedy.

No, when she thought of her world being blown apart, oddly it was not the front-page picture of her fiancé, James, running down the street in Glen Oak without a stitch on that was forefront in her mind. No, forefront was a boy leaving, seven years ago.

The next morning, out on her deck, nestled into a cushioned lounge chair, Lucy looked out over the lake and took a sip of her coffee. Despite the fact the sun was still burning off the early-morning chill, she was cozy in her pajamas under a wool plaid blanket.

The scent of her coffee mingled with the lovely, sugary smell of birch wood burning. The smoke curled out of Mama Freda's chimney and hung in a wispy swirl in the air above the water in front of Mama's cabin.

Birdsong mixed with the far-off drone of a plane.

What exactly did *I'll be there as soon as I can* mean?

"Relax," she ordered herself.

In a world like his, he wouldn't be able just to drop everything and come. It would be days before she had to face Macintyre Hudson. Maybe even a week. His website said his company had done 34 million dollars in business last year.

You didn't just walk away from that and hope it would run itself.

So she could focus on her life. She turned her attention from the lake, and looked at the swatch of sample paint she had put up on the side of the house.

She loved the pale lavender for the main color. She thought the subtle shade was playful and inviting, a color that she hoped would welcome and soothe the young girls and women who would someday come here when she had succeeded in transforming all this into Caleb's House.

Today she was going to commit to the color and order the paint. Well, maybe later today. She was aware of a little tingle of fear when she thought of actually buying the paint. It was a big house. It was natural to want not to make a mistake.

My mother would hate the color.

So maybe instead of buying paint today, she would fill a few book orders, and work on funding proposals for Caleb's House in anticipation of the rezoning. Several items had arrived for the silent auction that she could unpack. She would not give the arrival of Mac one more thought. Not one.

The drone of the plane pushed back into her awareness, too loud to ignore. She looked up and could see it, red and white, almost directly overhead, so close she could read the call numbers under the wings. It was obviously coming in for a landing on the lake.

Lucy watched it set down smoothly, turning the water, where it shot out from the pontoons, to silvery sprays of mercury. The sound of the engine cut from a roar to a purr as the plane glided over the glassy mirror-calm surface of the water.

Sunshine Lake, located in the rugged interior of British Columbia, had always been a haunt of the rich, and sometimes the famous. Lucy's father had taken delight in the fact that once, when he was a teenager, the queen had stayed here on one of her visits to Canada. For a while the premier of the province had had a summer house down the lake. Pierre LaPontz, the famous goalie for the Montreal Canadiens, had summered here with friends. Seeing the plane was not unusual.

It became unusual when it wheeled around and taxied back, directly toward her.

Even though she could not see the pilot for the glare of the morning sun on the windshield of the plane, Lucy knew, suddenly and without a shade of a doubt, that it was him.

Macintyre Hudson had landed. He had arrived in her world.

The conclusion was part logic and part instinct. And with it came another conclusion. That nothing, from here on in, would go as she expected it. The days when choosing a paint color was the scariest thing in her world were over.

Lucy had thought he might show up in a rare sports car. Or maybe on an expensive motorcycle. She had even considered the possibility that he might show up, chauffeured, in the white limo that had picked up Mama Freda last Mother's Day.

Take that, Dr. Lindstrom.

She watched the plane slide along the lake to the old dock in front of Mama Freda's. The engines cut and the plane drifted.

And then, for the first time in seven years, she saw him.

Macintyre Hudson slid out the door onto the pontoon, expertly threw a rope over one of the big anchor posts on the dock and pulled the plane in.

The fact he could pilot a plane made it more than evident he had come into himself. He was wearing mirrored aviator sunglasses, a leather jacket and knife-creased khakis. But it was the way he carried himself, a certain sureness of movement on the bobbing water, that radiated confidence and strength.

Something in her chest felt tight. Her heart was beating too fast.

"Not bald," she murmured as the sun caught on the luscious dark chocolate of his hair. It was a guilty pleasure, watching him from a distance, with him unaware of being watched. He had a powerful efficiency of motion as he dealt with mooring the plane.

He was broader than he had been, despite all the digging of ditches. All the slenderness of his youth was gone, replaced with a kind of mouthwatering solidness, the build of a mature man at the peak of his power.

He looked up suddenly and cast a look around, frowning slightly as if he was aware he was being watched.

Crack.

The sound was so loud in the still crispness of the morning that Lucy started, slopped coffee on her pajamas. Thunder?

No. In horror Lucy watched as the ancient post of Mama Freda's dock, as thick as a telephone pole, snapped cleanly, as if it was a toothpick. As she looked on helplessly, Mac saw it coming and moved quickly.

He managed to save his head, but the falling post caught him across his shoulder and hurled him into the water. The post fell in after him.

A deathly silence settled over the lake.

Lucy was already up out of her chair when Mac's head reemerged from the water. His startled, furious curse shattered the quiet that had reasserted itself on the peaceful lakeside morning.

Lucy found his shout reassuring. At least he hadn't been knocked out by the post, or been overcome by the freezing temperatures of the water.

Blanket clutched to her, Lucy ran on bare feet across the lawns, then through the ancient ponderosa pines that surrounded Mama's house. She picked her way swiftly across the rotted decking of the dock.

Mac was hefting himself onto the pontoon of the plane. It was not drifting, thankfully, but bobbing co-operatively just a few feet from the dock.

"Mac!" Lucy dropped the blanket. "Throw me the rope!"

He scrambled to standing, found the rope and turned to look at her. Even though he had to be absolutely freezing, there was a long pause as they stood looking at one another.

The sunglasses were gone. Those dark, melted-chocolate eyes showed no surprise, just lingered on her, faintly appraising, as if he was taking inventory.

His gaze stayed on her long enough for her to think, *He hates my hair.* And *Oh, for God's sake, am I in my Winnie-the-Pooh pajamas?*

"Throw the damn rope!" she ordered him.

Then the thick coil of rope was flying toward her. The throw was going to be slightly short. But if she leaned just a bit, and reached with all her might, she knew she could—

"No!" he cried. "Leave it."

But it was too late. Lucy had leaned out too far. She tried to correct, taking a hasty step backward, but her momentum was already too far forward. Her arms windmilled crazily in an attempt to keep her balance.

She felt her feet leave the dock, the rush of air on her skin, and then she plunged into the lake. And sank, the weight of the soaked flannel pajamas pulling her down. Nothing could have prepared her for the cold as the gray water closed over her head. It seized her; her whole body went taut with shock. The sensation was of burning, not freezing. Her limbs were paralyzed instantly.

In what seemed to be slow motion, her body finally bobbed back to the surface. She was in shock, too numb even to cry out. Somehow she floundered, her limbs heavy and nearly useless, to the dock. It was too early in the year for a ladder to be out, but since Mama no longer fostered kids she didn't put out a ladder—or maintain the dock—anyway.

Lucy managed to get her hands on the dock's planks, and tried to pull herself up. But there was a terrifying lack of strength in her arms. Her limbs felt as if they were made of Jell-O, all a-jiggle and not quite set.

"Hang on!"

Even her lips were numb. The effort it took to speak was tremendous.

"No! Don't." She forced the words out. They sounded weak. Her mind, in slow motion, rationalized there was no point in them both being in the water. His limbs would react to the cold water just as hers were doing. And he was farther out. In seconds, Mac would be helpless, floundering out beyond the dock.

She heard a mighty splash as Mac jumped back into the water. She tried to hang on, but she couldn't feel her fingers. She slipped back in, felt the water ooze over her head.

Lucy had been around water her entire life. She had a Bronze Cross. She could have been a lifeguard at the Main Street Beach if her father had not thought it was a demeaning job. She had never been afraid of water.

Now, as she slipped below the surface, she didn't feel terrified, but oddly resigned. They were both going to die, a tragically romantic ending to their story—after all these years of separation, dying trying to save one another.

And then hands, strong, sure, were around her waist, lifting her. Her head broke water and she sputtered. She was unceremoniously shoved out of the water onto the rough boards of the dock.

Lucy dangled there, her elbows underneath her chest, her legs hanging, without the strength even to lift her head. His hand went to her bottom, and he gave her one more shove—really about as unromantic as it could get—and she lay on the dock, gasping, sobbing, coughing.

Mac's still in the water.

She squirmed around to look, but he didn't need her. His hands found the dock and he pulled himself to safety.

They lay side by side, gasping. Slowly she became aware that his nose was inches from her nose.

She could see drops of water beaded on the sooty clumps of his sinfully thick lashes. His eyes were glorious: a brown so dark it melted into black. The line of his nose was perfect, and faint stubble, twinkling with water droplets, highlighted the sweep of his cheekbones, the jut of his jaw.

Her eyes moved to the sensuous curve of his lips, and she felt sleepy and drugged, the desire to touch them with her own pushing past her every defense.

"Why, little Lucy Lindstrom," he growled. "We have to stop meeting like this."

All those years ago it had been her capsized canoe that had brought them—just about the most unlikely of loves, the good girl and the bad boy—together.

A week after graduation, having won all kinds of awards and been voted Most Likely to Succeed by her class, she realized the excitement was suddenly over. All her plans were made; it was her last summer of "freedom," as everybody kept kiddingly saying.

Lucy had taken the canoe out alone, something she never did. But the truth was, in that gap of activity something yawned within her, empty. She had a sense of her own life getting away from her, as if she was falling in with other people's plans for her without really ever asking herself what *she* wanted.

A storm had blown up, and she had not seen the log hiding under the surface of the water until it was too late.

Mac had been over on the wild side, camping, and he had seen her get into trouble. He'd already been in his canoe fighting the rough water to get to her before she hit the log.

He had picked her out of the water, somehow not capsizing his own canoe in the process, and taken her to his campsite to a fire, to wait until the lake calmed down to return her to her world.

But somehow she had never quite returned to her world. Lucy had been ripe for what he offered, an escape from a life that had all been laid out for her in a predictable pattern that there, on the side of the lake with her rescuer, had seemed like a form of death.

In all her life, it seemed everyone—her parents, her friends—only saw in her what they wanted her to be. And that was something that filled a need in them.

And then Mac had come along. And effortlessly he had seen through all that to what was real. Or so it had seemed.

And the truth was, soaking wet, gasping for air on a rotting dock, lying beside Mac, Lucy felt now exactly as she had felt then.

As if her whole world shivered to life.

As if black and white became color.

It had to be near-death experiences that did that: sharpened awareness to a razor's edge. Because she was so aware of Mac. She could feel the warmth of the breath coming from his mouth in puffs. There was an aura of power around him that was palpable, and in her weakened state, reassuring.

With a groan, he put his hands on either side of his chest and lifted himself to kneeling, and then quickly to standing.

He held out his hand to her, and she reached for it and he pulled her, his strength as easy as it was electrifying, to her feet.

Mac scooped the blanket from the dock where she had dropped it, shook it out, looped it around her shoulders and then his own, and then his arms went around her waist and he pulled her against the freezing length of him.

"Don't take this personally," he said. "It's a matter of survival, plain and simple."

"Thank you for clarifying," she said, with all the dignity her chattering teeth would allow. "You needn't have worried. I had no intention of ravishing you. You are about as sexy as a frozen salmon at the moment."

"Still getting in the last shot, aren't you?"

"When I can."

Cruelly, at that moment she realized a sliver of warmth radiated from him, and she pulled herself even closer to the rock-hard length of his body.

Their bodies, glued together by freezing, wet clothing, shook beneath the blanket. She pressed her cheek hard against his chest, and he loosed a hand and touched her soaking hair.

"You hate it," she said, her voice quaking.

"It wasn't my best entrance," he agreed.

"I meant my hair."

"I know you did," he said softly. "Hello, Lucy."

"Hello, Macintyre."

Standing here against Mac, so close she could feel the pebbles of cold rising on his chilled skin, she could also feel his innate strength. Warmth was returning to his body and seeping into hers.

The physical sensation of closeness, of sharing spreading heat, was making her vulnerable to other feelings, the very ones she had hoped to steel herself against.

It was not just weak. The weakness could be assigned

to the numbing cold that had seeped into every part of her. Even her tongue felt heavy and numb.

It was not just that she never wanted to move again. That could be assigned to the fact that her limbs felt slow and clumsy and paralyzed.

No, it was something worse than being weak.

Something worse than being paralyzed.

In Macintyre Hudson's arms, soaked, her Winnie-the-Pooh pajamas providing as much protection against him as a wet paper towel, Lucy Lindstrom felt the worst weakness of all, the longing she had kept hidden from herself.

Not to be so alone.

Her trembling deepened, and a soblike sound escaped her.

"Are you okay?" he asked.

"Not really," she said as she admitted the full truth to herself. It was not the cold making her weak. It was him.

Lucy felt a terrible wave of self-loathing. Was life just one endless loop, playing the same things over and over again?

She was cursed at love. She needed to accept that about herself, and devote her considerable energy and talent to causes that would help others, and, as a bonus, couldn't hurt her.

She pulled away from him, though it took all her strength, physical and mental. The blanket held her fast, so that mere inches separated them, but at least their bodies were no longer glued together.

History, she told herself sternly, was *not* repeating itself.

It was good he was here. She could face him, puncture any remaining illusions and get on with her wonderful life of doing good for others.

"Are you hurt?" he asked, putting her away from him, scanning her face.

She already missed the small warmth that had begun to radiate from him. Again, she had to pit what remained of her physical and mental strength to resist the desire to collapse against him.

"I'm fine," she said tersely.

"You don't look fine."

"Well, I'm not hurt. Mortified."

His expression was one of pure exasperation. "Who nearly drowns and is mortified by it?"

Whew. There was no sense him knowing she was mortified because of her reaction to him. By her sudden onslaught of uncertainty.

They had both been in perilous danger, and she was worried about the impression her hair made? Worried that she looked like a drowned rat? Worried about what pajamas she had on?

It was starting all over again!

This crippling need. He had seen her once, when it seemed no one else could. Hadn't she longed for that ever since?

Had she pursued getting that message to him so incessantly because of Mama Freda? Or had it been for herself? To feel the way she had felt when his arms closed around her?

Trembling, trying to fight the part of her that wanted nothing more than to scoot back into his warmth, she reminded herself that feeling this way had nearly destroyed her. It had had far-reaching repercussions that had torn her family and her life asunder.

"This is all your fault," she said. Thankfully, he took her literally.

"I'm not responsible for your bad catch."

"It was a terrible throw!"

"Yes, it was. All the more reason you shouldn't have reached for the rope. I could have thrown it again."

"You shouldn't have jumped back in the water after me. You could have been overcome by the cold. I'm surprised you weren't. And then we both would have been in big trouble."

"You have up to ten minutes in water that cold before you succumb. Plus, I don't seem to feel cold water like other people. I white-water kayak. I think it has desensitized me. But under no circumstances would I have stood on the pontoon of my plane and watched anyone drown."

Gee. He wasn't sensitive, and his rescue of her wasn't even personal. He would have done it for anyone.

"I wasn't going to drown," Lucy lied haughtily, since only moments ago she had been resigned to that very thing. He'd just said she had ten whole minutes. "I've lived on this lake my entire life."

"Oh!" He smacked himself on the forehead with his fist. "How could I forget that? Not only have you lived on the lake your entire life, but so did three generations of your family before you. Lindstroms don't drown. They die like they lived. Nice respectable deaths in the same beds that they were born in, in the same town they never took more than two steps away from."

"I lived in Glen Oak for six years," she said.

"Oh, Glen Oak. An hour away. Some consider Lindstrom Beach to be Glen Oak's summer suburb."

Lucy was aware of being furious with herself for the utter weakness of reacting to him. It felt much safer to transfer that fury to him.

He had walked away. Not just from this town. He had walked away from having to give anything of himself. How could he never have considered all the possibilities? They had played with fire all that summer.

She had gotten burned. And he had walked away.

And he had never even said he loved her. Not even once.

CHAPTER THREE

"You know what, Macintyre Hudson? You were a jerk back then, and you're still a jerk."

"May I remind you that you begged me to come back here?"

"I did not beg. I appealed to your conscience. And I personally did not care if you came back."

"You were a snotty, stuck-up brat and you still are. Here's a novel concept," Mac said, his voice threaded with annoyance, "why don't you try thanking me for my heroic rescue? For the second time in your life, by the way."

Because of what happened the first time, you idiot.

"If I needed a hero," she said with soft fury, "you are the last person I would pick."

That hit home. He actually flinched. And she was happy he flinched. *Snotty, stuck-up brat?*

Then a cool veil dropped over the angry sparks flickering in his eyes, and his mouth turned upward, that mocking smile that was his trademark, that said *You can't hurt me—don't even try.* He folded his arms over the deep strength of his broad chest, and not because he was cold, either.

"You know what? If I was looking for a damsel in

distress, you wouldn't exactly be my first pick, either. You're still every bit the snooty doctor's daughter."

She felt all of it then. The abandonment. The fear she had shouldered alone in the months after he left. Her parents, who had always doted on her, looking at her with hurt and embarrassment, as if she could not have let them down more completely. The friends she had known since kindergarten not phoning anymore, looking the other way when they saw her.

She felt all of it.

And it felt as if every single bit of it was his fault.

"Just to set the record straight, maybe it's you who should be thanking me," she told him. "I came down here to rescue you. You were the one in the water."

"I didn't need your help...."

So, absolutely nothing had changed. She was, in his eyes, still the town rich girl, the doctor's snooty daughter, out of touch with what he considered to be real.

And he was still the one who didn't *need.*

"Or your botched rescue attempt."

The fury in her felt white-hot, as if it could obliterate what remained of the chill on her. Lucy wished she had felt *that* when she had seen him get knocked off the dock by the post. She wished, instead of running to him, worried about him, she had marched into her house and firmly shut the door on him.

She hadn't done that. But maybe it was never too late to correct a mistake. She could do the right thing this time.

She stepped in close, shivered dramatically, letting him believe she was weak and not strong, that she needed his body heat back. Mac was wary, but not wary enough. He let her slip back in, close to him.

Lucy put both her hands on his chest, blinked up at him with her very best will-you-be-my-hero? look and then shoved him as hard as she could.

With a startled yelp, which Lucy found extremely satisfying, Macintyre Hudson lost his footing and stumbled off the dock, back into the water. She turned and walked away, annoyed that she was reassured by his vigorous cursing that he was just fine.

She glanced back. More than fine! Instead of getting out of the water, Mac shrugged out of his leather jacket and threw it onto the dock. Then, making the most of his ten minutes, he swam back to his plane.

Within moments he had the entire situation under control, which no doubt pleased him no end. He fastened the plane to the dock's other pillar, which held, then reached inside and tossed a single overnight bag onto the dock.

She certainly didn't want him to catch her watching. Why was she watching? It was just more evidence of the weakness he made her feel. What she needed to be doing was to be heading for a hot shower at top speed.

Lucy had crossed back into her yard when she heard Mama's shout.

"*Ach!* What is going on?"

She turned to see Mama Freda trundling toward her dock, hand over her brow, trying to see into the sun. Then Mama stopped, and a light came on in that ancient, wise face that seemed to steal the chill right out of Lucy.

"Schatz?"

Mac was standing on the dock, and had removed his soaking shirt and was wringing it out. That was an unfortunate sight for a girl trying to steel herself against him. His body was absolutely perfect, sleek and strong, water sluicing down the deepness of his chest to the defined ripples of his abs.

He dropped the soaked shirt beside his jacket and sprinted over the dock and across the lawn. He stopped at Mama Freda and grinned down at her, and this time his grin was so genuine it could have lit up the whole lake. Mama reached up and touched his cheek.

Then he picked up the rather large bulk of Mama Freda as if she were featherlight, and swung her around until she was squealing like a young girl.

"You're getting me all wet," she protested loudly, smacking the broadness of his shoulders with delight. "*Ach*. Put me down, galoot-head."

Finally he did, and she patted her hair into place, regarding him with such affection that Lucy felt something burn behind her eyes.

"Why are you all wet? You'll catch your death!"

"Your dock broke when I tried to tie to it."

"You should have told me you were coming," Mama said reproachfully.

"I wanted to surprise you."

"Surprise, schmize."

Lucy smiled, despite herself. One of Mama's goals in life seemed to be to create a rhyme, beginning with *sch,* for every word in the English language.

"You see what happens? You end up in the lake. If you'd just told me, I would have warned you to tie up to Lucy's dock."

"I don't think Lucy wants me tying up at her dock."

Only Lucy would pick up his dry double meaning on that. She could actually feel a bit of a blush moving heat into her frozen cheeks.

"Don't be silly. Lucy wouldn't mind."

He could have thrown her under the bus, because Mama would not have approved of anyone being pushed into the water at this time of year, no matter how pressing the circumstances.

But he didn't. Her gratitude that he hadn't thrown her under the bus was short-lived as Mac left the topic of Lucy Lindstrom behind with annoying ease.

"Mama, I'm freezing. I hope you have *apfelstrudel* fresh from the oven."

"You have to tell me you're coming to get strudel fresh from the oven. That's not what you need, anyway. Mama knows what you need."

Lucy could hear the smile in his voice, and was aware again of Mama working her magic, both of them smiling just moments after all that fury.

"What do I need, Mama?"

"You need elixir."

He pretended terror, then dashed back to the dock and picked up his soaked clothing and the bag, tossed it over his naked shoulder. He returned and wrapped his arm around Mama's waist and let her lead him to the house.

Lucy turned back to her own house, her eyes still smarting from what had passed between those two. The love and devotion shimmered around them as bright as the strengthening morning sun.

That was why she had gone to such lengths to get

Macintyre Hudson to come back here. And if another motive had lain hidden beneath that one, it had been exposed to her in those moments when his arms had wrapped around her and his heat had seeped into her.

Now that it was exposed, she could put it in a place where she could guard against it as if her life depended on it.

Which, Lucy told herself through the chattering of her teeth, it did.

Out of the corner of his eye, Mac saw Lucy pause and watch his reunion with Mama.

"Is that Lucy?" Mama said, catching the direction of his gaze.

"Yeah, as annoying as ever."

"She's a good girl," Mama said stubbornly.

"Everything she ever aspired to be, then."

Only, she wasn't a girl anymore, but a woman. The *good* part he had no doubt about. That was what was expected of the doctor's daughter, after all.

Even given the circumstances he had noted the changes. Her hair was still blond, but it no longer fell, unrestrained by hair clips or elastic bands, to the slight swell of her breast.

Plastered to her head, it hadn't looked like much, but he was willing to bet that when it was dry it was ultra-sophisticated, and would show off the hugeness of those dazzling green eyes, the pixie-perfection of her dainty features. Still, Mac was aware of fighting the part of him that missed how it used to be.

She had lost the faintly scrawny build of a long-distance runner, and filled out, a fact he could not help but notice when she had pressed the lusciousness of her freezing body into his.

She seemed uptight, though, and the level of her anger at him gave him pause.

Unbidden, he wondered if she ever slipped into the lake and skinny-dipped under the full moon. Would she still think it was the most daring thing a person could do, and that she was risking arrest and public humiliation?

What made her laugh now? In high school it seemed as if she had been at the center of every circle, popular and carefree. That laugh, from deep within her, was so joyous and unchained the birds stopped singing to listen.

Mac snorted in annoyance with himself, reminding himself curtly that he had broken that particular spell a long time ago. Though if that was completely true, why the reluctance to return Lucy's calls? Why the aversion to coming back?

If that was completely true, why had he told Lucy Lindstrom, of all people, that his father had been a ditchdigger?

That had been bothering him since the words had come out of his mouth. Maybe that confession had even contributed to the fiasco on the dock.

"What's she doing?" Mama asked, worried. "Is she wet, too? She looks wet."

"We both ended up in the lake."

"But how?"

"A comedy of errors. Don't worry about it, Mama."

But Mama was determined to worry. "She should

have come here. I would look after her. She could catch her death."

Mama Freda, still looking after everyone. Except maybe herself. She was looking toward Lucy's house as if she was thinking of going to get her.

He noticed the grass blended seamlessly together, almost as if the lawns of the two houses were one. That was new. Dr. Lindstrom had gone to great lengths to accentuate the boundaries of his yard, to lower any risk of association with the place next door.

Despite now sharing a lawn with its shabby neighbor, the Lindstrom place still looked like something off a magazine spread.

A bank of French doors had been added to the back of the house. Beyond the redwood of the multilayered deck, a lawn, tender with new grass, ended at a sea of yellow and red tulips. The flowers cascaded down a gentle slope to the fine white sand of the private beach.

On the L-shaped section of the bleached gray wood of the dock a dozen canoes were upside down.

What was with all the canoes? He was pretty sure that Mama had said Lucy was by herself since she had come home a year ago.

A bird called, and Mac could smell the rich scent of sun heating the fallen needles of the ponderosa pine.

As he gazed out over the lake, he was surprised by how much he had missed this place. Not the town, which was exceptionally cliquey; you were either "in" or you were "out" in Lindstrom Beach.

Lucy's family had always been "in." Of course, "in" was determined by the location of your house on the lake, the size of the lot, the house itself, what kind of boat you had and who your connections were. “In” was determined by your occupation, your membership in the church and the yacht club, and by your income, never mentioned outright, always insinuated.

He, on the other hand, had been “out,” a kid of questionable background, in foster care, in Mama’s house, the only remaining of the original cabins that had been built around the lake in the forties. Her house, little more than a fishing shack, had been the bane of the entire neighborhood.

And so the sharing of the lawn was new and unexpected.

“Do you and Lucy go in together to hire someone to look after the grounds?” he asked.

“No, Lucy does it.”

That startled him. Lucy mowed the expansive lawns? He couldn’t really imagine her pushing a lawn mower. He remembered her and her friends sitting on the deck in their bikinis while the “help” sweated under the hot sun keeping the grounds of her house immaculate. But he didn’t want Lucy to crowd back into his thoughts.

“You look well, Mama,” he said, an invitation for her to confide in him. He should have known it wouldn’t be that easy.

“I look well. You look terrible.” She gave his freezing, naked torso a hard pinch. “No meat on your bones. Eating in restaurants. I can tell by your coloring.”

He thought his coloring might be off because he had just had a pretty good dunking in some freezing water, but he knew from long experience that there was no telling Mama.

They approached the back of her house. The porch

door was choked with overgrown lilacs, drooping with heavy buds. Mac pushed aside some branches and opened the screen door. It squeaked outrageously. He could see the floorboards of her screened porch were as rotten as her dock.

He frowned at the attempt at a repair. Had she hired some haphazard handyman?

"Who did this?" he said, toeing the new board.

"Lucy," she said, eyeing the disastrous repair with pride. "Lucy helps me with lots of things around here."

His frown deepened. Somehow that was a Lucy he could never have imagined, nails between teeth, pounding in boards.

Though Mama had said nothing, he had suspected for some time the house was becoming too much for her, and this confirmed it.

"You should come to Toronto with me," he said. It was his opening move. In his bag he had brochures of Toronto's most upscale retirement home.

"Toronto, schmonto. No, you should move back here. That big city is no place for a boy like you."

"I'm not a boy anymore, Mama."

"You will always be my boy."

He regarded her warmly, searching her face for any sign of illness. She was unchanging. She had seemed old when he had first met her, and she really had never seemed to get any older. There was a sameness about her in a changing world that had been a touchstone.

Why hadn't she told him she had lost her license?

She was going to be eighty years old three days before Mother's Day. He held open the inside door for her, and they stepped through into her kitchen.

It, too, was showing signs of benign neglect: paint chipping from the cabinets, a door not closing properly, the old linoleum tiles beginning to curl. There was a towel tied tightly around a faucet, and he went and looked.

An attempted repair of a leak.

"Lucy's work?" he guessed.

"Yes."

Again, the Lucy he didn't know. "You just have to tell me these things," he said. "I would have paid for the plumber."

"You pay for enough already."

He turned to look at Mama, and without warning he was fourteen years old again, standing in this kitchen for the first time.

Harriet Freda's had been his fifth foster home in as many months, and despite the fact this one had a prime lakeshore location, from the outside the house seemed even smaller and dumpier and darker than all the other foster homes had been.

Maybe, he had thought, already cynical, they just sent you to worse and worse places.

The house would have seemed beyond humble in any setting, but surrounded by the magnificent lake houses, it was painfully shacklike and out of place on the shores of Sunshine Lake.

That morning, standing in a kitchen that cheerfully belied the outside of the house, Mac had been fourteen and terrified. That had been his first lesson since the death of his father: never let the terror show.

She had been introduced to him as Mama Freda, and she looked stocky and ancient. Her hair was a bluish-white color and frizzy with a bad perm. She had more wrinkles than a Shar-Pei. Mac thought she was way too old to be looking after other people's kids.

Still, she looked harmless enough, standing at her kitchen table in a frumpy dress that showed off her chunky build, thick arms and legs, ankles swollen above sensible shoes. She had been wearing a much-bleached apron, once white, aged to tea-dipped, and covered with faded blotches of berry and chocolate.

The niceties were over, the social worker was gone and he was standing there with a paper bag containing two T-shirts, one pair of jeans and a change of underwear. Mrs. Freda cast him a look, and there was an unmistakable friendly twinkle in deep-set blue eyes.

Well, there was no sense her thinking they were going to be on friendly terms.

"I killed a man," he said, and then added, "With my bare hands." He thought the *with my bare hands* part was a nice touch. It was actually a line from a song, but it warned people to stay back from him, that he was dangerous and tough.

And if Macintyre Hudson had wanted one thing at age fourteen, it was for people to stay back from him. He had been like a wounded animal, unwilling to trust again.

Mama Freda glanced up from what she was doing, stretching out an enormous piece of dough, thin and elastic, over the edges of her large, round kitchen table. She regarded him, and he noticed the twinkle was gone from her eyes, replaced with an immense sorrow.

"This is a terrible thing," she said, sinking into a chair. "To kill a man. I know. I had to do it once."

He stared at her, his mouth open. And when she beckoned to the chair beside hers, he abandoned his meager bag of belongings and went to it, as if drawn to her side by a magnet.

"It was near the end of the war," she said, looking at her hands. "I was thirteen. A soldier, he was—" she glanced at Mac, trying to decide how much to say "—hurting my sister. He had his back to me. I picked up a cast-iron pan and I crept up behind him and I hit him as hard as I could over his head. There was a terrible noise. Terrible. He fell off my sister. I think he was already dead, but I knew if he ever got up we were all doomed, and so I hit him again and again and again."

Mac had never heard silence like he heard in Mama Freda's kitchen right then. The clock ticking sounded explosive.

"So I know what this thing is," she said finally, "to kill a man. I know how you carry it within you. How you think of his face, and wonder who he was before the great evil overcame him. I wonder what his mother felt when he never came home, and if his sisters grieve him to this day, the way I grieve the brother who went to war and never came home."

Her hand crept out from under her apron and she laid it, palm up, on the table. An invitation. And Mac surprised himself by not being able to refuse that invitation. He put his hand on the table, too. Her hand closed around his, surprisingly strong for such an old lady.

"Look at me," she said.

And he did.

She did not say a word. She didn't have to. He looked

deep into her eyes, and for the first time in a long, long time, he felt he was not alone.

That someone else knew what it was to suffer.

Later they ate the *apfelstrudel* she had finished rolling out on her kitchen table, and it felt as if his taste buds had come awake, as if he could taste for the first time in a long, long time, too, as if he had never tasted food quite so wondrous.

He started, in that moment, with warm strudel melting in his mouth, to do what he had sworn he would never do again. But he was careful never to call it that, and never to utter the words that would solidify it and make it real. For him, the admission of love was the holding of a samurai's sword that you would eventually plunge into your own heart.

But he had never altered the story he had told her that day, not even when she had said to him once, "I know, *schatz,* there is nothing in you that could kill another person. Or anything. Not even a baby robin that fell from its nest. I have watched you carry bugs outside rather than swat them."

But he had never doubted that she really had killed that soldier, and she, too, carried bugs outside rather than swatting them.

Mama, with her enormous capacity to care for all things, had saved him.

And he owed it to her to be there for her if she needed him. It was evident from the state of her house that he hadn't been there in the ways she needed. And that Lucy, the one he had called the spoiled brat, had been. He felt the faintest shiver of something.

Guilt?

"Go shower," Mama said, and he drew himself back to the present with a shake of his head. "Nice and hot."

She was already reaching up high into her cabinet and Mac shuddered when the ancient brown bottle of elixir came down, and he hightailed it for the tiny bathroom at the top of the stairs.

When he came down, in dry clothes, she had a tumbler of the clear liquid poured.

"Drink. It will ward off the cold."

"I'm not cold."

"The cold you will get if you don't drink it!" She had that look on her face, her arms folded over her ample bosom.

There was no sense explaining to Mama you didn't get colds from being cold, that you got them from coming in contact with one of hundreds of viruses, none of which were very likely to be living in the freezing-cold water of Sunshine Lake.

He took the tumbler, plugged his nose and put it back. It burned to his belly and he felt his toes curl.

He set the glass down, and wiped his watering eyes. "For heaven's sakes, its schnapps!"

"Obstler," she said happily. "Not peppermint sugar like they drink here. Ugh. Mine is made with apples. Herbs."

She was right, though—if there was any sneaky virus in him, no matter what the source, it would be gone now.

"Homemade, from my great-grandmother's recipe. Now, take some to Lucy. I have it ready." She passed him an unlabeled brown bottle of her secret elixir.

"I'm not taking it to Lucy." After that encounter on the dock, the less he had to do with Lucy the better.

He'd wanted to believe, after all this time, that Lucy, the girl who had not thought he was good enough, would have no power over him. He had seen the world. He'd succeeded. He'd expected Lucy and this town to be nothing more than a speck of dust from the past.

What he hadn't expected was the rush of feeling when he had seen her. Even dripping wet, near frozen, seeing Lucy on the dock calling to him, he had felt a pull so strong it felt as if his heart was coming from his chest. He'd been vulnerable, caught off guard, but still, there had always been something about her.

She still had that face, impish, unconventionally beautiful, that inspired warmth and trust, that took a man's guard right down, and left him in a place where he could be shoved into a lake by someone who weighed sixty pounds less than he did.

An old hurt surfaced, its edges knife-sharp.

I could never fall for a boy like you.

That was the problem with coming back to a place you had left behind, Mac thought. Old hurts didn't die. They waited. And those words, coming from Lucy, the one he had trusted with his ever-so-bruised heart…

"She needs the elixir! She'll catch her death."

Since he didn't want to tell Mama why he didn't want to see Lucy—because he had fully expected to be indifferent and had been anything but—now might be a good time to explain viruses. But his explanation, he knew, would fall on deaf ears.

"She's a doctor's daughter. I'm sure she knows what she needs."

Mama looked stubborn.

"Mama, it's probably illegal to make this stuff, let alone dispense it."

She regarded him, her eyes narrow, and then without warning, "Are you speaking to your mother yet, *schatz?*"

He glared at her stonily.

"Nearly Mother's Day. Just two weeks away. She must be lonely for you."

The only thing his mother had ever been lonely for was her bank account. But he wasn't being drawn into this argument. And he could clearly see Mama had grabbed on to it now, like a dog worrying meat off a bone.

"How many years?" she asked softly, stubbornly.

He refused to answer out loud, but inside, he did the math.

"It's time," she said.

On this, and only this, he had refused her from the first day he had come here. There would be no reconciliation with his mother.

"Just a card, to start," she said, as if they had not played out this scene a hundred times before. "I think I have the perfect one right here."

It was one of Mama's things. She always had a cupboard devoted to greeting cards. She had one suitable for every occasion.

Except son and mother estranged for fourteen years.

Without a word he picked up the bottle of homemade schnapps and went out the squeaking door. When he glanced back over his shoulder, Mama had her back to him, rummaging through the card cupboard, singing with soft satisfaction.

He noticed how hunched she was.

Frail, somehow, despite her bulk.

He noticed how badly the house needed repair, and felt guilty, again, that he had somehow let it get this bad.

Mac was not unaware that he had been back in Lindstrom Beach all of half an hour and all these uncomfortable feelings were rising to the surface. He didn't like feelings.

Lucy had been here when he had not. Well, he'd take over from her now.

It occurred to him that this trip was probably not going to be the quick turnaround he had hoped for. Still, a few days of intense work, and he'd be out of here, leaving all these uneasy feelings behind him.

"Make sure she drinks some," Mama shouted as the screen creaked behind him. "Make sure. Don't come back here unless she does."

And much as he didn't want Lucy to be right about anything, and much as he didn't like the unexpected feelings, he realized, reluctantly, she had been right to insist he come back here.

Mama needed him.

And yes, the time to honor his foster mother was definitely now. But he would leave the gala to Lucy, and honor his foster mother by making sure her house was livable before he left again.

CHAPTER FOUR

MAC CROSSED THE familiar ground between the two houses. He noted, again, that Lucy's property was everything Mama's was not. Even with the lawns melting together, the properties were very different: Mama's ringed in huge trees—that were probably hard to mow around—the Lindstrom place well-maintained, oozing the perfect taste of old money.

From the tidbits of information dropped by Mama, Mac knew Lucy had taken over the house from her mother a year or so ago. Hadn't there been something about a broken engagement?

How did she find time to do the work that it used to take an entire team of gardeners to do?

Unless she doesn't have a life.

Which, also from tidbits dropped by Mama, Lucy didn't. She ran some kind of online book business. A life, yes, but not the life he had expected the most popular girl in high school would have ended up with.

I don't care, Mac told himself, but if he really didn't, would he even have to say that to himself?

He debated going to the front of the house, keeping everything nice and formal, but in the end, he stayed in the back and went across the deck. He stopped and surveyed the house. The stately white paint was faded and peeling; a large patch of a sample paint color had been put up.

It was a pale shade of lavender. Several boards underneath it had samples of what he assumed would be trim color, ranging from light lilac to deep purple.

The paint color made him think he didn't know Lucy at all.

Which, of course, he didn't. She was no more the same girl she had been when he'd left than he was the same man. He became aware of the sound of water running inside the house, assumed Lucy was showering and was grateful for the reprieve from another encounter with her.

He wasn't a little kid anymore. And neither was Lucy. He respected Mama, but he couldn't take her every wish as a command. *Make sure she drinks it.* Lucy could find the bottle and make up her own mind whether to drink it.

He would take his chances. If he didn't return for a while, Mama might not question how he had completed his assignment. And, hopefully, she would be off the topic of his mother by then, as well.

Mac set Mama's offering at Lucy's back door, and then strolled down to her dock to look over the canoes. They weren't particularly good quality—different ages and makes and colors. Then he saw a sign, fairly new, nailed to a wharf post like the one that had broken at Mama's.

Lucy's Lakeside Rentals. It outlined the rates and rules for renting canoes.

Lucy was renting canoes? He *really* didn't know her anymore. In fact, it almost seemed as if their roles were reversed. He had arrived, he knew every success he had ever hoped for, and she was mowing lawns and scraping together pennies by renting canoes.

He thought he should feel at least a moment's satisfaction over that. A little gloating from the kind of guy Lucy could never fall for might be in order. But instead, Mac felt oddly troubled. And hated it that he felt that way.

He looked at the house. He could still hear water running. He eased a canoe up with his toe. The paddles were stored underneath it.

Then Mac maneuvered the canoe off the dock and into the water, got into it and began to paddle toward the other side of the lake.

Even more than Mama's embrace, the silent canoe skimming across the water filled him with what he dreaded most of all—a sense of having missed this place, a sense that even as he had tried to leave it all behind him, this was home.

An hour later, eyeing Lucy's house for signs of life and relieved to find none, Mac put the canoe back on the dock. He felt like a thief as he crept up to her back door. The elixir was gone. He could report to Mama with a clear conscience. Still, the feeling of being a thief was not relieved by sticking twenty bucks under a rock to cover the rental of the canoe.

"Hey," Lucy cried, "Wait!"

He turned and looked at her, put his hands into his pockets. He looked annoyed and impatient.

"What are you doing?" Lucy called.

"I took one of your canoes out. There's rental money under the rock." This was said sharply, as if it was obvious, and she was keeping him from something important.

"I never said you could rent my canoe."

"I have to pass a character test?"

Below the sarcasm, incredibly, Lucy thought she detected the faintest thread of hurt. After all these years, could it still be between them?

I could never fall for a boy like you.

No, he was successful and worldly, and it was written in every line of his stance that he didn't give a hoot what she thought of him.

"I didn't say that. You can't just take a canoe."

"I didn't just take it. I paid you for it."

"You need to tell me where you're going. What if you didn't come back?"

"I've been paddling these waters since I was fourteen. I've kayaked some of the most dangerous waters in the world. I think I can be trusted with your canoe."

Trust. There it was again. The missing ingredient between them.

"It's not the canoe I'm worried about. I need to give you a life jacket."

"You're worried about me, Lucy Lin?" Now, aggravatingly, he was pulling out the charm to try to disarm her.

"No!"

"So what's the problem?"

"You should have asked."

"Maybe I should have. But we both know I'm not the kind of guy who does things by the book."

Again she thought she heard faint challenge, a hurt behind the mocking tone.

She sighed. "I don't want your money, Mac. If you want to take a canoe, take one. But let someone know where you're going. At least Mama, if you don't want to talk to me."

She was unsettled to realize now she was the one who felt hurt. Not that she had a right to be. Of course he wouldn't want to talk to her. She'd pushed him into the lake. Though she had a feeling his aversion to her went deeper than that recent incident.

"I don't need your charity," he said, "I'd rather pay you."

"Well, I don't need your charity, either."

"You know what? I'll just have my own equipment sent up."

"You do that."

She watched him walk away, his head high, and felt regret. They needed to talk about Mama, if nothing else. But he hadn't returned her calls, and he didn't want to talk to her now, either.

Lucy picked up his twenty-dollar bill, stuck it in an envelope, scrawled his name across it. Not bothering to dress, she crossed the lawns between the two houses in her housecoat, but didn't knock on the door.

She followed his lead. She put the envelope under a rock and walked away. When she got home, she inspected the canoes, saw which one he had been using, and shoved a life jacket underneath it.

* * *

"What's this?" Mama said, handing him the envelope.

Mac looked in it and sighed with irritation. Trust Lucy. She was always going to have the last word.

Except this time she wasn't, damn her. He folded the envelope, tucked it in his pocket and went out the back door. The last person he would ever accept charity from was Lucy. He owed her for the canoe, fair and square, and the days of her—or anyone in this town—feeling superior to him were over.

He lifted his hand to knock on her back door to return the money to her. Raised voices drifted out the open French doors and he moved away from the paint and peered into Lucy's house.

"You're wrecking the neighborhood!" someone said shrilly.

"It's just a sample." That voice was Lucy's, low and conciliatory.

"Purple? You're going to paint your house purple? Are you kidding me? It's an absolute monstrosity. When Billy and I saw it from the boat the other day, I nearly fell overboard."

Lucy had a perfect opportunity to say, *too bad you didn't,* but instead she defended her choice.

"I thought it was funky."

"Funky? On Lakeshore Drive?"

No answer to that.

Mac tried the door, and it was unlocked. He pulled it open and slid in. After a moment, his eyes adjusted to being inside and he saw Lucy at her front door, still wrapped in a housecoat, her hands folded defensively over her chest, looking up at a taller woman, the other woman's slenderness of the painful variety.

Now, there was a face from the past. Claudia Mitchell-Franks. Dressed in a trouser suit he was going to guess was linen, her makeup and hair done as if she was going to a party. Her thin face was pinched with rage.

Lucy was everything Claudia was not. Fresh-scrubbed from the shower, her short hair was towel-ruffled and did not look any more sophisticated than it had fresh out of the drink. She was nearly lost inside a white housecoat, the kind that hung on the back of the bathroom door in really good hotels.

Her feet were bare, and absurdly that struck him as far sexier than her visitor's stiletto sandals.

"And don't even think you're renting canoes this year! Last summer it increased traffic in this area to an unreasonable level, and you don't have any parking. The street above your place was clogged. And I had riffraff paddling by my beach."

"There's no law against renting canoes," Lucy said, but without much force.

This was the same Lucy who had just pushed him into the water? Why wasn't she telling old Claudia to take a hike?

"I had one couple stop and set up a picnic on my front lawn!" Claudia snapped.

"Horrors," Lucy said dryly. He found himself rooting for her. *Come on, Lucy, you can do better than that.*

"I am not spending another summer explaining to people it's a private beach," Claudia said.

Shrilly, too, he was willing to bet.

"It isn't," Lucy said calmly. "You only own to the

high-water mark, which in your case is about three feet from your gazebo. Those people have a perfect right to picnic there if they want to."

Mac felt a little unwilling pride in her. That was information he'd given her all those years ago when he'd thumbed his nose at all those people trying to claim they owned the beaches.

"I hope you don't tell *them* that," Claudia said.

"I have it printed on the brochure I give out at rental time," she said, but then backtracked. "Of course I don't. But can't we share the lake with others?"

The perfectly coiffed Claudia looked as if she was going to have apoplexy at the idea of sharing the lake. Mac was pretty sure Claudia was one of the girls who used to sit on that deck painting her toenails while the "riffraff" slaved in the yard.

"Well, you won't be giving out any brochures this year, no, you won't! You'll need a permit to run your little business. And you're not getting one. And you know what else? You can forget the yacht club for your fund-raiser."

"I've already paid my deposit," Lucy said, clearly rattled.

"I'll see that it's returned to you."

"But I have a hundred confirmed guests coming. The gala is only two weeks away!" There was a pleading note in her voice.

"This is what you'll be up against if you even try rezoning. This is a residential neighborhood. It always has been and it always will be."

"That's what this is really about, isn't it?"

"We finally no longer have to put up with the endless parade of young thugs next door to this house, and you do this?"

He'd heard enough. He stepped across the floor. "Lucy, everything okay here?"

Lucy turned and looked at him. He could see her eyes were shiny, and he hoped he was the only person in the room who knew that meant she was close to tears.

He thought she might be angry that he had barged into her house, but instead he saw relief on her delicate features as he approached her. Despite the brave front, he could tell that for some reason she felt as if she was in over her head. Maybe because this attack was coming from someone who used to be her friend?

"You remember Claudia," she said.

He would have much rather Lucy told Claudia to get the hell out of her house instead of politely making introductions.

Claudia was staring at him meanly. Oh, boy, did he ever remember that look! The first time he'd taken Lucy out publicly, for an ice cream cone on Main Street, they had run into her, and she'd had that same look on her skinny, malicious face.

"I know you," she said tapping a hard, bloodred-lacquered fingernail against a lip that matched.

He waited for her to recognize him, for the mean look to deepen.

Instead, when recognition dawned in her eyes, her whole countenance changed. She smiled and rushed at him, blinked and put her claw on his arm, dug her talon in, just a little bit.

"Why, Macintyre Hudson." She beamed up at him.

"Aren't you the small-town boy who has done well for himself?"

He told himself he should find this moment exceedingly satisfactory, especially since it had happened in front of Lucy. Instead, he felt a sensation of discomfort—which Lucy quickly dispelled.

Because behind Claudia, Lucy crossed her arms over her chest and frowned. Then she caught his eye and pantomimed gagging.

He didn't want to be charmed by Lucy, but he couldn't help but smile. Claudia actually thought it was for her. He didn't let the impression last. He slid out from under her fingertips.

"I seem to remember being one of the young thugs from next door. *And* the riffraff who had the nerve to paddle by your dock. I might even have had the audacity to eat my lunch on your beach now and again."

She hee-hawed with enthusiasm. "Oh, Mac, such a sense of humor! I've always *adored* you. My kids—I have two boys now—won't wear anything but Wild Side. If it doesn't have that little orangey kayak symbol on it, they won't put it on."

He tried not to show how appalled he was that his brand was the choice of the elite little monkeys who lived around the lake.

"What brings you home?" Claudia purred.

Over Claudia's bony shoulder, he saw Lucy now had her hands around her own neck, the internationally recognized symbol for choking. He tried to control the twitching of his lips.

"Lucy's having a party to honor my mother. I wouldn't have missed it for the world."

Considering that it had given him grave satisfaction to snub Lucy by giving the event a miss, this news came as a shock to him.

"Oh. That. I wasn't expecting *you* would come for *that*. There's been a teensy problem with location. Anyway, it's not as if she's your *real* mother."

Unaware how insensitive that remark was, Claudia forged ahead, her red lips stretched over teeth he found very large.

"I'm afraid the committee has voted to revoke our rental to Lucy. And we don't meet again until next month, and that's too late. But you know, the elementary-school gym is probably available. I'd be happy to check for you."

"No thanks."

"Don't be mad at *me*. It's really Lucy's fault. Norman Avalon is president of the yacht club this year. Do you remember him?"

An unpleasant memory of a boy throwing a partially filled Slurpee cup on him while he was shoveling three tons of mud out of a ditch came to mind.

"They live right over there. If Lucy paints the place purple, his wife, Ellen—you remember Ellen, she used to be a Polson—will have to look at it all day. She's ticked. Royally. And that was before the rezoning application. Macintyre, it is just sooo nice seeing you."

He didn't respond, tried not to look at Lucy, who had her eyes crossed and her tongue hanging out, her hands still around her own throat.

"Congrats on your company's success. I know Billy would love to see you if you have time. We generally have pre-dinner cocktails at the club on Friday."

Behind Claudia, Lucy dropped silently to her knees, and was swaying back and forth, holding her throat.

"The club?" As if there was only one in town, which there was.

"You know, the yacht club."

"Oh, the one Lucy isn't renting anymore. To honor *my* mother."

"Oh." With effort, since her expression lines had been removed with Botox, Claudia formed her face into contrite lines and lowered her voice sympathetically. "If you wanted to drop by on Friday and talk to Billy about it, he might be able to use his influence for *you.*"

Lucy keeled over behind her, her mouth moving in soundless gasping, like a beached fish.

"Billy who?"

"Billy. Billy Johnson. Do you remember him?"

"Uh-huh," he said, noncommittal. He seemed to remember smashing his fist into the face of the lovely Billy after he had made a guess about his heritage.

Claudia held up a hand with an enormous set of rings on it. "That's me now, Mrs. Johnson. Don't forget—cocktails. We dress, by the way."

"As opposed to what?"

"Oh, Mac, you card, you. Toodle-loo, folks."

She turned and saw Lucy lying on the ground, feigning death.

She stepped delicately over her inert body, and hissed, "Oh, for God's sake, Lucy, grow up. This man's the head of a multimillion-dollar company."

And she was gone, leaving a cloying cloud of perfume in her wake.

For a moment Lucy actually looked as if she'd allowed Claudia's closing barb to land. Her eyes looked shiny again. But then, to his great relief, she giggled.

"Oh, for God's sake, Lucy," he said sternly, "grow up."

She giggled more loudly. He felt his defenses falling like a fortress made out of children's building blocks. He gave in to the temptation to play a little.

"Hey, I'm the head of a multimillion-dollar company. A little respect."

And then she started to laugh, and he gave in to the temptation a little more, and he did, too. It felt amazingly good to laugh with Lucy.

"You are good," he sputtered at her. "I got it loud and clear. Charades. Three words. *She's killing me.*"

He went over, took her hand and pulled her to her feet. She collapsed against him, laughing, and for the second time that day he felt the sweetness of her curves in his arms.

"Mac," she cooed, between gasps of laughter. "I've always *adored* you."

"The last time you looked at me like that, I got pushed in the lake."

She howled.

"What was that whole horrid episode with Claudia about?" he finally said, putting her away from him, wiping his eyes.

The humor died in her eyes. "Apparently if you even think of painting your house purple, you're off the approved list for renting the yacht club."

He had a sense that wasn't the whole story between the two women, but he played along.

"Boo-hoo," he said, and they were both laughing again.

"I haven't laughed like that for a long time."

She hadn't? Why? Suddenly, protecting himself did not seem quite as important as it had twenty minutes ago when he had come across her lawn to give her her money back.

"It's really no laughing matter," Lucy said, sobering abruptly. "Now I've gone and ticked her off—"

"Royally," he inserted, but she didn't laugh again.

"And I've got a caterer coming from Glen Oak, but they have to have a kitchen that's been food-safe certified. The school won't do."

"Don't worry. We'll fix it."

"We?" she said, raising an eyebrow at him, but if he wasn't mistaken she was trying valiantly not to look relieved.

"I told Claudia I came back for the party."

"But you didn't."

"When I saw Mama's place falling down, I realized I might be here a little longer than I first anticipated."

"Her place *is* in pretty bad repair," Lucy said. "I was shocked by it when I first came home. I've done my best."

"Thanks for that. I appreciate it. But don't quit your day job."

"She would love it if you were here for a while. Being at the gala would be a bonus. For her, I mean."

Mama *would* love it. But staying longer than he'd anticipated was suddenly for something more than getting Mama's house back in order. When he'd seen that barracuda taking a run at Lucy, he'd felt protective.

He didn't want to feel protective of Lucy. He wanted to hand her her money and go. He wanted to savor the fact she was on the outs with her snobbish friends.

But he was astonished to find that not only was he not gloating over Lucy's fall from grace, he felt as if he couldn't be one more bad thing in her day. Mama Freda would be proud: despite his natural inclination to be a cad, he seemed to be leaning toward being a better man.

Lucy seemed to realize she was in her housecoat and inappropriately close to him. She backed off, and looked suddenly uncomfortable.

"Claudia is right. I'm embarrassed. What made me behave like that? You, I suppose. You've always brought out the worst in me."

"Look, let's get some things straight. Claudia is *never* right, and I *never* brought out the worst in you."

"You didn't? Lying to my parents? Sneaking out? You talked me into smoking a cigar once. I drank my first beer with you. I—" Her face clouded, and for a moment he thought she was going to mention the most forbidden thing of all, but she said, "I became the kind of girl no one wanted sitting in the front pew of the church."

"That would say a whole lot more about the church than the kind of girl you were. I remember you laughing. Coming alive like Sleeping Beauty kissed by a prince. Not that I'm claiming to be any kind of prince—"

"That's good."

"I remember you being like a prisoner who had been set free, like someone who had been bound up by all these rules and regulations learning to live by your own guidelines. And learning to be spontaneous. I think it was the very best of you."

"There's a scary thought," she said, running a hand through her short, rumpled hair, not looking at him.

"I think the seeds of the woman who would paint her house purple were planted right then."

"You like the color?" she asked hopefully. "You saw my sample when you came in, didn't you?"

He hated it that she asked, as if she needed someone's approval to do what she wanted. "It only matters if you like the color."

"I wish that were true," she said ruefully.

"I remember when you used to be friends with Mrs. Billy-Goat Johnson," he said.

"I know. But I think the statute of limitations has run out on that one, so I won't accept responsibility for it anymore." She tried to sound careless, but didn't quite pull it off.

Suddenly it didn't seem funny. Lucy had changed. Deeply. And that change had not been accepted by the people around her. He suspected it went a whole lot deeper than her painting her house purple.

Well, so what? People did change. He had changed, too. Though probably not as deeply. He tended to think he was much the same as he had always been, a self-centered adrenaline junkie, driven by some deep need to prove himself that no amount of success ever quite took away. In other words, when Lucy had called him a jerk she hadn't been too far off the mark.

The only difference was that now he was a jerk with money.

She had helped Mama when he had not, and for that, if nothing else, he was indebted to her.

But now Lucy seemed somehow embattled, as if she desperately needed someone on her side.

Not me, he told himself sternly. He wasn't staying here. He owed Lucy nothing. He was getting a few of the more urgent things Mama needed done cleared up. Okay, it wouldn't hurt to stay a few more days for Lucy's party. That would make Mama happy. It wasn't about protecting Lucy from that barracuda. Or maybe it was. A little bit. But tangling his life with hers?

It occurred to him that he may have lied to himself about his reasons for never coming back to Lindstrom Beach. He had told himself it was because it was the town that had scorned him. The traditional place full of Brady Bunch families, where he'd been the kid with no real family and a dark, secret history.

He'd played on that and developed a protective persona: adrenaline junkie, renegade, James Dean of the high-school set. It had brought a surprising fan base from some of the kids, though not their parents.

Not the snooty doctor's daughter, either. Not at first.

But now, standing here looking at Lucy, it occurred to him none of that was the reason he had avoided returning to this place.

Had he always known, at some level, that coming home again would require him to be a better man?

But would that mean looking out for the girl who had rejected him?

"May I use your phone?" he asked. "My cell got wrecked in the lake."

Her expression asked if he had to, she suddenly

seemed eager to divest herself of him. But she looked around and handed him a cordless. Now that he had decided to be a better man, he was going to follow through before he changed his mind.

He could look at it as putting Claudia in her place as much as helping Lucy.

"Casey?" he said to his assistant. "Yeah, away for a few days...My hometown...You didn't know I had a hometown?...Hatched under a rock? Thanks, buddy." He waggled his eyebrows at Lucy, but she was pretending not to listen.

"Look, I need twenty thousand dollars of clothing products, sizes kid to teen, delivered to the food bank, boy's and girl's club and social services office of Lindstrom Beach, British Columbia. Make sure some of it gets to every agency that helps kids within a fifty-mile radius of that town...Yeah, giveaways.

"Of course you've never heard of Lindstrom Beach. When that's done—if you can have the whole area blanketed by tomorrow—take out a couple of ads on the local TV and radio stations thanking the Lindstrom Beach Yacht Club for donating their facilities for the Mother's Day Gala.

"Thanks, buddy. Don't know when I'll be back and don't bother with the cell. I made the mistake of not bringing the Wild Side waterproof case. Oh, throw some of those in with the other donations. I'll pick up another cell phone in the next few days."

Lucy was no longer pretending not to listen. She was staring at him as he found the button and turned off her phone. He handed it back to her. If he was not mistaken, she was struggling not to look impressed.

"Just admit it," he said. "That was great. Two birds with one stone."

"Everybody does not call you Mr. Hudson," she said, pleased. "Two birds?"

"Yeah. Claudia's stuck-up kids just became a whole lot less exclusive, and unless I miss my guess, you are *in* at the yacht club."

"You hate the yacht club," she reminded him.

"I've always had a strange hankering for anything anybody tells me I can't have."

Her arms folded more tightly over her chest and her eyes looked shiny again.

"I didn't mean you," he said softly.

"Let's not kid ourselves. That was part of the attraction. Romeo and Juliet. Bad boy and good girl."

"I don't think that was part of the attraction for me," he said, slowly. "It was more what I said before. It was watching you come into yourself, caterpillar to butterfly."

"Actually," she said, and she shoved her little nose in the air, reminding him of who she had been before he'd taught her you didn't go to hell for saying *damn*, "I don't want to have this discussion. In fact, if you don't mind, I need to get dressed."

"I have to give this to you first. Special delivery," he said, holding out the money to her. "What was that about rezoning?"

She ignored the envelope. "I think it had to do with the canoes. I think you're supposed to rezone to run a business."

But she suddenly wasn't looking at him. He was startled. Because, scanning her face, he was sure she was being deliberately evasive. What did renting canoes have to do with finally getting rid of the young thugs next door? Though it was Claudia they were dealing with. That was a leap in logic she could probably be trusted to make.

"I can put a lawyer on it if you want."

"I don't need you to fix things. I already told you I'm not in the market for a hero."

"Take your money."

"No. Are you in my house without an invitation?" she asked, annoyed.

"Boy, I saved you from drowning *and* from Claudia, and your gratitude, in both instances, seems to be almost criminally short-lived."

"Oh, well," she said.

"Anyone could come in your house without an invitation. You should consider locking the back door at least."

"Don't you dare tell me what to do! This is not the big city. And don't show up here after all these years and think you are going to play big brother. I don't need one."

But it was evident from what he had just seen that she needed something, someone in her court. Still, he was no more eager to play big brother to her than she was to cast him in that role.

But again, if that was what being a better man required of him, he'd suck it up. No looking at her lips, though. Or at the place her housecoat was gapping open slightly, revealing the swell of a deliciously naked breast.

"Lindstrom Beach may not be the big city," he said,

reaching out and gently pulling her housecoat closed. "But it's not the fairy tale you want to believe in, either."

She glanced down, slapped his hand away, and held her housecoat together tightly with her fist. "As a matter of fact, I gave up on fairy tales a long time ago."

"You did?" he said skeptically.

"I did," she said firmly.

He looked at her more closely, and there was that subtle anger in her again suddenly. He missed the girl who had lain on the floor, clutching her throat. He also felt the little ripple of unease intensify—the one that had started when he saw her clumsy repair job in Mama's porch. It was true. There was something very, very different about her.

In high school she had been confident, popular, perky, smart, pretty. She'd been born with a silver spoon in her mouth and had the whole world at her feet. Her crowd, including Claudia, expected it that way.

But Claudia had always had a certain hard smoothness to her, like a rock too polished. In Lucy, he remembered a certain dewy-eyed innocence, a girl who really did believe in Prince Charming, and for some of the happiest moments of his life, had mistakenly believed it was him.

But Lucy Lindstrom no longer had the look of a woman waiting for her prince.

In fact, from behind the barrier of her newly closed housecoat, she looked stubborn and offended. So, she did not want a hero. Or a prince. Good for her. And he was not looking for a damsel in distress. Or a princess.

So they were safe.

Except, he didn't really feel safe. He felt some danger he couldn't identify, so heavy in the air he might be able to taste it, the same way a deer could taste a threat on the wind.

"What happened to your fiancé?" he asked.

"What fiancé?"

"Mama told me you were going to get married."

"I changed my mind."

"She told me that, too."

"But she didn't give you the details?"

"No. Why would she know the details?"

"You're not from around these parts, are you, son?" She did a fairly good impression of a well-known TV doctor.

"I don't know what you mean."

"My engagement breakup was front-page news after my fiancé was chased naked down a quiet residential street in Glen Oak by a gun-wielding man who just happened to be the cuckolded husband of a woman who was my friend and the barista in our bookstore coffee shop."

It seemed Lucy Lindstrom's fall from grace had been complete. Mac ordered himself to feel satisfied. But that wasn't what he felt at all. He couldn't even pretend.

"Aw, Lucy." Her eyes had that shiny look again. He wanted to reach for her and hold her, but he knew if he did she would never forgive him.

"Don't feel sorry for me, please." She held up her hand. "Everything is on film these days. Someone caught the whole thing on their phone camera. It was a local sensation for a few days."

"Aw, Lucy," he said again, his distress for her genuine.

"Aren't you going to ask me if I never guessed something was going on? Everyone else asks that."

"No, I'm going to ask you if you want me to track him down and kill him."

"With your bare hands?" she asked, and though her voice was silky her eyes were shining again.

"Is he the one who made you quit believing in fairy tales?"

"No, Mac," she said quietly. "That happened way before him."

Her eyes lingered for just a moment on his lips, and then she licked hers, and looked away.

Mac turned from the sudden intensity, and made himself focus on the house—anything but her lips and the terrible possibility it was him who had made her stop believing in fairy tales.

"This isn't how I remember it."

Once, he had made the mistake of going to the front door when she was late meeting him at the dock for a canoe trip.

He'd stepped inside and it had reminded him of an old castle: dim and grim, the front room so crowded with priceless antiques that it felt hard to breathe. He found out he'd been invited inside to get a piece of her father's mind, and that's when he'd discovered that Lucy had been seeing him on the sly.

I forbid you to see my daughter.

After all these years Mac wasn't sure, but the word *riffraff* might have come into play. Of course, being *forbidden* to see Lucy had only made him come up with increasingly creative ways to spend time with her.

And it had intensified the pleasure of sneaking into this very room, when her parents were asleep upstairs, and kissing her until they had both been breathless with longing.

That first meeting with her father had been nothing in comparison to the last one.

There's been a rash of break-ins around the lake. My house is about to be broken into. The police are going to find the stolen goods next door, in your bedroom. You'll be arrested and it will be the final straw for that rotten place. I've always wanted to buy it. Someday, Lucy and the man she marries will live there.

Mac had known for a long time that he had to go. That there was no future for him in Lindstrom Beach and never would be.

He'd told her about her father's threat and said he couldn't stand it in this town for one more second. And that's when she had said it.

I could never fall for a boy like you.

Had her father convinced her he was a thief? That he was behind the break-ins that had happened that summer?

Or had she just come to her senses and realized it wasn't going to work? That a guy like him was never going to be able to give a girl like her the things she had become accustomed to?

It seemed to him that there was a lot of space between them that was too treacherous to cross. They'd caused each other pain, he was sure, but he was sure he had caused her more than she had caused him.

Maybe he had been the one who wrecked fairy tales for her.

But he'd already been a world away from fairy tales by the time he met her.

Safer to focus on the here and the now.

"There used to be a wall here," he said. *And a couch here.* He decided that focusing on the here and now meant not mentioning the couch. Not even thinking about it would have been good, too, but it was too late for that.

"My mom actually opened the walls ups after my dad died."

Which meant they were not, technically, even in the same room they had once made out in. The ghosts of their younger selves, breathless with need, were not here.

Mac somehow doubted her mother had achieved the almost tangible quality of sanctuary that the room had. Her mother, as he recalled her, had been much like Claudia. This room would have had the benefit of an interior designer, the magazine-shoot-perfect layout. It would have been designed with an eye for entertaining. And impressing.

But Lucy had created a space that was casual and inviting. It was a place where a person could read a book or stay in their housecoat all day. But there was something about it that he couldn't quite put his finger on.

Mac went through to the dining-room table to set down the envelope of money. There were papers stacked neatly on it. It was not the space of someone who entertained or had large dinner parties. He put his finger on it: her space had a feeling of surprising solitude clinging to it.

Lucy? Who had been at the heart of a crowd, directing all the action, without even knowing she was?

Imposing her standards on others as unconsciously as breathing?

Lucy? Who had been the most popular girl in her graduating class, not standing up for herself with the likes of Claudia Mitchell-Franks?

Lucy? Who had always been "in," now suddenly having to beg for use of the yacht club in the town named for her grandfather?

Lucy? Who had been as conservative as her parents before her, now tentatively painting her house purple and enraging the community by running a commercial venture from her dock?

"What happened to you?" he asked softly.

And he saw more than secrets in her eyes—enormous, green, dazzling. But if he didn't allow himself to be dazzled, he was sure he saw something he really didn't want to see. He saw fear.

CHAPTER FIVE

FOR ONE MOMENT Lucy was almost overcome by a desire to tell him. Everything. That after he had left that summer, her whole world as she had known it had changed irrevocably and forever.

But she was not giving in to impulses—she already regretted the charade behind Claudia's back—and especially not where Mac was concerned.

"Nothing happened to me. I grew up. That's all."

She didn't want him to look too closely at the table. The charitable foundation registration was sitting there. So was the rezoning application that would allow her to turn this house into a group home for unwed mothers.

She was not getting into that. Not with him. Not now and not ever.

Still clutching her housecoat closed, she went over and inserted herself between him and her secrets.

"Is there something on that table you don't want me to see?"

She was close enough that she could smell him, the scent of the pure lake water not quite eradicated by a faint soapy scent.

"No."

"Unlike Claudia," he said, "you are developing a little worry furrow right here."

He touched between her brows.

And she wanted, weakly, to lean into his thumb and share her burdens. She had secrets. She was worrying. It was none of his business. He was a man she had known back when he was a boy. To think she knew anything about him now, on the basis of that, would be pure folly.

Unless she remembered she couldn't trust him.

"Seven years," he said, peering over her shoulder. "What could possibly be on your table after seven years that you wouldn't want me to see?" He waggled his eyebrows at her in that fiendish way that he had. "The possibility of a lingerie catalog is making me look harder."

Enough. She snatched the money from where he had set it on the table, and looked at it with exaggerated interest. "I don't want this."

Mac shrugged. "Donate it to your favorite charity."

"All right," she said stiffly. There was an irony in that that he never had to know about. In fact, he did not need to know one more thing about her. She was all done laughing for the day. It felt like a total weakness that he coaxed that silly part from her. And the story of her broken engagement.

She didn't like how that had changed him, some wariness easing in him as he looked at her.

"Now, I have to go get dressed, so if you'll excuse me…"

"What *is* your favorite charity?"

She shook her head, felt put out that he was trying to make conversation with her instead of obediently heading for the door.

"Why? Do you want the receipt?"

He turned, and relieved, Lucy thought that she had insulted him and he was going. Instead, he went into her living room and sat down in one of her overstuffed chairs. If she was not mistaken, the only reason he was still here was that he was devilishly enjoying her discomfort.

At least he'd moved away from the rezoning documents.

He appeared totally relaxed, deeply enjoying the view out her window.

She cocked her head at him, unforthcoming. Who could outwait whom?

He picked up the book that was open on the arm, but she raced over and snatched it away—not quickly enough.

"Interesting reading material for a girl who has given up on fairy tales. *To Dance with a Prince?*"

She bit back an urge to defend her choice of reading material, but he had already moved on.

"I like what you've done to the place," he said. "Kind of ski-lodge chic instead of Victorian manor house. I doubt that was your mom. I bet the exterior paint color wasn't her choice, either. It's surprisingly Bohemian for this neck of the woods."

"The paint is barely dry and the neighbors have lost no time in letting me know they don't appreciate me indulging my secret wild side."

And then it was there, the danger. It sizzled in the air between them. Her secret wild side was interwoven with their history. Those heated summer nights of discovery, bodies melting together. That hunger they'd had, an almost desperate sense of not being able to get enough of each other.

She found his eyes on her lips and the memory was scalding.

She was shocked by what she wanted. To be wild. To taste him just one more time. To throw caution to the wind.

"I would have pictured you in a very different life, Lucy."

"Really?"

"Traditional. A big house. A busy husband. A van-load of kids, girls who need to get to ballet lessons, boys who need to be persuaded not to keep their frogs in the kitchen sink."

She was silent.

"I thought you would be living a life very similar to that of your parents, that you'd be hanging with all those kids you grew up with. Friday drinks with friends at the yacht club, water-skiing on weekends in the summer, trips to the ski hill in the winter."

She arched an eyebrow at him. "I'm surprised you pictured me at all."

It was his turn to be silent. The view out the window seemed to hold his complete attention. And then he said, quietly, "A man never forgets his first love."

Something trembled inside her. "I didn't know I was your first love."

"How could you not know? Those crazy weeks, Lucy. I'd wake up thinking of you. I'd go to sleep thinking of you. We spent every moment we could together. It felt as if I couldn't breathe unless you were there to give me air."

How well she remembered the intensity of those few weeks.

"You never said you loved me," she whispered.

He looked at her and smiled. She distrusted that smile. It could still turn her insides to jelly. That devil-may-care smile made him the most handsome man alive, but it said that nothing mattered to him. It was the wall he put up.

"I never say I love anyone," he said. "Not even Mama."

"You've never told Mama you love her?"

"I don't think so."

"Well, that just stinks."

"Anyway, those days are a long way behind us, Lucy."

Yes, they were and it would do nothing but harm to dredge them up. Even now, she could feel her heart beating way too quickly at his admission that he had spent night and day doing nothing but thinking of her. At the time, he certainly hadn't let on that's what was going on for him!

"So, what does the grown-up Lucy do for fun?"

The question took her aback. "Fun?" she asked uncomfortably.

"You were the girl at the center of the fun, as hokey and wholesome as I found it at the time. The water fight on the front lawn of the high school. The fund-raising car wash where they shut down Main Street and brought out the fire truck. The three-day bike excursion to Bartlett. The canoe trip across the lake, camping on the Point.

"I remember standing over at Mama's one night

when you had a group of kids here at your fire pit. You know what I couldn't believe? You had them all singing! All these kids who considered themselves cooler than cool, singing *Row Row Row Your Boat*."

"I thought those days were a long way behind us," she muttered. "Besides, you never participated in any of those things!"

"No, I didn't."

"Why?"

"I felt I didn't fit in."

It was an admission of something real about him, and for the second time Lucy was startled. He had never once said anything like that when they were together. He had revealed more about himself in the last ten minutes than he had the whole time they were together.

"That never showed," she said. "You always seemed so supremely confident. Everybody thought you were so cool. Unafraid, somehow. Bold. If you wore a pair of jeans with a rip in the knee, half the school had ripped their jeans by the next week."

"It wasn't that I didn't have the right stuff—the clothes, the great bike, though I didn't—it wasn't that. It was that your crowd was all so damn *normal*. Two parents. Nice houses. A dog. Allowances. Born into expectations of how they would behave and what they would become. I felt excluded from that. Like I could never belong, only be a visitor."

"I hope I never made you feel like that."

"No, Lucy, you never did. In fact, for those few weeks—" He stopped.

"For those few weeks what?" she breathed.

But he rolled his shoulders, like a fighter shrugging off a blow. "Nothing."

And the veil was down over his eyes, and that was what she remembered most about him. Get close, but not too close.

"You kind of bucked all those expectations of you, didn't you, Lucy?"

Oh, yeah. Because she had had one life before Mac and a completely different one after.

"My life may not be what my father and mother expected, but I have a really good life. I love what I do."

"Mama keeps me posted."

She felt mortified, and he saw it and laughed.

"Don't worry, nothing juicy, just tidbits of news. I heard about your online bookstore, and according to Mama, you do very well at it, too."

"Ah, well," Lucy said, wryly self-deprecating, "You know Mama. When she loves you, you can do no wrong."

"When did you two become so close? When I lived here there was always a kind of barrier, imposed by the doctor, between your family and her. You and Mama were polite to each other, and good neighbors, but you weren't mowing her lawn or repairing her house."

Again, Lucy had to fight with a voice inside her that said, *Wouldn't it be nice to tell him?*

But she reminded herself, firmly, that that summer when she had loved him, she had given and given and given until she had not a secret left. And he had not divulged anything about himself. Laughing at her efforts to find out.

I killed a man. With my bare hands.

"I don't remember the exact details," she lied. But oh, she remembered them so clearly. Flying across that lawn in the dark, the emotional pain in her so great, she was unaware she had stepped on a sharp rock and her foot was bleeding.

The door opening and Mama standing there.

Liebling! *What is it?*

"So, to get back to my original question, what do you do for fun?"

"My work's fun," she said firmly.

"I hope you're joking."

She felt mutinous. "What do you do for fun?"

"My work *is* fun. I developed a company that's all about fun. I think the roots of Wild Side started right here."

"So, your work is what you do for fun, too."

"Touché," he said. "But I do love the white-water kayaking. It is so physical and requires such intense concentration. It makes me feel more alive than just about anything I've ever done."

But a sudden memory flashed through his eyes and it was as if she could see it, too: lying in the sand beside him, the moonlight bathing them, never having ever felt quite so alive as that before.

Or since.

"I guess that's what I'm asking, Lucy. What makes you feel like that?"

"Like what?' she stammered.

"The way I feel when I am in a kayak. Alive. Totally engaged. Intensely in the moment. What makes you feel like that?"

If she said nothing, he would think she was a total

loser. And in fact there was something that made her feel exactly like that.

"I have something," she said reluctantly. And she did. "It makes me feel alive, but I'm pretty sure you wouldn't call it fun."

"Try me."

"Not today." To tell him would just make her feel way too vulnerable.

"Drink the schnapps and I'll ask again."

She marched into her kitchen, got down a shot glass, filled it from Mama's bottle and went back out. She slammed the liquid back. She blinked hard.

"Okay," he said. "What do you do for fun, Lucy Lin?"

"You already figured it out," she said, "I work. Now, shoo. Because I have a lot of that to do today."

Shoo. She wished she had worded that differently. He looked way too closely at her. He was too close to striking a nerve.

He turned to go. "I'll be back."

"I was afraid you would say that," she muttered as she watched him go. Even though she ordered herself not to, even though she knew she shouldn't, Lucy went and watched him cross the yards back to Mama's house.

He was whistling and the melody drifted in her open door, mingled with the scent of the trees, and tingled along her spine.

Rebel. It was a warning if she had ever heard one, and yet Lucy was aware that she felt alive in ways she had not for a long, long time.

Mac went back across the lawns, pensive. Something was so different about Lucy. What had changed in her?

He got the sense that maybe she had become an outcast from the Lindstrom Beach crowd, which was the most surprising thing of all.

As surprising as her mowing lawns and trying to fix floorboards and renting canoes.

Her new aloneness in this community, was it her choice or theirs?

What mattered, really, was that Lucy was shouldering all that responsibility for Mama and he had let her. She seemed alone, and she seemed just a little too grim about life.

Somewhere in her was a woman who wanted to paint her house purple, and probably wasn't going to.

Without an intervention. He was going to be the man Mama expected him to be.

Before he left here, he was going to help Lucy have some fun.

Lucy actually felt light-headed.

It was the schnapps, she told herself, not Mac Hudson crash-landing in her world. She went back upstairs and looked at herself critically in her bedroom's full-length mirror. First soaking wet, now in her housecoat! These were not the impressions she had intended!

She had intended to look sophisticated and coolly professional. Even if she did have a job where she could work in her pajamas if she wanted to.

Lucy found herself dressing for the potential of another meeting with him, and then made herself get to work. First, she turned on her computer and reviewed orders that had come in overnight. There were also a dozen more RSVPs for the Mother's Day Gala, three of them from girls she had gone to high school with, saying "will NOT be able to attend."

She felt something sag within her, and told herself it was not disappointment. It was pragmatic: the people refusing to come were the ones who could make the best donations to her cause.

But, of course, her cause was at odds with their vision for life around the lake.

Lucy forced herself to think of something else. She went into a spare room that had become the book room, retrieved the book orders and began to package them.

Later, she would review her rezoning proposal for Caleb's House, the documents lying out on her dining room table where she hadn't wanted Mac to see them.

As the day warmed, Lucy moved out onto her deck to work, as she often did. She told herself it was a beautiful day, but was annoyed at herself for sneaking peeks at Mama's house.

She could hear enormous activity—saws and hammers—but she didn't see Mac.

She wanted to go see what he was doing over there, but pride made her stay at home.

When she had finally succeeded in putting him out of her mind, the radio was on and she heard the ad about the donation of the Wild Side clothing in thanks for the donation of the yacht club for the Mother's Day Gala.

Within an hour she had been phoned by several representatives of the yacht club—notably not Claudia—falling all over themselves to make sure she knew she was most welcome to the space for the Mother's Day Gala, and that the regular charge had been waived.

Now, as evening fell, Lucy was once again cozy

in her pajamas, trying to concentrate on a movie. She found herself resentful that he was next door. She and Mama often watched a movie or a television show together in the evenings.

She hated it that she felt lonely. She hated it that she was suddenly looking at her life differently.

When had she allowed herself to become so boring? Her phone rang.

"Hello, Lucy."

"Mac," she said. "I've been meaning to call and thank you. The yacht club has confirmed."

He snickered. So did she.

"You didn't tell me Mama's car isn't even insured."

"Why would she insure a car she can't drive?"

"I took it to town three times for building materials before she remembered to tell me, ever so casually, that the insurance had lapsed. I could have been arrested!"

From loneliness to this: laughter bubbling up inside her.

"Anyway, Mama would like to see a movie tonight. Can you drive me to town so I can get one for her?"

"You're welcome to borrow my car anytime you need one."

"I'll keep that in mind, thanks, but Mama says I'm not allowed to pick a movie without you there. She says I'll bring home something awful. A man movie, she called it. You know. Lots of action. Blood. Swearing."

"Yuck."

"Just what Mama said. On the other hand, if we send you to get a movie without me, it'll probably be a two-hanky special, heavy on the violin music."

"Why don't you and Mama go get the movie?"

"She's making *apfelstrudel.*" He sighed happily. "She says it's at the delicate stage. It'll be ready by the time we bring the movie back. She says you have to come have some."

It was one of Mama's orders. Unlike an invitation, you could not say no. As if anyone could say no to Mama's strudel, anyway. Still, it was not as if Lucy was agreeing to spend time with him. Or plotting to spend time with him. It was just happening.

"She hasn't stopped cooking since you got there, has she?"

"No, because I also made a grocery run before I found out I was driving illegally. She made schnitzel for supper," he said happily. "You know something? Mama's schnitzel would be worth risking arrest for. She's already started a new grocery list. Would you mind if we picked up a few things while we're in for the movie?"

Lucy did mind. She minded terribly that she had been feeling sorry for herself and lonely, and that now she wasn't. That life suddenly seemed to tingle with possibility.

From going for a movie and to the grocery store.

Her life *had* become too boring.

Of course, she wasn't kidding herself. The tingle of possibility had nothing to do with the movie or groceries.

Sternly, Lucy reminded herself she was not a teenager anymore. Back then, being around Mac had seemed like pure magic. But she'd been innocent. As he had pointed out earlier, she had believed in fairy tales. She'd been a hopeless romantic and a dreamer and an optimist.

It would be good to see how Mac fared with her adult self! It would be good to do a few ordinary things with him. Certainly that would knock him down off the pedestal she had put him on when she was nothing more than a kid. It would be good to see how her adult self fared around Mac.

It was like a test of all her new intentions, and Lucy planned on passing it!

"Meet me in the driveway," she said. "In ten minutes."

Did she take extra care in choosing what to wear? Of course she did. It was only human that while she wanted to break her fascination with Mac, it would be entirely satisfying to see his with her increase.

She wanted to be the one in the power position for a change.

If she looked at her life that was the whole problem. She had always given away too much power to others. Fallen all over herself trying to win approval.

If she had a fatal flaw, it was that she had mistaken approval for love.

"You know," Mac said, a few minutes later, "they say that people's choice of cars says a lot about them."

Lucy looked at her car, a six-year-old compact in an almost indistinguishable color of gray.

She frowned. The car was almost a perfect reflection of the life she seemed to be newly reassessing. "It's reliable," she said defensively.

"I can cross driving off the list of things you do for fun."

"What do you drive?"

"What do you think?" he said.

"I'm guessing something sporty that guzzles up more than your fair share of the world's resources!"

"You'd be guessing right, then. I have two vehicles. One a sports car and the other an SUV great for hauling equipment around."

"Both bright red?" she asked, not approvingly.

"Of course. One's a convertible. You'd like it."

"Flashy," she said.

"I don't enjoy being flashy," he said without an ounce of sincerity. "I just want to find my vehicle in the parking lot. It's crowded in the big city."

They got in the car. She did not offer to let him drive. It wasn't that her car would be a disappointment after what he was accustomed to. It was that she was not letting him take charge. It was a small thing, but she hoped that it said something about her, too.

"I'm glad you came with me," he said after her disapproving silence about his flashy car lengthened between them.

Something in her softened. What was the point of being annoyed at him? He wanted to be with her. She ordered her heart to stop. She glanced at him, and he was frowning at the list.

"I didn't want to have to ask a clerk where to find this." He held the list under her nose.

"Hey! I'm trying to drive."

It was a good reminder that the point of being annoyed with him was to protect herself.

"It's after seven. There's no traffic on this road." Still he withdrew the list. "C-u-m-i-n."

"Cumin?"

"I wouldn't have pronounced it like that. What is it, anyway?

"A spice."

He rapped himself on the forehead. "See? I thought it had something to do with feminine hygiene."

"Mac. You're incorrigible! What an awful thing to say!"

"Why are you smiling then?"

"My teeth are gritted. Do not mistake that for a smile! I do not find off-color remarks funny."

"Now you sound like you've been at finishing school with Miss Claudia. Don't take life so seriously, Lucy. It's over in a blink."

That was twice as annoying because she had said almost the very same thing to herself earlier. Lucy simmered in silence.

CHAPTER SIX

"SAME OLD PLACE," Mac said, as they entered the town on Lakeshore Drive, wound around the edge of the lake, through a fringe of stately Victorian houses, and then passed under the wooden arch that pronounced it Main Street.

Lucy's house was two miles—and a world—away from downtown Lindstrom Beach. Main Street had businesses on one side, quaint shops that sold antiques and ice cream and rented bicycles and mopeds. Bright planters, overflowing with petunias, hung from old-fashioned light standards.

On the other side of the street mature cottonwoods formed a boundary to the park. Picnic tables underneath them provided a shaded sitting area in the acres of white-sand beach that went to the water's edge.

"Charming," she insisted.

"Sleepy," he said. "No. Make that exhausted."

The shops would be open evenings in the peak of the summer season, but now they were closed, their bright awnings rolled up, outdoor tables and chairs put away against the buildings. There were two teenagers sitting at one of the picnic tables. She was pretty sure they were both wearing Wild Side shirts.

They left downtown and the main road bisected a residential area. Lucy Lindstrom loved her little town, founded by her grandfather. This part of it had wide tree-shaded boulevards, a mix of year-round houses and enchanting summer cottages.

Under the canopy of huge trees, in the dying light, kids had set up nets and were playing street hockey. They heard the cry of "car!" as the kids raced to get their nets out of the way.

"I bet you don't see that in the big city."

"See?" he said. "You still believe in the fairy tale."

"I don't really think it's so much a fairy tale," she said, a trifle defensively. "This town, my house, the lake, they give me a sense of sanctuary. Of safety. Of the things that don't change."

In a few weeks, as spring melted into summer, the lake would come alive. Main Street Beach, which Lucy could see from her dock, would be spotted with bright umbrellas, generations enjoying it together.

There would be plump babies in sun hats filling buckets with sand, mothers slathering sunscreen on their offspring and passing out sandy potato chips and drinks, grandmothers and grandfathers snoozing in the shade or lazily turning the pages of books.

Along Lakeshore Drive, boards would come off the windows of the summer houses. Power boats, canoes and the occasional plane would be tied up to the docks. The floats would be launched and quickly taken over by rowdy teenagers pushing and shoving and shouting. There would be the smell of barbecues and, later, sparks from bonfires would drift into a star-filled sky.

"I'm unchanging. As incorrigible as ever."

"Can you ever be serious?"

"I don't see the point."

"I love this town," she said, stubbornly staying on the topic of the town, instead of the topic of *him*. "How could anyone not love it?"

Now, added to that abundance of charm that was Lindstrom Beach, Lucy had her dream, and it was woven into the peace and beauty and values of her town. The dream belonged here, even if Claudia Johnson didn't think so!

And so did she. Even if Claudia Johnson disapproved of her.

"How could anyone not like it here?" She could have kicked herself as soon as it slipped out. It sounded suspiciously like she cared that he didn't like it here.

"How much you like Lindstrom Beach depends on your pedigree." Suddenly he sounded very serious, indeed.

She glanced at him. His mouth had a firm line to it, and he took a pair of sunglasses out of his pocket and put them on. She was pretty sure those sunglasses had been in the lake yesterday.

"It does not."

"Spoken by the one with the pedigree. You have no idea what it was like to be a kid from the wrong side of the tracks in Lindstrom Beach."

This time the chill in the voice was hers. "That may be true, but it certainly wasn't for lack of trying."

Suddenly, the pain felt fresh between them, like fragile skin that had been burned only an hour or two before. He had been right. There was no point being so serious.

If she could, she would have left things as they were, lived contentedly in the lie that she was all over that, the summer she had spent loving Mac nothing more than the foolish crush of a woman barely more than a girl. She'd only been seventeen, after all.

He had teased her about it then. The perfect doctor's daughter having her walk on the wild side. When she had first heard the name of his company, she had wondered if he was taunting her for what she had missed. But he had never asked her to go on that journey with him. And besides, that brief walk on the wild side had been a mistake.

The repercussions had torn her oh-so-stable family apart. And then, there was the little place on a knoll behind the house, deeply shaded by hundred-year-old pines, that she went to, that reminded her what a mistake it had been.

Leave it, a voice inside her ordered. But she was not at all sure that she could.

"Macintyre Hudson," Lucy said, her voice deliberately reprimanding, "you lived next door to me, not on the wrong side of the tracks."

But underneath the reprimand, was she still hoping she could draw something out of him? That she could do today what she had not been able to do all those years ago?

Find out who he really was, what was just beneath the surface of the incorrigible facade he put on for the world?

He snorted. "The wrong side of the tracks is not a physical division. Your father hated Mama's old cottage, hardly more than a fishing shack, being right next door to his mansion. He hated it more that she brought children of questionable background there. His failures in life: he failed to have Mama's place shut down, and he failed to bully her in to moving."

Mac didn't know that, in the end, her father had considered *her* one of his failures, too.

"But it looks like Claudia Johnson née Mitchell-Franks has taken over where he left off," he said drily. And then he grinned, as if he didn't care about any of it. "I think we should attend her little shindig on Friday night at the yacht club."

The grin back, she knew her efforts to get below the surface had been thwarted. Again. She should have known better than to try.

"I wouldn't go there on Friday night if my life depended on it," she said.

"Really? Why?"

"First of all, I wasn't invited."

"You need an invitation?"

A little shock rippled through her. All those years ago, was it possible that he had never thought to invite her to go with him when he left Lindstrom Beach? That he had just thought if she wanted to go, she would have taken the initiative?

Lucy did not want to be thinking about ancient history. She was not allowing herself to dwell on what might have been.

But still, she said, "Yes, I need an invitation."

"Your grandfather built the damned place."

"I never renewed my membership when I came back."

"You're going to allow Claudia to snub you? I'd go just to tick her off. It could be fun."

But Lucy felt something dive in the bottom of her stomach at the thought of going somewhere where she wasn't wanted, all that old crowd looking at her as if she was the one who had most surprised them all, and not in a good way.

Fun. His diversionary tactic when anything got too serious, when anything threatened the fortress that was him.

"Well, showing up where I'm not wanted is not exactly my idea of a good time."

"I have a lot to teach you," he said, then, "And here we are at the grocery store. Which is open at—" he glanced at his watch "—half past seven. Good grief." He widened his eyes at her in pretended horror and whispered, "Lucy! Are they open Sunday?"

"Since I've moved back, yes."

"I'll bet there was a petition trying to make it close at five, claiming it would be a detriment to the town to have late-night and Sunday shopping. Ruin the other businesses, shut down the churches, corrupt the children."

She sighed. "Of course there was a petition."

The tense moment between them evaporated as he got out of the car and waited for her. "Come on, Lucy Lin, let's go find the cumin. And just for fun, we have to buy one thing that neither of us has ever heard of before."

"Would you quit saying the word *fun* over and over as if you don't think I know what it is? Besides, this is Lindstrom Beach, I don't think you'll find anything in this whole store that you've never heard of before."

"You're already wrong, because I'd never heard of cumin. Would you like to make a bet?"

Don't let him suck you into his world of irreverence, she ordered herself sternly.

"If I find something neither of us has ever heard of, you have to eat it, whatever it is," he challenged her.

"And if you don't?"

"You can pick something I have to eat."

It was utterly childish, of course. But, reluctantly she thought, it did seem like it might be fun. "Oh, goody. Pickled eggs for you."

"You remember that? That I hate those?"

Unfortunately, she remembered everything.

And suddenly it was there between them again, a history. An afternoon of canoeing, a picnic on an undeveloped beach on the far shore. Her laying out the picnic lunch she had packed with a kind of shy pride: basket, blanket, plates, cold chicken, drinks. And then the jar of eggs. Quail eggs, snitched from her mother's always well-stocked party pantry.

She had made him try one. He had made a big deal out of how awful it was. In fact, he had done a pantomime of gagging that surpassed the one she had done of Claudia yesterday. But, at that moment that he had started gagging on the egg, they had probably been going deeper, talking about something that mattered.

"I'm not worried about having to eat pickled eggs," he said. "I'm far too competitive to worry. I'll find something you've never heard of before. Unlike you, who are somewhat vertically challenged, I am tall enough to see what they tuck away on the top shelves."

As he grabbed a grocery cart, Lucy desperately wanted to snatch the list from him and just do it the way she had always done it. Inserting playfulness into everyday chores seemed like the type of thing that could make one look at one's life afterwards and find it very mundane.

And with Mac? There was going to be an afterward, because he was restless and he would never be content in a place like this.

"Here's something now," he said, at the very first aisle. "Sasquatch Bread. I mean, really?"

"It's from a local bakery. It's Mama's favorite."

"We'll get some, then. How about this?" He picked up a container. *"Chapelure de blé?"*

"What?"

"I knew it. Here less than thirty seconds, and I've already won."

She looked at what he was holding. "You're reading the French side. It's bread crumbs."

"Trust the French to make bread crumbs sound romantic. We'll take some of these, too. You never know when you might need romantic bread crumbs."

She was not sure she wanted to be discussing romance with Mac, not even lightly, but the truth was he was hard to resist. Even complete strangers could see how irresistible he was. She did not miss the sidelong glance of a mother with a baby in her buggy or the cheeky smile of leggy woman in short shorts.

But it seemed as if his world was only about her. He

didn't even seem to notice those other women, his focus so intent she could be giddy with it.

If she didn't know better than to steel herself.

But even with steeling herself against his considerable charm, just like that the most ordinary of things, shopping for groceries, was fun! He scoured the store for oddities, blowing dust from obscure items on the top shelves.

He thought he had her at quinoa, but when she said she made a really good salad with it, that went in the cart, too.

The strangest thing was that she was in a grocery store that she had been in thousands of times. And it felt as if she was discovering a brand-new world.

"Got it," he finally said. He held out a large jar to her. "You have never heard of this!"

"Rolliepops," she read. "Pickled herring wrapped around a savory filling. Ugh!"

"Gotcha!"

He bought the largest size he could find, and they found the rest of the things on the list, plus items he deemed essential for movie night: popcorn, red licorice and chocolate-covered raisins.

"You are really going to enjoy snacking on your Rolliepops during the movie," he told her as they strolled out of the store with their laden cart.

"I'd rather eat the bread crumbs."

"Then you shouldn't have admitted you knew what they were. Retribution for the quail eggs all those years ago," he said happily as he stowed all the things he had bought—most of them not on the list and completely impractical—in the trunk of her car.

The video store was also fun as they wrangled over movies. This was the part of being with him that she had forgotten: it was easy.

It had always astonished both of them what good friends they became and how quickly. They had thought they would be opposites. Instead, they made each other laugh. They thought their worlds would be miles apart, instead they were comfortable in the new world they created.

And now it was as if seven years didn't separate them at all. She felt as if she had seen him just yesterday.

Finally, after much haggling, they settled on a romantic comedy.

By the time they got back, it never even occurred to Lucy not to join him at Mama's house for the movie and fresh strudel. They parked the car back in her driveway and walked over with the groceries.

The strudel was excellent, the movie abysmal, Mama got up halfway through it and went to bed.

Suddenly, they were alone. Too late, Lucy remembered what else had come so easily and naturally to them.

When they were alone, an awareness of each other tingled in the air between them.

Back then, they had explored it. She with guilt, he with hunger, both of them with a sense of incredible discovery. The memory of that made her ache with wanting.

He was so close. She could smell the familiar, intoxicating scent of him. If she reached out, she could touch his arm.

"I have to go," she said, jumping up abruptly.

"Something urgent to do? Feed your fish? Put up a new swatch of color?"

"Something like that," she said.

"Don't forget, you owe me. You still have to eat a Rolliepop."

She grimaced. "I think I'd have nightmares. Herring wrapped around something 'savory'? Not my idea of a bedtime snack, but you know what? A bet is a bet."

"Yes, it is, but even though we had a deal, I'll let you off the hook. For tonight. I'll enjoy having something to hold over you."

He insisted on walking her back across the darkened lawns. A loon called on the lake and they both stopped to listen to its haunting cry.

"I don't like it that Mama was tired tonight," she said as they stood there. "She always insists on watching every movie to the end, even if it's awful. She told me once she always gives it a chance to redeem itself."

"People. Movies. She's all about second chances, our Mama. I'm concerned she's wearing herself out cooking for me. I told her to stop, but she won't."

"What rhymes with stop?" Lucy asked.

"Schnop," he said, and they shared a quiet laugh, but grew serious again as they continued walking across the backyard.

"I'm worried that it's not cooking that's wearing her out."

"Me, too."

It felt entirely too good to have someone to share these worries with.

"Has she said anything? About her health?" Lucy asked.

"No. I've been probing, too, but she says she's fine. While repairing the bathroom, I looked through the medicine cabinet. There was a prescription bottle, but she doesn't have internet, so I couldn't check what it's for."

"I can."

"I know, but it makes me feel guilty. Like I'm spying on her. It's kind of an affront to her dignity. So, I'm just going to hang out and fix the house, and keep my eyes and ears open and see if she tells me."

He stopped on her back porch.

"Good night, Lucy."

"Mac." It seemed to her suddenly she was a long way from her goal of proving to herself that he had no power over her anymore.

In fact, it felt like everything it had always felt like with him: as if the ordinary became extraordinary, as if she'd been sleeping and was coming awake, feeling the utter glory of life shimmering through her very pores.

The moonlight and the call of the loons wrapped her in their spell.

On an impulse she stepped in close to him. She needed to know.

On an impulse she stood up on her tiptoes. She needed to know if that was the same.

She wasn't sure why she had to do this. Maybe because she felt he believed she was way too predictable, from her car to her loyalty to her little town to what he presumed was the lack of fun in her life.

She had kissed other men since then. She had something to compare him to now. She had not back then. She would not be as easy to dazzle as that girl, a virgin whose only experiences with kisses had been spin-the-bottle at parties.

Or maybe she just had something to prove to herself when she took his lips.

That she could have the power. That she didn't need to wait for other people to instigate.

But whatever her intention was, it was lost the second their lips connected. He groaned and pulled her close to him, surrendered to her and claimed her at the very same time.

Oh, no. It was the same.

It was the same way as it had always been. She had never felt it before him, and never after, either. Certainly not with the man she had nearly married.

Oh, God, had she picked James precisely because he didn't make her feel like this? No wonder he had gone elsewhere for his passion!

When Mac's lips met hers, it was as if the world melted, as if the stars began to swirl in that dark sky, faster and faster until they melted right into it and everything became one. The stars, the sky, the loons, the lake, her, Mac.

All one incredible, swirling energy that was life itself.

How was it possible that she had convinced herself she could live without this?

She could feel the danger of being sucked right into the vortex of all that energy. She could feel the danger of wanting to be sucked into it.

Instead, she forced herself to yank away.

"Damn it all to hell," she said.

"Whoa. Not the normal reaction when a woman kisses me."

Was that often? Of course it was! Look at the man!

"You stud muffin, you," she said to hide how rattled she was.

"I have the feeling if we were on the dock, I'd be getting shoved in again. Why are you so angry with me, Lucy Lin?"

"I'm not!" she said.

And she wasn't. That was the whole problem. She wasn't angry with him at all. She loved it that he was making her laugh, and making ordinary things seem fun, and carrying the burden of Mama with her.

She loved the taste of his lips and the way his arms closed around her. It felt like a homecoming for one who had wandered too long in foreign lands.

She loved the way women looked at him in the grocery store, confirming what she always knew: Mac Hudson was about the most handsome man ever born.

And she hated herself for loving all those things.

She was angry with herself because she hadn't proved what she wanted at all. In fact, the exact opposite was true!

She had proved her life was empty and passionless, despite all her good causes!

She went in her house and closed the door, and forced herself not to look back to see him crossing the lawn in the moonlight.

"Stay on your own side of the fence!" she ordered herself grimly.

When Mac got back in, Mama was up, watching the end of the movie.

"I thought you were tired," he said.

"*Ach,* at my age, being tired doesn't mean you get to sleep. I thought the movie might redeem itself."

"Has it?"

"No. Why is this funny, people treating each other so badly?"

"I don't know, Mama." He sat down beside her, and she turned off the movie.

"What's wrong, *schatz?*"

"Mama, have I ever told you that I love you?"

"Of course," she said, with no hesitation. "Just not with words. You take time from your busy work and come to help me. What is that, if not love?"

"Too bad all women aren't as wise as you."

"When you look like me, you develop wisdom."

"I think you're beautiful," he said.

"See? What is that, if not love?"

"I'm worried about you, Mama. Living here by yourself. The house getting to be too much for you. I'm worried you're sick and not telling anyone."

"This is a good thing, my boy. To worry about someone else, hmm? It means you are not thinking of yourself all the time."

It was hard to be offended when it was true. He lived a hedonistic lifestyle. Self-indulgent. His business had allowed him to travel the world. Collect every toy. Seek increasing levels of adventure to fill himself, for a while. His lack of commitment made him responsible to no one but himself.

When he started feeling vaguely empty, he raced to the next rush, hoping it would be the thing that would fill him.

"When you feel pain, you have to do something for another."

"I can build you a new house."

"Would that make *you* feel better?"

"Wouldn't you like it?"

"I consider having more than what I need a form of stealing."

Hmm. Hadn't Lucy said something almost the same? About his vehicles. Taking more than his share of the world's resources?

"Everybody filling up their lives full, full, full with stuff," Mama said. "What is it they don't want to feel?"

"Lonely, I guess," he surprised himself by saying. "Less than."

"Do something for someone else."

"I am. I'm doing something for you."

"You should do something nice for Lucy."

Wasn't that what he'd already decided? But now, that kiss changed everything. He felt as if he was floundering.

"She seems angry at me."

"So, that stops you? You can only offer kindness if there is something in it for you? Why is she angry at you?"

"I don't know. I mean, you know we had a little thing that summer before I left. I knew she couldn't come with me. She loved it here. The little bit of time that she was with me put her at odds with her friends and family. Her dad threatened to have me arrested he was so put out by the whole thing. We were both stupidly young. How could that have worked?"

Mama was silent, and then she said, "You left her to

the only life she'd ever known. Maybe that was love, also, hmm, *schatz?*"

He was suddenly nearly blinded with a memory of how it had felt being with Lucy. Waking up with a smile on his face, needing to be with her. Practically on fire with the sensation of being alive.

He shook it off and sighed. "I'm not sure I'm capable of such nobility," he said. "She wanted more of me than I could give her."

"Ah."

"Maybe," he said hopefully, "it's not me that she's angry with. Her recent fiancé took a pretty good run at her self-esteem by the sounds of it. And something is going on with her old crowd. I hate it that Claudia Stupid-Johnson feels better than her."

"No," Mama said softly. "What you hate is that Lucy lets her."

He felt like he was getting a headache. This was all way too deep and complicated for a guy as dedicated to the rush as he was. But while he was tackling the hard stuff, there was no sense stopping halfway.

"You didn't answer me, Mama. Are you sick?" He hesitated, and said softly, feeling the anguish of it, "Are you going to die?"

"Yes, *schatz,* sooner or later. We are all dying. From the very minute we are born, we are marching toward the other end. Why does everybody act surprised when it comes? Why does everyone waste so much time, as if time is endless, when it is the most finite of all things?"

"I don't know," he said.

"Do something nice for Lucy. It will make you feel better. And send a card to your mother."

Mama patted his cheek, got up and went up the stairs.

Well, since he wasn't sending a card to his mother, that left doing something nice for Lucy. And he knew exactly what that was. She'd somehow lost sight of who she was. She was uncomfortable going to the yacht club! Hell, she should walk in there like the queen that she was!

He thought about her lips on his.

And wondered if Mama had any idea how complicated things could get.

CHAPTER SEVEN

LUCY WAS SITTING on her deck with her laptop. Her mother had sent her an email from Africa with a picture attached. Her mother looked happy. Her hair wasn't done, and she had a sunburn. It was odd, because Lucy didn't really recall her mother not having her hair done. And she was not what she would have ever called a happy person.

Her inbox had more RSVPs, two more from her old high-school crowd, saying no, they would not be able to attend the gala.

It didn't have quite the sting it had had previously. Of course, it was a beautiful mild spring day, the sun on the lake and her skin and in her hair. How could you feel bad on a day like this?

Was there a possibility she was able to dismiss negative things more easily and feel beautiful things more intensely since that kiss?

"Of course I'm not!" It was days ago! She hadn't, thank goodness, seen Mac since.

But think of the devil, and he will appear!

"Hey, Lucy Lin!" Mac was on the other side of her deck, peering through the slats of the deck railing at her. "Are you talking to yourself?"

Which would seem pathetic. Thankfully, she was not in her pajamas. It felt as if she was experiencing his sudden appearance intensely, too.

Her heart began to beat a little faster, her cheeks felt suddenly flushed. She was so aware of how incredibly handsome he was. And sexy. She was a little too aware of how his lips tasted.

He didn't wait for an answer.

"It doesn't look like you've made much progress on that paint."

"I'm not sure about the color anymore," she admitted a bit grumpily.

"Come and see what I found in Mama's shed."

She needed to pretend he wasn't there, go in her house and follow his suggestion of locking her doors.

But, of course, if she reacted like that, he would *know* he was affecting her way too deeply.

She set her laptop aside, got up and reluctantly padded over and looked over the railing, bracing herself. With Mac it could be anything, from a snake to an antique washboard.

He grinned up at her, and she knew that was what she really needed to brace herself against.

That, and the fact Mac was holding the handlebars of a bicycle built for two. It might have been gold once, now it was mostly rust. The leather seats were cracked.

"If you promise to keep your lips off of me, I'll take you for a ride."

"Look, let's get something straight. I didn't kiss you because I find you in any way attractive."

"Hey! That was just plain mean."

"Not that you aren't." Oh! This was going sideways.

"I kissed you as a way of saying thank you for caring so deeply about Mama."

"Well, I'm glad you cleared that up. Let's go for a ride."

She looked at him. She looked at the bike. She had cleared up the lip thing. Well, she hadn't really, but he had accepted her explanation. It was a beautiful day. An unexpected gift was being offered to her.

You are giving in to temptation, she told herself. "No," she told Mac.

"Look, princess, it's a bike ride or the Rolliepop. You owe me."

Her lips twitched. Once, for a few weeks, it had felt as if Macintyre Hudson was her best friend. She could tell him anything, be totally herself around him. In many ways, it felt as if she had found out what that meant—to be totally herself—around him.

She was aware of missing that.

Could they be friends? Without the complication of becoming lovers? What would it hurt to find out?

"You're even dressed for it," he said, sensing her weakening. "Aren't those things called pedal pushers?"

Those *things* were a pair of eighty-dollar trousers she had ordered well before her self-imposed austerity program. "It said capris when I ordered them online."

"Ah, well, you know, one born every minute."

And even though she had practiced saying no to him over and over again in her mind, she might as well not have practiced at all.

Because he was in possession of a bicycle built for two, and she wasn't in the mood to eat a Rolliepop. Plus, she was wearing an eighty-dollar pair of pedal pushers.

It seemed like it would be something of a waste not to try them out!

She came down off her deck, and they pushed the bike, which was amazingly heavy, up her steep driveway to the relative flatness of Lakeshore Drive above it.

“Hop on.” He took the front.

She folded her arms over her chest. “Why would you automatically get the front?”

“I assumed it would be harder.”

“I think you want control. That’s where the brakes are. And the steering.”

“Maybe *you* want control!”

“Maybe I do,” she admitted.

He sighed as if she was really trying his patience. “If you want the front, you can have it. Look, you even have the bell.” He rang a rusty old bell.

He surrendered the front, and she got on the bike. He got on the back. After a few false starts, they were off.

It felt as if she was pulling him. It was really the most awful experience. Because even though his handlebars were stationary and didn’t move, he acted as if they did, and every time he wrenched on them the whole bicycle shook precariously.

“Quit trying to steer!”

“I can’t help myself.”

“Are you pedaling?” she gasped.

“With all my might. Ring the bell and wave, we’re going by your neighbor gardening.”

She giggled, rang the bell and waved. The bike veered, and he tried to correct it with his handlebars that didn’t work. He nearly threw them both off the bicycle. Mrs. Feldman looked up, startled, and then smiled, unaware of the problems they were having, and waved back.

They rode by the houses with name plaques at the tops of the driveways. Her father had disapproved of naming the lake properties, saying he found it corny. But Lucy liked the names, ranging from whimsical: Bide Awhile, Pair-a-Dice, Casa Costallota, to the imposing: The Cliff House, Eagle's Rest, Thunder Mountain Manor. Sometimes you could catch a glimpse of the house from the road, other times lawns, gardens, trees, lake, the odd tennis court or swimming pool.

Had she been asked, Lucy would have said Lakeshore Drive was perfectly flat. Now, it was obvious that from her house toward town, it sloped substantially upward.

She was gasping for air. "Don't run over my tongue."

"Ready to trade places?"

She did, gladly.

Though the back position was slightly more relaxing than the front, the feeling of being out of control was terrible. She had to trust him.

"Hey, you got the easy part," she complained. The road that had been sloping upward crested, and began a gradual incline down.

"Woo-hoo! Look, no hands!"

"Put your hands back down."

"No, you put yours up. Come on, Lucy, fly!"

And so she did, and found herself shrieking with laughter as they catapulted down the hill, arms widespread, chins lifted.

His hands went back to the handlebars and so did hers.

"I think we need to slow down," she said. They were

approaching the bottom of the rise, the road banked sharply to the right.

"You think I'm not trying?"

In horror, she leaned by him to see he was squeezing the handbrakes with all his might. Nothing was happening.

"Try pushing backwards on the pedals."

He did. She did. The bike did not slow. They were coming up to the last curve into Lindstrom Beach.

He put his feet down to slow them. She was afraid he would break his leg. What his feet did was alter the course of the bike. It veered sharply left as the road went right. Her yanking away on her handlebars did nothing for their perilous balance.

They flew off the road and into a patch of thick bracken fern. She flew over her handlebars into him, and together they tumbled through the ferns. She landed on top of him, and the bike landed on top of her.

He reached up, and with one hand tenderly cupped the side of her face.

"Are you okay, Lucy Lin?" he asked with such gentleness it made her ache.

"I am," she heard herself saying. "I am okay. I haven't been for a long, long time, but I am right now."

"That's good. That's perfect. Did I mention where we were going before we were so rudely interrupted?" Mac asked her.

"I didn't think we were going anywhere. For a bike ride."

He reached around and shoved the bike off them. She sat up, then got up. The capris were probably ruined, a dark oily-looking smudge across the front leg, a grass stain on the other side.

“Ah, actually, no. We were going to cocktail hour at the yacht club.”

She glanced at him, realized he must be kidding. “You have to *dress,*” she reminded him, joking.

He was picking up the bike, inspecting it for damage. “We are dressed.”

“That’s not what she meant.”

“Claudia had her opportunity to clarify and she didn’t. So, we’re dressed or we’re naked. You pick.”

She suddenly saw he was serious.

“I’m not going. I’ve scraped my knee. I think there are leaves in my hair.”

He wheeled the bike over, picked the leaves out of her hair, bent down and inspected her knee. Then he kissed it.

“You’re going,” he said.

“There are smudges on the front of my pants.”

“Well, there’s one on your derriere, too.”

“I am not going to the yacht club all disheveled and smudged, with leaves in my hair! What would they think of me?”

“Why do you care what they think of you?” he asked softly.

“I wish I didn’t care, but I do, okay? So far, not one of them is coming to the Mother’s Day Gala.”

“Why not?”

“No one in this set has ever liked Mama. My father set the tone for that years ago. They’re all for doing good on paper, but they don’t do it in their backyard.”

"That makes me all the more committed to attending their little cocktail hour."

"Not me," she said with a shiver.

"We are going," he said, firmly. "And you're walking into that room like a queen. Do you understand me?"

She looked at him. He wasn't kidding.

"I don't want to go."

"Life's about doing lots of things you don't want to do. You're going."

And suddenly Lucy knew, with him beside her, she could do just what he had said. She could go. And she could hold her head high, too.

Suddenly, she knew he was absolutely right. She *had* to go.

She sighed. "I love it when you're masterful."

"Really? I'll have to try that more often. Back on the bike, wench."

And just like that she was riding toward what she had feared the most for a long, long time. Only, she didn't feel at all afraid.

They rode up on their now quite wobbly bicycle built for two. She would have left it at the back door, but Mac was in the control position, and he rode along the pathway that twisted to the front of the club, where it faced the lake. Some of the cocktail crowd were out on the deck.

There was a notable pause in the conversation as they parked the bike.

Mac threw his arm over her shoulder as they went up the steps, and she glanced at his face.

He had that smile on.

If you didn't know him, you might be charmed by it.

She said quiet hellos to people on the deck, sucked in her breath and, with Mac at her side, entered the yacht club.

"Macintyre Hudson!" Claudia squealed, just in case anyone hadn't recognized him, "I'm so glad you came. Look, folks—" she looped her arm through his "—Mac is back!"

If he cared that he was in shorts when every other man was in a sports jacket and slacks, you couldn't tell.

As always, he carried himself like a king.

And she took her cue from him. Claudia was pointedly ignoring her, so she pointedly ignored Claudia.

"Ellen!" she said, finding a familiar face, "I haven't seen you for ages. What's this I hear that you don't like my paint color on my house?"

"Don't you, Ellen?" Her husband, Norman, turned and looked at her. "I like it."

Claudia's mouth puckered and pointed down. "Let me get you a drink, Mac."

"I'll have lemonade. Lucy?"

"The same."

She grinned at Mac. He had Claudia fetching her a drink!

He winked at her.

And suddenly, in this crowd of people who had once been her friends, she felt lighthearted. Had she bumped her head on the bike?

Because all these people *had* once been her friends. The girls she had known and chummed with since kindergarten. They had stopped calling her. Looked the other way when she came into a room.

And suddenly, she really didn't care. Wasn't that

more about them than her? Why hadn't she picked up the phone? When had she forgotten who she was?

They all seemed so stuffy! The atmosphere in this room seemed subdued and stifling. Mac's question came back to her. *What do you do for fun?*

"Why are we all inside?" Lucy asked. "It's a gorgeous day. And Mac and I brought a bicycle built for two!"

People were looking at her! Good!

"Anyone want to try the bike?" she asked.

Silence. It was obvious no one here was dressed for this. But even so, how could they be so young and still so set in their ways? Where were their kids, for heaven's sake? Didn't they like being with their kids? That made her feel almost sorry for them.

Lucy felt determination bubbling up in her. Not to change who they were. No, not that at all. But not to hide who she was, either. Not anymore.

"There will be a prize," she said, "It's trickier than it looks!"

Still, silence. They were going to reject her. She didn't care! She was stunned by the freedom of not caring!

"The prize is complimentary tickets to the Mother's Day Gala. I have a few left."

Some of them looked uncomfortable then!

"I might throw in a free canoe rental for an afternoon. Much more romantic than those power boats tied up at the dock. That's if I'm still in business."

She was throwing their snubs back in their faces, and loving it.

"Don't pass up on this! Mac is going to serenade

you with that famous song about a bicycle built for two while you ride."

She was aware of Mac giving her a sidelong look, but also of a little smile tickling the edges of his mouth that was quite different from his devil-may-care smile.

"Well, that I can't resist!" And then quiet little Beth Adams, whom she had always liked, stepped forward. "I'll try it." She gave Lucy a quick, hard hug, and said quietly, "It is so good to see you."

It was so sincere that Lucy felt tears sting her eyes.

After that it was as if a dam had burst. People coming and hugging her, shaking Mac's hand, saying how good it was to see them both.

The party moved out onto the lawn as everyone lined up to watch Beth try the bike. Beth hitched up her skirt and kicked off her shoes. Lucy got on the backseat. There was laughter and encouragement as they wobbled down the path.

"Sing," Lucy ordered Mac.

He was a good sport.

"Ring the bell," Lucy called as they turned around at the parking lot and came back, the assembled crowd scattering off the walkway. "Don't get going too fast, the brakes are faulty."

Beth rang the bell, as Mac sang.

The way his eyes rested on her, it almost felt as if he was singing to her. He looked so proud of her!

Then Beth called her sister, Prue, to try it with her. Prue gamely hitched up her dress and tossed her shoes on the grass.

Mac started the song all over. Lucy sang with him.

And then to her amazement, everyone was singing.

Laughter flowed as others tried the bike, first some of the women together, and then couples.

It seemed everyone had to have a turn.

Mac nursed his lemonade, delivered to him and Lucy on the lawn by a very sulky Claudia. He was glad to be out of the clubhouse and back into the sunshine.

The yacht club had surprised him. Once, it had seemed like *the* place that meant you'd arrived, the exclusive enclave of the old and wealthy Lindstrom Beach families. He'd never been invited here when he lived here, nor had he attended the functions that had been open to the public, a kind of reverse snub.

Now, all these years later he'd been to places that were truly exclusive. Many of them.

And in comparison the Lindstrom Beach Yacht Club seemed like a three trying to be a nine. It had a "clubhouse" feel to it, but not in a good way. There was carpet, which was always a bad idea in a place close to water. The paneling was too dark and the paintings too somber.

He smiled as Lucy got everyone moving to the deck and then down on the lawn.

There was quite a gathering of people he'd gone to school with, some of them relatively unchanged, some changed for the worse. Most had arrived in the powerboats that were tied to the dock, and most of the women, at least, were "dressed," their opportunity to haul out the expensive cocktail dresses they normally wouldn't get a chance to wear.

Billy Johnson had aged poorly and had a tortured comb-over hairdo, and a potbelly.

Lucy was as he remembered her, finally. At the heart of it all. Encouraging them to laugh and have fun. Just as in the old days, they thought they were so cool, but they were chirping along to that hokey old song.

In her smudged pants and sleeveless top, with her knee bashed up, he thought she did look like queen.

He loved how she was getting everyone on that bicycle.

He loved how they were all singing that song, Lucy waving her arms around like a bandleader.

He noticed Claudia simmering beside him.

"You and Billy should try it," he said.

"Why would I?" she snapped.

"Come on, Claudia," Billy said. "Everybody but us has tried it. We could win the prize!"

She had been getting drinks when Lucy had announced the prize so Mac had to bite back a shout of laughter.

Annoyed, Claudia nonetheless did not want to seem like the only spoilsport on the lawn.

And Billy still had a bit of the captain of the football team in him. Or a few too many drinks. Because where everyone else had gone up the path and around the parking lot a few times, Billy began to go up the long steep driveway that people used to get their boats into the water.

At the top, he and Claudia disappeared onto Lakeshore Drive.

"Riding to town," someone guessed.

"Had a wreck," someone else said. "Impaired driving!"

"Oh, here they come!"

They had just turned around somewhere on the road. Claudia had obviously missed the part about the brakes, Billy had possibly already had too many drinks to get it.

As they whirred down the hill on the ancient bicycle, the little crowd burst into song.

The bike was wobbling but picking up speed. Billy was yelling, happily, "Faster! Faster!" He put his head down, pedaled with fury.

Claudia, her cocktail dress flying in the wind behind her was shrieking to him to slow down.

The crowd sang boisterously, saluting the couple with their wineglasses.

The bike careened down the hill and past the crowd. It went down the cement ramp that allowed boats to be backed gently into the lake.

Mac wasn't sure that Billy even tried the brake.

In fact, he seemed to be yelling "Ta-da" as they entered the water in a great spray of foam.

Claudia, on the backseat, flew off and into him, just as he and Lucy had done earlier.

It was spectacular! They both plunged into the water with a great splash.

Claudia floundered and squealed until Billy picked her up and hauled her out of the water. People swarmed around them. Claudia's dress looked as if it was made out of soggy toilet paper. Her hair hung in horrible ropes. Her makeup was running.

Her husband whirled her around. "Now, honey, *that* was fun! Hey, Lucy, did we win the prize?"

"Oh, you sure did," Lucy said. She was doubled over with laughter.

"What prize?" Claudia sputtered.

Mac could not take his eyes from Lucy. This is what he remembered. At the very center of it all. Only, there was something about it that was even better.

Because before, there had been no shadows in her.

And now that there were, it was twice as gratifying to see them go away. And now that there were, it was like seeing the sun after weeks of rain.

Beautiful.

The most beautiful thing he had ever seen.

CHAPTER EIGHT

"I've got to make some changes to the gala," Lucy panted. She was on the front of the bike, pedaling with all her might. They had left the yacht club and were on the final hill before her house. "I had it all wrong. It was like, when I was planning it, I was trying to win their approval. And none of them were even coming!"

"Well, they're all coming now," he said.

"That remains to be seen. They could all come to their senses before then."

"I think they just did come to their senses."

"I don't want it to be stuffy."

"Like cocktail hour was before you arrived?"

"Exactly. We need something more fun for the gala. I mean, still a dinner, and obviously it's too late to change the black-tie part, but what would you think of a comedian?"

"Lucy, please be quiet and pedal the bike!" She didn't even seem to be tired, bursting with a new energy. Mac wondered what the heck he had unleashed.

Since they knew the bike had no brakes, they walked the final decline in the road. Now that he had seen her light flicker back on, Mac felt honor bound to fan it to life, to keep it going, and it didn't take much.

Over the next few days, he did simple things. He brought a pack of hot dogs and some sticks to her place, and they roasted wieners over an open fire. And then cooked marshmallows, and ate them until their hands and faces were sticky.

He had the bike fixed and they rode it into town for ice cream.

He had one of his double kayaks sent up, and they began to explore the lake in the afternoons.

All this wholesome fun was great, but he wanted to show her more. He wanted to show her a bigger world than Lindstrom Beach. He wanted to show her he was more than the boy he had once been. That he had succeeded in a different place and moved in that place with comfort and confidence.

It occurred to him that his need to show her something more of himself was not strictly within the goal he had set for himself of showing Lucy some fun.

But since he already knew just how he would do it, he refused to ask the question whether he was going deeper than he had ever intended to go.

"Miss Lindstrom?" a deep voice, faintly muffled voice said.

"Yes?" Lucy shook herself awake, played along. She was still in bed. She looked at the clock. It was 6:00 a.m. A girl could live to wake up to the sound of his voice, even when he was trying to disguise it.

"You have won an all-expense-paid trip to Vancouver, B.C. Your flight is departing from the Freda dock in ten minutes."

That sounded so fun. And exciting. Lucy marveled

at this woman she had become. But maybe they'd better set some limits.

"Mac!"

His voice became normal. "How did you guess?"

"You're the only one I know with a plane tied up at Mama's dock. I can't come—for goodness' sake, the gala is days away. This is no time to be taking off."

"Literally, taking off."

"Ha-ha."

"I'm coming over."

Something in her sighed. Mac coming over, them passing back and forth between houses as if it was the most natural thing in the world.

The truth was she couldn't wait to see him. Seeing him for the first time in a day always felt so wonderful. She told herself she had to stop this. She told herself she was playing with fire.

But she had set it off, all those days ago when he had shown up with the bicycle to see if they could be friends.

And it seemed as if they could.

Okay, so she yearned to taste him. To hold him. To kiss him. But no, that had ruined everything last time.

This time she was going to be satisfied with friendship.

She wrapped her housecoat around her and went to the door. Mac looked incredible, of course, in a nice shirt and khakis.

"You spend an awful lot of time in that housecoat, Lucy Lin."

"It's six in the morning."

He grinned wickedly. "So, what do you say? You want to come play?"

"One of us has to be a responsible adult! The gala—"

"Part of the reason for the trip," he said with sincerity.

She folded her hands over her chest, waiting to see how he was going to pull this off.

"Mama found out it's not just about Mother's Day. That it's in her honor. She's quite impressed that something at the yacht club is being held in her honor. She considers it *swanky*."

"But it's supposed to be a surprise!"

"Come on. There are no secrets in Lindstrom Beach."

That, Lucy knew firsthand. "Did you tell her?"

He looked hurt. "No. Agnes Butterfield. It slipped out, apparently. Mama thinks it's a good thing she found out, because, according to her, she has nothing suitable to wear to such a *swanky* venue."

"Could you quit saying *swanky* like that? As if we're a bunch of small town hicks putting on airs?"

"Consider swanky banned from my vocabulary. If you'll come."

Really? A fly-in shopping trip to the big city? How on earth could she refuse that? Apparently he still thought she was resisting, and it was fun to make him try and convince her to do something she'd already decided she wanted to do.

"Mama says a galoot-head like myself cannot be trusted to help her pick a dress."

He was pushing all the right buttons. "Mac, she has more dresses and matching hats than the queen." But she said it weakly.

The carefree look melted from his face. He turned from her and looked over the inky darkness of the lake. His voice was low when he spoke. "She told me nothing she owns fits, that she lost a lot of weight last winter."

Lucy felt that ripple of fear. "I never noticed that," she said, biting a nail.

"I didn't, either. I thought it was because I hadn't seen her for a while. She said it's because she walks more, now that she doesn't have a driver's license."

Lucy closed her eyes, tried to swallow the fear and think rationally. She realized she was really dealing with two kinds of fear.

One, that something was wrong with Mama that had her losing weight and planning her own funeral.

And two, that Mac Hudson was standing on her back deck, and he still made her feel as though she was melting.

There was something quintessentially sexy about a man who could fly an airplane.

As if he knew she had given in, he said, "I told her I'd get her a new dress for her birthday. Lucy, we'll leave in a few minutes, shop, have a nice private birthday lunch with Mama and be home by early evening. It will be fun."

Oh, more fun. Didn't it seem like she was setting herself up for a heartbreak? Because he would leave and all the fun she was becoming so accustomed to would stop.

It was only a heartbreak if there was love involved she told herself. They were just friends. Besides, when was the last time she had just had a lighthearted shopping trip?

Come to think of it, Lucy realized, she was going to need a dress, too.

And come to think of it, she needed a dress that would show Mac she was not quite the stick-in-the-mud, fun-free creature he seemed to believe she was.

And maybe that she had come to believe she was, too!

Besides, wouldn't it be the best of exercises to prove that not only was she capable of embracing a spontaneous day of pure fun, but that she didn't have anything to fear from her reactions to Mac anymore?

She was a grown-up. So was he.

They could be friends. They had been proving that all week, with their strongest bond being their mutual caring for Mama Freda.

Still, this felt different than hanging out over a bonfire, eating marshmallows until they were sticky and sick.

Lucy found herself choosing what to wear very carefully. Finally, she settled on jeans, high heels, a white tailored shirt and a leather jacket. She'd finished with a dusting of makeup, a few curls in her too-short hair, and big gold hoop earrings. The look she was hoping for was casual but stunning.

And from the almost surprised male appreciation in his eyes, she had achieved it.

Mac helped Mama into the plane. Then it was her turn, and his hand closed around hers to hand her up. Given that the plane was bobbing on water, and they were stepping from the dock, this took more physical contact than Lucy had prepared herself for, but at least she didn't end up with his hand on her backside!

Her reaction to it, she told herself, was only evidence that it was time for her to stop being such a hermit.

Mama insisted on sitting in the back.

Apparently she was terrified of flying, a small detail that she was not going to allow to get in the way of a shopping trip and a new dress.

Mac leaned into the back to help her with her seat belt, but she refused the headset Mac passed to her. Instead, out of a gargantuan red handbag, she pulled a bulky eight-track tape player. After checking batteries, she plugged in an eight-track cassette. Then, she fished through the enormous purse, pulled out a book of word searches and a pencil and hunkered down in her seat.

"Mama, there's nothing to be worried about," Mac told her.

"Worried, schmurried," she muttered without looking up from the book.

He shrugged and grinned at Lucy, then helped her buckle in, and adjusted her headset for her. There was something entirely too sexy about Mac at the controls of the plane. He was confident and professional, on a two-way radio filing a flight plan, going through a series of checks.

As the plane taxied along the lake, Lucy looked over her shoulder to see Mama jacking up the volume of her eight track and squinting furiously at her book.

"Is that Engelbert Humperdinck?" Mac asked.

"I'm sure that's what she's listening to." Lucy confirmed.

She thought she heard a sound from Mama, but when she turned around again it was to see Mama glance out the window at the lakeshore rushing by them, go pale and jack up the volume yet again.

The plane wrested itself from gravity, left water and found air. Lucy found herself holding her breath as the plane lifted over the trees at the far end of the lake and then banked sharply.

"Have you ever been in a small plane before?"

"No."

"Nervous?"

Lucy contemplated that. "No," she decided. "It's exhilarating."

Mac flew back over her house and she knew he had done that just for her. Her house from the air was so cute, like a little dollhouse, all the canoes lined up like toys on her dock.

She thought it looked very nice in white.

"Is the lavender going to be a mistake?" she said into the headset. Then, "No! No, it isn't!"

He smiled at her as if she had passed a test—not that devil-may-care smile that held people at a distance. But a real smile, so genuine she could feel tears smart behind her eyes.

She turned and tried to get Mama's attention so she could see her own house from the air, but Mama was muttering along to her music, licking her pencil furiously, and scowling at her word-puzzle book, determined not to look out that window.

"What's Caleb's House?" Mac asked.

She went from feeling safe and happy to feeling as if she was on very treacherous ground. Lucy felt her heart race. "What? Why do you ask?"

"That's the charity Mama told me she wants the

money from the fund-raiser to go to. I'd never heard of it. She said to ask you."

She was aware she could tell him now. That there was something about hearing him say Caleb's name that made her want to be free of carrying it all by herself.

But the time was not right, and it might never be right. He was here only temporarily. Why share the deepest part of her life with him? Why act as though she could trust him with that part of herself?

She had trusted him way too much once before. She had talked and talked until she had no secrets left. Now, she had a secret.

After he had left here, seven years ago, Lucy had found out she was pregnant. Terrified, she had confided in one friend.

Claudia.

Claudia had felt a need to tell her mother and father, who had told Lucy's mother and father, and maybe a few other members of their church, as well.

Lucy's decent, upstanding family had been beyond dismayed.

"How could you do this to us?" her mother had whispered. "I'll never be able to hold up my head again."

Her father's disgust had been visited on her in icy silence. Her plans for college had gone up in smoke. Her friends had abandoned her. She had been terrified and alone, an outcast in her own town.

She had never felt so lonely.

And still, that life that grew within her had not felt like an embarrassment to her. It felt like the love she had known was not completely gone. She whispered to her baby. When she found out it was a boy, she went and bought him the most adorable pair of sneakers, and a little blue onesie.

When it had ended the way it had, in a miscarriage, it was as if everyone wanted to pretend it had never happened.

But by then she had already named him, crooned his name to him to make him feel welcome in a world where he was not really welcome to anybody but her. That was the night she had run to Mama's in her bare feet, needing to be somewhere where it would be okay to feel, to grieve, to acknowledge she could never pretend it hadn't happened.

That was the night she had spoken out loud the name of the little baby who had not survived.

Caleb.

Lucy was careful to strip her voice of all emotion when she answered.

"It's a house for young girls who are pregnant," she said. "It's still very much in the planning stages."

"One thing about Mama," he said wryly. "There's never any shortage of causes in her world."

To him it was just a cause. One of many. She took a deep breath. Was it possible he had changed as much as she had?

"Mac," she said, "tell me about you."

Part of her begged for him to see it for what it was, an invitation to go deeper.

Maybe it was different this time. If it was, would she tell him about Caleb?

"Remember I built that cedar-strip canoe?"

She nodded.

"My first sales were all those kind of canoes. It was

hard to make money at it, because they were so labor-intensive, but I loved doing it. I started getting more orders than I could keep up with, so I went into production. Pretty soon, I was experimenting with kayaks, too. Two things set me apart from others. Custom paint that no one had ever seen before—canoes were always green or red or yellow, some solid, nature-inspired palette, and I started doing crazy patterns on them. It appealed to a certain market."

As much as she genuinely enjoyed hearing about the building of his business, it hardly struck her as intimate.

"The other thing was, when you bought a canoe from me, you became part of a community. I kept in touch with people, put them in touch with other people who had purchased stuff from me. Eventually, it got big enough I had to do a newsletter and a website, a social-media page and all that stuff. I didn't realize I was setting something in place that was going to be marketing gold."

Was there something a little sad about him regarding the building of relationships as marketing gold?

"They didn't just buy a canoe. They belonged to something. They were part of Wild Side. Everybody wants to belong somewhere."

"It's kind of ironic," Lucy said. "Because you seemed like you didn't have that thing about belonging." *Even to me.*

"I guess I never found anything in Lindstrom Beach I wanted to belong to."

She looked swiftly out the window.

"I didn't mean that the way it sounded."

"No, it's okay," she said stiffly. "It was just a little

summer fling. I'm sure you moved on to bigger and better things. I mean, that's obvious."

"It's true I've become a successful businessman. And it's true I seem to have found my niche in life. But I've never been good at the relationship thing, Lucy. I have not improved with time. People want something I can't give them."

Was it a warning or a plea? She turned back and looked at him.

"And what is that?" she asked.

"They want to connect on a deep and meaningful level," he said, and there was that grin, devil-may-care and dashing. "And I just want to have fun."

She was not sucked in by the smile. "That sounds very lonely to me."

He raised an eyebrow. "I'm looking for someone to rescue me," he said, rather seductively, teasing.

Lucy turned back to the window and studied the panoramic views, water, earth and sky. He had always been like this. As soon as it started to go a little too deep, he turned up the wattage of that smile, kidded it away.

"Aren't you going to try and rescue me, Lucy Lin?" he prodded her.

"No," she said, and then looked back at him. "I'm going to get you a cat."

"I killed my last three houseplants."

"Wow. That takes commitment phobia to a new level. You can't even care about a plant?"

"Just saying. The cat probably isn't your best idea ever."

She sighed. "Probably not." Then she realized they

were in an airplane. It wasn't as if he could jump out. She could probe his inner secrets if she wanted to.

"You always seemed kind of set apart from everyone else. It seemed like a choice, almost as if you saw through all those superficial people and scorned them."

"I don't know if *scorn* is the right word," he said. "I've always liked being by myself. I'll still choose a tent in the woods beside a lake with not another soul around over just about anything else."

"It sounds to me like someone hurt you."

His face was suddenly remote.

"It sounds to me as if you don't trust anyone but yourself."

He didn't even glance at her, suddenly intently focused on the operation of the plane, and the instrument panel.

"I'm sure my father didn't help any. I'm sorry about the way Lindstrom Beach treated you. And especially my father. When you told me how he threatened you, said he was going to set you up as a thief, I was stunned. I was more stunned that you let it work. That you let him drive you away. I always figured you for the kind of guy who would stick around and fight for what you wanted."

"And I figured you would say something to your old man in my defense, but you never did, did you?"

All these years that she had nursed her resentment against Mac, and it had never once occurred to her that she had hurt him.

"That summer," he continued quietly, "I'd never felt like that with another person. So close. So connected. Not alone."

Lucy felt as if she couldn't breathe. It was the most Mac had ever said about how he was feeling.

"And the fact it was you, the rich girl, the doctor's daughter, loving *me*. Only, it was like you weren't the rich girl, the doctor's daughter. You stepped away from that role. You were so real, so authentic. And so was I around you. Myself. Whatever that was."

"Why didn't you at least ask me to go with you, Mac?"

"When you didn't take a stand with your dad, I guess I already knew what you would tell me later. That in the end, you would never fall for a boy like me. It would be too big a stretch for you. And unfair even to ask it."

But she was surprised by the pain, ever so briefly naked in his face. He had trusted her, and she had let him down. She could see his trust had been a most precious gift.

Lucy tried to explain. "It was only when it was obvious you were going, and you weren't going to ask me to go, that it was not even an option you had considered, that I said that. *I could never fall for a boy like you."*

He glanced at her, searching. "It cut me to the quick, Lucy. It made me so aware of everything that was different about us when I had been living and breathing everything that was the same. I guess before you said that, I thought we'd keep in touch. That I'd phone and write. And maybe come back to visit."

Now was the time to tell him that she hadn't meant it as in he wasn't worthy of her. She had meant it as in he was too closed, he couldn't be vulnerable with her.

"Mac, I'm so sorry."

But he suddenly looked uneasy, as if he had already

revealed more about himself than he wanted to, been as vulnerable as he cared to get. Some things didn't change, and she did not feel she could repair that hurt caused all those years ago by trying to clarify it now.

He must have felt the same way.

"It's all a long time ago," he said with an uncomfortable shrug. "Look where it led me. Hey, and look where we are. We're almost there. Look out your window. We'll be passing right over the Pacific Ocean in two minutes, and then making our approach to the Vancouver Flight Centre at Coal Harbour."

His face was absolutely closed. If she pursued this any farther, she was pretty sure if he had a parachute tucked behind his seat he was going to strap it on and jump.

They still had the trip home! And maybe he needed a rescuer, even as he kidded about it. She didn't know how long he was going to stick around, but she had him for today.

Maybe, just for today, neither of them needed to be lonely.

"It's only been two hours! It takes four or five times that long to drive here from Lindstrom Beach!"

"I know. It's great, isn't it?"

"It is," she said, and suddenly felt a new willingness to let go, to embrace whatever surprises the day held for her, to embrace the fact that for some reason fate had thrown her back together with the man who had left her pregnant all those years ago. Who had hurt her.

And whom she had hurt, too. Were they being given a second chance? Could they just take it and embrace it without completely rehashing the past? Lucy found herself hoping.

"Are we landing?" Mama demanded from the back.

"Yes."

She put her puzzle book away and fished through her bag. She drew out her rosary beads.

"Hail Mary..."

Whether it was Mama's prayers or his expertise, or some combination of both they landed without incident and docked at one of the eighteen float-plane spaces at the dock.

A chauffeur-driven limousine was waiting for them, and it whisked them by the Vancouver Convention Centre to the amazing Pacific Centre Mall.

He pressed them into a very posh-looking store. The salesclerks in those kind of stores always recognized power and money, even when it came dressed as casually as Mac was.

"My two favorite ladies need to see your very best in evening wear," he said.

The clerk took it as a mission. Lucy and Mama were whisked back to private dressing rooms. Mac was settled in a leather chair and brought a coffee.

"Would you like something to read? I have a selection of newspapers."

He shook his head, but after Mama and Lucy had modeled the saleslady's first few selections, he wandered off. Lucy assumed he was restless, and didn't blame him.

Lucy had grown up with privilege, but even so, it had been Lindstrom Beach. She had never worn designer labels like these. She and Mama were in awe of how good clothes fitted, the fabric, the drape of them. Of course, even if she weren't on an austerity program, she would never be able to afford dresses like these. Even so, it was so much fun to try them on.

Mac came back, a dress over each arm. "The black for Mama, the red for you."

"Red," she said, and wrinkled her nose. "You know I'm not flashy, so you must be afraid of losing me in the parking lot. Do you have any idea what dresses like these cost?"

"The saleslady asked for my gold card before she'd even take those down for me."

"I shouldn't even try it on," she said, but heard the wistfulness in her own voice.

"You're trying it on."

"What can I say? You know I love it when you're masterful."

And so she did. She wasn't going to buy this dress, and she certainly wasn't going to allow him to buy it for her, but why not just give herself over to the experience?

Mama went first. Lucy and Mac had "oohed" and "aahed" over the selection of designer dresses that had been brought out for Mama so far, but the one he had chosen was the best. Simple, black, silk: it was classic. Lucy and Mac applauded as Mama modeled, as if she had been on the runway all her life. She sauntered down the walkway between the change rooms, hand on her ample hip, turned, winked, flipped the matching scarf over her shoulder.

The salesclerk, Mac and Lucy applauded. Mama beamed. "This is it."

It was Lucy's turn. The clerk came into the fitting

room with her to help slide the yards of red silk over her head.

Even before she looked in the mirror, Lucy could tell by the way she felt that this dress was the kind of dress a woman dreamed of.

The clerk stared at her. "That man has taste," she said.

Lucy turned and looked in the mirror. The dress had slender shoulder straps and a neckline that was a sensual V without being plunging. It had an empire waistline, tight under her breasts, and then it floated in a million pleats to the floor.

She came out of the dressing room.

"Walk like a queen," the clerk said.

That's what Mac had said, too, when he had forced her to go to the yacht club. *Walk like a queen.* In a dress like this it was easy enough to do.

When Mac saw her, his reaction was everything she could ever hope for.

She had never seen him look anything but in control, but suddenly he looked flustered.

"You," he said hoarsely, "are not a queen. Lucy Lin, you are a goddess."

She could not resist walking with swaying hips, spinning in a swirl of rich color, tossing a look over her shoulder. She licked her lips and winked.

She was trying to add a bit of levity, but Mac, for once, did not seem to find it funny.

After she had taken off the dress, Lucy came out of the dressing room, feeling oddly out of sorts. What woman tried on a dress like that and then felt okay when she walked away from it?

She went and waited outside the store while Mac bought Mama the black dress to wear at the gala.

Mama was hugging her package to her and chastising him in a mix of German and English about spending too much money on her. But they could both tell she was utterly thrilled.

They went for a fabulous lunch at a waterfront restaurant, and then, almost as if the whole thing had been a dream, they were back in the plane.

They were home before supper.

He helped her get down from the plane, then they watched Mama waddle happily across the yard with all her bags.

“Thank you for a beautiful day, Mac. It was like something out of a dream. Honestly.”

He finished mooring the plane. He turned back to her.

“Okay,” he said. “That’s it. The whole show. I’ve shown you everything I do for fun. And you still haven’t shown me. You said there was something.”

“Oh.” She felt doubtful. And then she decided to be brave. What if, by showing him, she eased that loneliness that he wore like a shield? Even for a few more hours?

“Let me make some phone calls. I’ll call you in the morning.”

“Phone calls to arrange fun,” he said. “Skydiving? Horseback riding? I’ve got it! Bungee jumping!”

“I’m afraid I’m going to be a big disappointment to you, Mac.”

Or maybe to herself. Because once again, even though he had given nothing, she had made a decision to be vulnerable. She would show him that thing she did that made her feel so alive.

And he most likely wouldn't understand that there were ways a person could not feel lonely.

And how could that be anything but a good thing if he didn't understand how connected this one thing made her feel? She could have her world back the way it had been before he landed again.

Only, she had a feeling it was not going to be quite that simple.

Mac picked up the phone on the first ring in the morning.

"Are you ready for your big outing, Mr. Hudson?" Lucy asked. "Be ready in ten minutes."

"Should I be dressing for bungee jumping or horseback riding?"

"Actually, whatever you wear normally will be okay."

That could be anything from a wet suit to a suit suit, so Mac just put on some khakis and a sports shirt with the little kayak emblem on it.

He tried to take a clue from what Lucy was wearing and came to the conclusion it would be nothing too exciting. She might have been dressed for a day clerking at the bookstore. She was not the goddess he had seen in that dress yesterday.

And wasn't that a mercy?

Still, as they got in the car, he was so aware of her. Aware he liked being with her.

"We're going to Glen Oak."

They picked up coffees and conversation flowed freely between them. They talked of Mama and house repairs, the swiftly approaching gala and last-minute details, he made her laugh by doing an impression of Claudia receiving her free tickets to the gala, which he had delivered personally.

Having spent years in Lindstrom Beach, Mac was familiar with Glen Oak. Sixty miles from Lindstrom Beach, Glen Oak was the major city that serviced all the smaller towns around it. All the large chain stores had outlets there, there was an airport, hotels, golf courses and the regional hospital.

"Golfing," he guessed. "I have to warn you, I'm not much of a golfer. Too slow for me."

"That's okay, we're not golfing."

"Not even mini?" he said a little sadly as they passed a miniature golf course. He was aware he would like to go miniature golfing with her.

And horseback riding, for that matter. He wondered what it would take to talk her into bungee jumping.

He frowned as Lucy pulled into the hospital parking lot.

"We're going to a hospital for fun?" Mac asked. "Oh, boy, Lucy, you are in worse shape than I thought."

"I tried to warn you."

Perplexed, he followed her through the main doors. She did not stop at the main desk, but the receptionist gave her a wave, as if she knew her.

What if she was sick? What if that's what she was trying to tell him? Mac felt a wave of fear engulf him, but it passed as she pushed through doors clearly marked Neonatal.

She went to an office and a middle-aged woman

smiled when she saw her and came out from behind her desk and gave her a heartfelt hug.

"My very favorite cuddler!" she said.

Cuddler?

"This is Macintyre Hudson, the man I spoke to you about this morning. Mac, Janice Sandpace."

"Nice to meet you, Mr. Hudson. Come this way."

And then they were in a small anteroom. Through a window he could see what he assumed were incubators with babies in them.

"These babies," Janice explained, "are premature. Or critically ill. Occasionally we get what is known as a crack baby. We instigated a cuddling program several years ago because studies have shown if a baby has physical contact it will develop better, grow better, heal better, and have a shorter hospital stay. It also relieves stress on parents to know that even if they can't be here 24/7, and many can't because they have other children at home or work obligations, their baby is still being loved."

Lucy had already donned a gown with bright ducks all over it, and she turned for Janice to do up the back for her.

"You'll have to gown up, Mr. Macintyre."

He chose a gown from the rack. It had giraffes and lions on it. Lucy was already donning a mask and covering her hair.

Her eyes twinkled at him from above the mask.

He followed suit, as did Janice. She showed him how to give his hands a surgical scrub.

"Today we have multiples," Janice told him from behind her mask. "Twins. Preemies."

She gestured to a rocking chair. Lucy was already settled in one.

Side by side in their rocking chairs.

And then Janice brought Lucy the tiniest little bundle of life he had ever seen. Tightly swaddled in a pink blanket, the baby was placed in Lucy's arms. It stared up at her with curious, unblinking eyes.

"Amber," Janice said, smiling.

In seconds, Lucy was lost in that world. It was just the baby and her. She crooned to it. She whispered in its tiny little ear. She rocked.

This was what she did for fun.

Only, the look on her face said it wasn't just fun.

What Lucy did had gone way beyond fun. Her eyes on that baby had a light in them that was the most joyous thing he had ever seen.

Suddenly fun seemed superficial.

Lucy glanced at him. Even though she had a mask on, he could tell she was smiling. More than smiling—she was radiant.

"This is Sam," Janice said.

He looked up at her. His panic must have been evident.

"Don't worry," she said. "I'll walk you through it. Support his neck. See how Lucy is holding the baby?"

And then Mac found a baby in his arms. It looked up at him, eyes like buttons in the tiniest wrinkled face he had ever seen.

"Talk to him," Janice suggested.

"ET, call home," he said softly. If he was not mistaken, the baby sighed. "I was just kidding. You look more like Yoda. A very handsome Yoda."

He looked over at Lucy, crooning away as if she'd been born to this.

He didn't know what to say.

And then he did.

He sang softly.

It felt as if they had been there for only seconds when Janice came back in and took the now sleeping baby from him. "Thank you," she said.

"No, thank you."

And he meant it.

They were quieter on the way home. When she drove by the mini-golf course, he didn't feel like playing anymore.

Seeing her with that baby, he had known. He had known what he had wanted his whole life and had been so afraid of never being able to have that he had pretended he didn't want it at all.

She drove into her driveway. "I have so much to get done for the gala!"

But he wasn't letting her go that easily. "Is that a charitable organization, the baby thing?" he asked Lucy.

"Yes. It's called Cuddle-Hugs."

"Why aren't we doing Mama's fund-raiser in support of that?"

"Of course they need money to operate, but that's not what Mama chose."

"I'll talk to Corporate this afternoon. I'll have them call Janice. Anything they want. Anything. They'll get it."

"That's not why I took you there, to solicit a donation."

"I know. And we didn't go to Vancouver to buy you a dress, but I bought it for you anyway."

"You bought me that dress?" she gasped.

"So, what do you think now, Lucy Lin? Could you fall for a boy like me now?"

CHAPTER NINE

IT WAS ALL wrong. It was not what he had wanted to say at all.

Mac could have kicked himself. He didn't know where the question had come from. It certainly hadn't been on his agenda to ask something like that. That certainly hadn't been the reason for his donation, the reason for the fly-in shopping trip yesterday. He hadn't done it to impress her.

It was all just a gift to her. He had found his better side after all.

But now somehow he'd gone and spoiled it all by bringing up the past. Over the past few days Mac had convinced himself that they had pretty much put the past behind them.

But really, wasn't it was always there, the past? Wasn't that why he'd made her go to the yacht club and stand up for herself? Wasn't it true that he could not look at her without seeing her younger self, without remembering the joy of her trust in him, the way she had felt in his arms, the way her heated kisses had felt scattering across his face?

She took a startled step back from him. "Oh, Mac,"

she said, "when I said that all those years ago, it was never about what you had or didn't have."

He gave her his most charming smile. "It wasn't? You could have fooled me."

"I guess I did fool you. Because I didn't want you to know how deeply it hurt me that you never, ever told me a single thing about you. Not one single thing about you that mattered. And then when you left, you didn't even ask me to go with you. It seems nothing has changed. Even these gifts, so wonderful and grand, are like a guard you put up. That smile you are smiling right now? That's the biggest defense of all."

"You want to know why I never asked you to go with me, Lucy? It wasn't because I wasn't willing to fight for you. It was because you loved this place more than me. It was because I could see your family being torn up and your friends looking at you sideways as if you'd lost your mind. I gave you your life back. The part I don't get is that you didn't take it back. At all."

"No," she said, quietly, "I didn't."

"Why?"

"This isn't how it works, Mac, with you keeping everything to yourself, while I spill my guts."

"You know what? I've had about as much of Lindstrom Beach as I can handle. I wish I had never come back here."

"I wish you hadn't, either!"

He watched, stunned, as she walked away, went into her house and closed the door behind her.

With a kind of soft finality.

"Mama," he said a few minutes later, "something's

come up. I have to go back to Toronto. I bought that dress for Lucy. Will you give it to her?"

"Give it to her yourself," Mama said, and went up the stairs. He heard her bedroom door slam.

Both the women he loved were mad at him.

Wait a minute! He loved Lucy? Then he was getting out of here just in the nick of time....

Lucy listened to Mac's plane take off.

"I don't care if he's gone," she told her cat. "I don't. I always knew he wasn't staying."

She had a gala to finish organizing. She had her dream of Caleb's House to hold tight to.

She burst into tears.

When the phone rang, she rushed to it. Maybe it was him. Could he phone her from the plane? Was he telling her he was turning around?

"Hello from Africa, Lucy!"

Her mother was brimming with excitement. She'd seen an elephant that day. She'd seen a lion. Somehow, Lucy didn't remember her mother like this.

"Anyway," her mother said, "I know you'll be busy on Mother's Day, so I thought I'd phone today. I didn't want you having to track me down adding an extra stress to your day."

That was unusually thoughtful for her mother. It made Lucy feel brave.

"Mom," she said, "do you mind if I paint the house purple? I mean, it's not purple, exactly, a kind of lavender."

It was kind of a segue to *Do you mind if I turn our old family home into a house for unwed mothers?*

"Lucy! I don't care what color you paint the house. It's your house!"

"Mom, did you give me this house because you felt sorry for me? Because you thought I'd never get my life together without help from you?"

"No, Lucy, not at all. I gave you that house because I hated it."

"What?"

"It was the perfect house, I was the perfect doctor's wife and you were the perfect doctor's daughter."

"Until I ruined everything," Lucy said.

"It's only in the last while that I've seen how untrue that is, Lucy. When you got pregnant, it blew a hole in the facade. When you miscarried, I thought we could patch up the hole. That everything would be the same. That you would be the same.

"But you didn't come back. You didn't want what you had always wanted anymore. I think, at first, we were all angry with you for not coming back to your old life. Me, certainly. Your friend Claudia, too.

"Now I can see how we were really all prisoners in that house. Trying to live up to your father's expectations of us. Which was a nearly impossible undertaking. Everything always had to look so good. But keeping it that way took so much energy—without my even knowing it, had sucked the life force out of me.

"That hole you blew in all our lives? I glimpsed freedom out that hole. If your dad hadn't died, I would have left him."

Lucy was stunned.

"Lucy, paint the house purple. Swim naked in the moonlight. Dream big and love hard. I'm glad you didn't marry James. He was like your father—in every way, if you get my drift. He was cold and withholding and a control freak. And he was a philanderer."

"Mom? Mac came back." Somehow this was the talk she had always dreamed of having with her mother.

"And?"

"I love him!" she wailed. "And he left again!"

"Sweetie, I can't be there. If I was I would take you on my lap and hold you and comb your hair with my fingers until you had no tears left. That's what I wish I had done all those years ago. The night the baby died."

A baby. Not a fetus. "Thanks, Mom."

"Life has a way of working out the way it's supposed to, Lucy. I am living proof of that. I love you."

"You, too, Mom. I'll be thinking of you on Mother's Day."

"Now, go eat two dishes of chocolate ice cream. Then go and skinny-dip in the lake!"

Lucy was laughing as she hung up the phone. Her mother was right. Everything would work out the way it was supposed to.

Mac was gone.

But she still had Mama, and the gala, and the babies to cuddle. Sometime, somewhere, she had become a woman who would paint her house purple, and who had a dream that was bigger than she was.

And he was part of that. Loving him was part of that.

He hadn't ruined her life. Her mother had made her so aware of that. He had given her a gift. He had broken her out of the life she might have had. He had made her see things differently and want things she had not wanted before.

That's what love did. It made people better. Even if it hurt, it was worth the pain.

Lucy was going to cry. And eat the ice cream. She'd skip the dip in the lake. She was going to feel every bit of the glorious pain.

Because it meant she had loved. And her mother was right. Love, in the end, could only make you better. Not worse.

Mac was aware he was cutting things very close to the wire. He'd gone back to Toronto. His life had seemed empty and lonely, and no amount of adrenaline had been able to take the edge off his pain.

He loved her. He loved Lucy. He always had.

He had to give that a chance. He had to. And if it required more of him, then he had to dig deep and find that.

He was aware he was cutting things close. He arrived back in Lindstrom Beach the night before the gala.

He had never felt fear the way he felt it when he crossed back over those lawns and knocked on Lucy's door.

"Can I come in?"

When she saw it was him, Lucy looked scared to open that door. And he didn't blame her. But hope won out. She stood back from the door.

"You're in your housecoat," he said.

"It *is* nighttime." She scanned his face. "Come sit down, Mac."

The room was beautiful at night. She had a small fire burning in the hearth, and it cast its golden light across fresh tulips in a vase, a cat curled up on the rug in front of it, a book open on its spine on the arm of the chair. What would it be like to have a life like this?

Not a life of adrenaline rush after adrenaline rush, but one of quiet contentment?

A life of Lucy sharing evenings with him?

He couldn't think about that. Not until she knew the full truth. He sat on the couch, she took the chair across from him, tucked those delectable little toes up under her folded legs.

"Lucy, if you care to listen, I'm going to tell you some things I've never told anyone. Not even Mama."

Why was he doing this?

But he knew why. He could see it all starting again. She loved him. She wanted more from him. She always had.

She was leaning toward him, and he could see the hope shining in her face.

He considered himself the most fearless of men. No raging chute of white water ever put fear into his heart, only anticipation.

But wasn't this what he had always feared? Being vulnerable? Opening up to another? Tackling a foaming torrent of raging water was nothing in comparison to opening your heart. Nothing in comparison to letting someone see all of you.

But once she knew all his secrets would she still love him? Could she? Now seemed like the time to find out.

Mac took a deep breath. It was time. It was time to let it all go. It was time to tell someone. It involved the scariest thing of all. It involved trust. Trusting her.

He hesitated, looking for a place to start. There was only one starting point.

"When I was five, my mom left my dad and me. I remember it clearly. She said, I'm looking for something. I'm looking for something *more.*

"As an adult, I can understand that. We didn't have much. My dad was a laborer on a construction crew in a small town, not so different from Lindstrom Beach. He didn't make a pile of money, and we lived pretty humbly in a tiny house. As I got older I realized it was different from my friends' houses. No dishwasher, no computer, no fancy stereo, no big-screen TV. We heated with a wood heater, the furniture was falling apart and we didn't even have curtains on the windows.

"To tell you the truth, I don't know if he couldn't afford that stuff, or if it just wasn't a priority for him. My dad loved the outdoors. Since I could walk, I was trailing him through the woods. In retrospect, I think he thought of *that* as home. Being outside with his rifle or his fishing rod or a bucket for picking berries. And me.

"Mom left in search of something *more,* and I don't remember being traumatized by it or anything. My dad managed pretty well for a guy on his own. He got me registered for school, he kept me clean, he cooked simple meals. When I was old enough, he taught me how to help out around the place. We were a team.

"My mom called and wrote, and showed up at Christmas. She always had lots of presents and stories about her travels and adventures. She was big on saying 'I love you.' But even that young, I could tell she *hated* how my dad lived, and maybe even hated him for being content with so little.

"When she left, there was always a big screaming match about his lack of ambition and her lack of responsibility. I was overjoyed when she came, and guiltily glad when she left.

"Then she found her something *more.* Literally. She found a very, very rich man. I was eight at the time, and she came and got me and took me to Toronto for a visit with her and the new man. Walden, her husband, had a mansion in an area called the Bridle Path, also called Millionaire's Row. They had a swimming pool. She bought me a bike. There was a computer in every room. And a theater room.

"That first time I went for a visit with them, I couldn't wait to get home. But what I didn't know was that the visit there was the opening shot in a campaign.

"My mom started phoning me all the time. Every night. Why didn't I come live with them? They could give me so much *more.*

"I love you. I love you. I love you.

"What I didn't really get was how she had started undermining my dad, how she was working at convincing me only her kind of love was good. She would ask questions about him and me and how we lived, and then find flaws. She'd say, in this gentle, concerned tone, '*Little boys should not have to cook dinner.*' Or do laundry. Or cut wood. Or she'd say, mildly shocked, '*He did what? Oh, Macintyre, if he really cared about you, you would have gotten that new computer you wanted. Didn't you say he got a new rifle?*'

"In one particularly memorable incident, I told her my dad wouldn't let me play hockey because he couldn't afford it.

"She expressed her normal shock and dismay over his priorities, and then told me she would pay for hockey. I was over the moon, and I ran and told my dad as soon as I hung up the phone.

"I can play hockey this year. My mom's going to pay for it!"

"You know, I'd hardly ever seen my dad really, really mad, but he just lost it. Throwing things around and breaking them. Screaming, 'She's never paid a dentist's bill or for school supplies, but she's going to pay for hockey? She's never coughed up a dime when you need new sneakers or a present to bring to a birthday party, but she's going to pay for hockey? What part of hockey? The fee to join the team? The equipment? The traveling? The time I have to take off work?' And then the steam just went out of him, and he sat down and put his head in his hands and said, 'Forget it. You are not playing hockey.'

"This went on for a couple of years. Her planting the seeds of discontent, literally being the Disneyland Mama while my dad was slugging it out in the trenches.

"When I was twelve, I went and spent the summer with her and Walden. I made some friends in her neighborhood. I had money in my Calvin Klein jeans. I was swimming in my own pool. She bought me a puppy. She didn't have rules like my dad did. It was kind of anything goes. She actually let me have wine with dinner, and the odd beer.

"And when summer was over, she sat down on the side of my bed and wept. She loved me so much, she couldn't bear for me to go back to *that* man. She told me I didn't have to go back. She said I didn't have to think about my dad or his feelings. I should have seen the irony in that—that my dad's feelings counted for nothing, but hers were everything, but I didn't.

"I was twelve, nearly thirteen. At home, my dad made me work. By then, I was in charge of keeping our house supplied with firewood. I did a lot of the cooking. Sometimes he took me to work with him and handed me a shovel. I was allowed to go out with my friends only if I'd met all my obligations at home.

"And here she was offering me a life of frolic. And ease. I saw all the *stuff* I could ever want. I could be one of the rich, privileged kids at school instead of Digger Dan's son.

"I phoned my dad and told him I was staying. I could hear his heart breaking in the silence that followed. But she had convinced me that didn't matter. Only *I* mattered.

"And that's what I acted like for the next few months. Like only I mattered. She encouraged that. When my dad called, sometimes I blew him off. I was supposed to spend Christmas with him, but I didn't want to miss my best friend's New Year's Eve party, so I begged off going to be with him."

Mac took a deep shuddering breath. "Do you remember, a long time ago, I told you I killed a man?"

"With your bare hands," she whispered.

"Not with my bare hands. With my self-centeredness. With my callousness. With my utter insensitivity.

"He died. My dad died on Christmas Day."

"Oh, Mac," she whispered.

"At home, all by himself. He managed to call for help, but by the time they got there he was gone. They said it was a massive heart attack, but I knew it wasn't. I knew I'd killed him."

"Oh, Mac."

"Killed that man who had been nothing but good to me. He might not have been big on words. I don't think I heard him say 'I love you' more than twice in my whole life. But he was the one who had been there when no one else was, who had stepped up to the plate, who had done his best to provide, who had taught me the value of hard work and honesty. I had traded everything he taught me for a superficial world, and I hated myself for it.

"And her. My mother. I hated her. When she told me she didn't see the point in me going to the funeral, that was the last straw. I ran away and went back. To his funeral, to sort through our stuff.

"I never lived with her again. I couldn't. When they tried to make me go back to her, I ran away. That's how I ended up in foster care.

"I haven't spoken to her in fourteen years. I doubt I ever will again. I can see right through her clothes and her makeup, her perfect hair and her perfect house. She plays roles. For a while I was the role and she could play at being the fun-loving, cool mom, because it filled something in her. It relieved her of any guilt she felt about leaving me when I was little.

"But underneath that veneer she was mean-spirited and manipulative, and basically the most selfish and self-centered person ever born. She was using me to meet her needs, and I was done with her.

"I went through a series of foster homes, crazy with grief and guilt. And then I came here. To Mama Freda.

"And Mama saw the broken place in me, and didn't even try to fix it. She just loved me through it.

"I owe Mama my life."

The silence was so long. There, Lucy had it all. She knew the truth about him. He was the man who had killed his own father.

"When you told me, all those years ago, that you had killed a man, I thought you were blowing me off," Lucy whispered.

When had she moved beside him? When had her hand come to rest on his knee?

"I started to tell you. Back then. I saw the look on your face and retreated to the default defense. I always told people that when I was trying to drive them away, protect myself. I added the part about *with my bare hands* because it seemed particularly effective."

"You feel as if you killed your father," she said, looking at him. The firelight reflected off her face. In her eyes he saw the same radiance he had seen when she held the baby.

It hadn't been pity for the baby. And it wasn't pity for him.

It was love. It was the purest love he'd ever seen.

"I did kill my father," he whispered, daring her to love him anyway.

"No," she said, firmly, with almost fierce resolve. "You didn't."

Three words. So simple. *No. You. Didn't.*

Her hand came to his face, and her eyes were so intent on his.

It felt like absolution. It felt as if, by finally naming

it out loud, the monster that had lived in the closet was forced to disappear when exposed to light.

He'd been a teenage boy who did what teenage boys do, so naturally. He had been selfish and thoughtless and greedy. He'd thought only of himself.

It didn't have to be who he was today. It wasn't who he was today.

"You're terrified of love," she said.

"Terrified," he whispered, and knew he had never spoken a truer word.

And she didn't try to fix him. Or convince him. She laid her head on his chest, and wrapped her arms hard around him. He felt her tears warm, soaking through his shirt, onto the skin of his breast.

Her tenderness enveloped him.

And he knew another truth.

That she would see him through it.

Mama's love had carried him so far. Now it was time to go the distance. If he was strong enough to let her. If he was strong enough to say yes to something he had said no to for the past fourteen years.

Love.

He suddenly felt so tired. So very tired. And with her arms wrapped around him, with his head on her breast, he slept, finally, the sleep of a man who did not have to go to his dreams to do battle with his guilt.

When he awoke in the morning, she was gone. The coffee was on, and there was a note.

"Sorry, three zillion things to do. The gala is tonight!"

He went back over to Mama's. Overnight the population there had exploded. Her many foster children wandered in and out, many of them with children of their own. There were tents on the lawn and inflatable mattresses on the floor.

"You stayed with Lucy?" Mama asked, in a happy frenzy of cooking.

"Not in the way you think. Mama, come outside with me for a minute." He found a spot under the trees, and took a deep breath. "Lucy asked some of your foster children to speak at the gala tonight. She chose a few. I was one of them and I've said no. But I think, with your permission, I'll change my mind. But only if you'll allow me to share that story you told me all those years ago."

"*Ach.* For what purpose, *schatz?*"

"For the same purpose you told it to me. To let everyone know that in the end, if you hold tight, love wins."

Her eyes searched his. She nodded.

The gala was sold out. He had seen Lucy flitting around in her red dress. He had told her he would speak.

But it seemed to him strange that with the big day here, the day that she had given her heart and soul to, she seemed wan.

"Are you not feeling well?" he asked her.

"Oh," she said. "No. I'm fine. I thought my doing this…" Her voice faltered. "Mother's Day is hard on me."

"Why? Because your own mother is so far away?"

"I'm just being silly," she said. "Sorry. I think I'm a little overwhelmed."

"Everything looks incredible. The silent auction is racking up bids."

She smiled, but it still seemed wan, disconnected.

He had the awful thought it might be because of what he had shared with her last night.

"I think the custom-painted Wild Ride kayak is going to be the high earner of the night."

"It will be. I keep pushing up the bid on it."

He expected her to laugh. She ran a hand through her hair, looked distracted.

"Oh," she said brightening slightly. "He's here."

"Who?"

"I couldn't find a comedian on such short notice. I found something Mama will like even better. An Engelbert impersonator."

He waited for her to smile. But she didn't. She looked as if she was going to cry.

"Later," she said, and walked away.

After dinner, some of Mama's foster children spoke. Ross Chillington talked about his parents being killed in an accident and about coming to Mama's house, how she was the first one who ever applauded his skill in acting.

Michael Boylston told how Mama had given him the courage and confidence to take on the world of international finance and how now he lived a life beyond his wildest dreams in Thailand.

Reed Patterson told of a drug-addicted mother and a life of pain and despair before Mama had made him believe he could take on the world and win.

And then it was his turn. But he didn't talk about himself.

"A long time ago," he said, "in a world most of us in this room had not yet been born into, there was a terrible war." And then he told Mama's story.

When he finished, the room was as silent as it had been that day fourteen years ago when he had first heard this story.

Into the silence he laid his next words with tenderness, with care.

"Mama spent the rest of her life finding that soldier. She found him over and over again. She found him in every lost boy she took into her home. She found him and she saved him. She saved him before the great evil had a chance to overcome him.

"I am one of those boys," he said quietly, proudly. "I am one of the boys who benefited from Mama's absolute belief in redemption, in second chances.

"I am one of those boys who was saved by love. Who was redeemed by it. And as a result, finally, was able to love back.

"Mama." He looked right at her. "I love you."

The words felt so good. She was weeping. As was most of the audience. His eyes sought Lucy. It wasn't hard to find her in her bright red dress. She had her face buried in her hands, crying.

Mac realized right then that he had a new mission in life. He had not killed his father. But it was possible that he had contributed to his death.

He could not change that. But he could try to redeem himself. He could spend the rest of his life on that. Make up for every wrong he had ever done by loving Lucy. And their children. By believing all that love was a light, and when it grew big enough it would envelop the darkness. Obliterate it.

Lucy still didn't look right. She was in her element,

surrounded by people. She had just pulled off something incredible. But she was still crying.

And suddenly she spun around and went into the night.

He waited for her to come back, especially when the Engelbert impersonator geared up and the tables were cleared away for dancing.

Mama stood right in front of the stage. She took off her scarf and threw it at the man's feet.

He picked it up and wiped his sweaty brow, and tossed it back to Mama, who looked as if she was going to die of happiness. Michael Boylston came and asked her to dance. Mac watched and shook his head.

If Mama was unwell, there was no sign of that now. None.

It occurred to Mac that there was something of the miraculous in this evening.

Those foster kids who had grown into adults seemed to be the first to take to the floor, having embraced so much of Mama's enthusiasm and joy for life. They were asking others to dance with them, and, in some instances, were dancing with the people who had once snubbed them as the riffraff from Mama's house.

Claudia was trying to get Ross to sign a movie poster with him on it. Over in the corner, Billy was drinking too much and talking football with Reed Patterson.

Lucy had done what she always did best. She had brought people together.

It hit him out of nowhere.

Things on her dining-room table she didn't want him to see.

Rezoning that had the neighbors in an uproar.

Caleb's House: a home for unwed mothers.

Finding joy in holding little babies.

Mother's Day is hard on me.

It hit him out of nowhere: all her plans had been altered. Claudia feeling superior to her. Her friends not being her friends anymore. No college. Moving away from here. And coming back. Changed.

"Oh my God," he said out loud, and he headed for the door.

There was still, thankfully, a little light in the evening sky. If it had been darker, he might not have been able to see her.

But as it was, her red dress was like a beacon in the thick greenery above her house.

Mac went toward that beacon as if he was a sailor lost at sea. There was a trail, well-traveled along the side of her house, that led him to her.

She was in a small clearing above her house, sitting on a small stone bench. There was a little flower bed cut from the thick growth. In the center of that bed was a stone, hand-painted in the curly cursive handwriting of a girl.

Caleb.

He went and sat beside her on the bench. "There was a baby," he said, and it was a statement not a question. His mouth had the taste of dust in it.

"They said not to name him," she choked. "They said he wasn't even a baby yet. A fetus. They wouldn't let me bury him. He was disposed of as medical waste."

She was sobbing, and he felt a grief as deep as anything he had ever felt.

"He was mine, wasn't he?"

"Yes, Mac, he was yours."

So many questions, and all of them poured out, one on top of the other. "Why didn't you tell me? Were you planning on telling me? Would you have told me if he lived?"

"Mac, I was at the scared-out-of-my-mind stage. I knew Mama would know where you were. I'd decide to tell you. I'd even cross the lawn to Mama's house. And then I'd talk myself out of it. I felt that you would come back—not for love, but because I'd trapped you into it."

"I had a right to know."

"Yes," she said softly, ever so softly, "Yes, you did. And I think, eventually, I would have finished that million-mile journey across her lawn. But then the baby was gone, and the pain was so bad that the last person I was thinking of was you."

Mac was silent. He could feel that pain unfurling in him. *His baby. His and hers.* It made life as he had lived it so far seem unreal. How would he have been different if he had known?

"When were you going to tell me?" he finally asked.

"Soon," she whispered. "I hoped to get through Mother's Day. If you hadn't come back I was going to call you. I knew it was time. To trust you with it."

He looked at her, and knew it was true. And he knew something else. That he had to rise to the fragile trust she was handing him. This had been her secret, her intensely personal grief, but it was no longer. This pain would be an unbreakable bond between them.

Something that they, and they alone, would know the full depth of.

In this instant he sat beside her and felt her grief, and he felt his own. He felt a momentary hurt that he had been excluded from one of the biggest events of his own life.

And yet looking into her eyes, he felt his hurt dissolve and he was taken by the bravery he saw in her. Her hands were clutched around something, and he unfolded them from around it.

It was a small box.

"I bring it with me when I come here."

"May I look?" His voice sounded gruff, hoarse with unshed emotion.

Lucy nodded through her tears, her eyes on his face, begging him.

Inside was a tiny pair of sneakers. A blue onesie with a striped bear embossed on it. And an ultrasound picture.

Begging him to what? To love her anyway, when everyone else had stopped? That was a given.

He touched the little sneakers to his lips. He had not wept since his father died. But he wept now, on Mother's Day, for the baby who would have been his son.

And that's when he saw what she was really begging him for. Someone to share this love with him. The love she had carried alone for too long.

He vowed to himself she would not be alone with it anymore. Not ever.

He saw so clearly what was being given to them both. A chance at redemption. A chance to make good come from bad.

A chance for love to grow from this garden where there had been sorrow.

A long time later they sat in silence, their hands intertwined. The sounds from the party below them grew more boisterous.

The sounds of "I Can't Take My Eyes Off You" floated up through the air.

"You know we would have never made it if I'd asked you to come with me all those years ago."

"I know."

"But I think we could make it now."

She turned to him, her eyes wide with love and hope.

Mac felt now what he could never have felt back then, as a callow youth. The complexity of loving someone.

"I'm asking you to marry me, Lucy Lin, I'm half crazy all for the love of you."

"Yes," she whispered, and then stronger, "Yes."

"You know, Lucy," he said, softly, his voice still gruff with emotion, "it won't all be a bicycle built for two. There are going to be hurts. And misunderstandings. I have places in me that are so tender they will bruise if you try to touch them. It's going to be a lifelong exercise in building trust."

She leaned her head on his shoulder. "I know what I'm getting into."

He watched the moonlight in her eyes and saw that the light coming from them was radiant.

"I do believe you do, Lucy Lin."

Mac took Lucy in his arms, and her soft warmth melted into him and he thanked God for second chances.

EPILOGUE

MACINTYRE HUDSON SIGHED AS a rush of girlish laughter filled the air. Mother's Day was still a whole week away, but Caleb's House, next door to this one, was filled to capacity. There were two trucks with campers on them parked up on the road. No doubt Claudia would be by shortly to complain about that.

There was no official Mother's Day celebration at Caleb's House, but they always came back, those girls, turned into young women, who had stayed there.

They came back whether they had kept their babies or given them up for adoption.

They were drawn back there as if by a spell. Every year, at the same time, they came.

Some came with families—mothers and fathers they had reconciled with, or young husbands who had accepted their history and stepped up to the plate for their future. They came with new young babies and toddlers.

They joined whoever was in residence now, and pretty soon the giggling started and carried across the lawns of that beautiful lavender house to this one.

Mama's house was long since gone. He'd torn it down, and he and Lucy had built a new one. It had what was called a mother-in-law suite, but they moved back and forth between the two living spaces seamlessly. Mama particularly liked their kitchen with all its shiny stainless-steel appliances, even though she didn't make *apfelstrudel* very often anymore.

But it was still *her* house, and ever since the gala, so many of those children Mama had fostered came back on Mother's Day weekend. Came back to the place where they had learned the meaning of home.

Right now, this part of Lakeshore Drive looked like a carnival.

"Did you see this?" Lucy came up behind him.

The funeral-planning kit was out on the table, where they could not miss it.

"Do you know what it's about?" she asked, that cute little worry line puckering her forehead.

"She was staring out the window the other day, lamenting the fact she might not see our children before she dies."

"I guess we should tell her, hmm?" Lucy said.

"No! I don't want her thinking every time she produces that brochure we're going to have a baby for her. Aren't there enough of them next door?"

"Ach," Lucy said, imitating Mama, "a baby is always a blessing."

Those words were a motto, and hung on a smaller sign right below the one that read Caleb's House.

Lucy wrapped her arms around him from behind, nestled into him for a moment and sighed with utter contentment. Then she went to the fridge and took out a jar of Rolliepops.

She popped one in her mouth.

"Those things can't be good for the baby."

"Who are you kidding? You hate kissing me after I've had one. Can't help it. Cravings." She removed a large stainless-steel bowl of potato salad.

"Potluck at Caleb's tonight," Lucy said. "Between Mama's kids and my kids, I think there must be a hundred people out there. Have you seen my mom?"

"She went through here with Donald on her hip a while ago, muttering about diapers." Donald was the baby she had brought back from Africa.

Next year there would be one more added to this amazingly diverse, huge and loving family Mac found himself a part of.

"Are you coming?" Lucy asked. "They'll be starting in a few minutes."

"Give me a minute."

Funny how even after all this time, the sound of his son's name, the son whom had never been born and who he had never known, still squeezed at his heart.

Mac went back to the table. Beside the funeral-planning kit, Mama had set out a card.

He picked it up. On the front it said, "Happy Mother's Day." Inside was completely blank. He set it back down, then went and stood at the window and looked over the familiar sparkling waters of Sunshine Lake.

His own child would be coming into this world soon. It would require more of him.

Love required more of him. He had thought it would be a lifetime exercise to build trust, but he had never been so wrong.

He trusted Lucy implicitly. He trusted himself to be the man she and Mama believed he was. He trusted in life. Hadn't it become joyous and sweet beyond his wildest dreams?

Mac fished through the junk drawer until he found a pen, and then he went and sat down at the old kitchen table that they could never replace. It was the *apfelstrudel* table. He stared at the card for a long time, and then opened it.

How to start?

And so he started like this.

Dear Mom,

Not too much. A few lines. That she would be a grandmother soon. That she had not met his wife yet. That maybe they could get together the next time he was down east.

He signed it, licked the envelope, addressed it and put a stamp on. Maybe, just maybe, they would have a chance to redeem themselves.

Mama waddled in and went right to the fridge. "Where's the potato salad? My German one. Not like the stuff they call potato salad here."

"Lucy took it already."

"Are you coming, my galoot-head? Listen. They're singing grace."

All those voices raised in a joyous song of thanks. His Lucy would be at the very center of it, where she belonged.

"I'll be along in minute. I'm going to run up to the mailbox first."

Mama's eyes shot to the table, where the card had been.

Mac thought you could live for moments like this: a heart filled with love, the sound of gratitude drifting in the window and a smile like the one Mama gave him.

* * * * *

IT STARTED WITH A CRUSH. . .

BY
MELISSA McCLONE

With a degree in mechanical engineering from Stanford University, the last thing **Melissa McClone** ever thought she would be doing was writing romance novels. But analysing engines for a major US airline just couldn't compete with her 'happily-ever-afters'. When she isn't writing, caring for her three young children or doing laundry, Melissa loves to curl up on the couch with a cup of tea, her cats and a good book. She enjoys watching home decorating programmes to get ideas for her house—a 1939 cottage that is *slowly* being renovated. Melissa lives in Lake Oswego, Oregon, with her own real-life hero husband, two daughters, a son, two loveable but oh-so-spoiled indoor cats and a no-longer-stray outdoor kitty that decided to call the garage home.

Melissa loves to her from her readers. You can write to her at PO Box 63, Lake Oswego, OR 97034, USA, or contact her via her website: www.melissamcclone.com.

For all the people who generously volunteer their time to coach kids—especially those who have made such a difference in my children's lives. Thank you!

Special thanks to: Josh Cameron, Brian Verrinder, Ian Burgess, Bernice Conrad and Terri Reed.

CHAPTER ONE

EVERY day for the past four weeks, Connor's school bus had arrived at the corner across the street no later than three-thirty. Every day, except today. Lucy Martin glanced at the clock hanging on the living-room wall.

3:47 p.m.

Anxiety knotted her stomach making her feel jittery. Her nephew should be home by now.

Was it time to call the school to find out where the bus might be or was she overreacting? This parenting—okay, surrogate parenting—thing was too new to know for certain.

She stared out the window, hoping the bus would appear. The street corner remained empty. That wasn't surprising. Only residents drove through this neighborhood on the outskirts of town.

What to do? She tapped her foot.

Most contingencies and emergencies had been listed in the three-ring binder Lucy called the survival guide. Her sister-in-law, Dana, had put it together before she left. But a late school bus hadn't been one of the scenarios. Lucy had checked. Twice.

No need to panic. Wicksburg was surrounded by farmland, a small town with a low crime rate and zero excitement except for harvests in the summer, Friday-night football games in the fall and basketball games in the winter. A number of things could have delayed the bus. A traffic jam due to slow-moving farm equipment, road construction, a car accident…

A chill shivered down Lucy's spine.

Don't freak out. Okay, she wasn't used to taking care of anyone but herself. This overwhelming need to see her nephew right this moment was brand-new to her. But she'd better get used to it. For the next year she wasn't only Connor's aunt, she was also his guardian while his parents, both army reservists, were deployed overseas. Her older brother, Aaron, was counting on Lucy to take care of his only child. If something happened to Connor on her watch…

Her muscles tensed.

"Meow."

The family's cat, an overweight Maine Coon with a tail that looked more like a raccoon's than a feline's, rubbed against the front door. His green-eyed gaze met Lucy's.

"I know, Manny." The cat's concern matched her own. "I want Connor home, too."

Something caught the corner of her eye. Something yellow. She stared out the window once again.

The school bus idled at the corner. Red lights flashed.

Relief flowed through her. "Thank goodness."

Lucy took a step toward the front door then stopped. Connor had asked her not to meet him at the bus stop. She understood the need to be independent and wanted to make him happy. But not even following his request these past two and a half weeks had erased the sadness from his eyes. She knew better than to take it personally. Smiles had become rare commodities around here since his parents deployed.

Peering through the slit in the curtains gave her a clear view of the bus and the short walk to the house. Connor could assert his independence while she made sure he was safe.

Lucy hated seeing him moping around like a lost puppy, but she understood. He missed his parents. She'd tried to make him feel better. Nothing, not even his favorite desserts, fast-food restaurants or video games, had made a difference. Now that his spring soccer team was without a coach, things had gone from bad to worse.

The door of the bus opened. The Bowman twins exited. The

seven-year-old girls wore matching pink polka-dot dresses, white shoes and purple backpacks.

Connor stood on the bus's bottom step with a huge smile on his face. He leaped to the ground and skipped away.

Her heart swelled with excitement. Something good must have happened at school.

As her nephew approached the house, Lucy stepped away from the window. She wanted to make sure his smile remained. No matter what it took.

Manny rubbed against her leg. Birdlike chirping sounds came from his mouth. Strange, but not unexpected from a cat that barked when annoyed.

"Don't worry, Manny." She touched the cat's back. "Connor will be home in three…two…one…"

The front door flung open. Manny dashed for the outside, but Connor closed the door to stop his escape.

"Aunt Lucy." His blue eyes twinkled. So much like Aaron. Same eyes, same hair color, same freckles. "I found someone who can coach the Defeeters."

She should have known Connor's change of attitude had to do with soccer. Her nephew loved the sport. Aaron had coached his son's team, the Defeeters, since Connor started playing organized soccer when he was five. A dad had offered to coach in Aaron's place, but then had to back out after his work schedule changed. No other parent could do it for a variety of reasons. That left the team without a coach. Well, unless you counted her, which was pretty much like being coachless.

The thought of asking her ex-husband to help entered her mind for about a nanosecond before she banished it into the far recesses of her brain where really bad ideas belonged. Being back in the same town as Jeff was hard enough with all the not-so-pleasant memories resurfacing. Lucy hadn't seen him yet nor did she want to.

"Fantastic," she said. "Who is it?"

Connor's grin widened, making him look as if he'd found a million-dollar bill or calorie-free chocolate. He shrugged off his backpack. "Ryland James."

Her heart plummeted to her feet. Splat! "*The* Ryland James?"

Connor nodded enthusiastically. "He's not only best player in the MLS, but my favorite. He'll be the perfect coach. He played on the same team with my dad. They won district and a bunch of tournaments. Ryland's a nice guy. My dad said so."

She had to tread carefully here. For Connor's sake.

Ryland *had* been a nice guy and one of her brother's closest friends. But she hadn't seen him since he left high school to attend the U.S. Soccer Residency Program in Florida. According to Aaron, Ryland had done well, playing overseas and now for the Phoenix Fuego, a Major League Soccer (MLS) team in the U.S. Coaching a recreational soccer team comprised of nine-year-olds probably wasn't on his bucket list.

Lucy bit the inside of her cheek, hoping to think of something—anything—that wouldn't make this blow up in her face and turn Connor's smile upside down.

"Wow," she said finally. "Ryland James would be an amazing coach, but don't you think he's getting ready to start training for his season?"

"MLS teams have been working out in Florida and Arizona since January. The season opener isn't until April." Connor spoke as if this was common knowledge she should know. Given soccer had always been "the sport" in the Martin household, she probably should. "But Ryland James got hurt playing with the U.S. Men's Team in a friendly against Mexico. He's out for a while."

Friendly meant an exhibition game. Lucy knew that much. But the news surprised her. Aaron usually kept her up-to-date on Ryland. Her brother would never let Lucy forget her schoolgirl crush on the boy from the wrong side of town who was now a famous soccer star. "Hurt as in injured?"

"He had surgery and can't play for a couple of months. He's staying with his parents while he recovers." Connor's eyes brightened more. "Isn't that great?"

"I wouldn't call having surgery and being injured great."

"Not him being hurt, but his being in town and able to coach us." Connor made it sound like this was a done deal. "I bet Ryland James will be almost as good a coach as my dad."

"Did someone ask Ryland if he would coach the Defeeters?"

"No," Connor admitted, undaunted. "I came up with the idea during recess after Luke told me Ryland James was at the fire station's spaghetti feed signing autographs. But the whole team thinks it's a good idea. If I'd been there last night..."

The annual Wicksburg Fire Department Spaghetti Feed was one of the biggest events in town. She and Connor had decided not to go to the fundraiser because Dana was calling home. "Don't forget, you got to talk to your mom."

"I know," Connor said. "But I'd like Ryland James's autograph. If he coaches us, he can sign my ball."

Signing a few balls, mugging for the camera and smiling at soccer moms didn't come close to the time it would take to coach a team of boys. The spring season was shorter and more casual than fall league, but still...

She didn't want Connor to be disappointed. "It's a great idea, but Ryland might not have time."

"Will you ask him if he'll coach us, Aunt Lucy? He might just say yes."

The sound of Connor's voice, full of excitement and anticipation, tugged at her heart. "Might" likely equaled "yes" in his young mind. She'd do anything for her nephew. She'd returned to the same town where her ex, now married to her former best friend, lived in order to care for Connor but going to see Ryland...

She blew out a puff of air. "He could say no."

The last time Lucy had seen him had been before her liver transplant. She'd been in eighth grade, jaundiced and bloated, carrying close to a hundred pounds of extra water weight. Not to mention totally exhausted and head over heels in love with the high-school soccer star. She'd spent much of her time alone in her room due to liver failure. Ryland James had fueled her adolescent fantasies. She'd dreamed about him letting her wear his jersey, asking her out to see a movie at the Liberty Theater and inviting her to be his date at prom.

Of course, none of those things had ever happened. She'd hated being known as the sick girl. She'd rarely been able to get up the nerve to say a word to Ryland. And then…

The high-school soccer team had put on two fundraisers—a summer camp for kids and a goal-a-thon—to help with Lucy's medical expenses. She remembered when Ryland handed her the large cardboard check. She'd tried to push her embarrassment and awkwardness aside by smiling at him and meeting his gaze. He'd surprised her by smiling back and sending her heart rate into overdrive. She'd never forgot his kindness or the flash of pity in his eyes. She'd been devastated.

Lucy's stomach churned at the memory. She wasn't that same girl. Still, she didn't want to see him again.

"Ryland is older than me." No one could ever imagine what she'd gone through and how she'd felt being so sick and tired all the time. Or how badly she'd wanted to be normal and healthy. "He was your dad's friend, not mine. I really didn't know him."

"But you've met him."

"He used to come to our house, but the chances of him remembering me…"

"Please, Aunt Lucy." Connor's eyes implored her. "We'll never know unless you ask."

Darn. He sounded like Aaron. Never willing to give up no matter what the odds. Her brother wouldn't let her give up, either. Not when she would have died without a liver transplant or when Jeff had trampled upon her heart.

Lucy's chest tightened. She should do this for Aaron as much as Connor. But she had no idea how she could get close enough to someone as rich and famous as Ryland James.

Connor stared up at her with big, round eyes.

A lump formed in her throat. Whether she wanted to see Ryland James or could see him didn't matter. This wasn't about her. "Okay. I'll ask him."

Connor wrapped his arms around her. "I knew I could count on you."

Lucy hugged him tight. "You can always count on me, kiddo."

Even if she knew going into this things wouldn't work out the way her nephew wanted. But she could keep him smiling a little while longer. At least until Ryland said no.

Connor squirmed out of her arms. "Let's go see him now."

"Not so fast. This is something I'm doing on my own." She didn't want her nephew's image of his favorite soccer player destroyed in case Ryland was no longer a nice guy. Fame or fortune could change people. "And I can't show up empty-handed."

But what could she give to a man who could afford whatever he wanted? Flowers might be appropriate given his injury, but maybe a little too feminine. Chocolate, perhaps? Hershey Kisses might give him the wrong idea. Not that he'd ever known about her crush.

"Cookies," Connor suggested. "Everyone likes cookies."

"Yes, they do." Though Lucy doubted anything would convince Ryland to accept the coaching position. But what was the worst he could say besides no? "Does chocolate chip sound good?"

"Those are my favorite." Connor's smile faltered. "It's too bad my mom isn't here. She makes the best chocolate-chip cookies."

Lucy mussed his hair to keep him from getting too caught up in missing his mom. "It is too bad, but remember she's doing important stuff right now. Like your dad."

Connor nodded.

"How about we use your mom's recipe?" Lucy asked. "You can show me how she makes them."

His smile returned. "Okay."

Lucy wanted to believe everything would turn out okay, but she knew better. As with marriage, the chance of a happy ending here was extremely low. Best to prepare accordingly. She would make a double batch of cookies—one to give to Ryland and one for them to keep. She and Connor were going to need something to make them feel better after Ryland James said no.

* * *

The dog's whimpering almost drowned out the pulse-pounding rock music playing in his parents' home gym.

Ryland didn't glance at Cupcake. The dog could wait. He needed to finish his workout.

Lying on the weight machine's bench, he raised the bar overhead, doing the number of reps recommended by the team's trainer. He used free weights when he trained in Phoenix, but his parents wanted him using the machine when he worked out alone.

Sweat beaded on his forehead. He'd ditched his T-shirt twenty minutes ago. His bare back stuck to the vinyl.

Ryland tightened his grip on the handles.

He wanted to return to the team in top form, to show them he still deserved the captaincy as well as their respect. He'd already lost one major endorsement deal due to his bad-boy behavior. For all he knew, he might not even have a spot on the Fuego roster come opening day. And that…sucked.

On the final rep, his muscles ached and his arms trembled. He clenched his jaw, pushing the weight overhead one last time.

"Yes!"

He'd increased the amount of weight this morning. His trainer would be pleased with the improvements in upper-body strength. That and his core were the only things he could work on.

Ryland sat up, breathing hard. Not good. He needed to keep up his endurance while he healed from the surgery.

Damn foot. He stared at his right leg encased in a black walking-cast boot.

His fault. Each of Ryland's muscles tensed in frustration. He should have known better than to be showboating during the friendly with Mexico. Now he was sidelined, unable to run or kick.

The media had accused him of being hungover or drunk when he hurt himself. They'd been wrong. Again. But dealing with the press was as much a part of his job as what happened for ninety minutes out on the pitch.

He'd appeared on camera, admitted the reason for his

injury—goofing off for the fans and the cameras—and apologized to both fans and teammates. But the truth had made him look more like a bad boy than ever given his red cards during matches the last couple of seasons, the trouble he'd gotten into off the field and the endless "reports" on his dating habits.

The dog whined louder.

From soccer superstar to dog sitter. Ryland half laughed.

Cupcake barked, as if tired of being put off any longer.

"Come here," Ryland said.

His parents' small dog pranced across the padded gym floor, acting more like a pedigreed champion show dog than a full-blooded mutt. Ryland had wanted to buy his mom and dad a purebred, but they adopted a dog from the local animal shelter, instead.

Cupcake stared up at him with sad, pitiful brown eyes. She had mangy gray fur, short legs and a long, bushy tail. Only his parents could love an animal this ugly and pathetic.

"Come on, girl." Ryland scooped her up into his arms. "I know you miss Mom and Dad. I do, too. But you need to stop crying. They deserve a vacation without having to worry about you or me."

He'd given his parents a cruise for their thirty-second wedding anniversary. Even though he'd bought them this mansion on the opposite side of town, far away from the two-bedroom apartment where he'd grown up, and deposited money into a checking account for them each month, both continued to work in the same low-paying jobs they'd had for as long as their marriage. They also drove the same old vehicles even though newer ones, Christmas presents from him, were parked in the four-car garage.

His parents' sole indulgence was Cupcake. They spoiled the dog rotten. They hadn't wanted to leave her in a kennel or in the care of a stranger while away so after his injury they asked Ryland if he would dog sit. His parents never asked him for anything so he'd jumped at the opportunity to do this.

Ryland hated being back in Wicksburg. There were too many

bad memories from when he was a kid. Even small towns had bullies and not-so-nice cliques.

He missed the fun and excitement of a big city, but he needed time to get away to repair the damage he'd done to his foot and his reputation. No one was happy with him at the moment, especially himself. Until getting hurt, he hadn't realized he'd been so restless, unfocused, careless.

Cupcake pawed at his hands. Her sign she wanted rubs.

"Mom and Dad will be home before you know it." Ryland petted the top of her head. "Okay?"

The dog licked him.

He placed her on the floor then stood. "I'm getting some water. Then it's shower time. If I don't shave, I'm going to start looking mangy like you."

Cupcake barked.

His cell phone, sitting on the countertop next to his water bottle, rang. He read the name on the screen. Blake Cochrane. His agent.

Ryland glanced at the clock. Ten o'clock here meant seven o'clock in Los Angeles. "An early morning for you."

"I'm here by six to beat the traffic," Blake said. "According to Twitter, you made a public appearance the other night. I thought we agreed you were going to lay low."

"I was hungry. The fire station was having their annual spaghetti feed so I thought I could eat and support a good cause. They asked if I'd sign autographs and pose for pictures. I couldn't say no."

"Any press?"

"The local weekly paper." With the phone in one hand and a water bottle in the other, Ryland walked to the living room with Cupcake tagging alongside him. He tried hard not to favor his right foot. He'd only been off crutches a few days. "But I told them no interview because I wanted the focus to be on the event. The photographer took a few pictures of the crowd so I might be in one."

"Let's hope whatever is published is positive," Blake said.

"I was talking with people I grew up with." Some of the

same people who'd treated him like garbage until he'd joined a soccer team. Most accepted him after he became a starter on the high-school varsity team as a freshman. He'd shown them all by becoming a professional athlete. "I was surrounded by a bunch of happy kids."

"That sounds safe enough," Blake admitted. "But be careful. Another endorsement deal fell through. They're nervous about your injury. The concerns over your image didn't help."

Ryland dragged his hand through his hair. "Let me guess. They want a clean-cut American, not a bad boy who thinks red cards are better than goals."

"You got it," Blake said. "I haven't heard anything official, but rumors are swirling that Mr. McElroy wants to loan you out to a Premier League team."

McElroy was the new owner of the Phoenix Fuego, who took more interest in players and team than any other head honcho in the MLS. He'd fired the coach/manager who'd wanted to run things his way and hired a new coach, Elliot Fritz, who didn't mind the owner being so hands-on. "Seriously?"

"I've heard it from more than one source."

Damn. As two teams were mentioned, Ryland plopped into his dad's easy chair. Cupcake jumped onto his lap.

"I took my eye off the ball," he said. "I made some mistakes. I apologized. I'm recovering and keeping my name out of the news. I don't see why we all can't move on."

"It's not that easy. You're one of the best soccer players in the world. Before your foot surgery, you were a first-team player who could have started for any team here or abroad. Not many American footballers can say that," Blake said. "But McElroy believes your bad-boy image isn't a draw in the stands or with the kids. Merchandising is important these days."

"Yeah, I know. Being injured and getting older isn't helping my cause." As if twenty-nine made Ryland an old man. He remembered what the team owner had said in an interview. "McElroy called me an overpaid liability. But if that's the case, why would an overseas team want to take me on?"

"The transfer period doesn't start until June. None have said they want the loan yet."

Ouch. Ryland knew he had only himself to blame for the mess he found himself in.

"The good news is the MLS doesn't want to lose a home-grown player as talented as you. McElroy's feathers got ruffled," Blake continued. "He's asserting his authority and reminding you that he controls your contract."

"You mean, my future."

"That's how billionaires are."

"I'll stick to being a millionaire, then."

Blake sighed.

"Look, I get why McElroy's upset. Coach Fritz, too. I haven't done a good job handling stuff," Ryland admitted. "I'll be the first to admit I've never been an angel. But I'm not the devil, either. There's no way I could do everything the press says I do. The media exaggerates everything."

"True, but people's concerns are real. This time at your parents' house is critical. Watch yourself."

"I'm going to fix this. I want to play in the MLS." Ryland had already done an eleven-year stint in the U.K. "My folks are doing fine, but they're not getting any younger. I don't want to be an ocean away from them. If McElroy doesn't want me, see if the Indianapolis Rage or another club does."

"McElroy isn't going to let a franchise player like you go to another MLS team," Blake said matter-of-factly. "If you want to play stateside, it'll be with Fuego."

Ryland petted Cupcake. "Then I'll have to keep laying low and polishing my image so it shines."

"Blind me, Ry."

"Will do." Everyone always wanted something from him. This was no different. But it sucked he had to prove himself all over again with Mr. McElroy and the Phoenix fans. "At least I can't get into trouble dog sitting. Wicksburg is the definition of boring."

"Women—"

"Not here," Ryland interrupted. "I know what's expected of

me. I also know it's hard on my mom to read the gossip about me on the internet. She doesn't need to hear it firsthand from women in town."

"You should bring your mom back with you to Phoenix."

"Dude. Keeping it quiet and on the down low is fine while I'm here, but let's not go crazy," Ryland said. "In spite of the reports of me hooking up with every starlet in Hollywood, I've been more than discreet and discriminate with whom I see. But beautiful women coming on to me are one of the perks of the sport."

Blake sighed. "I remember when you were this scrappy, young kid who cared about nothing but soccer. It used to be all about the game for you."

"It's still about the game." Ryland was the small-town kid from the Midwest who hit the big-time overseas, playing with the best in the world. Football, as they called it everywhere but in the U.S., meant everything to him. Without it… "Soccer is my life. That's why I'm trying to get back on track."

A beat passed and another. "Just remember, actions speak louder than words."

After a quick goodbye, Blake disconnected from the call.

Ryland stared at his phone. He'd signed with Blake when he was eighteen. The older Ryland got, the smarter his agent's advice sounded.

Actions speak louder than words.

Lately his actions hadn't been any more effective than his words. He looked at Cupcake. "I've put myself in the doghouse. Now I've got to get myself out of it."

The doorbell rang.

Cupcake jumped off his lap and ran to the front door barking ferociously, as if she weighed ninety pounds, not nineteen.

Who could that be? He wasn't expecting anyone.

The dog kept barking. He remained seated.

Let Cupcake deal with whomever was at the door. If he ignored them, maybe they would go away. The last thing Ryland wanted right now was company.

CHAPTER TWO

LUCY'S hand hovered over the mansion's doorbell. She fought the urge to press the button a third time. She didn't want to annoy Mr. and Mrs. James. Yes, she wanted to get this fool's errand over with, but appearing overeager or worse, rude, wouldn't help her find a coach for Connor's team.

"Come on," she muttered. "Open the door."

The constant high-pitch yapping of a dog suggested the doorbell worked. But that didn't explain why no one had answered yet. Maybe the house was so big it took them a long time to reach the front door. Lucy gripped the container of cookies with both hands.

The dog continued barking.

Maybe no one was home. She rose up on her tiptoes and peeked through the four-inch strip of small leaded-glass squares on the ornate wood door.

Lights shone inside.

Someone had to be home. Leaving the lights on when away wasted electricity. Her dad used to tell her that. Aaron said the same thing to Connor. But she supposed if a person could afford to live in an Architectural Digest–worthy home with its Georgian-inspired columns, circular drive and manicured lawn that looked like a green carpet, they probably didn't worry about paying the electricity bill.

Lucy didn't see anyone coming toward the door. She couldn't see the dog, either. She lowered her heels to the welcome mat.

Darn it. She didn't want to come back later and try again. A chill shivered down her spine. She needed to calm down.

She imagined Connor with a smile on his face and soccer cleats on his feet. Her anxiety level dropped.

If no one answered, she would return. She would keep coming back until she spoke with Ryland James.

The dog's barking became more agitated.

A sign? Probably not, but she might as well ring the bell once more before calling it quits.

She pressed the doorbell. A symphony of chimes erupted into a Mozart tune. At least the song sounded like Mozart the third time hearing it.

The door opened slightly. A little gray dog darted out and sniffed her shoes. The pup placed its stubby front paws against her jean-covered calves.

"Off, Cupcake." The dog ran to the grass in the front yard. A man in navy athletic shorts with a black walking-cast on his right leg stood in the doorway. "She's harmless."

The dog might be, but not him.

Ryland James.

Hot. Sexy. Oh, my.

He looked like a total bad boy with his short, brown hair damp and mussed, as if he hadn't taken time to comb it after he crawled out of bed. Shaving didn't seem to be part of his morning routine, either. He used to be so clean-cut and all-American, but the dark stubble covering his chin and cheeks gave him an edge. His bare muscular chest glistened as if he'd just finished a workout. He had a tattoo on his right biceps and another on the backside of his left wrist. His tight, underwear model–worthy abs drew her gaze lower. Her mouth went dry.

Lucy forced her gaze up and stared into the hazel eyes that had once fueled her teenage daydreams. His dark lashes seemed even thicker. How was that possible?

The years had been good, very good to him. The guy was more gorgeous than ever with his classically handsome features, ones that had become more defined, almost refined, with age. His nose, however, looked as if it had been broken at least once. Rather than detract from his looks, his nose gave him character, made him appear more…rugged. Manly. Dangerous.

Lucy's heart thudded against her ribs. "It's you."

"I'm me." His lips curved into a charming smile, sending her already-racing pulse into a mad sprint. "You're not what I expected to find on my doorstep, but my day's looking a whole lot better now."

Her turn. But Lucy found herself tongue-tied. The same way she'd been whenever he was over at her house years ago. Her gaze strayed once again to his amazing abs. Wowza.

"You okay?" he asked.

Remember Connor. She raised her chin. "I was expecting—"

"One of my parents."

She nodded.

"I was hoping you were here to see me," he said.

"I am." The words rushed from her lips like water from Connor's Super Soaker gun. She couldn't let nerves get the best of her now that she'd accomplished the first part of her mission and was standing face-to-face with Ryland. "But I thought one of them would answer the door since you're injured."

"They would have if they'd been home." His rich, deep voice, as smooth and warm as a mug of hot cocoa, flowed over her. "I'm Ryland James."

"I know."

"That puts me at a disadvantage because I don't know who you are."

"I meant, I know you. But it was a long time ago," she clarified.

His gaze raked over her. "I would remember meeting you."

Lucy was used to guys hitting on her. She hadn't expected that from Ryland, but she liked it. Other men's attention annoyed her. His flirting made her feel attractive and desired.

"Let me take a closer look to see if I can jog my memory," he said.

The approval in his eyes gave her goose bumps. The good kind, ones she hadn't felt in a while. She hadn't wanted to jump back into the dating scene after her divorce two years ago.

"I *have* seen that pretty smile of yours before," he continued. "Those sparkling blue eyes, too."

Oh, boy. Her knees felt wobbly. Tingles filled her stomach.

Stop. She wasn't back in middle school.

Lucy straightened. The guy hadn't a clue who she was. Ryland James was a professional athlete. Knowing what to say to women was probably part of their training camp.

"I'm Lucy." For some odd reason, she sounded husky. She cleared her throat. "Lucy Martin."

"Lucy." Lines creased Ryland's forehead. "Aaron Martin's little sister?"

She nodded.

"Same smile and blue eyes, but everything else has changed." Ryland's gaze ran the length of her again. "Just look at you now."

She braced herself, waiting to hear how sick she'd been and how ugly she'd looked before her liver transplant.

He grinned. "Little Lucy is all grown up now."

Little Lucy? She stiffened. His words confused her. She hadn't been little. Okay, maybe when they first met back in elementary school. But she'd been huge, a bloated whale, and yellow due to jaundice the last time he'd seen her. "It's been what? Thirteen years since we last saw each other."

"Thirteen years too long," he said.

What was going on? Old crushes were supposed to get fat and lose their hair, not get even hotter and appear interested in you. He sounded interested. Unless her imagination was getting the best of her.

No, she knew better when it came to men. "It looks as if life is treating you well. Except for your leg—"

"Foot. Nothing serious."

"You had surgery."

"A minor inconvenience, that's all. Nothing like what you suffered through," he said. "The liver transplant seems to have done what Aaron hoped it would do. All he ever wanted was for you to be healthy."

"I am." She wondered why Aaron would have talked about

her illness to Ryland. All they'd cared about were soccer and girls. Well, every other girl in Wicksburg except her. "I take medicine each day and have a monthly blood test, but otherwise I'm the same as everybody else."

"No, you're not." Ryland's gaze softened. "There's nothing ordinary about you. Never has been. It sucked that you were sick, but you were always so brave."

Heat stole up her neck toward her cheeks. Butterflies flapped in her tummy. Her heart…

Whoa-whoa-whoa. Don't get carried away by a few nice words from a good-looking guy, even if that guy happened to be the former man of her dreams. She'd been a naive kid back then. She'd learned the hard way that people said things they didn't mean. They lied, even after saying how much they loved you. Lucy squared her shoulders.

Time to get this over with. She handed Ryland the cookies. "These are for you."

He removed the container's lid. His brows furrowed. "Cookies?"

Ryland sounded surprised. She bit the inside of her mouth, hoping he liked them. "Chocolate chip."

"My favorite. Thanks."

He seemed pleased. Good. "Aaron's son, Connor, helped me make them. He's nine and loves soccer. That's why I'm here. To ask a favor."

Ryland looked at the cookies, then at her. "I appreciate your honesty. Not many people are so up-front when they want something. Let's talk inside."

She hesitated, unsure of the wisdom of going into the house. Once upon a time she'd believed in happily ever after and one true love. But life had taught her those things belonged only in fairy tales. Love and romance were overrated. But Ryland was making her feel things she tried hard not to think about too much—attraction, desire, hope.

But the other part of her, the part that tended to be impulsive and had gotten her into trouble more than once, was curious. She wanted to know if his parents' house was as nice on the inside as the exterior and front yard. Heaven knew she would never live in an exclusive neighborhood like this one. This might be her only chance to find out.

Ryland leaned against the doorway. The casual pose took weight off his right foot. He might need to sit down.

"Sure." She didn't want him hurting. "That would be nice."

He whistled for the dog.

Cupcake ran inside.

Lucy entered the house. The air was cooler than outside and smelled lemony. Wood floors gleamed. A giant chandelier hung from the twenty-foot ceiling in the foyer. She clamped her lips together so her mouth wouldn't gape. Original watercolor paintings in gilded frames decorated the textured walls. Tasteful and expensive.

She stepped through a wide-arched doorway into the living room. Talk about beautiful. The yellow and green décor was light, bright and inviting. The colors, fabrics and accessories coordinated perfectly. What she liked most was how comfortable the room looked, not at all like some of those unlivable magazine layouts or model homes.

Family pictures sat on the wooden-fireplace mantle. A framed poster-size portrait of Ryland, wearing a U.S. National team uniform, hung on the wall. An open paperback novel rested cover-side up on an end table. "Your parents' house is lovely."

"Thanks."

He sounded proud, making her wonder about his part in his parents' house. She'd guess a big part, given his solid relationship with his mom and dad when he'd been a teen.

"My mom thought the house was too big, but I convinced her she deserved it after so many years of apartment living." Ryland motioned to a sofa. "Have a seat."

Lucy sat, sinking into the overstuffed cushions. More comfortable than the futon she'd sold before leaving Chicago. She'd gotten rid of her few pieces of furniture so she wouldn't have to pay for storage while living at Aaron and Dana's house.

Cupcake hopped up next to her.

"Is she allowed on the couch?" Lucy asked.

"The dog is allowed everywhere except the dining-room table and kitchen counters. She belongs to my parents. They've spoiled her rotten." Ryland sounded more amused than angry. He sat on a wingback chair to her right. "Mind if I have a cookie?"

"Please do."

He offered her the container. "Would you like one?"

The chocolate chips smelled good, but she would be eating cookies with Connor later. Better not overdo the sweets. The trips to the ice-cream parlor and Rocket Burger with her nephew were already adding up. "No, thanks."

Ryland took one. "I can't remember the last time someone baked anything for me."

"What about your mom?"

"I don't spend as much time with my parents as I'd like due to soccer. Right now I'm dog sitting while they're away." Cupcake circled around as if chasing her own tail, then plopped against the cushion and placed her head on Lucy's thigh. "She likes you."

Lucy ran her fingers through the soft gray fur. She'd never had a dog. "She's sweet."

"When she wants to be." Ryland bit into the cookie. He took his time eating it. "Delicious."

The cookies were a hit. Lucy hoped they worked as a bribe. She mustered her courage. Not that she could back out now even if she wanted to. "So my nephew…"

"Does he want an autograph?" Ryland placed the cookie container on the coffee table. "Maybe a team jersey or ball?"

"Connor would love it if you signed his ball, but what he really wants is a coach for his spring under-9 rec. team." She didn't want to waste any more of Ryland's time. Or hers. "He wanted me to ask if you could coach his team, the Defeeters."

Ryland flinched. "Me? Coach?"

"I know that's a big request and likely impossible for you to do right now."

He looked at his injured foot. “Yeah, this isn’t a good time. I hope to be back with my team in another month or so.”

“I’m sure you will be. Aaron says you’re one of the best players in the world.”

“Thanks. It’s just… I’m supposed to be laying low while I’m here. Staying out of the press. The media could turn my coaching your nephew’s team into a circus.” Ryland stared at the dog. “I’m really sorry I can’t help you out.”

“No worries. I told Connor you probably couldn’t coach.” Lucy knew Ryland would never say yes. He’d left his small-town roots behind and become famous, traveling all over the U.S. and the world. The exotic lifestyle was as foreign to her as the game of soccer itself. But maybe she could get him to agree to something else that wouldn’t take so much of his time. “But if you happen to have an hour to spare sometime, Connor and his teammates would be thrilled if you could give them a pep talk.”

Silence stretched between them. She’d put him on the spot with that request, too. But she’d had no choice if she wanted to help her nephew.

“I can do that,” Ryland said finally.

Lucy released the breath she hadn’t realized she was holding. “Thanks.”

“I’m happy to talk to them, sign balls, pose for pictures, whatever the boys want.”

She hoped the visit would appease Connor. “That will be great. Thanks.”

Ryland’s eyes darkened, more brown than hazel now. “Who will you get to coach?”

“I don’t know,” she admitted. “Practices don’t start until next week so I still have a little time left to find someone. I can always coach, if need be.”

Surprise flashed across his face. “You play soccer?”

Lucy hadn’t been allowed to do anything physical when she was younger. Even though she no longer had any physical limitations, she preferred art to athletics. “No, but I’ve been reading up on the game and watching video clips on the internet, just in case."

His lips narrowed. "Aaron was great with those kids when we put on that camp back in high school. Why doesn't he coach the team?"

"Aaron's coached the Defeeters for years, but he's overseas right now with the army. Both he and his wife were deployed with their Reserve unit last month. I'm taking care of Connor until they return next year."

"Aaron talked about using the military to pay for college," Ryland said thoughtfully. "But I lost track of him, of everyone, when I left Wicksburg."

"He joined the army right after high school." Lucy's medical expenses had drained their college funds, her parents' saving account and the equity in their house. Sometimes it felt as if she was still paying for the transplant years later. Aaron, too. "That's where he met his wife, Dana. After they completed their Active Duty, they joined the Reserves."

"A year away from home. Away from their son." Ryland dragged his hand through his hair. "That has to be rough."

Lucy's chest tightened. "You do what you have to do."

"Still..."

"You left home to go to Florida and then England."

"To play soccer. Not protect my country," Ryland said. "I had the time of my life. I doubt Aaron and his wife can say the same thing right now."

Lucy remembered the tears glistening in Connor's eyes as he told her his mom sounded like she was crying on the phone. "You're right about that."

"I respect what Aaron and his wife, what all of the military, are doing. The sacrifices they make. True heroes. Every one of them."

Ryland sounded earnest. She wanted to believe he was sincere. Maybe he was still a small-town guy at heart. "They are."

Cupcake rolled over on her back. She waved her front paws in the air.

Lucy took the not-so-subtle hint and rubbed the dog's stomach.

"So you've stuck around Wicksburg," Ryland said.

"I left for a while. College. I also lived in Chicago." Aaron had accused her of running away when her marriage failed. Maybe he'd been right. But she'd had to do something when her life crumbled around her. "I moved back last month."

"To care for your nephew."

She nodded. "Saying no never entered into my mind. Not after everything Aaron has done for me."

"He was so protective of you."

"He still is."

"That doesn't surprise me." Ryland rubbed his thigh above the brace he wore. He rested his foot on an ottoman. "Did you leave your boyfriend behind in Chi-town or did he come with you?"

She drew back, surprised by the question. "I, uh, don't have a boyfriend."

He grinned wryly. "So you need a soccer coach and a boyfriend. I hope your brother told you the right qualities to look for in each."

Aaron always gave her advice, but she hadn't always listened to him. Lucy should have done so before eloping. She couldn't change the past. But she wouldn't make that same mistakes again.

"A soccer coach is all I need." Lucy figured Ryland had to be teasing her, but this wasn't a joking matter. She needed a boyfriend as much as she needed another ex-husband. She shifted positions. "I have my hands full with Connor. He's my priority. A kid should be happy and carefree, not frowning and down all the time."

"Maybe we should get him together with Cupcake," Ryland said. "She goes from being happy to sad. I'm a poor substitute for my parents."

Lucy's insecurities rushed to the surface. She never thought she would have something in common with him. "That's how I feel with Connor. Nothing I do seems to be…enough."

Ryland leaned forward. His large hand engulfed hers. His touch was light. His skin was warm. "Hey. You're here to see me about his team. That says a lot. Aaron and his family, especially Connor, are lucky to have you."

Ryland's words wrapped around Lucy like a big hug. But his touch disturbed her more than it comforted. Heat emanated from the point of contact and spread up her arm. She tried not to think about it. "I'm the lucky one."

"Maybe some of that luck will rub off on me."

"Your injury?" she asked.

"Yeah, and a few other things."

His hand still rested upon hers. Lucy hadn't been touched by a man in over two years. It felt...good.

Better not get used to it. Reluctantly, she pulled her hand from beneath his and reached for her purse.

"If you need some luck, I've got just the thing for you." Lucy removed a penny from her change pocket and gave it to Ryland. "My grammy told me this is all a person needs to get lucky."

Wicked laughter lit his eyes. "Here I thought it took a killer opening line, oodles of charm and an expensive bottle of champagne."

Oh, no. Lucy realized what she'd said. Her cheeks burned. "I meant to change their luck."

He winked. "I know, but you gave me the opening. I had to take the shot."

At least he hadn't scored. Not yet, anyway. Lucy swallowed. "Aaron would have done the same." She needed to be careful, though. Ryland was charming, but he wasn't her big brother. Being near him short-circuited her brain. She couldn't think straight. That was bad. The last time she allowed herself to be charmed by a man she'd ended up with a wedding ring on her finger.

"You said your nephew loves soccer," Ryland said.

She nodded, thankful for the change in subject. "Yes. Connor and Aaron are crazy about the sport. They wear matching jerseys. It's cute, though Dana says it's annoying when they get up at some crazy hour to watch a game in Europe. But I don't think she minds that much."

Lucy cringed at her rambling. Ryland didn't care about Aaron's family's infatuation with soccer. She needed to shut up. Now.

"That's great they're so into the game." A thoughtful expression crossed Ryland's face. "I haven't been back in town for a while, but I bet some of the same people are still involved in soccer. I'll ask around to see if there's someone who can coach your nephew's team."

Her mouth parted in surprise. She liked being self-reliant and hated asking for help, but in this case Ryland had offered. She'd be stupid to say no when this meant so much to Connor. "I'd appreciate that. If it's not too much trouble."

"No trouble. I'm happy to do it. Anything for…"

You, she thought.

"…Aaron."

Of course, this was for her brother. Ryland's childhood and high-school friend and teammate. She ignored the twinge of disappointment. "Thanks."

Ryland held the penny between the pads of his thumb and index finger. "You've made me cookies, given me a lucky penny. What do I get if I find a coach?"

Lucy wondered if he was serious or teasing her. His smile suggested the latter. "My undying gratitude?"

"That's a good start."

"More cookies?"

"Always appreciated, especially if they're chocolate chip," he said. "What else?"

His lighthearted and flirty tone sounded warning bells in her head. Ryland *was* teasing her, but Lucy no longer wanted to play along. His charm, pretty much everything about him, unsettled her. "I'm not sure what else you might want."

He gave her the once-over, only this time his gaze lingered a second too long on her lips. "I can think of a couple things."

So could Lucy. The man was smokin' hot. His lips looked as if they could melt her insides with one kiss. Sex appeal oozed from him.

A good thing she'd sworn off men because she could tell the

soccer pitch wasn't the only place where Ryland James played. Best not to even start that game. She'd only lose. Again.

Not. Going. To. Happen.

Time to steer this conversation back to where it needed to be so she could get out of here.

"How about you make a list?" Lucy kept a smile on her face and her tone light and friendly. After all, he was going to try to find Connor's team a coach. But if Ryland thought she was going to swoon at his feet in adoration and awe, he had another think coming. "If you find the team a coach, we'll go from there."

Ryland's smile crinkled the corner of his eyes, taking her breath away. "I always thought you were a cool kid, Lucy Martin, but I really like who you are now."

Okay, she was attracted to him. Any breathing female with a pulse would be. The guy was appealing with a capital *A*.

But Lucy wasn't stupid. She knew the type. His type.

Ryland James spelled T-R-O-U-B-L-E.

Once he visited the Defeeters, she never wanted to see him again. And she wouldn't.

It was so good to see Lucy Martin again.

Ryland sat in the living room waiting for her to return with Cupcake, who needed to go outside. Lucy had offered to take the dog to the backyard so he wouldn't have to get up. He'd agreed if only to keep her here a little while longer.

He couldn't get over the difference in her.

She'd been a shy, sweet girl with freckles, long braids and yellowish whites surrounding her huge blue eyes. Now she was a confident, sweet woman with a glowing complexion, strawberry-blond hair worn in a short and sassy style, and mesmerizing sky-blue eyes.

Ryland had been wrong about not wanting company this morning. Sure she'd shown up because she wanted something. But she'd brought him cookies—a bribe, no doubt—and been straightforward asking him for a favor.

He appreciated and respected that.

Some women were devious and played up to him to get what they wanted. Lucy hadn't even wanted something for herself, but for her nephew. That was…refreshing.

Cupcake ran into the living room and hopped onto the couch.

Lucy took her same spot next to the dog. "Sorry that took so long, the dog wanted to run around before she got down to business."

"Thanks for taking her out." Lucy had brightened Ryland's mood, making him smile and laugh. He wanted her to stick around. "You must be thirsty. I'll get you something to drink. Coffee? Water? A soda?"

Lucy shifted on the couch. "No, thanks."

Years ago, Aaron had told Ryland that his sister had a crush on him so to be nice to her. He had been. Now he was curious to know if any of her crush remained. "It's no trouble."

But he could get in trouble wondering if she were still interested in him. He was supposed to be avoiding women.

Not that he was pursuing her. Though he was…curious.

She grabbed her purse. "Thanks, but I should be going."

Lucy was different than other women he knew. Most would kill for that kind of invitation from him, but she didn't seem impressed or want to hang out with him. She'd eagerly taken Cupcake outside while he stayed inside. Almost as if she'd wanted some distance from him.

Interesting. His charm and fame usually melted whatever feminine resistance he faced. Not with Lucy. He kind of liked the idea of a challenge. Not that it could go anywhere, he reminded himself. "I'd like to hear more about Aaron."

"Perhaps another time."

"You have somewhere to be?"

Her fingers curled around the leather strap. "I have work to do before Connor gets home from school."

Ryland would have liked it if she stayed longer, but he would see her again. No doubt about that. He rose. "I'll see you out."

She stood. Her purse swung like a pendulum. "That's not necessary. Stay off your foot. I know where the door is."

"My foot can handle it."

Lucy's gaze met his. "I can see myself out."

He found the unwavering strength in her eyes a big turn-on. "I know, but I want to show you out."

After what felt like forever, she looked away with a shrug. "It's your foot."

He bit back a smile. She would be a challenge all right. A fun one. "Yes, it is."

Ryland accompanied Lucy to her car, a practical looking white, four-door subcompact. "Thanks for coming by and bringing me cookies. I'll give you a call about a coach and talking to the team."

She removed something from an outside pocket of her purse and handed it to him. "My cell-phone number is on my business card. Aaron has a landline, but this is the best way to reach me."

He stared at the purple card with white and light blue lettering and a swirly border. That looked more like Lucy. "Freelance graphic designer. So you're still into art."

"You remember that?"

She sounded incredulous, but the way her eyes danced told him she was also pleased.

"You'd be surprised what I remember."

Her lips parted once again.

He'd piqued her interest. Good, because she'd done the same to him. "But don't worry, it's all good."

A charming blush crept into Lucy's cheeks.

"We'll talk later." Ryland didn't want to make her uncomfortable, but flirting with her came so easily. "You have work to do now."

"Yes, I do." She dug around the inside of her purse. As she pulled out her keys, metal clanged against metal. "Thanks. I'm… I look forward to hearing from you."

"It won't be long." And it wouldn't. Ryland couldn't wait to talk to her again. "I promise."

CHAPTER THREE

THAT afternoon, the front door burst open with so much force Lucy thought a tornado had touched down in Wicksburg. She stood her ground in the living room, knowing this burst of energy wasn't due to Mother Nature—the warning siren hadn't gone off—but was man, er, boy-made.

Manny usually couldn't wait for Connor to get home and make another escape attempt, but the cat hightailed it into the kitchen. A ball of dark fur slid across the linoleum before disappearing from sight.

Connor flew into the house, strands of his strawberry-blond hair going every which way. He was lanky, the way his dad had been at that age, all limbs with not an ounce of fat on him. The set of his jaw and the steely determination in his eyes made him seem more superhero than a four-and-a-half-foot third grader. All he needed was a cape to wear over his jersey and jeans.

"Hey." Lucy knew he wanted to know about her visit to Ryland, but the sexy soccer player had been on her mind since she'd left him. Much to her dismay. She didn't want to start her time with Connor focused on the guy, too. "Did you have a good day at school? You had a spelling quiz, right?"

He slammed the front door closed. The entire house shook. His backpack hung precariously off one thin shoulder, but he didn't seem to care. "Did you talk to Ryland James?"

Connor had the same one-track mind as her brother. When Aaron had something he wanted to do, like joining the military, he defined tunnel vision.

Lucy might as well get this over with. "I went to Mr. and Mrs. James's house this morning. Ryland liked the cookies we baked."

The backpack thudded against the entryway's tile floor. Anticipation filled Connor's blue eyes. "Is he going to coach the Defeeters?"

This was the part she hadn't been looking forward to since leaving the Jameses' house. "No, but Ryland offered to see if he can find the team a coach. He's also going to come out and talk to the team."

Different emotions crossed Connor's face. Sadness, anger, surprise. A thoughtful expression settled on his features. "I guess he must be really busy."

"Ryland's trying to heal and stay in shape." Her temperature rose remembering how he looked in only a pair of shorts and gleam of sweat. "He doesn't plan on being in town long. Maybe a month or so. He wants to rejoin his team as soon as he can."

Manny peered around the doorway to the kitchen, saw Connor and ran to him.

Connor picked up the cat. "I guess I would want to do that, too."

Poor kid. He was trying to put on a brave face. She wished things could be different for him. "There's still time to find the Defeeters a coach."

He stared over the cat's head. "That's what you said last week. And the week before that."

"True, but now I have help looking for a coach." Lucy hoped Ryland had been serious about his offer and came through for… the boys. "A good thing, otherwise, you'll be stuck with me."

Connor nodded.

She ruffled his hair. "Gee, thanks."

"You're the one who said it." He flashed her a lopsided grin. "But no matter what happens, having you for a coach is better than not playing at all."

Lucy hoped he was right. "I'll do my best if it comes down to that."

"It won't." Connor sounded so confident.

"How do you know?"

"If Ryland James said he'd find us a coach, he will."

She'd been disappointed too many times to put that much faith into someone. Ryland had seemed sincere and enthusiastic. But so had others. Best not to raise Connor's hopes too high on the chance his favorite player didn't come through after all. "Ryland said he'd *try.* He's going to call me."

"Have you checked your voice mail yet?" Connor asked.

His eagerness made her smile. She'd been wondering when the call might come herself. They both needed to be realistic. "I just saw Ryland a couple hours ago."

"Hours? He could have found us five coaches by now."

She doubted that.

"All Ryland James has to do is snap his fingers and people will come running," Connor continued.

Lucy could imagine women running to the gorgeous Ryland. She wasn't so sure the same could be said about coaches. Not unless they were female.

"Check your cell phone," Connor encouraged.

The kid was relentless…like his dad. "Give Ryland time to snap his fingers. I mean, make calls. I know this is important to you, but a little patience here would be good."

"You could call him."

No, she couldn't. Wouldn't. "He said he'd call. Rushing him wouldn't be nice."

She also didn't want to give Ryland the wrong impression so he might think she was interested in him. A guy like him meant one thing—heartbreak. She'd had enough of that to last a lifetime.

"Let's give him at least a day, maybe two, to call us, okay?" she suggested.

"Okay," Connor agreed reluctantly.

She bit back a laugh. "How about some cookies and milk while you tell me about school?"

Maybe that would get Ryland James out of Connor's thoughts. And hers, too.

"Sure." As he walked toward the kitchen, he looked back at her. "So does Ryland James have a soccer field in his backyard?"

Lucy swallowed a sigh. And then maybe not.

After dinner, Ryland retreated with Cupcake into the media room aka his dad's man cave. He had all he needed—laptop, cell phone, chocolate-chip cookies, Lucy's business card and a seventy-inch LED television with ESPN playing. As soon as Ryland found Lucy a coach for her nephew's team, he would call her with the good news.

Forget the delicious cookies she'd made. The only dessert he wanted was to hear her sweet voice on the opposite end of the phone.

Ryland laughed. He must need some feminine attention if he felt this way.

But seeing Lucy again had made him feel good. She also had him thinking about the past. Many of his childhood memories living in Wicksburg were like bad dreams, ones he'd pushed to the far recesses of his mind and wanted to keep there. But a few others, like the ones he remembered now, brought a welcome smile to his face.

Cupcake lay on an Indianapolis Colts dog bed.

Even though Ryland played soccer, his dad preferred football, the American kind. But his dad had never once tried to change Ryland's mind about what sport to play. Instead, his father had done all he could so Ryland could succeed in the sport. He would be nowhere without his dad and his mom.

And youth soccer.

He'd learned the basic skills and the rules of the game playing in the same rec. league Aaron's son played in. When Ryland moved to a competitive club, playing up a year from his own age group, his dad's boss, Mr. Buckley, who owned a local farm, bought Ryland new cleats twice a year. Not cheap ones, but the good kind. Mr. Martin, Aaron and Lucy's dad, would drive Ryland to away games and tournaments when his parents had to work.

Lucy taking care of Aaron's son didn't surprise Ryland. The Martins had always been a loyal bunch.

In elementary school, other kids used to taunt him. Aaron stood up for Ryland even before they were teammates. Once they started playing on the same team, they became good friends. But Ryland had wanted to put Wicksburg behind him when he left.

And he had.

He'd focused all his effort and energy into being the best soccer player he could be.

Now that he was back in town, finding a soccer coach was the least he could do for his old friend Aaron. Ryland pressed the mute button on the television's remote then picked up his cell phone. This wouldn't take long.

Two hours later, he disconnected from yet another call. He couldn't believe it. No matter whom he'd spoken with, the answer was still the same—no. Only the reason for not being able to coach changed.

"Wish I could help you out, Ryland, but I'm already coaching two other teams."

"Gee, if I'd known sooner…"

"Try the high school. Maybe one of the students could do it as a class project or something."

Ryland placed his cell phone on the table. Even the suggestion to contact the high school had led to a dead end. No wonder Lucy had asked him to coach Connor's team.

Ryland looked at Cupcake. "What am I going to do?"

The dog kept her eyes closed.

"Go ahead. Pretend you don't hear me. That's what everyone else has done tonight."

Okay, not quite. His calling had resulted in four invitations to dinner and five requests to speak to soccer teams. Amazing how things and his status in town had changed. All his hard work had paid off. Though he was having to start over with Mr. McElroy and the Fuego.

"I need to find Lucy a coach."

Cupcake stretched.

Something flashed on the television screen. Highlights from a soccer match.

Yearning welled inside him. He missed the action on the field, the adrenaline pushing through him to run faster and the thrill of taking the ball toward the goal and scoring. Thinking about playing soccer was making him nostalgic for days when kids, a ball and some grass defined the game in its simplest and purest form.

Lucy's business card caught his eye.

Attraction flared to life. He wanted to talk to her. Now.

Ryland picked up his cell phone. He punched in the first three digits of her number then placed the phone back on the table.

Calling her tonight would be stupid. Saying he wanted to hear her voice might be true, but he didn't want to push too hard and scare her off. Other women might love a surprise phone call, but Lucy might not. She wasn't like the women he dated.

That, he realized, surprisingly appealed to him. Sitting in his parents' living room eating cookies and talking with a small-town girl had energized him in a way no visit to a top restaurant or trendy club with a date ever had.

Ryland stared at the cell phone. He wanted to talk to her, but if he called her he would have to admit his inability to find her a coach. That wouldn't go over well.

With him, he realized with a start. Lucy wouldn't be upset. She'd thank him for his efforts then take on the coaching role herself.

I can always coach, if need be.

You play soccer?

No, but I've been reading up on the game and watching coaching clips on the internet just in case.

He imagined her placing a whistle around her graceful neck and leading a team of boys at practice. Coaching would be nothing compared to what Lucy went through when she was sick. She would figure out the basics of what needed to be done and give the boys her all.

But she shouldn't *have* to do that. She was doing enough taking care of her nephew. The same as Aaron and his wife.

His gaze focused on Lucy's name on her business card. The script might be artistic and a touch whimsical, but it showed strength and ingenuity, too.

Ryland straightened. He couldn't let people saying no stop him. He was tougher than that. "I might have screwed up my career, but I'm not going to mess up this."

The dog stared at him.

"I'll find Lucy and those kids a coach."

No matter what he had to do.

Two days later, Lucy stood in the front yard kicking a soccer ball to Connor. The afternoon sun shone high in the sky, but the weather might as well be cloudy and gray due to the frown on her nephew's face. Practices began next week and the Defeeters still didn't have a coach. Ryland hadn't called back, either.

She tapped the ball with her left foot. It rolled too far to the left, out of Connor's reach and into the hedge separating the yard from the neighbor's. Lucy grimaced. "Sorry."

Connor didn't say a word but chased the ball. She knew what he was thinking because his expression matched her thoughts. The team needed someone who knew soccer better than she did, someone who could teach the kids the right skills and knew rules without having to resort to a book each time.

Her efforts to find a coach had failed. That left one person who could come to her—and the team's—rescue.

It won't be long. I promise.

Ryland's words returned to her in a rush. Pathetic, how quick she'd been to believe them. As if she hadn't learned anything based on her past experiences.

Okay, it had been only a couple of days. "Long" could mean a few days, a week, even a month. But "promise" was a seven-letter word that held zero weight with most of the people in this world.

Was Ryland one of them?

Time would tell, but for Connor's sake she hoped not. He kicked the ball back to her.

She stopped the ball with her right foot the way she'd seen someone do on a video then used the inside of her foot to kick the ball back. She had better control this time. "Your teacher liked your book report."

"I guess."

"You got an A."

Connor kicked the ball her way without stopping it first. "Are you sure he hasn't called?"

He equaled Ryland. Connor had been asking that question nonstop, including a call during lunchtime using a classmate's cell phone.

Lucy patted her jeans pocket. "My phone's right here."

"You checked your messages?"

"I did." And rechecked them. No messages from Ryland. From anyone for that matter. She hadn't made any close friends in Chicago. The ones who lived in Wicksburg had remained friends with her ex-husband after Lucy moved away. That made things uncomfortable now that she was back. The pity in their eyes reminded her of when she'd been sick. She wanted no part of that ever again. "But it's only been a couple of days."

"It feels like forever."

"I know." Each time her cell phone rang, thinking it might be Ryland filled her stomach with tingles of anticipation. She hated that. She didn't want to feel that way about any guy calling her, even if the reason was finding a coach for her nephew's soccer team. "But good things come to those who wait."

Connor rolled the ball back and forth along the bottom of his foot. "That's what Mom and Dad say. I'm trying to be patient, but it's hard."

"I know it's hard to wait, but we have to give Ryland time."

Connor nodded.

Please come through, Ryland. Lucy didn't want Connor's favorite player letting him down at the worst possible time. She didn't want her nephew to have to face the kind of betrayal and disappointment she'd suffered due to others. Not when he was only nine, separated from his parents by oceans and continents.

He kicked the ball to her. "Maybe Ryland forgot."

Lucy didn't want to go there. The ball rolled past her toward the sidewalk. She chased after it. "Give him the benefit of the doubt."

Connor didn't say anything.

She needed him to stop focusing so much on Ryland. "Your dad wants to see videotapes of your games. He can't wait to see how the team does this spring."

She kicked the ball back. Connor touched the ball twice with his foot before kicking it to her.

"Next time only one touch," she said.

Surprise filled his blue eyes. "That's what my dad says."

"It might come as a shock, but your aunt knows a few things about the game of soccer." She'd found a book on coaching on the living-room bookcase and attended a coaching clinic put on by the league last night while Connor had dinner over at a friend's house. "How about we kick the ball a few times more, then go to the pizza parlor for dinner? You can play those video games you like so much."

"Okay."

Talk about an unenthused reaction.

An old beat-up, blue pickup truck pulled to the curb in front of the house. The engine idled loudly, as if in need of a tune-up. The engine sputtered off. The truck lurched forward a foot, maybe two.

The driver's door opened. Ryland.

Her heart thumped.

It won't be long. I promise.

Tingles filled her stomach. He hadn't let her down. He was still the same nice guy he'd been in high school.

Ryland rounded the front of the truck. He wore a white polo shirt with the Fuego logo on the left side, a pair of khaki shorts and the boot on his right foot. He wore a tennis shoe on his left. His hair was nicely styled. He'd shaved, removing the sexy stubble.

Even with his clean-cut look, she knew not to let her guard down. The guy was still dangerous. The only reason she was happy to see him was Connor.

A little voice inside her head laughed at that. She ignored it.

"It's him." Awe filled Connor's voice. "Ryland James."

"Yes, it's him," she said.

Ryland crossed the sidewalk and stood near them on the lawn. "Hello."

Lucy fought the urge to step back and put some distance between them. "Hi."

He acknowledged her with a nod, but turned his attention to the kid with the stars in his eyes. "You must be Connor."

Her nephew nodded.

Lucy's heart melted. Ryland knew how important this moment must be for her nephew.

Connor wiped his right hand against his shorts then extended his arm. "It's nice to meet you, Mr. James."

As Ryland shook his hand, he grinned. "Call me Ryland."

Connor's eyes widened. He looked almost giddy with excitement. "Okay, Ryland."

He motioned to the soccer ball. "Looks like you've been practicing. It's good to get some touches on the ball every day."

Connor nodded. The kid was totally starstruck. Lucy didn't blame him for being wowed by Ryland. She was, too.

Better be careful.

Ryland used his left foot to push the ball toward Connor. "Let's see you juggle."

Connor swooped up the ball and bounced it off his bony knees. He used his legs and feet to keep the ball from touching the ground.

"You're doing great," Ryland encouraged.

Connor beamed and kept going.

Ryland glanced at her. "He reminds me of Aaron."

"Two peas in a pod," she agreed.

The ball bounced away. Connor ran after it. "I'll try it again."

"The more you practice, the better you'll get," Ryland said.

"That's what Aunt Lucy told me."

His gaze met hers. Lucy's pulse skittered at the flirtatious gleam in Ryland's hazel eyes.

"Your aunt is a smart woman," he said.

Lucy didn't feel so smart. She wasn't sure what to make of her reaction to Ryland being here. Okay, the guy was handsome. Gorgeous, really. But she knew better than to be bowled over by a man and sweet talk.

So why was she practically swooning over the sexy soccer star? Ryland showing up and the way he was interacting with Connor had to be the reason. Nothing else made sense.

She straightened. "I thought you were going to call."

"I decided to stop by, instead."

Warning bells rang in her head. "The address isn't on my business card. How did you find this place?"

"I went into the café for a cup of coffee and asked where Aaron lived," Ryland explained. "Three people offered directions."

"That's Wicksburg for you," she said. "Friendly to a fault."

"No kidding," he agreed. "I received a friendly reminder about the difference between a tornado watch versus a tornado warning. More than one person also suggested I drop my dad's old truck off at the salvage yard before he gets home from vacation. But it's a good thing he has it. The truck is the only vehicle that has enough room so I can drive with my left foot."

"You went to so much trouble. A phone call would've been fine."

He motioned to her nephew. "Not for him."

A big grin brightened Connor's face. The heartache of the last few weeks seemed to have vanished. He looked happy and carefree, the way a nine-year-old boy should be.

Words didn't seem enough, but gratitude was all Lucy could afford to give Ryland. "Thank you."

"Watch this," Connor said.

"I'm watching," Ryland said, sounding amused.

Her nephew juggled the ball. His face, a portrait in concentration.

"Keep it going," Ryland encouraged.

"You're all he's talked about for the last two days," she said quietly. "I'm so happy you're here. I mean, Connor's happy. We're both happy."

"That makes three of us," Ryland said.

"Did you find a coach for the Defeeters?" Connor asked.

"Not a head coach, but someone who can help out for now."

"I knew it!" Connor screamed loud enough for the entire town to hear. The ball bounced into the hedge again.

Ryland had done his part, more than Lucy had expected. Warmth flowed through her. Not good. She shouldn't feel anything where he was concerned. She wanted him to give his talk to the team ASAP so she could say goodbye. "Thanks."

"So who's going to help coach us?" Connor asked eagerly.

Ryland smiled, a charming lopsided grin that made her remember the boy he used to be, the one she'd fallen head over heels for when she'd been a teenager.

"I am," he said.

CHAPTER FOUR

THE next week, on Monday afternoon, Ryland walked through the parking lot at Wicksburg Elementary School. Playing soccer here was one of the few good memories he had of the place.

He hoped today's soccer practice went well. He was looking forward to spending time with Lucy, and as for the boys… how hard could it be to coach a bunch of eight- and nine-year-olds?

Ryland adjusted the strap of the camp-chair bag resting on his left shoulder. He hated the idea of sitting during any portion of the practice, but standing for an entire hour wouldn't be good if his foot started hurting.

Healing was his number one priority. He had to be smart about helping the Defeeters. Not only because of his foot. His agent and the Fuego's front office might not consider a pseudo coaching gig "laying low." He'd sent an email to all the boys' parents explaining the importance of keeping his presence with the team quiet.

A car door slammed.

He glanced in the direction of the sound. Lucy's head appeared above the roof of a car.

Ryland hoped she was happier to see him today. The uncertainty in her eyes when he'd said he would help with the Defeeters had surprised him. When he explained no one else wanted to coach, so he'd decided to do it himself, a resigned smile settled on her lips. But she hadn't looked happy or relieved about the news.

He'd wanted a challenge. It appeared he'd gotten one.

She bent over, disappearing from his sight, then reappeared. Another door shut.

Her strawberry-blond curls bounced. His fingers itched to see if the strands felt as silky as they looked.

Lucy stepped out from between two cars with a bag of equipment in one hand and a binder in the other. She was alone.

He hoped her nephew wasn't sick. At least Lucy had shown up.

That made Ryland happy. So did the spring weather. He gave a quiet thanks for the warm temperature. Lucy had ditched the baggy hoodies she'd worn at his parents' house and at Aaron's. Her sweatshirts and pants had been hiding treasures.

Her outfit today showed off her figure to perfection. A green T-shirt stretched tight across her chest. Her breasts were round and high, in proportion and natural looking. Navy shorts accentuated the length of her legs. Firm and sexy. Ryland preferred the pale skin color to the orangey fake tan some women had.

Little Lucy Martin was a total hottie. Ryland grinned. Coaching the Defeeters was looking better and better.

Her gaze caught his. She pressed her lips together in a thin, tight line.

Busted. He'd been staring at her body. Practically leering. Guilt lodged in his throat.

A twinge of disappointment ran through him, too. Her reaction made one thing clear. She no longer had a crush on him.

He wasn't surprised. Crushes came and went. Over a decade had passed since they knew each other as kids. But Ryland didn't get why Lucy looked so unhappy to see him. If not for him, she would be on her own coaching the boys. He didn't expect her to fall at his feet, but a smile—even a hint of one—would have been nice.

She glanced toward the grass field.

He half expected her to walk away from him, but instead she headed toward him. Progress? He hoped so. "Hello."

"Hi," she said.

"Where's Connor?"

"He went home from school with a boy from the team. They should be here soon."

"A playdate and the first practice of spring. Connor is a lucky kid."

"I wanted to make today special for him."

"You have." Ryland liked how Lucy did so much for her nephew, but she seemed to give, give, give. He wondered if she ever did anything for herself. Maybe that was how he could get on her good side. "The first practice is always interesting. Getting to know a new coach. Sizing up who has improved over the break. Making friends with new teammates. At least that's how I remember it."

"All I know is Connor has been looking forward to this for weeks," she said. "He's been writing letters and sending emails to Aaron and Dana counting down the days to the start of practice, but they must be somewhere without computer access. They haven't replied the past couple of days."

That didn't sound good. "Worried?"

Lucy shrugged but couldn't hide the anxiousness in her eyes. "Aaron said this could happen. Connor just wants to hear what his dad thinks about you working with the team."

She hadn't answered Ryland's question about being worried, but he let it go. "I hope I live up to Connor's expectations."

"You really don't have to do this."

"I don't mind showing up early to practice."

"I was talking about coaching."

That wasn't what he'd expected her to say, but Lucy didn't seem to mince words. She also wore her heart on her sleeve. He didn't like seeing the tight lines around her mouth and narrowed eyes. He wanted to put her at ease. "It might be the last thing I expected to be doing while I'm in Wicksburg. But I want to do this for Aaron and his son."

For Lucy, too. But Ryland figured saying that would only upset her more.

"What if someone finds out?" she asked.

That thought had crossed his mind many times over the past

few days. Someone outside the team would recognize him at some point and most likely wouldn't be able to keep quiet.

But he was a man who took chances.

Besides how much trouble could he get into helping a bunch of kids? Community involvement was a good thing, surely? "I'll deal with that if it happens, but remember, I'm not coaching. I'm only helping."

A carefully laid out distinction that made a world of difference. At least he hoped so.

He waited for her to say something, to rattle off a list of reasons why his assisting the Defeeters was a bad idea or to tell him she'd found someone else to coach the team.

Instead, she raised the bag of equipment—balls and orange cones—in the air. "I picked up the practice gear. I also have a binder with emergency and player information."

Interesting. He'd expected her to put up more of a fight. He'd kind of been looking forward to it. When Lucy got emotional, silvery sparks flashed in her irises. He liked her blue eyes. And the rest of her, too. "Thanks."

"So what do you want to do with the cones?" she asked. "I've never been to a soccer practice before."

This was why Ryland wanted—no, needed—to help. He wouldn't be working only with the kids. He would be teaching Lucy what to do so she'd be all set when fall season rolled around. He didn't want the Defeeters split up as a team in September because they didn't have a coach for fall league. That wouldn't be good for the boys or for Aaron when he returned home. Lucy might end up feeling bad, too. "I'll show you."

With Lucy at his side, Ryland stepped from the asphalt onto the field. The smell of fresh grass filled his nostrils, the scent as intoxicating as a woman's perfume. He inhaled to take another sniff. Anticipation zinged through him, bringing all his nerve endings to life.

Neither soccer nor women had been part of his life since his foot surgery. He shot a sideward glance at Lucy. At least one of them would be now. Well, sort of.

"It's good to be back," he said, meaning it.

"In town?" she asked.

"On this field." For the last eleven years, no matter what level he played, soccer had meant packed stadiums, cheering crowds and vuvuzelas being blown. Shirtless men with painted faces and chests stood in the stands. Women with tight, tiny tops wanted body parts autographed. Smiling, he motioned to the field in front of him. "It doesn't matter whether I'm at an elementary school for a practice or at a sold-out stadium for a World Cup game. This is…home."

A dreamy expression formed on Lucy's face.

He stared captivated wondering what she was thinking about.

"I felt that way about this loft in Chicago." The tone of her voice matched the wistfulness in her eyes. "They rented studio space by the hour. The place smelled like paint and thinner, but that made it even more perfect. I couldn't afford to rent time that often, but when I did, I'd stay until the last second."

All the tension disappeared from around her mouth and forehead. Joy lit up her pretty face.

Warmth flowed though his veins. This was how Lucy should always look.

"Do you have a place to work on your art here?" he asked, his voice thick.

"No. It's just something I pursue in my spare time. I don't have much of that right now between Connor and my graphic-design business."

He didn't like how she brushed aside her art when talking about the studio loft made her so happy. "If you enjoy it…"

"I enjoy spending time with Connor." She glanced at her watch. "We should get ready for the boys to arrive."

Ryland would have rather found out more about her art and her. But he still had time.

"So the cones?" she asked again.

Her practical, down-to-business attitude didn't surprise him, but he was amused. He couldn't wait to break through her hard shell. "How do you think they should be set up?"

She raised her chin slightly. “You tell me. You’re the coach.”

“Officially, you are.” Lucy had listed herself as the head coach with the league, which kept Ryland’s name off the coach’s list and league website. Besides, he wouldn’t be here for the whole season. “I’m your helper.”

“I may be listed as the head coach,” she said. “But unofficially, as long as you’re here to help, my most important job is to put together the snack list.”

“That job is almost as important as coaching. Snacks after the game were my favorite part of rec. soccer.”

Though now that Ryland had seen her go-on-forever legs, he might have to rethink that. A mole on the inside of her calf just above her ankle drew his attention. He wondered what her skin would taste like.

“Ryland…”

Lucy’s voice startled him. He forced his gaze onto her face.

Annoyance filled her blue eyes, but no silver sparks flashed. “The cones.”

Damn. He’d been caught staring twice now, but all her skin showing kept taking him by surprise. He wondered how she’d look in a bikini or…naked. Pretty good, he imagined. Though thinking about Lucy without any clothes on wasn’t a smart idea. He needed to focus on the practice. “Two vertical lines with a horizontal connecting them at the top. Five cones on each side.”

She dropped the equipment bag on the grass. “While I do that, set up your chair and take the weight off your foot. You don’t want anything to slow down your recovery.”

And your departure from town. The words may not have been spoken, but they were clearly implied.

Before he could say anything, she walked away, hips swaying, curls bouncing.

Too bad she was out-of-bounds.

Ryland removed his chair from the bag and opened it up. But he didn’t sit. His foot didn’t hurt.

He ran over the practice in his mind. His injury would keep him from teaching by example. He needed someone with two working feet to show the boys what needed to be done. Someone like…

"Lucy."

"Just a minute." She placed the last cone on the grass. "What do you need?"

You. Too bad that wasn't possible. But a brilliant albeit somewhat naughty idea formed in his mind. "I'm going to need you to show the boys what to do during warm-ups and drills."

Her eyes widened. "I've never done anything like this before. I have no idea what you want me to do."

Ryland wanted her. It was as simple as that. Or would be if circumstances were different. "I'll show you."

"O-kay."

Her lack of enthusiasm made him smile. "It's soccer not a walk down death row."

"Maybe not from your point of view," she said. "Show me."

"I want the boys to do a dynamic warm-up," he explained. "They'll break up into two groups. One half will go on the outside of the cones, the other half on the inside. Each time around they'll do something different to warm up their muscles."

"That sounds complicated."

"It's easy."

"Maybe for a pro soccer star."

Star, huh? He was surprised she thought of him that way. But he liked it. "Easy for a nine-year-old, too."

She followed him to the cones.

"The first lap I want you to jog around the outside of the cones."

"The boys know how to do that."

"I want them to see how to do it the right way."

Ryland watched her jog gracefully around the cones.

"Now what?" she asked.

"Backward."

She walked over to the starting point and went around the cones backward.

Each time he told her what to do, whether skipping and jumping at each cone or reaching down to pull up the toe of her tennis shoe. A charming pink colored her cheeks from her efforts. Her breasts jiggled from the movement.

This had to be one of his best ideas ever. Ryland grinned wickedly, pleased with himself. “Face the cones and shuffle sideward.”

She did something that looked like a step from the Electric Slide or some other line dance popular at wedding receptions.

“Let me help you.” He walked over, kneeled on his good leg and touched her left calf. The muscles tightened beneath his palms. But her skin felt as soft as it looked. Smooth, too. “Relax. I’m not going to hurt you.”

“That’s what they all say,” she muttered.

Ryland had no idea what she meant or who “they all” might be, but he wanted to find out.

“Bring your foot to the other one, instead of crossing the leg behind.” He raised her boot off the ground and brought it over to the other foot. “Like this.”

Her cheeks reddened more. “You could have just told me.”

He stood. “Yeah, but this way is more fun.”

“Depends on your definition of fun.”

Lucy shuffled around the cones.

Ryland enjoyed watching her. This was as close as he’d gotten to a female next to the housecleaner his mom had hired while she was away. Mrs. Henshaw was old enough to be his mother.

“Anything else?” Lucy asked when she’d finished.

There was more, but he didn’t want to do too many new things at the first practice. Both for Lucy’s and the boys’ sakes.

“A few drills.” The sound of boys’ laughter drifted on the air. “I’ll show you those when the time comes. The team is here.”

“Nervous?”

“They’re kids,” Ryland said. “No reason to be nervous.”

Lucy studied him. “Ever spend much time with eight- and nine-year-olds?”

Not unless you counted signing autographs, posing for photographs and walking into stadiums holding their hands. “No, but I was a kid once.”

She raised an arched brow. "Once."

He winked.

Lucy smiled.

Something passed between them. Something unexpected and unwelcome. Uh-oh.

A loud burp erupted from behind them followed by laughter.

Whatever was happening with Lucy came to an abrupt end. Good, because whatever connection Ryland had felt with her wasn't something he wanted. Flirting was one thing, but this couldn't turn into a quick roll in the sheets. He couldn't afford to let that happen while he was here in Wicksburg. "The Defeeters have arrived."

Lucy looked toward the parking lot. "Aaron told me coaching this age is a lot like herding cats," Lucy explained. "Except that cats don't talk back."

Another burp sounded. More laughter followed.

"Or burp," Ryland said.

As she nodded, boys surrounded them. He'd played in big games in front of millions of people, but the expectant look in these kids' eyes disconcerted him, making him feel as if he was stepping onto the pitch for the very first time.

"Hey, boys. I'm Ryland." He focused on the eager faces staring up at him, not wanting to disappoint them or Lucy. "I'm going to help out for a few games. You boys ready to play some football?"

Nine—or was it ten?—heads, ranging in size and hair color, nodded enthusiastically.

Great. Ryland grinned. This wouldn't be difficult at all.

A short kid with long blond hair scrunched his nose. "This isn't football."

"Everywhere else in the world soccer is called football," Ryland explained.

The kid didn't look impressed. "It's called soccer here."

"We'll talk more about that later." Soccer in America was nothing like soccer in other parts of the world. No sport in the

U.S. could compare with the passion for the game elsewhere. "I want you to tell me your name and how long you've played."

Each boy did. Justin. Jacob. Dalton. Tyler. Marco. The names ran into each other. Ryland wasn't going to be able to remember them. No worries. Calling them dude, bud and kid would work for today. "Let's get working."

"Can you teach us how to dive?" a boy with beach-blond hair that hung over his eyes asked.

Some soccer players dived—throwing themselves on the field and pretending to be hurt—to draw a penalty during the game. "No," Ryland said firmly. "Never dive."

"What if it's the World Cup?" a kid with a crew cut asked.

"If you're playing in the World Cup, you'll know what to do." Ryland clapped his hands together. "Time to warm up."

The boys stood in place.

He knew the warm-up routine, and so did his Fuego teammates, but based on these kids' puzzled looks, they hadn't a clue what he was talking about. "Get in a single file line behind the first cone on the left side."

The boys shuffled into place, but it wasn't a straight line. Two kids elbowed each other as they jockeyed for the spot in front of Connor. A couple kids in the middle tried to trip each other. The boys in the back half didn't seem to understand the meaning of a line and spread out.

This wasn't working out the way he'd planned. Ryland dragged his hand through his hair.

"Meow," Lucy whispered.

"So where can I find a cat herder?" he asked.

Her coy smile sent his pulse racing. "Look in the mirror. Didn't you know cat herder is synonymous with coach?"

"That's what I was afraid you'd say."

The hour flew by. Lucy stood next to Ryland on a mini-field he'd had her set up using cones. She hadn't known what to expect with the boys' first practice, but she begrudgingly gave him credit. The guy could coach.

After a rocky start, he'd harnessed the boys' energy with

warm-up exercises and drills. He never once raised his voice. He didn't have to. His excitement about the game mesmerized both the boys and Lucy. Out on the field, he seemed larger-than-life, sexier, despite the boot on his foot. Thank goodness practice was only sixty minutes, twice a week. That was more than enough time in his presence. Maybe even too much.

Ryland focused on the boys, but her gaze kept straying to him. The man was so hot. She tried hard to remain unaffected. But it wasn't easy, especially when she couldn't forget how it felt when he'd moved her leg earlier.

Talk about being a hands-on coach. His touch had surprised her. But his tenderness guiding her leg had made her want… more.

And when he'd stood behind her, his hard body pressed against her backside, helping her figure out the drills so she could show the boys…

Lucy swallowed. More wasn't possible, no matter how appealing it might sound at the moment. Being physically close to a man had felt good. She'd forgotten how good that could be. But getting involved with a guy wasn't on her list of things to do. Not when she had Connor to take care of.

"Great pass, Tyler." Ryland turned to her. "Do you know if Aaron uses set plays?"

"I have no idea," she admitted. "I have his coaching notebook if you want to look through it."

"I would. Thanks."

"I should be thanking you," she said. "The boys have learned so much from you today. More than I could have taught them over an entire season."

"I appreciate that, but you'll be ready to do this when the time comes."

She doubted that.

All but two of the boys surrounded the ball.

Ryland grimaced.

Lucy appreciated how seriously he took practice, because she needed to figure out what should be happening on the field. "Something went wrong, but I have no idea what."

He pointed to the cluster of boys. "See how the players are gathered together and focused only on the ball?"

She nodded.

"They need to spread out and play their position." He pointed to the fastest kid on the team—Dalton. "All that kid wants is the ball. Instead of playing in the center, where he should be, he's back on the left side chasing down the ball and playing defender. See how that black-haired kid, Mason—"

"Marco," she corrected.

"Yeah, Marco," Ryland said. "You've got Marco and Dalton and those other players all in the same area."

Ryland's knowledge of the game impressed her. Okay, he was a professional soccer player. But he never stopped pointing things out to her and helping the boys improve. She should have brought a notebook and pen so she could write down everything he said. It was like being enrolled at Soccer University and this was Basic Ball Skills 101. She, however, didn't feel like she had the prerequisites to attend.

"So what do you do?" she asked.

Ryland raised the silver whistle around his neck. "This."

As he blew the whistle, she wondered what his lips would feel like against her skin. Probably as good as his hands. Maybe even better.

Stop thinking about it.

The boys froze.

"This isn't bunch ball," Ryland said. "Don't chase the ball. Spread out. Play your position. Try again."

The boys did.

Ryland directed them to keep them from bunching again. He clapped when they did something right and corrected them when they made mistakes.

As she watched Ryland coach, warmth pooled inside Lucy. She forced her gaze back on the boys.

The play on the field reminded her of an accordion. Sometimes the boys were spread out. Other times they came together around the ball.

"Will telling them fix the problem?" she asked.

"No. They're still very young. But they'll start realizing what they're supposed to do," he said. "Only practice and game time will make the lesson stick."

Lucy wondered if that was what it took to become a competent coach. She had a feeling she would be doing her best just to get by.

The energy on the field intensified. Connor passed the ball to Dalton who shot the ball over the goalie's head. Goal!

"Yes!" Ryland shouted. "That's how you do it."

The boys gave each other high fives.

"That score was made possible by Connor moving to a space. He has good instincts just like his dad." Ryland's smile crinkled the corners of his eyes.

Her pulse quickened. "Wish you could be out there playing?"

He shrugged. "I always want to play, but being here sure beats sitting on my dad's easy chair with a dog on my lap."

His comment about his dad made Lucy look toward the parking lot. A line of parents waited to pick up their boys. She glanced at her watch. Uh-oh. She'd lost track of the time. "Practice ended five minutes ago."

"That was fast." Ryland blew the whistle again. "I want everyone to jog around the field to cool down. Don't run, just a nice easy pace."

The boys took off, some faster than the others.

"The team did well," Ryland said to her.

"So did you."

He straightened. "This is different from what I'm used to."

"You rose to the occasion." Lucy couldn't have worked the boys like he had. She usually preferred doing things on her own. But she needed Ryland's help with the team. Thank goodness she'd listened to Connor and taken a chance by going to see Ryland. "I learned a lot. And the boys had fun."

"Soccer is all about having fun when you're eight and nine."

"What about when you're twenty-nine?" she asked, curious about his life back in Phoenix.

"There are some added pressures and demands, but no complaints," he said. "I'm living the dream."

"Not many can say that." She sure couldn't, but maybe someday. Nah, best not to get her hopes up only to be disappointed. "Aaron says you worked hard to get where you are."

"That's nice of him. But it's amazing what being motivated can do for a kid."

"You wanted to play professionally."

"I wanted to get out of Wicksburg," he admitted. "I didn't have good grades because I liked kicking a ball more than studying so that messed up any chance of getting a football scholarship."

Football? She was about to ask when she remembered what he'd said at the beginning of practice. Soccer was called football overseas. That was where he'd spent the majority of his career. "Small-town boy who made it big."

"That was the plan from the beginning."

His wide smile sent her heart beating triple time. Lucy didn't understand her response. "I'd say you succeeded splendidly."

Whereas she… Lucy didn't want to go there. But she knew someone successful like Ryland would never be satisfied living in a small, boring town like Wicksburg. He must be counting the weeks, maybe even the days, until he could escape back to the big city. While she would remain here as long as she was needed.

As the boys jogged toward them, Ryland gave each one a high five. "Nice work out there. Practice your juggling at home. Learning to control the ball will make you a better player. Now gather up the cones and balls so we can get out of here. I don't know about you, but I'm hungry."

The boys scattered in search of balls like mice looking for bits of cheese. They dribbled the balls back. Lucy placed them inside the mesh bag. The boys picked up their water bottles then walked off the field to their parents.

Connor's megawatt smile could light up half of Indiana. "That was so much fun."

"You played hard out there," Ryland said.

Her nephew shot her a quick glance. "All that running made me hungry, too."

"I've got dinner in the slow cooker," Lucy said.

"Want to eat with us, Ryland?" Connor asked. "Aunt Lucy always makes enough food so we can have leftovers."

Spending more time with Ryland seemed like a bad idea, but she was more concerned about Connor. She couldn't always shield him from disappointment, but with him adjusting to his parents being away, she wanted to limit it. "That's nice of you to think of Ryland. We have enough food to share, but I'm sure he has somewhere else to be tonight."

There, she'd given Ryland an easy out from the dinner invitation. No one's feelings would be hurt.

"I'm free tonight," he said to her dismay. "But I wouldn't want to intrude."

"You're not." Connor looked at Lucy for verification.

She was still stuck on Ryland being free tonight. She figured he would have a date, maybe two, lined up. Unless he had a girlfriend back in Phoenix.

"Tell him it's okay, Aunt Lucy." Her nephew was using his lost puppy-dog look to his full advantage. "Ryland's coaching the team. The least we can do is feed him."

"You sound like your mom." Lucy's resolve weakened. "She's always trying to feed everyone."

Connor nodded. "That's how we ended up with Manny. Mom kept putting tuna out for him. One day he came inside and never left."

Ryland smiled. "He sounds like a smart cat."

"We call him Manny, but his full name is Manchester," Connor said.

Amusement filled Ryland's eyes. "After the Red Devils."

Connor nodded. "Man U rules."

"If Manny was a girl, I'm guessing you wouldn't have named her Chelsea."

Connor looked aghast. "Never."

Ryland grinned. "At least I know where your loyalties lie."

"I have no idea what you're talking about," Lucy admitted.

"Manchester United and Chelsea are teams in the Premier League in England," Ryland explained.

"Rivals," Connor added. "Can Ryland come over, please?"

Lucy could rattle off ten reasons not to have him over, but she had a bigger reason to say yes—Connor.

"You're welcome to join us." If Lucy didn't agree, she would never hear the end of it from her nephew. Besides, she liked how he smiled whenever Ryland was around. It was one meal. No big deal. "We have plenty of food."

"Thanks," he said. "I'm getting tired of grilling."

Connor's eyes widened. "You cook?"

"If I don't cook, I don't eat," Ryland explained. "When I moved to England, I had to cook, clean and do my own laundry. Just like my mom made me do when I was growing up."

His words surprised Lucy. She would have expected a big-shot soccer star to have a personal chef or eat out all the time, not be self-sufficient around the house. Her Jeff, her ex-husband, did nothing when it came to domestic chores.

"I'll have to learn how to do those things," Connor said with a serious expression.

"You're on your way," Ryland encouraged. "You already make great chocolate-chip cookies."

Connor's thin chest puffed slightly. "Yeah, I do."

Lucy shook her head. "You're supposed to say thank you when someone compliments you."

"Even if it's true?" Connor asked.

Ryland's smiled widened. "Especially then."

Connor shrugged. "Okay. Thank you."

Having Ryland over was exactly what Connor needed. But a part of her wondered if it was what she needed, too.

Now that was silly.

Ryland was coming over for dinner because of her nephew. Just because she might like the idea of being around him a little longer didn't mean anything at all.

CHAPTER FIVE

In the kitchen, the smell of spices, vegetables and beef simmering in the slow cooker lingered in the air. The scents brought back fond memories of family dinners with Aaron and her parents. But other than the smell, tonight wasn't going to be as comfortable as any of those dinners growing up.

Lucy checked the oven. Almost preheated to the correct temperature.

Ryland had heated her up earlier. She couldn't stop thinking about how he'd touched her at practice. His large, warm hand against her skin. Leaning against the counter, she sighed.

The guy really was…

She bolted upright.

Lucy needed to stop fantasizing and finish making dinner. She was a divorced twenty-six-year-old, not a swooning teenager. She knew better than to be crushing on any man, let alone Ryland James. The guy could charm the pants off everybody. Well, everyone except for her.

She placed the uncooked biscuits on a cookie sheet.

The sounds of laser beams from a video game and laughter from all the fun drifted into the kitchen. Ryland's laugh was deep and rich, thick and smooth, like melted dark chocolate.

Lucy opened the oven door and slid the tray of biscuits onto the middle rack. Would he taste as good as he sounded?

The pan clattered against the back of the oven.

"Need help?" Ryland yelled from the living room.

Annoyed at herself for thinking about *him* that way when

she knew better, she straightened the pan then closed the oven door. "Everything's fine."

Or would be when he was gone.

Okay, that wasn't fair. Connor was laughing and having fun. Her nephew needed Ryland, so did the team. That meant she needed him, too.

Watching a couple of videos and reading some books weren't the same as having Ryland show her what needed to be done at practice. The boys would have been the ones to suffer because of her cluelessness. Feeding Ryland dinner was the least she could do to repay him. It wasn't as if she'd had to go to any extra trouble preparing the meal.

Nor was it Ryland's fault he was gorgeous and seemed to press every single one of her buttons. Being around him reminded her that a few of the male species had redeeming qualities. Ones like killer smiles, sparkling eyes, enticing muscles, warm hands and a way with kids. But she knew better than to let herself get carried away.

"I'm going to win," Connor shouted with glee.

"Not so fast," Ryland countered. "I'm not dead yet."

"Just you wait."

The challenge in her nephew's voice loosened her tight shoulder muscles. Boys needed a male influence in their lives. Even if that influence filled her stomach with butterflies whenever he was nearby.

No worries, Lucy told herself. She hadn't been around men for a while. That had to be the reason for her reaction to Ryland.

She tossed the salad. The oven timer buzzed.

With the food on the table, she stood in the doorway to the kitchen with a container of milk in one hand and a pitcher of iced tea in the other. "Dinner's ready."

Connor took his normal seat. He pointed to a chair across, the one next to where Lucy had been sitting since she arrived a month ago. The "guest spots" at the table. "Sit there, Ryland. The other chairs are my mom's and dad's."

Ryland sat. The table seemed smaller with him there, even though it seated six.

Ignoring her unease, Lucy filled everyone's glasses. She sat, conscious of him next to her.

Her leg brushed his. Lucy stiffened. The butterflies in her stomach flapped furiously. She tucked her feet beneath her chair to keep from touching Ryland again. Next time…

There wouldn't be a next time.

Her nephew grabbed two biscuits off the plate. "These are my favorite."

Ryland took one. "Everything smells delicious."

The compliment made Lucy straighten. She hadn't cooked much after the divorce so felt out of practice. But Connor needed healthy meals so she was getting back in the habit. "Thanks."

As she dished up the stew, Ryland filled his salad plate using a pair of silver tongs. His arm brushed hers. Heat emanated from the spot of contact. "Excuse me."

"That's okay." But the tingles shooting up her arm weren't. Lucy hated the way her body reacted to even the slightest contact with him. She pressed her elbows against her side. No more touching.

Flatware clinked against bowls and plates. Ryland and Connor discussed the upcoming MLS season. She recognized some of the team names, but nothing else.

"Who's your favorite team?" Ryland asked her.

She moved a carrot around with her fork. Stew was one of her favorite dishes, but she wasn't hungry. Her lack of appetite occurred at the same time as Ryland's arrival at the house. "The only soccer games I watch are Connor's."

"That was when you lived here with Uncle Jeff," Connor said. "After you moved away you didn't come to any."

"That's true." Curiosity gleamed in Ryland's eyes, but she ignored it. She didn't want to discuss her ex-husband over dinner or in front of Connor. No matter how badly Jeff had betrayed her and their marriage vows, he'd been a good uncle and still sent Connor birthday and Christmas presents. "But I'll get to see all your games now."

Lucy reached for the salt. Extra seasoning might make the

stew more appealing. She needed to eat something or she'd find herself starving later. That had happened a lot when she moved to Chicago. She didn't want a repeat performance here.

Ryland's hand covered hers around the saltshaker.

She stiffened.

He smiled. "Great minds think alike."

Too bad she couldn't think. Not with his large, warm hand on top of hers.

Darn the man. Ryland must know he was hot stuff. But he'd better think twice before he put any moves on her. She pulled her hand away, leaving the salt for him.

Ryland handed the shaker to her. "You had it first."

Lucy added salt to her stew. "Thanks."

"I forgot to tell you, Aunt Lucy. Tyler got a puppy," Connor said, animated. "His parents took him to the animal shelter, and Tyler got to pick the dog out himself." Connor relayed the entire story, including how the dog went potty on the floor in the kitchen as soon as they arrived home. "I bet Manny would like to have a dog. That way he'd never be lonely."

Oh, no. Lucy knew exactly where her nephew was going with this. Connor had used a similar tactic to get her to buy him a new video game. But buying an inanimate object was different than a living, breathing puppy.

"Manny is rarely alone." She passed the saltshaker to Ryland. "I work from home."

Connor's forehead wrinkled, as if he were surprised she hadn't said yes right away. "But you don't chase him around the house. When I'm at school he just lays around and sleeps."

Ryland feigned shock. "You don't chase Manny?"

Lucy wanted to chase Ryland out of here. She hated how aware she was of him. Her blood simmered. She drank some iced tea, but that didn't cool her down. "Cats lay around and sleep. That's what they like to do during the day. I don't think Manny is going to be too keen on being chased by a dog. He's not a kitten anymore."

"Don't forget. Dogs make big messes outside," Ryland said. "You're going to have to clean it all up with a shovel or rake."

Connor scrunched his face. "I'm going to have to scoop up the poop?"

Okay, maybe having Ryland here wasn't so bad. She appreciated how skillfully he'd added a dose of dog-care reality to the conversation. He might make her a little hot and bothered, but he'd saved her a lot of back and forth by bringing up the mess dogs left in the yard. A fair trade-off in the grand scheme of things. At least she hoped so.

"Yes, you would have to do that." No matter how badly Connor wanted a puppy she couldn't make that decision without Aaron and Dana. Getting a pet wasn't a commitment to make lightly. "A dog is something your parents have to decide on, not me. Owning a dog is a big responsibility."

"Huge," Ryland agreed, much to Lucy's relief. "I've been taking care of my parents' dog Cupcake. I never knew something so little would take so much work. She either wants food or attention or to go outside on a walk."

"I've never taken a dog on a walk," Connor said.

"Maybe you could take Cupcake for a walk for me," Ryland suggested.

Connor nodded enthusiastically. "If it's okay with Aunt Lucy."

The longing in his blue eyes tugged at her heart. She couldn't say no to this request, even if it meant seeing Ryland outside of soccer again. "I'm sure we can figure out a time to take Cupcake for a walk."

"You can get a glimpse of what having a dog is like," Ryland said. "It might also be a good idea to see what Manny thinks of Cupcake. Cats and dogs don't always get along."

His words were exactly what a nine-year-old dog-wannabe owner needed to hear. The guy was turning into a knight in a shining soccer jersey. She would owe him dozens of chocolate-chip cookies for all he was doing for Connor.

Ryland smiled at her.

A feeling of warmth traveled from the top of her head to the tips of her toes. She'd better be careful or she was going to turn into a pile of goo. That would not be good.

"Did you ever have a dog?" Connor asked her.

"No, but we had cats and a few other animals," she replied. "Fish, a bird and reptiles."

As Ryland set his iced tea on the table, she bit into a biscuit. "Has your aunt told you about Squiggy?"

Lucy choked on the bread. She coughed and swallowed. "You remember Squiggy?"

Mischief danced in his eyes. "It's a little hard to forget being asked to be dig a grave and then rob it on the same day."

Connor's mouth formed a perfect O. "You robbed a grave?"

"Your dad and I did," Ryland said. "It was Squiggy's grave."

Connor leaned forward. "Who's Squiggy?"

Ryland winked at her.

Oh, no. He wouldn't tell… Who was she kidding? The mischievous gleam in his eyes was a dead giveaway he would spill every last detail. Might as well get it over with.

"Squiggy was my turtle. He was actually a tortoise," she explained. "But Squiggy was…"

"The best turtle in the galaxy," Ryland finished for her. "The fastest, too."

Lucy stared at him in disbelief. Those were the exact words she used to say to anyone who asked about her Squiggy. Other kids wanted dogs. She loved her hard-shelled, wrinkled reptile. "I can't believe you remember that."

"I told you I remembered a lot of stuff.

He had, but she thought Ryland was talking about when she'd been a teenager and sick. Not a seven-year-old girl who'd thought the sun rose and set on a beloved turtle.

"Your aunt doted on Squiggy," Ryland said. "Even painted his shell."

Lucy grinned. "Polka dots."

He nodded. "I recall pink and purple strips."

Memories rushed back like water over Cataract Falls on Mill Creek. "I'd forgotten about those."

"Your aunt used to hand-feed him lettuce. Took him on walks, too."

She nodded. "Squiggy might have been the fastest turtle around, but those walks still took forever."

"You never went very far," Ryland said.

"No, we didn't," she admitted. "Wait a minute. How did you know that?"

His smile softened. "Your mom had us watch you."

Her mother, make that her entire family, had always been so overprotective. Lucy had no idea they'd dragged Ryland into it, too. "And you guys accused me of following you around."

"You did follow us."

"Okay, I did, but that's what little sisters do."

Connor reached for his milk glass. "I wouldn't want a little sister."

"I never had a little sister," Ryland said. "But it felt like I had one with Lucy spying on us all the time."

She stuck her tongue out at him.

He did the same back to her.

Connor giggled.

Sitting here with Ryland brought back so many memories. When she was younger, she used to talk to him whenever he was over at the house with Aaron. Puberty and her crush had changed that. The awkward, horrible time of hormones and illness were all she'd remembered. Until now.

"Why did you have to rob Squiggy's grave?" Connor asked him.

Ryland stared into her eyes. His warm hazel gaze seemed to pierce through her. Breaking contact was the smart thing to do, but Lucy didn't want to look away.

For old times' sake, she told herself.

A voice inside her head laughed at the reasoning. A part of her didn't care. Looking was safe. It was all the other stuff that was…dangerous.

"Do you want to tell him or should I?" Ryland asked.

Emotion swirled inside her. Most of it had to do with the uncertainty she felt around him, not the story about her turtle. "Go ahead. I'm curious to hear your side of the story."

"I want to hear both sides," Connor announced.

"You will, if Ryland gets it wrong," she teased.

"I have a feeling you may be surprised," Ryland said.

She had a feeling he was right.

"Your aunt came to your dad and me with big crocodile tears streaming down her cheeks," Ryland explained. "She held a shoebox and said her beloved Squiggy had died. She wanted us to dig a hole so she could bury him."

"Before you go any further, I wanted to have a funeral, not just bury him. I would also like to remind Connor that I was only seven at the time."

Amusement gleamed in Ryland's eyes. "Age duly noted."

Connor inched forward on his chair. "What happened?"

"Your dad and I dug a hole. A grave for Squiggy's coffin."

"Shoebox," Lucy clarified.

Ryland nodded. "She placed the shoebox into the hole and tossed wilted dandelions on top of it. While your dad and I refilled the hole with dirt, your aunt Lucy played 'Taps' on a harmonica."

"Kazoo," she corrected. Still she couldn't believe all he remembered after so many years.

"A few words were spoken."

"From my favorite book at the time *Franklin in the Dark,*" she said.

"Who is Franklin?" Connor asked.

"A turtle from a series of children's books," Lucy explained. "It was turned into a cartoon that was shown on television."

"Aaron said a brief prayer," Ryland said. "Then your aunt stuck a tombstone made of Popsicle sticks into the ground and sprinkled more dandelions over the mound of dirt."

Lucy nodded. "It was a lovely funeral."

"Yeah," Ryland said. "Until you told us that Squiggy wasn't actually dead, and we had to unbury him so he wouldn't die."

Connor stared at her as if she were a short, green extraterrestrial with laser beams for eyes. "You think some video games are too violent and you buried a live turtle?"

She squirmed under his intense scrutiny. "Some games

aren't appropriate for nine-year-olds. And nothing bad happened to Squiggy."

Fortunately. What had she been thinking? Maybe burying Barbie dolls had gotten too boring.

Ryland grinned. "But it was a race against time."

She had to laugh. "They dug so fast dirt flew everywhere."

"Aaron and I were sure we would be blamed if Squiggy died."

As her gaze collided with Ryland's again, something passed between them. A shared memory, she rationalized. That was all it could be. She looked at her untouched food. "But your dad and Ryland didn't get in trouble. They saved Squiggy."

Connor leaned over the table. "Squiggy didn't die under all that dirt?"

Ryland raised his glass. "Nope. Squiggy was alive and moving as slow as ever."

But that was the last time she'd thrown a funeral for anything living or inanimate. Her parents had made sure of that.

"So why did you bury him and have a funeral?" Connor asked.

Lucy knew this question would be coming once more of the story came out. "You know how some kids play house or restaurant?"

"Or army," Connor suggested.

She nodded. "One of the games I played was funeral."

"That's weird." Connor took another biscuit from the plate. "In school Mrs. Wilson told us turtles live longer than we do. Whatever happened to Squiggy?"

"He ran away," Lucy said. "Your dad and I grew up in a house that was near the park with that nice lake. We'd see turtles on tree trunks at the water's edge. Your dad told me Squiggy was lonely and ran away to live with the other turtles. I was sad and missed him so much, but your dad said I should be happy because Squiggy wanted to be in the park."

A beat passed. And another. Connor looked at Ryland. "So what really happened to Squiggy?"

Her mouth gaped.

A sheepish expression crossed Ryland's face.

Realization dawned. "Squiggy didn't run away."

Connor gasped. "Squiggy died!"

Ryland nodded once, but his gaze never left hers. "I thought you'd figured out what happened."

She'd been so quick to believe Aaron… Of course she'd wanted to believe it. "I never thought something bad might have happened to Squiggy."

"I'm sorry." The sincerity in Ryland's voice rang clear, but the knowledge still stung. "Aaron didn't want to put you through a real funeral because he knew how much Squiggy meant to you so we buried him one night in the park after you went to bed."

Lucy had imagined the adventures Squiggy had experienced at the pond. But the lie didn't surprise her. Few told her the truth once she'd gotten sick. It must have been the same way before she was so ill. "I should have figured that out."

"You were young," Ryland said. "There's nothing wrong with believing something if it makes us happy."

"Even if it's a lie?" she asked.

"A white lie so you wouldn't hurt so badly," he countered. "You know Aaron always watched out for you back then."

That much was true. Lucy nodded.

"My dad told me it's important to look out for others, especially girls." Connor scrunched his nose as if that last word smelled bad.

"He's right," Ryland said. "That's what your dad was doing with your aunt when Squiggy died. It's what he always did and probably still does with her and your mom."

Connor sat taller. "I'll have to do the same."

Ryland looked as proud of her nephew as she felt. "We all should," he said.

Her heart thudded. The guy was a charmer, but he sounded genuine.

But then so had Jeff, she reminded herself.

The harsh reality clarified the situation. She needed to rein in her emotions ASAP. Thinking of Ryland as anything other than the Defeeters' coaching assistant was not only dangerous but also stupid. She wasn't about to risk her heart with someone like that again.

She scooted back in her chair. "Who's ready for dessert?"

While Lucy tucked Connor back into bed, Ryland stared at the framed photographs setting on the fireplace mantel. Each picture showed a different stage in Aaron's life—army, marriage, family, college graduation. Those things were as foreign to Ryland as a three-hundred-pound American football linebacker trying to tackle him as he ran toward the goal.

Footsteps sounded behind him. "I think Connor's down for the count this time," Lucy said.

Finally. The kid was cool and knew a lot about soccer, but he hadn't left them alone all evening. Twice now Connor had gotten out of bed after they'd said good-night. "Third time's the charm."

"I hope so."

Ryland did, too. A repeat performance of today's practice with some touching would be nice, especially if she touched back. Having a little fun wouldn't hurt anyone. No one, not Mr. McElroy or Blake or Ryland's mom, would have to know what went on here tonight.

She sat on the couch. "Looking at Aaron's pictures?"

"Yeah." Ryland ran his fingertip along the top of a black wood frame, containing a picture of Aaron and Connor fishing. That was something fathers and sons did in Wicksburg. "Aaron's looks haven't changed that much, but he seems like quite the family guy."

Many professional players had a wife, kids and pets. When Ryland first started playing overseas, he hadn't wanted to let anything get in the way of his new soccer career and making a name for himself. He'd been a young, hungry hotshot.

Wait a minute. He still was. Only maybe not quite so young…

"It's hard to believe Aaron's only thirty. He's done a lot for his age," Lucy said with a touch of envy in her voice. "You both have."

Ryland shrugged. "I'm a year younger and have four, maybe five, years left to play if I'm lucky."

"That's not long."

Teams used up and threw away players. But he wasn't ready for that to happen to him. He also didn't want to hang on past his time and be relegated to a few minutes of playing time or be on a team in a lower league. "That's why I want to make the most of the time I have left in the game."

"Soccer is your priority."

"It's my life." He stared at Aaron's wedding picture. Knowing someone was there to come home to must be nice, but he'd made the decision not to divide his focus. Soccer was it. Sometimes Ryland felt a sense of loneliness even when surrounded by people. But occasionally feeling lonely wasn't a reason to get involved in a serious relationship. "That's why I won't start thinking about settling down until my career is over with."

"Playing the field might be hard to give up," she commented.

"Is that the voice of experience talking?"

"Someone I knew," she said. "That's not my type of…game."

A picture of Aaron wearing fatigues and holding a big rifle caught Ryland's attention. His old friend might consider him a foe for putting the moves on Lucy. He nudged the frame so the photo of Aaron looking big, strong and armed didn't directly face the couch.

Ryland flashed her his most charming smile. "What kind of games do you play?"

"None."

He strode to the couch. "That doesn't sound like much fun."

She shrugged. "Fun is in the eye of the beholder."

Holding her would be fun. He sat next to her.

Lucy smelled like strawberries and sunshine. Appealing and intoxicating like sweet ambrosia. He wouldn't mind a taste. But she seemed a little tense. He wanted the lines creasing her forehead to disappear so they could get comfortable and cozy. "I see lots of family photographs. Is any of your artwork here?"

"Yes."

"Show me something."

Her eyes narrowed suspiciously. "Are you asking to see my etchings?"

"I was thinking more along the lines of sketches and paintings, but if you have etchings and they happened to be in your bedroom…" he half joked.

She glanced toward the hallway he assumed led to the bedrooms. Interest twinkled in her eyes. Her pursed lips seemed to be begging for kisses. Maybe Lucy was more game than she let on.

Anticipation buzzed through him. All he needed was a sign from her to make his move. Unless she took the initiative. Now that would be a real turn-on.

Her gaze met his. "Not tonight."

Bummer. He didn't think she was playing hard to get so he had to take her words at face value. "Another time, maybe."

"I'll…see."

Her response didn't sound promising. That…bugged him. Some women would be all over him, trying to get him to kiss, touch, undress them. Lucy wanted nothing to do with him. At least outside of soccer practice.

Calling it a night would be his best move. A challenge was one thing, but there was no sense beating his head against the goalpost. He wasn't supposed to be flirting let alone wanting to kiss her. Too bad he didn't want to leave yet. "Anything I can do to help my cause?"

Her blue-eyed gaze watched him intently. "Not tonight."

Same answer as before. At least she was consistent.

Ryland stood. "It's getting late. Cupcake's been out in the dog run since before practice. She has a cushy doghouse, but she's going to be wondering where I've been. Thanks for dinner. A home-cooked meal was the last thing I was expecting tonight."

Lucy rose. “I wasn’t expecting a dinner guest.”

Ryland wished tonight could be ending differently, but he liked that she was honest and up-front. “We’re even.”

“I’d say your helping with the team outweighs my cooking dinner.”

He wasn’t quite ready to give up. “You could always invite me over for more meals.”

Lucy raised an eyebrow. “Taking another shot?”

“Habit.” A bad one under the circumstances. Not many would call him a gentleman, but Lucy deserved his respect. “Which means it’s time for me to go. Practice is at five o’clock on Wednesday, right?”

She nodded.

He took a step toward the door. “See you then.”

“Ryland…”

As he looked at her, she bit her lower lip. He would like to nibble on her lip. Yeah, right. He wanted to kiss her until she couldn’t breathe and was begging for more.

Not tonight.

“Thanks,” she said. “For coaching. I mean, helping out with the team. And being so nice to Connor.”

Her warm eyes were as appealing as her mouth. “Your nephew is a great kid.”

She nodded. “Having you here is just what we…he needed.”

Ryland found her slip of the tongue interesting. Maybe she wasn’t as disinterested as she claimed to be. He hoped she changed whatever opinion of him was holding her back. Earning her respect ranked right up there with tasting her kisses. “Anytime.”

That was often a throwaway line, but he meant it with her.

Time to get the hell out of here before he said or did anything he might regret.

Lucy was the kind of woman you took home to meet your mother. The kind of woman who dreamed of a big wedding, a house with a white picket fence and a minivan full of kids. The kind of woman he normally avoided.

Best to leave before things got complicated. His life was far from perfect with all the demands and pressures on him, unwanted media attention and isolation, but his career was on the line. What was left of it, anyway. His reputation, too.

No woman was worth messing up his life for, not even the appealing, challenging and oh-so-enticing Lucy Martin.

CHAPTER SIX

ON WEDNESDAY afternoon, Lucy shaded an area on her sketch pad. The rapid movement of her pencil matched the way she felt. Agitated. Unnerved.

She'd filled half a sketch pad with drawings these past two days. An amazing feat considering she hadn't done any art since she'd left Chicago to return to Wicksburg. But she'd had to do something to take her mind off Ryland.

She took a closer look at the sketch. It was *him.* Again. If she wasn't thinking about Ryland, she was drawing him.

Lucy moved her pencil over the paper. She lengthened a few eyelashes. Women would kill for thick, luscious lashes like his. Heaven knew a tube of mascara couldn't come close to making her eyes look like that. So not fair.

Lucy shaded under his chin then raised her pencil.

Gorgeous.

Not the drawing, the man. The strength of his jaw, the flirtatious gleam in his eyes, his kissable lips.

Attraction heated her blood. What in the world was she doing drawing Ryland this way?

And then she realized…

She had another crush. But this felt different from when she'd been a teenager crushing on Ryland, stronger even than when she'd started dating her ex-husband.

Stupid.

Lucy closed the cover of her sketch pad, but every line,

curve and shadow of Ryland's face was etched on her brain. She massaged her aching temples.

Connor ran from the hallway to the living room. "I'm ready for practice."

He wore his soccer clothes—blue shirt, shorts and socks with shin guards underneath. As the shoelaces from his cleats dragged on the ground, he bounced from foot to foot with excitement.

Soccer practice was the last place she wanted to go. The less time she spent with Ryland, the better. She was too old to be feeling this way about him. About any guy. But skipping out wasn't an option. She was the head coach, after all. "Let me get my purse."

On the drive, Lucy glanced in the rearview mirror. Connor sat in the backseat, his shoulders hunched, as he played a game on his DS console. He was allowed a certain amount of video-game time each day, and he liked playing in the car. At least that kept him from talking about Ryland. Connor had a serious case of hero worship.

But that didn't mean she had to have one, too. Ryland hadn't known about her crush before. He didn't need to know about this one.

She would stay focused on soccer practice. No staring, admiring or lusting. No allowing Connor to invite him over for dinner tonight, either.

With her resolve firmly in place, Lucy parked then removed the soccer gear from her trunk. As Connor ran ahead of her, she noticed Ryland, dressed in his usual attire of shorts and a T-shirt, talking with Dalton's mom, Cheryl.

Lucy did a double take. Cheryl wore a tight, short skirt and a camisole. The clothing clung to every curve, showing lots of tanned skin and leaving little to the imagination. Not that Ryland would have to wait long to sample Cheryl's wares. She stood so close to him her large chest almost touched him.

Lucy gripped the ball bag in her hand.

Ryland didn't seem to mind. He stood his ground, not trying to put any distance between them.

Okay, maybe they weren't standing that close, but still…

Emotions swirled through her. She forced herself to look away.

No reason to be upset or jealous. She'd had her chance Monday night, but turned him down. Oh, she'd been tempted to have him stay and get comfy on the couch, but she was so thankful common sense had won over raging hormones. Especially now that he'd moved on to someone more…willing.

No worries. What two consenting adults did was none of her business. But like a moth drawn to a flame, she glanced over at them. She'd never considered herself masochistic, but she couldn't help herself.

Cheryl batted her mascara-laden eyelashes at him.

Ryland's grin widened. He'd used that same charming smile on Lucy after Connor had gone to bed.

Her stomach churned. Maybe she shouldn't have eaten the egg-salad sandwich for lunch. Maybe she needed to chill.

She quickened her pace. Not that either would notice her. They were too engrossed with each other.

No big deal. Ryland was a big boy, a professional athlete. He knew what he was getting into. He must deal with women hitting on him on a daily basis, ones who wouldn't think of telling him *not tonight.*

As she passed the two, Lucy focused on the boys. Seven of them stood in a circle and kicked the ball to one another while Marco ran around the center trying to steal the ball away.

Cheryl laughed, a nails-on-chalkboard sound that would make Cupcake howl. Lucy grimaced. If Ryland wanted to be with that kind of woman, he'd never be satisfied with someone like her. Not that she wanted to be with him.

Stop thinking about it! About him!

But she couldn't. No doubt this was some lingering reaction to Jeff's cheating. She'd thought it was great how her husband and her best friend since junior high, Amelia, got along. Lucy hadn't even suspected the two had been having an affair.

Better off without him. Without any of them. Men and best friends.

"Lucy."

Gritting her teeth, she glanced over her shoulder. Ryland was walking toward her. She waited for him. Even with the boot on his injured right foot, he moved with the grace of a world-class athlete, but looked more like a model for a sportswear company.

She didn't want to be impressed, but she couldn't blame Cheryl for wanting to get to know Ryland better. The guy was hot.

Maybe if Lucy hadn't taken a hiatus—more like a sabbatical—from men…

No. Even if she decided to jump back into the dating scene, he wasn't the right man for her. He wasn't the kind of guy to settle down let alone stick around. A superstar like Ryland James had too many women who wanted to be with him and would do anything to get close to him. He'd admitted he wouldn't start thinking about settling down until his career was over with. Why should he? Ryland had no reason to tie himself to only one woman and fight temptation on a daily basis.

Or worse, give in to it as Jeff had.

Ryland was smart for staying single and enjoying the… benefits that came with being a professional athlete.

He stopped next to her. "You sped by so fast I thought we were late starting practice."

He'd noticed her? With sexy Cheryl right there? Lucy was so stunned she almost missed the little thrill shooting through her. "I like being punctual."

The words sounded stupid as soon as she'd spoken them. She did like being on time, but that wasn't the reason she'd rushed by him. Telling him she'd been jealous of Cheryl wasn't happening. Not in this lifetime. She didn't need to boost his ego and decimate hers in one breath.

Ryland pulled out his cell phone and checked the time. He glanced at the boys on the field. "Practice doesn't start for ten minutes. We're still missing players."

Lucy noticed he didn't wear a watch or jewelry. She liked

that he didn't flaunt his wealth by wearing bling as some athletes she'd seen on television did.

Not that she cared what he wore.

Feeling flustered, she set the equipment bag on the grass. "That'll give me plenty of time to set up."

His assessing gaze made Lucy feel as if she were an abstract piece of art that he couldn't decide was valuable or not. She didn't like it. If he was looking for a list of her faults, she could give him one. Jeff had made it clear where she didn't stack up in the wife department.

She placed her hands on her hips. "What?"

"You okay?" Ryland asked.

"Fine." The word came out quick and sharp. "Just one of those days," she added.

Two more women, Suzy and Debbie, joined Cheryl. Both wore the typical soccer-mom uniform—black track pants and T-shirts. The women waved at Ryland. He nodded in their direction before turning his attention back to Lucy.

"Anything I can do to help?" he offered.

"You've done enough." She realized how that might sound. She shouldn't be taking her feelings out on him. Like it or not, she needed his help if she was going to learn enough about soccer to be helpful to the boys. Not just for the spring season, but fall if no one else stepped up to coach. "I mean, you're doing enough with the team. And Connor."

"I'm happy to do more for the boys and for you."

She should be grateful, but his offer irritated Lucy. She liked being self-sufficient. Competent. Independent. Yet she was having to depend on Ryland to help with the team, to teach her about soccer and to keep a smile on Connor's face. She felt like a failure…again. No way could she have him do more. "Let's get set up so we can start on time."

As she removed the cones from the bag, she glanced up at him.

Ryland stood watching her. With the sun behind him, he looked almost angelic except the look in his eyes made her feel as if he wanted to score with her, not the ball.

Lucy's heart lurched. Heat pooled within her. Common sense told her to ignore him and the hunger in his eyes. But she couldn't deny he made her feel sexy and desired. If only…

Stop. Now.

He was charming, handsome, and completely out of her league. An unexpected crush was one thing. It couldn't go any further than that.

"I can put them out," Ryland said.

No. Lucy didn't want any more help from him. She lowered her gaze to his mouth. His lips curved into a smile. Tingles filled her stomach.

And no matter how curious she might get or how flirtatious he might be, she didn't want any kisses from him, either. "Thanks, but I've got it."

A week later, Ryland gathered up the cones from the practice field. The sun had started setting a little later. Spring was his favorite time of year with the grass freshly cut, the air full of promise and the game fast and furious.

A satisfied feeling flowed through him. The boys were getting it. Slowly, but surely. And Lucy…

What was he going to do about her?

He'd had a tough time focusing during today's practice due to how cute she looked in her pink T-shirt and black shorts. Those sexy legs of her seemed to have gotten longer. Her face glowed from running around.

Look, don't touch. Ryland had been reminding himself of that for the past hour. Okay, the last week and a half.

She held the equipment bag while he put the cones inside. Her sweet scent surrounded him. Man, she smelled good. Fresh and fruity. He took another sniff. Smelling wasn't touching.

"The boys had a good practice today," she said.

"We'll see how they put it to use in their first match."

"Connor said they've never beaten the Strikers." She tightened the pull string on the bag. "Will they be ready?"

"No, but soccer at this age is all about development."

"Scores aren't reported."

He was used to being surrounded by attractive women, but with Lucy her looks weren't her only appeal. He appreciated how she threw herself into learning about soccer, practicing the drills and studying the rules at home. "Maybe not, but the boys will know the score. And I'd be willing to bet so will the majority of the parents."

"Probably," she said, sounding rueful.

Empathy tugged at him. "You might have to deal with that. Especially toward the end of the season."

She nodded, resigned. "I can handle it."

Pride for her "can do" attitude swelled in his chest. "I know you can."

Lucy's unwavering smile during practices suggested she might be falling in love with the game. Too bad she couldn't fall for him, too.

But that wasn't going to happen. She didn't look at him as anything other than her helper.

Many women wanted to go out with a professional athlete. Lucy wasn't impressed by what he did. He could pump gas at the corner filling station for all she cared. She never asked him anything about his "job" only how his foot was doing. Her indifference to him bristled, even if he knew it was less complicated that way.

She scanned the field. "Looks like we've got everything."

Without waiting for a reply, she headed toward the parking lot. He hobbled along behind her, watching her backside and biting his lip to keep from commenting on how sexy she looked in her gym shorts.

Flirting with her came so naturally, he'd tried hard during practices to keep the conversation focused on soccer. Maybe he should try to be more personable. She was back in town, just like him. She could be...lonely.

Ryland fell into step next to Lucy. Maybe he was the one who was lonely. He'd had offers for company from one of the soccer moms and from several other women in town. None had interested him enough to say yes, but something about Lucy...

He knew all the reasons to keep away from her, but he

couldn't stop thinking about her or wanting to spend time with her outside of practice.

Lines creased her forehead, the way they did when she was nervous or worried. "Uh-oh. Look how many parents stayed to watch practice today."

He'd been too busy with the boys and sneaking peeks at Lucy to notice the row of chairs along the edge of the grass. The different colors reminded him of a rainbow. Several dads sat alongside the moms who had come to the last two practices. Some of the men were the same ones who had either ignored or bullied him in elementary school. It wasn't until he'd proven his worth on the pitch that he'd became a real person in their eyes. Now they clamored to talk to him about their sons. "I thought they were too busy or working to be at practices."

"That's what they said when I asked if one of them could coach."

"At least no one can use that excuse now."

Her eyes widened. "You're leaving already?"

Interesting. Lucy sounded upset. Maybe she wasn't as indifferent to him as she appeared to be. "Not yet. But when I do you'll need a new assistant. Maybe two."

"Oh, okay," she said. "It's just the boys like having you around, especially Connor."

"What about you?"

She flinched. "Me?"

Ryland had put her on the spot. He didn't care. The way she reacted to his leaving suggested this wasn't only about the team. If that were true, he wanted to know even if it wouldn't change anything between them. Or change it that much. "Yes, you."

"You're an excellent coach. I'm learning a lot."

"And..."

"A nice guy."

"And...

The color on her cheeks deepened. "A great soccer player."

"Yes, but you haven't seen me play."

"Modest, huh?"

He shrugged.

"Aaron and Connor told me how good you are."

Ryland wouldn't mind showing her just how good he was at a lot more than soccer.

Bad idea. Except…

He knew women. Lucy was more interested in him than she was letting on. His instincts couldn't be that off. Not with her. "You haven't answered my question."

She looked at the grass. "I appreciate you being here."

"Do you like having me around?"

"It doesn't suck," Lucy said finally.

Not a yes, but close enough. The ball had been passed to him. Time to take the shot.

"Bring Connor over tonight. He can walk Cupcake." Ryland might want to be alone with Lucy, but he knew that wasn't going to happen. A nine-year-old chaperone was a good idea, anyway. The last thing this could turn into was a date. "I'll have pizza delivered."

Her jaw tightened. "You don't have to do this."

"Do what?"

"Repay me for dinner."

"I'm not."

"So this is…"

"For Connor." That was all it could be. *For now,* a little voice whispered.

A beat passed. And another. "He'd like that."

Ryland would have preferred hearing she would like that, too. "I'll order pizza, salad and breadsticks."

"I'll bring dessert."

If he told her not to bother, she'd bring something anyway. And this wasn't a date. "Sounds great."

"Ice-cream sundaes, okay?"

"Perfect."

He could think of lots of ways to use the extra whipped cream with Lucy. The cherries, too. Ryland grinned.

But not tonight. He pressed his lips together. Maybe not any night. And that, he realized, was a total bummer.

The Jameses' kitchen was four times the size of Aaron and Dana's and more "gourmet" with granite countertops, stainless-steel top-of-the-line appliances and hi-tech lighting. The luxurious setting seemed a stark contrast to the casual menu. But no one seemed to notice that except Lucy.

She felt as if she were standing on hot coals and hadn't been able to relax all evening. The same couldn't be said about Connor. A wide grin had been lighting her nephew's face since they'd left practice. He seemed completely at home, hanging on Ryland's every word and playing with Cupcake.

That pleased her since she'd accepted Ryland's invitation for Connor's sake. And *Starry Night* hadn't been painted from within the confines of an asylum, either.

Lucy grimaced. Okay, a part of her had wanted to come over, too.

Insane.

She had to be crazy to torture herself by agreeing to spend more time with Ryland outside of practice. Hanging out with him was working about as well as it had when she'd been in middle school. Her insides quivered, making her feel all jittery. She rinsed a dinner plate, needing the mundane task to steady her nerves.

It didn't help much.

Ryland entered the kitchen. The large space seemed smaller, more…intimate.

She squared her shoulders, not about to let him get to her.

"Connor is chasing Cupcake around the backyard," Ryland said. "It's lighted and fenced so you won't have to worry about him."

She loaded the plate into the dishwasher. As long as the conversation remained on Connor she should be fine. "What makes you think I worry?"

"Nothing, except you pay closer attention to your nephew than an armored car guard does to his cargo."

Lucy rinsed another plate. "I'm supposed to watch him."

"I'm kidding." Ryland placed the box with the leftover pizza slices into the refrigerator. "Aaron has nothing to worry about with you in charge."

She thought about her brother and sister-in-law so far away. "I hope you're right. Sometimes…"

"Sometimes?" he asked.

Lucy stared into the sink, wishing she hadn't said anything. Letting her guard down was too easy when Ryland was around. Strange since that was exactly the time she should keep it up.

"Tell me," he said.

Warm water ran over her hands, but did nothing to soothe her. "Until Aaron and Dana deployed, I had no idea what having someone totally rely on you meant. It's not as easy as I thought it would be. Sometimes I don't think I'm as focused on Connor as I should be."

Especially the past week and a half with Ryland on her mind so much.

"Any more focused and you'd be obsessing." He smiled. "Don't worry. Connor is happy. All smiles."

She placed the plate in the dishwasher. "That's because of you."

"Yeah, you're right about that."

Ryland's lighthearted tone told her that he was joking. She turned and flicked her hands at him. Droplets of water flew in his direction.

He jumped back. Amusement filled his gaze.

"Gee, thanks," she joked.

"Seriously, you're doing a great job," Ryland said. "Your kids will be the envy of all their friends."

Her kids? Heat exploded through Lucy like the grand finale of Fourth of July fireworks. Jeff had said she was too independent to be a decent wife. He'd told her that she would be a bad mother. Funny, how his liking a self-reliant girlfriend when they were dating turned out to be one-hundred-and-eighty percent different from his wanting a needy wife to stroke his fragile ego after they married.

"Thanks." She placed a plate in the rack next to the other. "I suppose being a surrogate parent now will help if I ever have a family of my own."

"If?"

She shrugged. "I've got too much going on with Connor to think about the future."

"Nothing wrong with focusing on the present," he said.

Yeah, she imagined that was what he did. But his situation was different from hers. He was doing something with his life. And she…

Lucy picked up the last plate and scrubbed. Hard.

A longing ached deep inside her. She wanted to do something, too. Be someone. To matter…

Uh-oh. She didn't want to end up throwing herself a pity-party. Not with Ryland here. Time to get things back on track.

She loaded the plate. "Connor has been writing his parents about soccer practices and telling them how well you coach."

"I bet Aaron sees right through that."

"Probably."

Ryland raised a brow. "Probably?"

"You said it," she teased.

He picked up the can of whipped cream with one hand and the red cap with his other. "You didn't have to agree."

"Well, Connor did say you're *almost* as good a coach as his dad."

"Almost, huh?" With a grin, Ryland walked toward her. "I thought we were on the same team, but since we're not…"

He pointed the can of whipped cream in her direction.

She stepped back. Her backside bumped into the granite counter. The lowered dishwasher door had her boxed in on the left. Ryland blocked the way on the right. Trapped. It didn't bother her as much as it should. "You wouldn't."

Challenge gleamed in his eyes. "Whipped cream would go well with your outfit."

His, too. They could have so much fun with the whipped cream. Anticipation made her smile.

What was she thinking? Forget about the whipped cream. Forget about him.

Self-preservation made her reach behind and pull the hand nozzle from the sink. She aimed it at him. The surprise in his eyes made her feel strong and competent. Her confidence surged. “I wonder how you’ll look all wet.”

A corner of his mouth curved and something shifted between them. The air crackled with tension, with heat. His gaze smoldered.

Heaven help her. She swallowed. Thank goodness for the counter’s support or she’d be a puddle on the floor.

“I’m game if you are,” he said.

For the first time in a long time, Lucy was tempted to…play. But nerves threatened to get the best of her. She knew better to play with fire.

Unsure of what to do or say next, she clutched the nozzle as if it could save her. From what, she wasn’t sure.

Still Lucy wasn’t ready to back down. Surrendering wasn’t an option, either. “What if I’m out of practice and don’t remember how to play?”

He took a step toward her. “I’m an excellent coach. I can show you.”

She bet he could. She could imagine all kinds of things he could show her. Her cheeks burned. “What are the rules?”

He grinned wryly. “Play fair. Don’t cheat.”

A little pang hit her heart. “Those sound like good rules. I don’t like cheaters.”

“Neither do I.”

His gaze captured hers. She didn’t know how long they stood there with their weapons ready. It didn’t matter. Nothing did except this moment with him.

Lucy wanted…a kiss. The realization ricocheted through her, a mix of shock and anticipation. No wonder she held a water nozzle in her hand ready to squirt him. She wanted Ryland to kiss her senseless. If only…

Not possible. She didn’t want to get burned. Again.

Still her lips parted slightly. An invitation or a plea of desperation, she wasn't certain.

Desire flared in his eyes.

Please.

She wasn't brave enough to say the word aloud.

"How do I know this isn't a trap?" he asked with mock seriousness.

"I could say the same thing."

"We could put our weapons down on three."

"Fair play."

He stood right in front of her. "Exactly."

She nodded, still gripping the nozzle. "One, two…"

Ryland lowered his mouth to hers. The touch of his lips sent a shock through her. He tasted warm with a hint of chocolate from the hot-fudge topping.

His tender kiss caressed. She felt cherished and important. Ways she hadn't felt in years. Her toes curled. She gripped the nozzle.

This was what had been missing, what she needed.

Bells rang. Mozart. Boy, could Ryland kiss.

She wanted more. Oh-so-much-more.

A dog barked.

Lucy leaned into Ryland, into his kiss. She brought her right arm around him and her left…

Water squirted everywhere.

Ryland jumped back, his shirt wet.

She glanced down. Hers hadn't fared much better. Thank goodness she was wearing a camisole underneath her T-shirt.

Laughter lit his eyes. "At least you got the playing fair part. We're both wet."

Lucy attempted to laugh. She couldn't. She tried to speak. She couldn't do that, either. Not after being so expertly and thoroughly kissed. Ryland's kiss had left her confused, wanting more and on fire despite the water socking her shirt and dripping down her legs.

A crush was one thing. This felt like…

No, it was nothing but some hot kisses.

Lucy straightened. Letting him kiss her had been a momentary lapse in judgment. She should have ended the kiss as soon as his mouth touched hers. But she hadn't. She…couldn't. Worse, her lips wanted more kisses.

Stupid. The word needed to be tattooed across her forehead for the world to see. Correction, for her to see, a reminder of the mistakes she'd made when it came to men.

"Aunt Lucy." Connor ran into the kitchen with Cupcake at his heels. Her nephew stared at her and Ryland with wide eyes. "What happened?"

"An accident," Ryland answered.

Did he mean the kiss or the water? The question hammered at her. She wasn't sure she wanted to know the answer, either.

A sudden realization sent a shiver down Lucy's spine. For the few minutes she'd been kissing Ryland, she hadn't thought once about Connor. He'd been left unattended in a strange house. Okay, Cupcake had been with him and Lucy had only been in the kitchen, but still…

Ryland's kiss had made her forget everything, including her nephew. That could not happen again. She adjusted the hem of her shirt, smoothed her hair and looked at her nephew. "You okay?"

Connor nodded. "But there's a man at the front door. He said his name is Blake. He's here to see Ryland."

CHAPTER SEVEN

STANDING in his parents' living room, Ryland dragged his hand through his hair. Uncomfortable didn't begin to describe the atmosphere. Blake's nostrils flared. A thoroughly kissed and embarrassed Lucy stared at Connor, who sat on the carpet playing with Cupcake, oblivious to what was going on.

Not that any of the adults had a clue.

At least Ryland didn't.

He was trying to figure out what had happened in the kitchen. He couldn't stop thinking about Lucy's kisses. About how silver sparks had flashed when she'd opened her eyes. About how right she felt in his arms.

Not good since the last thing he needed was a woman in his life. Even one as sweet and delicious as Lucy Martin. But this wasn't the time to think about anything except damage control.

Blake hadn't seen them kissing, but Lucy's presence was going to be a problem. A big one.

"Let me introduce everyone," Ryland said.

Polite words were exchanged. Obligatory handshakes given.

Thick tension hung on the air, totally different from the sizzling heat in the kitchen a few minutes ago. That was where Ryland wished he could be now—in the kitchen kissing Lucy.

Whoa. He must have taken a header with a ball too hard and not remembered. Ryland was in enough trouble with his agent. He needed to stop thinking about kisses. And her. Not even flings were in his playbook at the moment.

"What brings you to Wicksburg?" Lucy asked Blake.

Ryland wanted to know the answer to that question, too. Blake never dropped by unannounced. Something big must have happened with either Fuego or his sponsors.

Good news, Ryland hoped. But given the muscle flicking on Blake's jaw and the tense lines around his mouth, probably not.

"I was in Chicago for a meeting." That explained Blake's designer suit, silk tie and Italian-leather shoes. Not exactly comfortable traveling attire, but Blake always dressed well, even when he was straight out of law school and joining the ranks of sports agents. "I thought I'd swing by Indiana and see how Ryland was doing on his own."

Swing by? Yeah, right. No one swung by Wicksburg when the nearest airport was a two-hour drive away. Blake must have rented a car to get here. Something was up. The question was what.

The edges of Lucy's mouth curved upward in a forced smile. The pink flush that had crept up her neck after he'd kissed her hadn't disappeared yet. "That's nice of you."

Blake Cochrane and the word "nice" didn't belong in the same sentence. Of course Lucy wouldn't know that. He had the reputation of being a shark when it came to contract negotiations and pretty much anything else. His hard-nosed toughness made him a great agent. Blake eyed Lucy with suspicion. "I can see my concerns about Ryland being lonely are unfounded."

The agent's ice-blue eyes narrowed to slits. He focused first on Lucy then moved to Ryland.

The accusation in Blake's voice and gaze left no doubt what the agent thought was going on here. Ryland grimaced. He didn't like Lucy being lumped in with other women he'd gone out with. He squared his shoulders. "I invited Lucy and Connor over to take Cupcake on a walk for me and have some pizza."

"And ice-cream sundaes," Connor added with a grin.

Blake's brow slanted. His gaze lingered on Lucy's damp shirt that clung to her breasts like a second skin. "A water fight, too, I see."

Ryland tried hard not to look at her chest. Tried and failed.

The color on Lucy's face deepened. She looked like she wanted to bolt.

His jaw tensed. He didn't like seeing her so uncomfortable. "Faucet malfunction."

"Hate when that happens," Blake said.

Damn him. Blake wasn't happy finding Lucy here, but he didn't have to be such a jerk about it. Ryland's hands balled. "Nothing that can't be fixed."

His harsh tone silenced the living room. Only Connor and the dog seemed at ease.

"Well, it's been nice meeting you, Blake. It's a school night so we have to get home," Lucy said. "Thanks for having us over for dinner, Ryland."

"Yeah, thanks. I had fun with Cupcake." Connor stood, stifling a yawn. "This is a cool house. The backyard is so big we could hold our practices here."

"You play soccer?" Blake asked.

Connor nodded.

Blake studied the kid, as if sizing up his potential. Scouts could recognize talent at a young age. In the United Kingdom, the top prospects signed with football clubs in their teens. "What position do you play?"

Connor raised his chin, a gesture both his dad and Lucy made. "Wherever I'm told to play."

Blake's sudden smile softened his rugged features. "With that kind of attitude you'll go far."

Connor beamed. "I want to be just like Ryland when I grow up."

The words touched him. He mussed Connor's hair. Working with the boys reminded him of the early years of playing soccer, full of fun, friendship and laughter. "Thanks, bud."

Ryland turned his attention to Lucy. He wanted to kiss her good-night. Who was he kidding? He wanted to kiss her hello, goodbye and everything in between. She was sexy and sweet, a potent, addictive combo. He should have his head examined soon. There wasn't room in his life for a serious girlfriend, especially one who lived in Wicksburg. He couldn't afford to lose his edge now. "I'll see you out."

Lucy nodded.

That surprised him. He'd expected her to say it wasn't necessary like the first time she'd visited.

"I'll stay here," Blake said.

Ryland accompanied them to the driveway where Lucy's car was parked. Lights on either side of the garage door illuminated the area. Cupcake ran around the car barking. She didn't seem to want Connor to go. Ryland felt the same way about Lucy.

That made zero sense. They weren't playing house. Being with her wasn't cozy. More like being on a bed of hot knives. She needed to leave before he got the urge to kiss her again.

Connor climbed into the backseat. Cupcake followed, but Ryland lifted the dog out of the car and held on to her. As soon as Connor fastened his seat belt, his eyelids closed.

"He's out," Ryland said.

She glanced back at the house. "You're in trouble."

The word "no" sat on the tip of his tongue and stayed there. He didn't want to worry Lucy, but he also didn't want to lie. Blake's surprise visit concerned Ryland. "I don't know."

Lines creased Lucy's forehead. Her gaze, full of concern and compassion, met his. "Blake doesn't look happy."

Ryland was a lone wolf kind of guy. He wasn't used to people being concerned about him. It made him…uncomfortable.

Best not to think about that. Or her. "Blake's intense. No one would ever accuse him of being mild-mannered and laid-back."

"I wouldn't want to meet him in a dark alley. A good thing he's on your side."

"Blake's my biggest supporter after my folks." The agent had always been there for Ryland. One of the few people who had believed in him from the beginning. "He fights for his clients. I've been with him for eleven years. I was the second client to sign with him."

"You both must have been young then."

"Young and idealistic." Those had been the days before all

the other stuff—the business stuff—became such a priority and a drag. "But we've grown up and been through a lot."

"You've probably made him a bunch of money over the years."

They were both rich men now. "Yeah."

But her words made Ryland think. Those closest to him, besides his parents, were people who made money off him. His agent, his PR spokesperson, his trainer, the list went on. His friends were plentiful when he was covering the tab at a club or throwing a party, but not so much now that he was stuck in the middle-of-nowhere Indiana. Bitterness coated his mouth.

Was that the reason Blake had dropped by? To make sure his income from "Ryland James" endorsements and licensing agreements wouldn't dry up?

Ryland hoped not. He wanted to think he was considered more than just a client after all the years.

The tip of her pink tongue darted out to moisten her lips.

He wouldn't mind another taste of her lips. He fought the urge to pull her against him and kiss her until the worry disappeared. "About what happened in the kitchen..."

The lines on her forehead deepened. She glanced at Connor who was asleep. "That shouldn't have happened. It was a... mistake."

Ryland studied her, trying to figure out what she was thinking. He couldn't. "It didn't feel like a mistake."

"I..."

He placed his finger against her lips, remembering how soft they'd felt against his own. They needed to talk, but this wasn't the time, and maybe the words needed to remain unsaid. "It's late."

"Blake's waiting for you."

"Don't let the suit and attitude fool you. He's not in charge here. I am," Ryland said. "Take Connor home. We'll talk soon."

She nodded.

"Blake's bag was in the entryway. He's staying the night." An ache formed deep in Ryland's gut. He wanted to kiss Lucy. More than he'd wanted anything in a long time. He didn't understand why he was feeling that way. Staying away from her was the smart thing to do. Though come to think of it, no one had ever accused him of being smart. "I'll call you tomorrow. Promise."

So much for playing it safe. But something about Lucy made him forget reason and make promises.

She started to speak then stopped herself. "Good luck with Blake."

"Thanks, but I've got all the luck I need thanks to your penny."

Her eyes widened. "You kept it?"

Bet she'd be surprised to know the penny had been sitting on his nightstand for the past two weeks. "Never know when I'll need it to get lucky."

The color on her cheeks deepened again. "That's my cue to say good-night."

Sweet and smart. It was a good thing Blake was going to be his houseguest tonight and not Lucy. Ryland opened the car door for her. "Drive safe."

After the taillights of Lucy's car faded from view, he went inside. He couldn't put off his conversation with Blake any longer.

His agent stood in the entryway. He'd changed into shorts, a T-shirt and running shoes.

"Tell me what you're really doing here," Ryland said.

"I've been on airplanes or stuck at conference tables for the last two days," Blake said. "Let's work out."

In the home gym, Ryland hopped on the stationary bike. His physical therapist had increased the number of things he could do as his foot healed. He liked being able to do more exercises, but working out was the furthest thing from his mind. Thoughts about Lucy and her hot kisses as well as his agent's purpose for coming here filled his brain.

Blake stepped on the treadmill. He adjusted the settings on the computerized control panel. "I knew you couldn't go that long without a woman."

Ryland's temper flared. But after receiving more red cards

these past two seasons than all the seasons before, he'd learned not to react immediately. He accelerated his pedaling, instead. "You're checking up on me."

"Sponsors are nervous." Blake's fast pace didn't affect his speech or breathing. "They aren't the only ones."

So now his agent had added babysitter to his list of duties. Great. Ryland's fingers tightened around the handlebars. "You."

"I don't get nervous." Blake accelerated his pace. "But I am…concerned. You'll be thirty soon. We need to make the most of the next few years whether you're playing with Fuego or across the pond."

His agent had stressed the need for financial planning to Ryland since he was eighteen years old. But he'd never set out to amass a fortune, just be the best soccer player he could be. "I'm set for life."

"You can never have too much money when you're earning potential will drastically diminish once you stop playing."

Ryland had more money than he could ever spend, but dissatisfaction gnawed at him. He might be injured, but he wasn't about to be put out to pasture just yet.

"Don't be concerned. I'm laying low," he said. "Tonight is the first time I've had anyone over to the house other than the housekeeper, who's old enough to be my mom. I made sure Lucy and I had a chaperone."

"Nice kid," Blake said. "Is it his team you're coaching?"

Damn. Ryland slowed his pedaling. He reached for his water bottle off the nearby counter then took a long swig. The cool liquid rushing down his throat did little to refresh him. "Where'd you hear that?"

"Someone tweeted you were coaching a local rec. team." Blake kept a steady pace. "Tell me this was some sort of one-off rah-rah-isn't-soccer-great pep talk."

"I'm helping Lucy with Connor's team." Ryland placed his water bottle on the counter. "Her brother coaches the team, but he's on deployment with his Reserve unit. No other parent stepped up so she took on the role as head coach even though she knows nothing about soccer. I offered to help."

"Lucy's so hot she could get a man to do most anything," Blake said. "Those legs of hers go on forever."

The appreciative gleam in his agent's ice-blue eyes bugged Ryland. Women always swarmed around Blake. He didn't need to be checking out Lucy, too.

Ryland's jaw tensed. "I'm coaching for both her and the boys."

"Mostly Lucy, though." Blake grinned. "That's a good thing."

"It is?"

"Your coaching becomes a nonissue if you have a personal connection and aren't showing favoritism to one team."

"Favoritism?" Ryland didn't understand what Lucy had to do with this. "I'm helping the Defeeters, but I've also spoken to two other teams this week and will visit with three more next week."

"No need to get defensive," Blake said. "A guy helping out his girlfriend isn't showing favoritism."

Girlfriend? A knot formed in the pit of Ryland's stomach. Everything suddenly made sense. "So if Lucy and I aren't..."

He couldn't bring himself to say the word.

Blake nodded. "If you weren't dating Lucy, you wouldn't be able to coach the team."

Ryland's knuckles turned white. "What do you mean?"

As Blake moved from the treadmill to the stair-climber machine, he wiped the sweat from his face with a white towel. "You're public property. The face of the Phoenix Fuego. Showing favoritism to one team without a valid personal connection would be a big no-no for a player of your caliber. Especially one on shaky ground already."

Ryland gulped.

"But we don't need to worry about that," Blake added.

Emotion tightened Ryland's throat. His agent had always been overprotective. No doubt watching over his investment. Ryland understood that, but he wasn't going back on his word to help Lucy with the team. She needed him. "No worries."

If his agent believed a romance was going on between

Ryland and Lucy, Blake wouldn't feel the need to play mother hen. No one would have to know the truth. Not the sponsors or the Fuego, not even Lucy…

Play fair. Don't cheat.

Not saying anything wasn't cheating, but it wasn't exactly fair, either.

"I must admit I'm a little surprised," Blake said. "Lucy's not your usual type."

Ryland wasn't sure he had a type, but the kind of women he met at clubs couldn't hold a candle to a certain fresh-faced woman with a warm smile, big heart and legs to her neck. Someone who didn't care how much he made or the club he played for or what car he drove. Someone whose kisses had rocked his world.

"I've known Lucy since she was in kindergarten," Ryland explained. "Her brother was one of my closest friends and teammates when I was growing up."

Blake's brows furrowed. "We might be able to use this to our advantage. McElroy is big on family. Childhood sweethearts reunited would make a catchy headline."

Whoa, so not going there. "Lucy was too young for me to date when we were in school. Don't try to milk this for something it's not. I'll be leaving town soon."

"The two of you seem cozy. Serious."

Ryland climbed off the bike. "I don't do serious."

"You haven't done serious. That doesn't mean you can't," Blake said. "Lucy could be a keeper."

Definitely.

The renegade thought stopped Ryland cold. Lucy might be a keeper, but not for him. Fame and adoring women hadn't always satisfied him, but things would improve now that he'd had a break. This time away was what he needed. He could concentrate on his career and get back on track with the same hunger and edge that had made him a star player.

Besides Lucy needed a guy who would be around to help her with Connor. Someone who could make her a priority and give her the attention she deserved. He couldn't be that kind of guy, not when he played soccer all over the world, lived in Arizona and wasn't about to start thinking in the long-term until his career was over.

Ryland picked up his water bottle. "The only keeper I want in my life is a goalkeeper."

There wasn't room for any other kind. There just couldn't be.

While a tired Connor brushed his teeth, Lucy laid out his pajamas on his bed. She couldn't stop thinking about Ryland. About his kissing her. About what he might be saying to his agent right now.

Lucy wished she could turn back the clock. She would have turned down his offer to come over tonight. That way he wouldn't be in trouble and she wouldn't want more of his kisses.

Pathetic.

Crushing on Ryland didn't mean she should be kissing him. Crushes were supposed to be fun, not leave her with swollen lips and a confused heart.

Not her heart, she corrected herself. Her mind.

Her heart was fine. Safe. She planned on keeping it that way. Keeping her distance from Ryland would be her best plan of action. She wasn't supposed to see him again until the Defeeters' game on Saturday. Though he'd promised he would call tomorrow…

He'd used the word "promise" again. He hadn't let her down the first time. She hoped he wouldn't this time, but she had no idea. She didn't trust herself when it came to men.

Lucy's fingers twitched. Touching her tingling lips for the umpteenth time would not help matters. She needed to hold a pencil and sketchbook. She needed to draw.

As soon as Connor was in bed…

He was her priority. Not her art. Definitely not Ryland.

The phone rang.

Her heart leaped. Ryland. Oh, boy, she had it bad.

Connor darted out of the bathroom as if he'd gotten his second wind. He picked up the telephone receiver. "Hello, this is Connor, may I ask who's calling…Dad!"

The excitement in that one word brought a big smile to Lucy's face. Relief, too. Aaron must have returned to a base where phone calls could be made. Her brother was safe. For now.

"I'm so glad you got my emails." Connor leaned against the wall. "Yeah. Ryland knows a lot about soccer. He's cool. But no one is as good a coach as you…We had dinner at his house tonight…Pizza…No, just me and Aunt Lucy. I got to walk his parents' dog. Her name is Cupcake…Can we get a dog?…Ryland said they were a lot of work…" Connor nodded at whatever Aaron said to him. "Yeah, he's a nice guy just like you said…Okay…I love you, too." Connor handed Lucy the phone. "Dad wants to talk to you."

That was odd. Usually she emailed Aaron and Dana so they could spend their precious phone minutes speaking with Connor. She raised the phone to her ear. "Hey, Bro. Miss you."

"Ryland James?" Aaron asked.

Her brother's severe tone made her shoo Connor into his bedroom. "Ryland's helping with Connor's team."

"Dinner at his house has nothing to do with the *team.*"

She walked down the hallway to put some distance between her and her nephew. "Connor likes spending time with him."

"And you're hanging with Ryland for the sake of Connor?"

"Yes. Connor's the reason I accepted the dinner invitation." She kept her voice low so her nephew wouldn't hear. "He misses you and Dana so much. But ever since Ryland started working with the team, Connor's been happy and all smiles."

"What about you?" Aaron asked. "You had a big crush on him."

"That was years ago," she said.

"Ryland James is a player, Luce. You don't follow soccer, but I do. The guy has a bad reputation when it comes to women. He'll break your heart if he gets the chance."

"I'll admit he's attractive," she said. "But after Jeff, I know better than to fall for a guy like Ryland James."

"I hope so."

Her brother sounded doubtful. "Don't worry. Ryland isn't going to be around much longer."

"Stay away from him."

"Hard to do when he's helping me with the team and teaching me what I need to coach."

"Limit your interaction to soccer. I hate to think he might hurt you," Aaron said. "Damn. Out of time. Love you. Be careful, Luce."

The line disconnected.

A lump of emotion formed in her throat. Aaron had tried to warn her about Jeff before she eloped, but Lucy hadn't listened. She couldn't make the same mistake again. Because she knew Aaron was right. Ryland James was dangerous. He could break her heart. Easily. She'd survived when that happened with Jeff. She wasn't sure she could survive that type of heartache again.

Lucy put away the phone receiver and made her way to Connor's bedroom. Aaron's words echoed through her head. She felt like an idiot. She'd questioned whether she could trust Ryland, yet she'd kissed him tonight and still wanted more kisses.

So not good.

But she couldn't wallow or overanalyze. She'd done enough of that when her marriage had ended. She knew what to do now—start a new project. As soon as her nephew was tucked into bed, she would gather her art supplies.

Forget a pencil and sketchbook. Time to pull out the big guns—brushes, paints and canvas. Painting was the only thing that might clear her thoughts enough so she could forget about Ryland James and his kisses.

CHAPTER EIGHT

AFTER Connor left for school the next morning, Lucy worked. She enjoyed graphic design—creative, yet practical—but the painting she'd started last night called to her in a way her normal work never had. She emailed a proof to one client and uploaded changes to another's website. The rest of the items on her To Do list could wait until later.

Lucy stood in front of the painting. The strong, bright, vivid colors filled the canvas. The boldness surprised her.

She wasn't that into abstract art. She preferred subjects that captured a snapshot of life or told a story. But thanks to Ryland, her thoughts and emotions were a mismatched jumble. Geometric shapes, lines and arcs were about all she could manage at the moment.

Still the elements somehow worked. Not too surprising, Lucy supposed. She'd always found solace in art, when she was sick and after her marriage ended. The only difference was this time neither her health nor heart were involved.

She wouldn't allow her heart to be involved. That internal organ would only lead her astray.

Stop thinking. Just paint.

Time to lose herself in the work. Lucy dipped her brush into the paint.

She worked with almost a manic fervor. Joy and sorrow, desire and heartache appeared beneath her brush in bold strokes, bright colors, swirls and slashes.

The doorbell rang.

The sound startled her. She dripped paint onto her hand.

A quick glance at the clock showed she'd been painting for the past two hours. She'd lost track of time. A good thing she'd been interrupted or she could have stayed here all day.

Using a nearby rag, she wiped her hands then headed to the front door. Most likely the UPS man. She'd ordered some paper samples for a client.

Lucy opened the door.

Ryland stood on the porch. Her breath caught and held in her chest. He wore warm-up pants and a matching jacket with a white T-shirt underneath. The casual attire looked stylish on him. His hair was styled, but he hadn't shaved the stubble from his face this morning. Dark circles ringed his eyes, as if he hadn't slept much last night.

Like her.

Though she doubted she'd played a role in his dreams the way he'd starred in hers.

He smiled. "Good morning."

Ryland was the last person she expected to see. He'd told her he would call, not show up in person. But a part of her was happy to see him standing here.

That bothered her. She blew out a breath. Remember what Aaron had said. Ryland was the last person she should want to spend any time with. Yet…

Her gaze slid from his hazel-green eyes to his mouth. Tingles filled her stomach. Her lips ached for another kiss.

Lucy clutched the doorknob. For support or ease in slamming shut the door, she wasn't certain. "What are you doing here?"

Her tone wasn't polite. She didn't care. His presence disturbed her.

His smile faltered a moment before widening. "Let's go for coffee."

"I'm not sure that's such a good idea."

Talk about a wimpy response. She knew going out would be a very bad idea.

"We need to talk about my coaching the Defeeters," he added.

He would bring up coaching and the Defeeters. She was torn. Seeing him over something soccer-related didn't make Ryland James any less dangerous. She glanced down at her paint-splattered shirt and sweatpants. "I'm not dressed to go out."

His gaze took in her clothes and her hands with splotches of purple on them. "You've been painting."

She didn't understand why he sounded so pleased. "Yes."

"We can stay here," he said. "I'd like to see what you're working on."

Lucy didn't feel comfortable sharing her work with Ryland. No way did she want to expose such an intimate part of herself. Not after kissing him had brought up all these feelings. Speaking of kissing him, being alone in the house wasn't a good idea at all. "We can go to the coffee shop. Let me wash up and get my purse."

A few minutes later, refreshed and ready, she locked the front door. "Do you want to meet there?"

"We can ride together."

That was what she was afraid he would say. "I'll drive."

"Your car is nicer than my dad's old truck."

"My car is closer." She motioned to her car parked on the driveway. "Less walking for you."

He headed to her car. "That's thoughtful."

More like self-preservation. She would also be in control. She could determine when they left, not him.

Lucy unlocked the car and opened the door for him. "Do you need help getting in?"

He drew his brows together. "Thanks, but I can handle it."

She walked around the front of the car, slid into her seat and turned on the engine. "Buckled in?"

Ryland patted the seat belt. "All set."

The tension in the air matched her tight jaw. She backed out of the driveway. "So what did you want to talk about?"

"Let's wait until we get to the coffee shop," Ryland said.

They were only five minutes away. She turned on the radio. A pop song with lyrics about going home played. The music was better than silence, but not by much. She tapped her thumbs on the steering wheel. “Does it have anything to do with Blake?”

Ryland nodded. “But no need to worry.”

Easier said then done.

Lucy turned onto Main Street. Small shops and restaurants lined the almost-empty street. A quiet morning in Wicksburg. She parked on the street right in front of the Java Bean, a narrow coffee shop with three tables inside and two out front on the sidewalk.

A bell jangled when Ryland opened the door for her. She stepped inside. The place was empty. As they walked to the counter, he placed his hand at the small of her back. His gentle touch made her wish she were back in his arms again, even if that was the last place she should be.

Lucy ordered a cappuccino. He got a double espresso. She went to remove her wallet, but he was handing the barista a twenty-dollar bill.

“You can buy the next time,” he said.

Going out to coffee with Ryland was not something she planned on doing again. She’d figure out another way to repay him.

Once their order was ready, she sat at a small, round table. Jazzy instrumental music played from hidden speakers.

Ryland sat across from her. His left foot brushed hers. “Excuse me.”

“Sorry.” Lucy placed her feet under her chair. The sooner they got this over with the better. She wrapped her hands around the warm mug. “So what’s going on?”

Ryland took a sip of his coffee. “Somebody tweeted I was coaching a team of kids in Wicksburg.”

“Blake saw the tweet?”

“A PR firm I use did.”

She drank from her cup. “No wonder Blake looked so upset.”

“He calmed down after you left,” Ryland said. “Turns out

helping my girlfriend coach a team is a perfectly acceptable thing for me to do."

Girlfriend? She stared at him confused. "Huh?"

"Blake thinks you and I are dating," Ryland explained.

Dating. The word echoed through her head. Even if the idea appealed to her a tiny, almost miniscule bit, she knew it would never happen. "How did he react when you told him we weren't dating?"

"I didn't tell him." Ryland wouldn't meet her gaze. "I didn't deny we were dating, but I didn't say we were a couple, either."

She stared in disbelief. "So Blake thinks we are—"

"I had no choice."

"There's always a choice." She knew that better than anyone. Sometimes the hard choice was the best option.

"I made my choice."

"You had to do what you thought was best for your career. I get that." He'd gotten into this mess with his agent for helping the Defeeters. She couldn't be angry. "I know how much soccer means to you."

His eyes narrowed. "It's not only about my career. If I'd told Blake we weren't dating, I wouldn't be able to help you and the team."

His words sunk in. Ryland hadn't been thinking of himself. He'd done this for her, Connor and the boys.

Her heart pounded so loudly she was sure the barista behind the counter could hear it.

"I wasn't sure if I should tell you," Ryland admitted.

"Why did you?" she asked.

"Fair play."

Play fair. Don't cheat. She remembered the rules he'd told her last night. Right before he'd kissed her senseless. "Thank you for being honest."

"If it's any consolation, I told Blake we weren't serious about each other."

She was glad they were on the same page about not getting involved except she couldn't ignore a twinge of disappointment.

Silly reaction given the circumstances. "Understatement of the year."

Amusement gleamed in his eyes. "True, but people will believe what they want if we don't deny it. And this way I can keep helping you and the team."

Her heart dropped. "You want us to pretend to be dating."

"It's not what I want, but what we have to do." Ryland's smile reached all the way to his eyes. "After those kisses last night, I'm not sure how much pretending is going to be involved."

Heat flooded her face. "We agreed kissing was a mistake."

"You said that. I didn't." His gaze held hers. "There's chemistry between us."

A highly combustible reaction, but she would never admit it. If she did, Ryland could use it to his advantage. She wouldn't stand a chance if he did.

"This is crazy." Lucy's voice sounded stronger than she felt. She tightened her grip on the coffee-cup handle to keep her hand from shaking. "No more kissing. No pretend dating, either."

"Then you'd better find yourself a new assistant before the game on Saturday."

"Seriously?"

He nodded once.

Darn. Lucy watched steam rise from her coffee cup. She didn't know what to do. She needed to protect herself, but she also had to think about Connor.

Connor.

He was the reason she'd approached Ryland in the first place. Her nephew would be the one to suffer if he couldn't continue coaching the Defeeters. She couldn't allow that to happen.

She tried to push all the other stuff out of her mind, including her own worries, doubts and fears, and to focus on Connor. "What's important here is…the team."

"Especially Connor," Ryland said.

She nodded. What was best for Connor might not be the best thing for her, but so what? She had to put her nephew first even if it put her in an awkward position. "You're leaving soon. Until then I'm willing to do whatever it takes so you can keep coaching the team. I can't imagine it'll be that big a deal to pretend to date since your agent lives in California."

"The other coaches in the rec. league have to believe it, or there could be trouble," Ryland clarified. "The parents, too."

Maybe a bigger deal than she realized. But for her nephew she would do it. "Okay."

"Right now there's no press coverage, but that could change."

This had disaster written all over it. If Aaron found out... She couldn't think about him. Connor was her priority, not her brother.

No matter what life had thrown at Lucy, she'd proven she was capable and able to handle anything. She would do the same here. "It's only for a few weeks, right?"

Ryland nodded. "It'll be fun."

There was that word again. She doubted this would be fun. But as long as he was working with the team, keeping a smile on Connor's face and teaching her how to coach, it would be... doable.

Besides they were just pretending. What could go wrong?

Pretending to date wasn't turning out to be all that great. So far "dating" had amounted to several texts being exchanged about soccer and an impromptu dinner at the pizza parlor with the entire team. He'd have to step things up as soon as this game was over.

It couldn't end quickly enough for Ryland. He forced himself to stay seated on the bench. The Defeeters were outmatched and losing. He couldn't do a single thing about it, either.

"Great job, Defeeters!" Lucy stood along the sideline in a blue T-shirt with the name of the soccer league across the front and warm-up pants. She held a clipboard with a list of when players should be substituted to ensure equal playing time and waved it in the air when she got excited during the game. "You can do it!"

The way she cheered was cute. If only the team could pull

off a victory, but that would take a miracle given their competition today.

Lucy glanced back at him with a big smile on her face. "The boys have improved over the past two weeks."

Ryland nodded. They had lots of work to do at the next practice.

Lucy checked the stopwatch she wore around her neck. "There can't be much time left."

He glanced at his cell phone. "Less than four minutes."

Connor stole the ball from a small, speedy forward. He passed the ball to Marco, who ran toward the field. He dribbled around a defender and another one.

Parents cheered. Lucy waved the clipboard. Ryland shook his head. Marco needed to pass before the ball got stolen.

The kid sped across the center line.

No way could he take the ball all the way to the goal alone. Not against a skilled team like the Strikers.

"Pass," Ryland called out.

Lucy pointed to Jacob, who stood down field with no defenders around him.

"Cross, Marco," Ryland yelled. "To Jacob."

Marco continued dribbling. A tall, blond-haired defender from the opposite team ran up, stole the ball and kicked it to a teammate. Goal.

The Defeeter parents sighed. The Striker parents cheered.

The referee blew the whistle.

Game over. The Defeeters had lost six–three. Not that the league kept score, but still…

Ryland would add some new drills and review the old ones. The boys needed to learn to pass the ball and talk to each other out on the field. This was a soccer match, not Sunday services at church.

Each of the teams shouted cheers. Great. The kids had found their voices now that the game was over.

The players lined up with the coaches at the end and shook hands with their opponents. Several of the Strikers grabbed their balls and asked Ryland to sign them. He happily obliged and posed for pictures.

By the time he finished, Lucy was seated on the grass with the boys. He walked their way, passing through a group of Defeeter parents.

Suzy, one of the moms, smiled at him. "They played well out there."

Cheryl nodded. "The last time they played the Strikers it was a shutout."

Marco's dad, Ewan, patted Ryland on the back. "This is the most competitive they've ever been. You've done a great job preparing them."

Interesting. Ryland would have thought the parents would be upset, but they sounded pleased. The boys were all smiles, too.

"Did you see?" Connor asked him. "We scored three goals."

Ryland had never seen so many happy faces after a loss. "Nice match, boys."

"Coach Lucy said if we could score one more goal than the last time we'd played the Strikers that would be a win in her book," Marco said.

Dalton pumped his fists in the air. "We needed one goal, but we scored three!"

Ryland had been so focused on winning he'd forgotten there was more to a game than the final score. Especially when skills development, not winning the game, was the goal. But Lucy, who might not have the technical knowledge, had known that.

She sat with a wide smile on her face and sun-kissed cheeks. Lovely.

A warm feeling settled over Ryland. They really needed to spend more time together.

"In the fall, we lost nine–zero," Connor explained.

Ouch. Ryland forced himself not to grimace. No wonder there was so much excitement over today's match. "You gave them a much better game today."

Dalton nodded. "We play them again at the end of the season."

"Let's not get ahead of ourselves. This is our first game," Lucy said. "We have lots to work on before that final match."

"I'll second that," Ryland agreed. "But that's what practice is for. All of you played so well today it's time for a celebration."

"Snacks!" the boys yelled in unison.

Suzy, the snack mom for today's game, passed out brown lunch bags filled with juice, string cheese, a package of trail mix and a bag of cookies. The boys attacked the food like piranhas.

Ryland walked over to Lucy, who jotted notes on her clipboard. "Snacks have improved since I played rec. soccer."

"Yes, but the game's still the same."

He didn't want things to stay the same between them.

Sitting behind her, he placed his hands on her shoulders.

Her muscles tensed beneath his palms.

Ryland didn't care. They were supposed to be dating. Might as well start pretending now. Kisses might be off-limits, but she hadn't said anything about not touching. As he placed his mouth by her ear, her sweet scent enveloped him.

"I wanted to congratulate you," he whispered, noticing curious looks from parents and the other coaches. "Excellent job, Coach."

She turned her head toward him. Her lips were mere inches from his. It would be so easy to steal a kiss. But he wasn't going to push it. At least not yet.

Wariness filled her eyes, but she smiled at him. "Thanks, but I have the best assistant coach in the league. The boys wouldn't have scored any goals without his help."

Her warm breath against his skin raised his temperature twenty degrees. He could practically taste her. His mouth watered. Pretend kisses would probably feel just as nice as real ones.

"Though you're going to have to explain the offside rule to me again," she continued. "I still don't get it."

Ryland laughed. Here he was thinking about kisses, and she

was still talking soccer. "I'll keep explaining until you understand it."

Waiting until Monday afternoon to see her again was unacceptable. He doubted she'd agree to a date, not even a pretend one. But she'd agreed to the pretending because of Connor. The kid would give Ryland the perfect reason to see Lucy before the next practice.

Not cheating, he thought. Perhaps not playing one hundred percent fair, but being able to spend some time with her was worth it. Once they were alone, she might even agree.

Ryland stood. "The way you boys played today deserves a special treat." He looked each boy in the eyes. "Who's up for a slushie?"

Sitting on a picnic bench outside Rocket Burgers, Lucy placed her mouth around the straw sticking out of her cup and sipped her blue-raspberry slushie. Suzy, Cheryl, Debbie and the other moms from the team sat with her.

Ryland and the dads sat with the boys on a grassy area near a play structure.

Suzy set her cup on the table. "Ryland is so nice to treat us all to slushies."

"I'm sure he can afford it. You are so lucky Lucy to spend so much time with him." Cheryl pouted. "I thought I had a chance, but it's better he chose you since I'm not divorced."

Suzy smiled at Lucy. "I thought you guys looked a little chummier at the pizza party, but I didn't realize you were dating until today."

"He is a total catch," Debbie said. "The two of you make a cute couple."

Happiness shot all the way to the tips of Lucy's hot-pink painted toenails. Not for her, she countered. But for Connor. This charade was for him. She repositioned her straw. "Thanks."

Lucy was not going to confirm or deny anything about their "dating." The less she said, the less dishonest she would feel. She drank more of her slushie.

The men laughed. The boys, too. Through the cacophony

of noise, the squeals and giggles, Lucy singled out Ryland's laughter. The rich sound curled around her heart and sent her temperature climbing. She sipped her slushie, but the icy drink did nothing to cool her down.

No biggie. She would be heading home soon and wouldn't have to see Ryland until Monday afternoon.

As the women talked about a family who'd moved to Iowa, Lucy glanced his way. Ryland sat with Connor on one side and Dalton on the other, the only two boys on the team without fathers here today.

While the other boys spoke with their fathers, Ryland talked to Connor and Dalton. The boys looked totally engaged in the conversation. Smiles lit up their faces. They laughed.

A soccer ball–size lump formed in her throat.

Ryland James might have a reputation as a womanizer, but she could tell someday he would be a great dad. The kind of dad she had. The kind of dad her brother was.

He flashed her a lopsided grin and winked.

Lucy had been caught staring. She should look away, but she didn't want to. She realized since they were pretending to date she didn't have to.

The fluttery sensations in her stomach reminded her of when she was thirteen and head over heels in love with Ryland. But she knew better than to fantasize about a happily ever after now with a guy like him. Besides she knew happy endings were rare, almost nonexistent these days.

A dad named Chuck said something to Ryland. He looked at him, breaking the connection with her.

Lucy turned her attention to the table. The other women had gotten up except for Suzy.

"Well, this has been fun." Cheryl motioned to her son Dalton and gazed longingly at Ryland. "See you at practice on Monday."

"The boys will have their work cut out for them," he said.

Families said goodbye and headed to their cars. Several boys lagged behind, not wanting to leave their friends. Marco and Connor ran up to the picnic table. Ryland followed them.

"Can Connor spend the night?" Marco asked his mom.

"Sure. We have no plans other than to hang out and watch a DVD." Suzy glanced at Lucy. "Is it okay with you?"

Connor stared at her with an expectant look. "Please, Aunt Lucy?"

"He's had sleepovers at our house before," Suzy added.

Dana had provided Lucy with the names of acceptable sleepover and playdate friends. Marco had been at the top of the list. "Okay."

The boys gave each other high fives.

"But you're going to have to come home with me first. You need to shower and pack your things," she said.

"I have to run by the grocery store. We can pick him up on our way home," Suzy offered.

"Thanks." Lucy hugged her nephew. "This will be my first night alone since I've been back in Wicksburg. I don't know what I'll do."

Connor slipped out of her embrace. "Ryland can keep you company tonight."

She started to speak, but Ryland beat her to it.

"I have no plans tonight," he said. "I'd be happy to make sure your aunt doesn't miss you too much."

The mischievous look on Ryland's face made her wonder if he'd planned this whole thing. She wouldn't put it past him. But a part of her was flattered he'd go to so much trouble to spend time with her.

Remember, it's pretend.

"Then we're all set." Suzy grinned. "See you in an hour or so."

As Marco and his parents headed to their SUV, Connor watched them go. "Tonight is going to be so much fun."

Maybe for him. Anxiety built inside Lucy. She had no idea if Ryland was serious about tonight. A part of her hoped he was serious about keeping her company. Not because she was going to be lonely, but because she wanted to see him.

Ridiculous. She blew out a puff of air.

"I'll see you at five," Ryland said.

Before she could say anything he walked off toward the old beat-up truck.

Okay, he was serious. But what exactly did he have in mind?

Connor bounced on his toes. "We'd better get home."

She wrapped her arm around his thin shoulders. "You have plenty of time to get ready for your sleepover."

"I'm not worried about me, but Dad says it takes Mom hours to get ready. You're going to need a lot of time."

His words and sage tone amused her. "What for?"

"Your date with Ryland."

Lucy flinched. She hadn't wanted to drag Connor into the ruse. "Date?"

"Ryland's taking you out to dinner." A smug smile settled on Connor's freckled face. "I told him Otto's was your favorite restaurant, and you liked the cheese fondue best. I also told him it was expensive and only for special occasions, but Ryland said he could probably afford it."

"He can." He could probably afford to buy the entire town.

"If you and Ryland got married, that would make him my new uncle, right?" Connor asked.

Oh, no. The last thing she needed was Connor mentioning marriage to Aaron. "Marriage is serious business. Ryland and I are just going out to eat."

"But it would be pretty cool, don't ya think?"

Maybe if she were nine she would think it was cool. But she was twenty-six and pretending to be dating a soccer star. Marriage was the last thing on her mind while she took care of Connor for the next year. She wasn't even sure if she wanted to get married again. Not after Jeff.

"When two people love each other, marriage can be very cool," Lucy said carefully. "But love is not something you can rush. It takes time."

"My dad knew the minute he saw my mom he was going to marry her," Connor said. "They didn't date very long."

"That's true, but what happened with your mom and dad doesn't happen to many people."

Definitely not her and Jeff.

"But it could happen with you and Ryland," Connor said optimistically.

She gave him a squeeze. "I suppose anything is possible."

But in her and Ryland's case, highly unlikely.

CHAPTER NINE

STANDING on Lucy's front door step on Saturday night, Ryland held the single iris behind his back. At the flower shop, he'd headed straight for the roses because that was what he usually bought women, but the purple flower caught his eyes. The vibrant color reminded him of Lucy, so full of life. He hoped she liked it.

Anticipation for his "date" buzzed through Ryland. He hadn't gone to this much trouble for a woman before. Not unless you counted what he did for his mom on Mother's Day, her birthday in July and Christmastime. But like his mother, Lucy was worth it. Even if this wasn't a "real" date.

He wanted her to see how much fun they could have together. And it would be a memory he could take with him when he left Wicksburg. One he hoped Lucy would look back on fondly herself. Smiling, he pressed the doorbell.

A moment later, the door opened.

Lucy stood in the doorway. Mascara lengthened her eyelashes. Pink gloss covered her lips. He couldn't tell if she was wearing any other makeup. Not that she needed any with her high cheekbones and wide-set eyes.

She never wore any jewelry other than a watch, but tonight dangling crystals hung from her earlobes. A matching necklace graced her long neck.

Her purple sleeveless dress hugged all the right curves and fell just above her knees. Strappy high-heeled shoes accentuated her delicate ankles and sexy calves.

Beautiful.

Lucy was a small-town girl, but tonight she'd dressed for the big city. Whether this was a real date or not, she'd put some effort into getting ready. That pleased him.

"You look stunning."

She smiled softly. "I figured since we were going to Otto's..."

"Connor told you."

"Nine-year-olds and magpies have a lot in common," she explained. "So what did it cost you to enlist him and Marco as your partners in crime?"

Manny lumbered over toward the door. Lucy blocked his way so he couldn't get out of the house. The cat rubbed against her bare leg. Ryland wished he could do the same.

"Twenty bucks," he said, unrepentant.

Her mouth gaped. If this were a real date, he would have been tempted to take advantage of the moment and kiss her. But it wasn't, so he didn't.

"You paid the boys that much?" she asked.

He shrugged. "They earned it."

"Paying someone to do your dirty work gets expensive."

But worth every dollar. "A man does what he has to do."

"Even for a pretend date?" she said.

"A date's a date."

"That explains your clothes." Lucy's assessing gaze traveled the length of him. The brown chinos and green button-down shirt were the dressiest things he'd brought with him to Wicksburg. Going out hadn't been on his list of things to do here. "You clean up well."

He straightened, happy he'd pulled out all the stops tonight. "You sound surprised."

A half smile formed on her lips. "Well, I've only seen you in soccer shorts, jerseys and T-shirts."

Ryland remembered the first day she'd shown up at his parents' house. He raised a brow. "And shirtless."

Her cheeks turned a charming shade of pink. "That, too."

He handed her the iris. The color matched her dress perfectly. "For you."

"Thank you." She took the flower and smelled it. "It's real."

"Not everything is pretend."

She smiled. "I've always liked irises better than roses."

Score. "It reminded me of you."

Her eyes widened. "You don't have to say stuff like that. No one is watching us."

He held his hands up, his palms facing her. "Just being honest."

She kept staring at the flower. "Let me put this in some water before we go."

With an unexpected bounce to his step, Ryland entered the house and closed the door behind him. He followed Lucy, enjoying the sway of her hips and the flow of her dress around her legs. Her heels clicked against the floor. Manny trotted along behind him.

In the kitchen, she filled a narrow glass vase with water. She studied the flower, turning it 360 degrees, then stuck the stem into the vase. "I want to paint this."

Satisfaction flowed through him. "I'd like to see your work."

"We need to get to Otto's."

"There's no rush," he said. "I called the restaurant. No reservations unless it's a party of six or more."

She tilted her chin. "You're going to a lot of trouble for a pretend date."

"Connor doesn't want you to be lonely tonight."

"Connor, huh?"

Ryland's gaze met hers. Such pretty blue eyes. "I don't, either."

And that was the truth. Which surprised him a little. Okay, a lot. This was supposed to be all make-believe, but the more time he spent with Lucy, the more he cared about her. He wanted to make her smile and laugh. He wanted to please her.

This had never happened to him with a woman before. He wasn't sure what to think or even if he liked it.

Silence stretched between them, but if anything, the quiet drew them closer together not apart.

The sounds of the house continued on. Ice cubes dropped inside the freezer. A motor on the refrigerator whirred. Manny drank water from his bowl.

Funny, but Ryland had never felt this comfortable around anyone except his parents. He needed to figure out what was going on here. "So your paintings..."

"I'm really hungry."

So was Ryland. But what he wanted wasn't on any menu. She was standing right next to him. "Then let's go."

As Ryland held open the door to Otto's, Lucy walked into the restaurant. The din of customers talking and laughing rose above the accordion music playing. She inhaled the tantalizing aromas of roasting pork and herbs lingering in the air.

Her stomach rumbled. She'd been too nervous about the soccer game to eat lunch. Big mistake because now she was starving.

For food and for...

She glanced over her shoulder at Ryland. The green shirt lightened his hazel eyes. He looked as comfortable in dressier clothes as casual ones. He'd gone out of his way to make tonight special. She appreciated that even if none of this was for real. "Thanks for taking me out tonight."

"Thanks for going out with me."

Otto's was packed. Not surprising given it was a Saturday night and the best place in town. The last time she'd been here was right before Aaron and Dana deployed—a going away dinner for them.

Customers crammed into booths and tables. Servers carried heavy trays of German food and large steins full of beer. People waited to be seated. Some stood near the hostess stand. Others sat on benches.

Ryland approached the hostess, who was busy marking the seating chart. The woman in her early twenties looked up with a frown. But as soon as she saw him, a dazzling smile broke across her young, pretty face.

Lucy was beginning to realize wherever Ryland went female attention was sure to follow. But she saw he did nothing to make women come on to him. Well, except for being an extremely good-looking and all-around good guy. She stepped closer to him, feeling territorial. Silly considering this wasn't a real date.

"Hello. I'm Emily. Welcome to Otto's." She smoothed her hair. "How many in your party?"

"Two," he said.

She fluttered her eyelashes coquettishly. "Your name, please?"

"James."

The hostess wrote the information on her list. "You're looking at a thirty-minute wait, but I'll see what I can do."

Lucy was surprised the woman didn't ask for Ryland's phone number or hand him hers. More women, both staff and customers, stared at him.

He shot Lucy a sideward glance. "Half hour okay?"

"The cheese fondue is worth the wait."

Ryland raised a brow. "Even when you're hungry?"

"Especially then."

Other customers made their way out of the restaurant while more entered. He moved closer to her to make room in the small, crowded lobby area. "Connor told me how much you love the cheese fondue here."

"It's my favorite."

"Not chocolate?"

"Chocolate, cheese. I'm not that particular as long as it's warm and…"

"Gooey."

"Lucy?" a familiar male voice asked.

No. No. No. Every muscle in her body tensed. She squeezed her eyes shut in hopes she was dreaming, but when she opened them she was still standing in Otto's. Her ex-husband, Jeff Swanson, and his wife, Amelia, weaved through the crowd toward her. Jeff's receding hairline had gotten worse. And Amelia. She looked different…

Lucy narrowed her gaze for a better look.

Pregnant.

Pain gripped her chest. Life wasn't fair. She sighed.

Ryland stiffened. "You okay?"

"No." Not unless aliens were about to beam her up to the mother ship would she be okay. Being probed and prodded by extraterrestrials would be better than having to speak with the two people who had hurt her most. "But I'll survive."

At least she hoped so.

Jeff crowded in next to them. "I almost didn't recognize you."

The smell of his aftershave brought a rush of memories she'd rather forget. The bad times had overshadowed any good ones that might have existed at the beginning. "It's me."

"I see that now." Jeff's gaze raked over her. "But you cut your hair short. And you must have lost what? Twenty-five pounds or more?"

Stress had made eating difficult after the divorce. Going out solo or fixing a meal for one wasn't much fun, either. She'd also discovered Zumba classes at a nearby gym when she moved to Chicago. "Fifteen."

"Good for you," Amelia said. "It seems like we never stopped dieting when we were in high school. Remember that soup diet? I still can't stand the sight or smell of cabbage."

Until finding out about the affair, Lucy had been thankful to have Amelia for a best friend. Lucy had always felt inadequate, an ugly duckling compared to pretty Amelia with her jade-green eyes and shoulder-length blond hair. Amelia's hair now fell to her mid-back. Jeff liked long hair. That was why Lucy had chopped hers off.

Jeff extended his arm to shake hands. "Ryland James. I'm surprised to see you back in town."

His jaw tensed. "My parents still live here."

"Amelia, do you remember Ryland?" Jeff asked. "Soccer player extraordinaire."

"Of course." Amelia smiled sweetly. "Lucy had the biggest crush on you when we were in middle school."

"I know," Ryland said.

Lucy's heart went splat against the restaurant's hardwood floor. "You did?"

He nodded.

Aaron must have told Ryland. But why would her brother have done that? Her crush was supposed to be a secret.

"I didn't know," Jeff announced.

"Husbands." Amelia shook her head. "I mean, ex-husbands are always the last to know."

Ignore her. Ignore her. Ignore her.

Lucy repeated the mantra in her head so she didn't say anything aloud. The words wanting to come out of her mouth were neither ladylike nor appropriate for a public setting.

So what if she would have rather told Ryland about her failed marriage? Amelia was not worth causing a scene over.

Ryland put his arm around Lucy and pulled her against him. He toyed with her hair, wrapping a curl around his finger.

Her heart swelled with gratitude. She hated needing anyone. She'd been so weak when she'd been younger she wanted to be strong now that she was healthy. But she needed him at this moment.

She sunk against Ryland, soaking up his warmth and his strength, feeling his heart beat. The constant rhythm, the sound of life, comforted her.

Lucy smiled up at him.

He smiled back.

Both Jeff and Amelia stared with dumbfounded expressions on their faces.

Ryland had been right. Words weren't always necessary. People believed what they wanted, even if their assumptions might be incorrect.

Amelia's eyes darkened. She pressed her lips into a thin line.

Jeff's gaze bounced between Lucy and Ryland. "The two of you are…together?"

Lucy understood the disbelief in his voice. She and Ryland

made an unlikely pair, but still she nodded. She didn't like dishonesty after all the lies people had told her, but this didn't bother her so much. They were having dinner together tonight. Not the "together" Jeff had been talking about, but "together" nonetheless.

"I'd heard you were back in town taking care of Connor, but I had no idea about the two of you," Jeff said, not sounding pleased at all.

Good. Let him stew in his own cheating, miserable, arrogant juices.

Biting back a cutting retort, she glanced up at Ryland.

He kept playing with her hair with one hand while the other kept a possessive hold around her. His gaze held Lucy's for a long moment, the kind that elicited envious sighs from movie audiences. She'd owe him big-time for pretending like this, but she would gladly pay up.

"Soccer isn't that big in the U.S.," Ryland said. "But I played in the U.K. where the media coverage is insane so I try to keep a low profile with my personal life."

Amelia's face scrunched so much it looked painful. "But you're not staying here, are you? I thought you played on the West Coast somewhere."

"Phoenix." Ryland's gaze never wavered from Lucy's, making her insides feel all warm and gooey. "Though I wouldn't mind playing for Indianapolis so I could be closer to Wicksburg."

A thrill rushed through her. That was only a couple of hours away.

"We're having a baby," Amelia blurted as if no one had noticed her protruding belly. "It's a boy."

"Congratulations," both Lucy and Ryland said at the same time.

"I know how badly you wanted children when you were with Jeff," Amelia said to her. "Maybe something happened because of your liver. All those medicines you took and the transplant. But adoption is always an option."

After two years of trying to conceive, she hadn't been able to get pregnant. The doctors said there was no medical reason why she shouldn't be able to have a baby. Amelia knew that. So did Jeff. And it wasn't as if the two of them had gotten pregnant right away. Still feelings of inadequacy pummeled Lucy. Her shoulders slumped.

Ryland cuddled her close, making her feel accepted and special. "Kids aren't easy to handle. But you should see how great Lucy is with Connor."

Amelia patted her stomach. "Jeff and my best friend, Madison, are throwing me a baby shower. They've been planning it for weeks. I can't wait."

The words reminded Lucy of something she'd buried in the far recesses of her mind. Pain sliced through her, sharp and unyielding, at the betrayal of trust by Jeff and Amelia.

"I remember when the two of you spent all that time planning my birthday party." The words tasted bitter on Lucy's tongue. "That's when your affair started, right?"

Amelia gasped. She glared at a contrite-looking Jeff then stormed out of the restaurant.

"Damn." Jeff ran after her calling, "It's not what you think."

Lucy looked toward the door. "I almost feel sorry for her."

"Don't. She knew who and what she was marrying. Swanson is a complete moron." Ryland kept his arm around her. Lucy felt safe and secure in his embrace. His presence took the sting out of the past. "Any guy who would choose that woman over you doesn't have a brain cell in his head."

"Thanks," she said, grateful for his support in the face of her bad judgment. "But the truth is, I should have never married a guy like him."

"Why did you?" Ryland asked.

At a small table for two in the corner of the restaurant, candlelight glowed from a glass votive holder, creating a dancing circle against the white linen tablecloth. Ryland sat across from Lucy, their knees brushing against each other. A bowl of cheese fondue, a basket of bread cubes and a plate with two Bavarian Pretzels were between them.

As Lucy talked about Jeff Swanson, Ryland wished he could

change the past and erase the pain she'd experienced from her disastrous marriage.

"People warned me about Jeff." Lucy kept her chin up, her gaze forward, not downcast. But the hurt in her voice was unmistakable. "Told me to break up with him while we were dating. Aaron. Even Amelia. But I thought I knew better than all of them. I thought I could trust Jeff, but he had me so fooled."

"I doubt you're the only one he fooled."

She nodded. "After we eloped, I discovered Jeff hadn't been honest with me. He didn't like how independent and self-reliant I'd been while we were dating. He expected me to turn into his needy little wife. One who stayed home, cooked, cleaned and doted upon him. I admit I was far from the ideal spouse he expected. Amelia is more the doting type he wanted." Lucy stabbed her fork into a piece of bread. "But that didn't give him a reason to cheat."

"Jeff treated girls badly in high school, but they still wanted to go out with him."

She poked the bread again. "I don't think he knew I existed in high school. But when we bumped into each other in college, he laid on the charm. He knew what girls wanted to hear. At least what this girl needed to hear."

Her piece of bread had been stabbed so many times it was falling apart. He didn't think Lucy realized what she was doing with her appetizer fork. "There's not much left of that piece of bread. You might want to try another cube."

"Sorry." She stuck her fork into another piece and dipped the bread into the cheese. It fell into the pot. "I know I played a part in the breakup. It takes two people to make a marriage. But I wish Jeff had been more up-front and honest about what he wanted from me."

Ryland respected how she took responsibility, not laying all the blame on a cheating spouse. "If you could do it over…"

"I wouldn't," she said firmly. "I'm better off without him, but I'll admit it's hard being back in town. So many people know what happened. I'm sure they're pitying me the way they did when I was sick and talking behind my back."

"What people say doesn't matter." He wanted to see her smile, not look so sad. "Forget about them. Don't let it get to you. You're strong enough to do that."

"Strong?" Her voice cracked. "I'm a wimp."

"You came back to Wicksburg."

"Only because Aaron asked me," she admitted. "I couldn't have taken this leap on my own."

Damn Jeff Swanson. He'd not only destroyed Lucy's trust in others, but also in herself. "Give it time. Go slow."

She winced. "I'm trying. It's just when we were dating, Jeff made me feel…"

Ryland didn't want to push, but curiosity got the best of him. "What?"

Her gaze met his. The depth of betrayal in her eyes slammed into him, as if he'd run headfirst into the left goalpost. He reached across the table and laced his fingers with hers.

She took a deep breath and exhaled slowly. "You know about my liver transplant."

Ryland nodded.

"Someone died so I could live." Her tone stressed the awfulness of the situation and made him wondered if she somehow felt guilty. "I always wondered—I still wonder—whether that person's family would think I was living up to their expectations. I mean, their child's death is what enabled me to have the transplant. Given that ultimate sacrifice, would they be disappointed with what I've done with my life? What I'm doing or not doing now?"

Ryland's heart ached for her. That was a heavy load for anyone to carry. Especially someone as sensitive and sweet as Lucy. He squeezed her hand.

"Jeff's real appeal, I think, was that he made me believe we could achieve something big, something important together. With his help, I could prove I deserved a second chance with a new liver." Her mouth turned down at the corner. Angst clouded her eyes. "But we didn't. It was all talk. He no longer cared about that once we were married."

The sorrow in her voice squeezed Ryland's heart like a vice grip.

"I wanted to make a difference because of the gift I was given." Her mouth twisted with regret. "But I didn't do that when I was married to Jeff. I haven't done anything on my own, either. I doubt I ever will."

Her disappointment clawed at Ryland. "You're making a huge difference for Connor. For Aaron and his wife, too."

She shrugged. "But it's not something big, world changing."

"For your family it is." Did Lucy not know how special she was? "Look at yourself. You graduated college. You run your own business. That's a lot for someone your age."

"I'm twenty-six," she said with wry sarcasm. "Divorced. In debt with college loans and a car payment. I'm living at my brother's house, and all my possessions fit inside my car."

"You beat liver disease," Ryland countered. "Your being here—alive—is more than enough."

She stared at him as if she was trying to figure him out. A soft smile teased the corners of her mouth. "Where have you been all my life? Well, these past two years?"

Ryland was wondering the same thing. The realization should bother him more than it did.

"Thank you." Gratitude filled her eyes. Her appreciation wasn't superficial or calculated, but from her heart and made him feel valued. She squeezed his hand. "For tonight. For listening to me."

He stroked Lucy's hand with his thumb. "Thanks aren't necessary. I asked you to tell me. I've also been there myself."

Oops. Ryland hadn't meant to say that. He pulled his hand away and took a sip from his water glass.

She pinned him with a questioning gaze. "You?"

He tightened his grip on the glass, wanting to backpedal. "It's not the same. Not even close."

"I've spilled my guts," Lucy said. "It's your turn."

Ryland never opened up the way she had with him. People only valued him for what he could give them. If they knew him, the real him, they would think he wasn't worth much off the pitch. He took another sip of water then placed the glass on the table.

The tilt of her chin told him she wasn't going to let this drop. Of all the people in his life, Lucy didn't care about his fortune or fame. She had never asked him for anything for herself. She was always thinking of others. That included him. If he could tell anyone the truth, it was Lucy.

He swallowed around the emotion clogging his throat. "When I was in elementary school, I was bullied."

"Verbally?"

He nodded. "Sometimes…a lot of times…physically."

Lucy gasped. She placed her hand on top of his, the way he'd done with hers only moments before. "Oh, Ryland. I'm so sorry. That had to be horrible."

"Some days I felt invisible. As if kids were looking right through me." He'd never told anyone about this. Not even his parents. He thought telling Lucy would be hard, but the compassion in her eyes kept him going. "Those were the good days. Otherwise I would get pushed around, even beat up."

He'd felt like such a loser, a nobody, but he'd soon realized bullies were the real losers. Bullies like Jeff Swanson. Ryland would never tell Lucy her ex-husband had been one of the kids who terrorized students like him at Wicksburg Elementary School. That would only upset her more.

Concern knotted her brow. "I had no idea that went on."

"You were a little girl." He remembered her with ponytails and freckles playing hopscotch or swinging at recess. Seemingly without a care in the world. He hadn't known until later that she was so sick. "Some older kids like Aaron knew, but if they stood up to the bullies, they got beat up, too."

Her mouth formed a perfect O. "The time Aaron said he'd fallen off the monkey bars and gotten a black eye."

"One kid couldn't do much. Even a cool guy like your brother." Ryland remembered telling Aaron not to interfere but the guy wouldn't listen. "I hated going to school so much. I hated most everything back then. Except football. Soccer."

Lucy's smile filled him with warmth, a way he'd never felt

when thinking about this part of his past. "You found your passion at a young age."

"I liked being part of a team," he admitted. "It didn't matter that I lived in a dumpy apartment on the wrong side of town or was poor or got beat up all the time. When I put on that jersey, I fit in."

She squeezed his hand. "Thank goodness for soccer."

"It was my escape. My salvation." He took a sip of water. "With my teammates alongside me, the bullies had to leave me alone."

She smiled softly. "Your teammates took care of their star player."

He nodded. "Football gave me hope. A way out of Wicksburg so I could make something of myself. Be someone other than the scrawny kid who people picked on."

Kindness and affection reflected in her eyes. "You've done that. You've accomplished so much."

His chest tightened. She was one of a kind. "So have you."

Her hand still rested on his, making everything feel comfortable and natural. Right.

Ryland was in no hurry to have her stop touching him. He had no idea what was going on between them. Pretend, real… He didn't care.

Slowly, almost reluctantly, Lucy pulled her hand away. "Wicksburg holds some bad memories for both of us."

He missed her softness and her warmth. "Some good ones, too."

Like the memories they were creating right now.

She tried to pull the lost bread cube out of the fondue bowl. "At first I wasn't sure about us pretending to date. I don't like being dishonest. But after seeing Jeff and Amelia, I'm thankful you were with me tonight. I know this is what's best for Connor. And the only way for you to help the team."

"And help you."

"And me."

"We're not being that dishonest," he said. "If you think about it, what we're doing is kind of like the funeral."

Her eyes widened. "Funeral?"

Lucy reminded him of Connor. "Playacting at Squiggy's funeral."

She laughed. "You mean his first funeral. Not the top-secret one I wasn't supposed to know about."

Ryland smiled at her lighthearted tone. "Now this is more like it. No more being upset over an idiot like Jeff. It's time for laughter and fun."

"That's exactly what I need."

She raised the piece of fondue-covered bread to her mouth. Her lips closed around it.

So sexy. Ryland's temperature soared. He took another sip of water. Too bad she also didn't need some kisses.

A drop of cheese remained at the corner of her mouth. Ryland wished he could lick it off. "You have a little cheese on your mouth."

She wiped with a napkin, but missed the spot.

Reaching across the table, he used his thumb to remove the cheese, ignoring how soft her lips looked or how badly he wanted to taste their sweetness again. "It's gone."

Her eyes twinkled with silver sparks. "Thanks."

Lucy wouldn't be thanking him if she knew what he was thinking. "You're welcome."

The server arrived with their main courses. Sauerbraten, spatzle noodles and braised red cabbage for Lucy. Jagerschnitzel with mashed potatoes for him. The food smelled mouthwateringly delicious.

As they ate, Ryland couldn't stop thinking about what would happen after dinner and dessert were finished. When it was the two of them back at her house. Alone. This might be a pretend date, but he wanted to kiss her good-night.

For real.

CHAPTER TEN

RIDING in the old, blue truck, Lucy glanced at Ryland, who sat next to her on the bench seat. With his chiseled good looks, his handsome profile looked as if it had been sculpted, especially with the random headlights casting shadows on his face. But there was nothing hard and cold about the man. He was generous, caring and funny. He might be portrayed as being a bad boy in the press, but she'd glimpsed the man underneath the façade and liked what she saw.

He turned onto the street where she lived.

After spilling secrets, she and Ryland had spent the rest of dinner laughing over jokes, stories and memories. Too bad the evening had to end.

"I can't believe we ate that entire apple strudel after all the fondue and dinner," she said.

"We," he teased. "I only had two bites."

"More like twenty-two."

He parked at the curb and set the gear. "Math's never been a strong point. Which is why soccer is the perfect sport for me. Scores rarely reach two digits."

She grinned. "That's why they invented calculators. For all us right-brained people who can't tell the difference between Algebra and Calculus."

"What about addition and subtraction?" With a wink, he removed the key from the ignition. "Stay there. I'll get the door for you."

His manners impressed Lucy. Okay, she may have assumed

athletes had more in common with Neanderthals than gentlemen, but Ryland was proving her wrong. About many things tonight.

The passenger door opened. He extended his arm. "Milady?"

Lucy didn't need Ryland's help, but accepted it anyway. He wasn't offering because she was incapable or unhealthy. He was doing this to be polite. She would gladly play along. "Thank you, kind sir."

The touch of her fingers against his skin caused a spark. Static electricity from the truck's carpet? Whatever it was, heat traveled through her, igniting a fire she hadn't felt in a long time and wasn't sure what to do with.

As soon as she was out of the truck and standing on the sidewalk, Ryland let go of her. A relief, given her reaction, but she missed his touch.

"You must be cold," he said.

Even with the cool night air and her sleeveless dress, she wasn't chilly. Not with Ryland next to her.

"I'm fine." Thousands of stars twinkled overhead. She'd forgotten what the night sky looked like in the country compared to that in a city. "It's a beautiful night."

"Very beautiful."

She glanced his way.

He was looking at her, not the sky. Her body buzzed with awareness. She could stand out here with him all night.

His smile crinkled the corners of his eyes and did funny things to her heart rate.

Tearing her gaze away, Lucy headed up the paved walkway toward the front porch. Ryland followed her, his steps sounding against the concrete.

Uncertainty coursed through Lucy. Ryland made her feel so special tonight, listening in a way Jeff never had and sharing a part of himself with her.

This wasn't a real date. Except at some point this evening, she hadn't been pretending. Ryland hadn't seemed to be, either. That...worried her.

Lucy didn't trust herself when it came to men, especially

Ryland. Best to say a quick good-night and make a hasty retreat inside. Alone. So she could figure this out.

On the porch, she reached into her purse with a shaking hand and pulled out her keys. "I had a great time. Thanks."

"The night's still young."

Anticipation revved her blood. She wanted to invite him in. Who was she kidding? She wanted to throw herself into his arms and kiss him until they ran out of air. Or the sun came up.

Lucy couldn't deny the flush of desire, but if they started something would she be able to stop? Would she want to stop? To go too far would be disastrous. "I'm thinking we should call it a night."

He ran his finger along her jawline. "You think?"

Lucy gulped. "I'm not ready for taking any big leaps."

"What about a small one?"

His lips beckoned. Hers ached. Maybe just a little kiss…

She lifted her chin and kissed him on the mouth. Hard.

Ryland pressed his mouth against Lucy's with a hunger that matched her own. He wrapped his arms around her, pulling her closer. She went eagerly, arching against him. This was what she wanted…needed.

The keys dropped from her fingers and clattered on the step. She placed her hands on his shoulders, feeling the ridges of his muscles beneath her fingertips.

His lips moved over hers. She parted her lips, allowing their tongues to explore and dance.

Pleasurable sensations shot through her. She clung to him and his kiss. Longing pooled low in her belly. A moan escaped her lips.

Ryland drew the kiss to an end. "Wow."

That pretty much summed it up. She took a breath and another. It didn't help. Her breathing was still ragged. And her throbbing lips…

She fought the urge to touch them to see that what she'd experienced hadn't been a dream. "I've been trying to curb my impulsive side. Looks like I failed."

"I'd give you an A+ and recommend letting yourself be more impulsive." Wicked laughter lit his eyes. He kept his arms around her. "We could go inside and see where our impulses take us."

Most likely straight into the bedroom. Lucy's heart slammed against her chest.

A sudden fear dampened her desire. She'd been hurt too badly, didn't trust her judgment or the feelings coursing through her right now. Especially with a man who had more opportunity to cheat than her ex-husband ever had.

Ryland James is a player, Luce. He'll break your heart if he gets the chance.

Aaron's words echoed through her head. "We can't. I mean, I can't."

Ryland combed his fingers through her hair. "If you think I'm pretending, I'm not."

"Me, either." Her resolve weakened. "But I have to think of Connor."

"He's spending the night with Marco."

Her mouth went dry with the possibilities. "You're leaving town soon."

"True, but we can make the most of the time I have left," Ryland said, his voice husky and oh-so tempting. "You said you didn't want a boyfriend. I'm not looking for a girlfriend."

"Not a real one at least."

"Touché."

"This has nowhere to go. I'm not up for a fling. Aaron thinks if we get involved, you'll break my heart."

Ryland stiffened. "Your brother said that?"

"The other night when he called."

His mouth quirked. "So let's just keep doing what we've been doing."

"Pretending."

"We'll date, but keep it light," he said. "No promises. No guarantees."

"No sex."

"You've made that clear." He sounded amused, not upset. "Except how do you feel about pretend sex?"

"Huh?"

"Never mind," he said. "We'll just have fun and enjoy each other's company until it's time for me to go back to Phoenix."

Lucy wasn't one to play with fire. She'd done everything in her power these past two years to keep from getting burned again. But this was different. She knew where she stood with Ryland. He'd been honest with her. They could make this work. But she would keep a fire extinguisher handy in case the flames got out of control. Getting burned was one thing. She didn't want to wind up a pile of ash. "Okay. We can keep doing what we've been doing."

On Sunday afternoon, Ryland knocked on Lucy's front door. He'd done the same thing less than twenty-four hours ago. But he felt more anticipation today.

She'd been on his mind since last night. Her kisses had fueled his fantasies, making him want more.

But she wasn't ready to give more. At least not the more he wanted.

I don't sleep around.

I'm not up for a fling.

No sex.

She hadn't said anything about no kisses. He'd settle for those. Maybe Lucy would change her mind about the physical part of their…not relationship…hanging out.

The front door opened. Connor smiled up at him with a toothy grin. "Fuego plays in an hour."

This was the second game of the season for his team. They were in L.A. to play against the Galaxy. Ryland had missed not being at the season opener earlier this week when the team lost to the Portland Timbers. He'd felt like he was letting down his teammates and fans down being unable to play. He looked at his foot.

The orthopedist had told Ryland he might get the boot off in another week or two. That meant he would be able to return to the team, but in order to do that he would have to leave Wicksburg.

Wait a minute. Leaving town would be a good thing. Nothing was holding him here. Well, except his parents who would be returning home this week.

And Lucy. But he couldn't let himself go there. When he could play again, soccer would have to be his total focus. He couldn't afford any distractions. She would be a big one.

"Aunt Lucy told me to cheer loudly." Connor grabbed Manny who was darting between his legs, trying get out of the house. "I have to finish my math homework first. Aunt Lucy said so."

"Better get to it, bud." Ryland entered the house. He closed the door behind him. "I don't want to watch the game without you."

Connor ran off to his bedroom to finish his homework. Ryland walked to the kitchen.

The scents of cheese and bacon filled the air. His mouth watered, as much for whatever was baking as the woman unloading the dishwasher. Lucy wore a pair of jean shorts. Her T-shirt inched up in the back showing him a flash of ivory skin in the back as she bent over to grab silverware. Her lime V-neck T-shirt gaped revealing the edge of her white-lace bra.

Beautiful.

He stepped behind and wrapped his arms around Lucy. Her soft-in-all-the-right-places body fit perfectly against his. Knowing they were alone while Connor did his math, Ryland showered kisses along her jawline.

She faced him. Silver sparks flashed in her eyes. "Is this how you normally say hello?"

"No, I prefer this way."

He lowered his mouth to hers. His lips soaked in her warmth and sweetness. His heart rate tripled. The blood rushed from his head.

She arched against him, taking the kiss deeper. He followed her lead, relieved she was as into kissing as he was. He liked kissing Lucy. He wanted to keep on kissing her.

Forever.

Ryland jerked back.

He didn't do forever.

She stared up at him with flushed cheeks and swollen lips. The passion in her eyes matched the desire rushing through his veins. Definitely a keeper. If he was looking for one…

Lucy grinned. "I like how you say hello."

He liked it, too. Especially with her.

But he had to remember to keep things light. No thoughts about forever. They had two weeks, if they were lucky. No reason to get carried away.

And he wouldn't. That wouldn't be fair to Lucy. Or her brother.

He owed Aaron that much, even if his old friend was wrong about Ryland breaking Lucy's heart. He wouldn't do that to her.

He inhaled. "Whatever you're cooking smells delicious."

"Macaroni and cheese." She turned on the oven light so he could see the casserole dish baking inside. "Dana marked her cookbooks with Connor's favorite recipes."

"I smell bacon."

Lucy smiled coyly. "That's one of the secret ingredients."

"I didn't know you were allowed to divulge secret ingredients."

She shrugged. "We shared our secrets last night so I figured why not."

The vase containing the iris he'd given her sat on the counter. Paintbrushes dried alongside it. "If we have nothing left to hide, show me your paintings."

Her lips quirked. "You really want to see them?"

She sounded surprised by his interest in her art. "I do, or I wouldn't keep asking."

"I—I don't show my work to a lot of people."

"It's just me."

Uncertainty flickered in her eyes. "Exactly."

Ryland didn't understand what she meant. "Show me one."

She raised a brow. "That'll be enough to appease your curiosity?"

He wasn't sure of anything when it came to Lucy. But he

would take what he could get. "Yes. I'll leave it up to you if you want to show me more."

She glanced at the oven timer. "I suppose we have time now."

Not the most enthusiastic response, but better than a no. "Great."

Lucy led him down a hallway covered with framed photographs. One picture showed a large recreational vehicle that looked more like a bus.

"Is that your parents' RV?" he asked.

"Yes," she said. "How did you know about that?"

"Connor told me his grandparents were living in a camper and traveling all over the country."

"Yes, that's how they dreamed of spending their retirement. They finally managed to do it three months ago." She peeked in on Connor, who sat at his desk doing his homework. "They're in New Mexico right now."

Ryland wondered what Lucy dreamed of doing. He considered asking, but any of her dreams would be on hold until Aaron and his wife returned. Ryland admired Lucy's sacrifice. He'd thought watching Cupcake had been a big deal. Not even close. He followed her through another doorway.

The bedroom was spotless with nothing out of place. The queen-size bed, covered with a flower-print comforter and matching pillow shams, drew his attention. This was where Lucy slept. Alone, but the bed was big enough for two.

Don't even think about it. He looked away.

She went to the closet.

Ryland knew what to expect from a typical twenty-something woman's closet—overflowing with clothing, shoes and purses.

Lucy opened the door.

Only a few clothing items hung on the rack. A sheet of plastic covered the closet floor. Five pairs of shoes sat on top. Not a handbag in sight. Instead, the backsides of different-size canvases and boxes of art supplies filled the space.

Not typical at all.

Given this was Lucy he shouldn't have been surprised.

"This is something I painted when I was living in Chicago."

As she reached for the closest painting, her hand trembled.

Ryland touched her shoulder. He wanted to see her work, but he didn't want to make her uncomfortable. Her bare skin felt soft and warm beneath his palm. "We can do this another time."

"Now is fine." She glanced back at him. "It's just a little hard…"

"To show this side of yourself."

She nodded.

The vulnerability in her eyes squeezed his heart. Her affect on him unnerved Ryland. He lowered his arm from her shoulder. "If it's any consolation, I know nothing about art. I'm about as far removed from an art critic as you can get."

"So if you like it, I'll remember not to get too excited."

He smiled.

She smiled back.

His heart stumbled over itself. His breath rushed from his lungs as if he'd played ninety minutes without a break at halftime.

What was going on?

All she'd done was smile. Something she'd done a hundred times before. But he could hardly breathe.

She pulled out the canvas. "Ready?"

No. Feeling unsteady, he sat on the bed.

"Sure." He forced the word from his tight throat.

Lucy turned the canvas around.

Ryland stared openmouthed and in awe. He'd expected to see a bowl of fruit or a bouquet of flowers. Not a vibrant, colorful portrait full of people having fun. The painting depicted a park with people picnicking, riding bicycles, pushing baby strollers and flying kites.

A good thing he was sitting or he would have fallen flat on his butt. The painting was incredible. Amazing. He felt transported, as if he were in the park seeing what she'd seen, feeling what she'd felt. Surreal.

He took a closer look. "Is that guy eating a hot dog?"

She nodded. "What's a day in the park without a hot dog from a vendor?"

Drops of yellow mustard dripped onto the guy's chin and shirt. The amount of detail amazed Ryland. He noticed a turtle painted next to the pond. An homage to Squiggy? "You're so talented."

"You know nothing about art," she reminded him.

"True, but I know quality when I see it," he said. "This is a thousand times better than any of the junk hanging on my walls in Phoenix."

She raised a brow. "I doubt those artists would consider their work junk."

He waved a hand. "You know what I mean."

"Thank you."

"No, thank you." This painting told him so much about Lucy. He could see her in each stroke, each character, each detail. Life exploded from the canvas. The importance of community, too. "I know a couple of people who own art galleries."

Her lips pursed. "Thanks, but I'm not ready to do that."

"You're ready," he encouraged. "Trust yourself. Your talent."

"I don't think I should do anything until Aaron and Dana get home."

Ryland hated to see Lucy holding back like this. "Think about it."

"I will. Would you like to see another one?" she asked to his surprise. "Not all of them are so cheery as this one. I went through a dark stage."

"Please." Looking at her work was like taking a peek inside her heart and her soul. He wanted to see more, as many paintings as she allowed him to see. "Show me."

Lucy would have never thought the best date ever would include mac and cheese, her nine-year-old nephew and a televised soccer game, but it had tonight. At first she'd been so nervous about showing Ryland her work, afraid of exposing herself like that and what he might think. He not only liked her paintings, but also understood them. Catching details most people overlooked.

She stood at the doorway to her nephew's bedroom while Ryland, by request, tucked Connor into bed.

The two talked about the game. Even though Fuego lost 0–1 to the Galaxy, both agreed it was a good game.

"They would have won if you'd been there," Connor said.

Ryland ruffled Connor's hair. "We'll never know."

"I can't wait to see you play."

As the soccer talk continued, Lucy leaned against the hallway wall.

Thanks to Ryland, her nephew was a happy kid again. Connor still missed his parents, but a certain professional soccer player had made a big difference. At least for now.

Lucy wondered if Connor realized when Ryland could play again he wouldn't be coaching. But if the Fuego played the Indianapolis Rage, maybe they could get tickets. She would have to check the match schedule.

Seeing Ryland play in person might be just the ticket to keep a smile on her nephew's face. Lucy had to admit she would like that, too.

"Good night, Connor." Ryland turned off the light in the bedroom. "I'll see you at practice tomorrow."

"'Night."

In the hallway, he laced his fingers with hers and led her into the living room. "I finally have you all to myself."

"We don't have to watch the post-match commentary?" she teased.

"I set the DVR so I wouldn't have to subject you to that." He pulled her against him. "But I will subject you to this."

Ryland's lips pressed against hers. His kiss was soft. Tender. Warm.

She leaned against him, only to find herself swept up in his arms. But his lips didn't leave hers.

He carried her to the couch and sat with her on his lap. Lucy wrapped her arms around him. Her breasts pressed against his hard chest.

As she ran her hands along his muscular shoulders and wove her fingers through her hair, she parted her lips. She wanted more of his kisses, more of him.

The pressure of his mouth against hers increased, full of hunger and heat. Her insides felt as if they were melting.

Ryland might be a world-class soccer player, but he was a world-class kisser, too.

Pleasurable sensations shot through her. Tingles exploded. If she'd been confused about the definition of chemistry, she understood it now.

Thank goodness he had his arms around her or she'd be falling to the floor, a mass of gooey warmth. Not that she was complaining. She clung to him, wanting even more of his kisses.

Slowly Ryland loosened his hold on her and drew the kiss to an end. "Told you this would be fun."

"You did." A good thing he wasn't going to be around long enough or this could become habit forming. Her chest tightened.

Lucy couldn't afford for anything about Ryland to become habit. She couldn't allow herself to get attached.

Neither of them was in a place to pursue a relationship. Neither of them could commit to anything long-term.

This was about spending time together in the short-term and having fun. And sharing some very hot kisses.

That had to be enough. Even if a part of her was wishing there could be…more.

CHAPTER ELEVEN

As the days passed, the temperature warmed. The sun stayed out longer. The Defeeters won more games than they lost. But Lucy wasn't looking forward to the end of spring. She didn't want Ryland to leave.

Being with him was exciting. Wicksburg no longer seemed like a boring, small town as they made the most of their time together. Practice twice a week. Dinner with Connor. Lunch when her work schedule or his physical therapy allowed. When she was alone, her painting flourished with heightened senses and overflowing creativity.

After Mr. and Mrs. James returned from their vacation, they became fixtures at games and invited everyone to dinner following a practice.

That Monday evening, a bird chirped in a nearby cherry tree in the Jameses' backyard. The cheery tune fit perfectly with the jubilant mood. The boys kicked a soccer ball on the grass while Cupcake chased after them barking.

Standing on the patio, Lucy watched the boys play.

"Connor reminds me of his father," Mrs. James said. She wore her salt-and-pepper hair in a ponytail, a pair of jeans and a button-down blouse. "Though he's a little taller than Aaron was at this age."

"Connor's mom is tall." Lucy glanced at Mrs. James. "Thank you for having us over tonight."

"Our pleasure. It's so nice to have children here." She stared at the boys running around. "I've been telling Ryland to settle down so I can have grandchildren to spoil, but that boy has only one thing on his mind."

"Soccer," Lucy said at the same time as his mother.

Mrs. James eyed her curiously. "You know him well."

Lucy shifted her weight between her feet. "He's been helping me with the team."

"And going out with you." Mrs. James smiled. "Hard to keep things secret in a town Wicksburg's size."

They hadn't tried hiding anything. The more people who knew they were going out, the better. Lucy wanted nothing more than to enjoy her time with Ryland, but she felt as if she was trying to hold on to the wind. He would be blowing out of her life much too soon.

"It's so nice Ryland is with someone who knew him before he became famous," Mrs. James said.

"He was always a star player around here."

Ryland shouted something to the boys. Laughter filled the air.

"Yes, but he thinks of himself as a footballer, nothing else," Mrs. James explained. "Ryland needs to realize that there's a life for him off the pitch, too. I hope being here and getting reacquainted with you and others will help him see that."

"Soccer is his only priority." Lucy had been reminding herself that for days now. All the smiles, laughter and kisses they shared would be coming to an end. But she didn't want to turn into a sighing lump because he was leaving. "He's not interested in anything else."

"I wonder if soccer would be as important to him if he thought there was somewhere else he belonged."

I liked being part of a team. It didn't matter that I lived in a dumpy apartment on the wrong side of town or was poor or got beat up all the time. When I put on that jersey, I fit in.

Lucy remembered what he'd told her. "Belonging is important to him, but Ryland doesn't think he belongs in Wicksburg."

Mrs. James's eyes widened. "You've talked about this?"

Lucy hoped she wasn't opening a can of worms for Ryland, but his mother seemed genuinely concerned. "A little."

"That's a start." Mrs. James's green eyes twinkled with pleasure. "It's going to take Ryland time to realize where he belongs, and that he's more than he thinks he is."

"Maybe when he gets back to Phoenix." Lucy's chest tightened. "He doesn't have much time left here."

"He can always come back."

Lucy nodded. She hoped Ryland would return after the MLS season ended, but that was months away.

"Well, I'd better finish getting the taco bar ready," Mrs. James said. "The boys must be starving."

"What can I do to help?" Lucy asked.

"Enjoy yourself."

As Mrs. James walked away, Cheryl came up. She held an iPad. "Getting on the mother's good side is smart. I should have done that with my mother-in-law."

"It's not too late," Lucy said.

"Well, the divorce papers haven't been filed yet. But I don't want to talk about my sorry situation." Cheryl showed Lucy an article from a U.K. tabloid's website. "Guess this is what happens when you're with one of the hottest footballers around."

Lucy stared at the iPad screen full of pictures of her and Ryland. "Why would they do this?"

Cheryl sighed. "Because it's so romantic."

Romantic, perhaps. But not…real. The photos made it appear as if Lucy and Ryland were falling for each other. Falling hard.

The top photograph was from the Defeeters' first game when Ryland kneeled behind her and whispered in her ear, but it looked as if he were kissing her neck. The second showed them in a booth at the pizza parlor sitting close together and gazing into each other's eyes. The last one captured their quick congratulatory peck after the team's first win, but the photograph made it seem like a long, tongue shoved down each other's throats full-on make-out session. Okay, they'd had a couple of those, but not where anyone could see them let alone take a picture.

As Lucy read the article, the blood rushed from her head.

The world spun. The pictures didn't imply a serious relationship. The words suggested an imminent engagement.

Oh, no. This was bad. "I can't believe this."

"I didn't realize things were so serious."

"Me, neither." Ryland wasn't going to like this. Lucy reread a paragraph. "They call me a WAG. Is that a British euphemism for hag or something?"

Cheryl laughed. "WAG stands for Wives and Girlfriends. Many women aspire to be one."

The acronym wasn't accurate. Surprisingly the thought of being Ryland's girlfriend didn't sound so bad. Unease slithered down Lucy's spine. She knew better to think that way. Dating Ryland didn't include being his girlfriend. Except everyone reading the article… "I hope people don't believe all this."

"You and Ryland care about each other. That's all that matters."

Care.

Yes, Lucy cared about Ryland. She cared…a lot.

As she stared at one of the photographs, a deeper attraction and affection for Ryland surfaced, accompanied by a sinking feeling in her stomach.

Oh, no. She'd been ignoring and pretending certain feelings didn't exist, but the article was bringing all that emotion out. She couldn't deny the truth any longer.

Lucy didn't just care about Ryland.

I love him.

The truth hit her like a gallon of paint dropped on her head. She'd fallen in love with Ryland James. Even though she'd known all the reasons why she shouldn't.

Stupid, stupid, stupid.

"You look pale," Cheryl said. "Are you okay?"

"I don't know," Lucy admitted. "I really don't know."

Ryland had pursued her. She'd pretended she couldn't be caught, but she'd been swept up by his charm and heart the minute he'd turned them on her.

Lucy wanted people to be honest with her, but she'd lied to

herself about how safe it was to date Ryland, to hang out with him, to kiss him.

“Don’t let a gossip column bother you. Talk to Ryland about it,” Cheryl suggested. “I’m sure he’s dealt with this before.”

Gossip, yes. But Lucy wasn’t sure how many women had fallen in love with him. She couldn’t imagine being the first, but she wasn’t sure she wanted to know the number of women who had gone down this same path.

Talk to Ryland about it.

She’d experienced a change of heart about wanting a relationship. Maybe he’d had one, too. And if not…

No. This wasn’t a crush. Her feelings weren’t one-sided. His kisses were proof of that as was his wanting to spend time with her. He had feelings for her. She knew he did.

Lucy had shared her secrets and art with him. How hard could it be to tell him she’d lost her heart to him, too?

She would talk to Ryland and see where their feelings took them.

After dinner, Ryland carried in the leftovers from the taco bar while a soccer match between kids and adults was being fought to determine bragging rights.

In the kitchen, he set the pan of ground beef on the counter. “That’s the last of it.”

His mother handed him a plastic container. “I like Lucy.”

“So do I.”

“Good, because it’s about time you got serious with a woman.”

Ryland flinched. He stared at his mom in disbelief. “Who said anything about getting serious?”

“Your father and I aren’t getting any younger. We’d like grandkids while we can still get around and play with them. You and Lucy would have cute babies.”

“Whoa, Mom.” Ryland held up his hands, as if that could stop a runaway train like his mom. “I like Lucy. That’s a long way from having babies with her. I need to focus on my career.”

His mom shrugged. "A soccer ball won't provide much comfort after you retire."

He spooned the meat into the container. "I'll settle down once I stop playing."

"That's years away."

Ryland covered the ground beef with a lid. "I hope so."

"That's not what your mother wants to hear."

"It's the truth," he admitted. "If I put down any kind of roots, I'm not going to be able to finish out my career the way I want to."

"A woman like Lucy won't wait around forever. She won't have to in a town like Wicksburg." His mom filled a plastic Ziploc baggie with the leftover shredded cheese. "While you're off playing football and partying with WAG wannabes, another man will sweep Lucy off her feet. She'll have a ring on her finger before Christmastime."

Ryland clenched his hands. Wait a minute. His mom had no idea what she was saying. "Lucy doesn't want a ring. Not from me or anyone else."

"You sound confident."

"I am," he admitted. "We talked about it."

"It?"

"Relationships. Lucy and I are on the same page." He wished his mom wasn't sticking her nose into his business. He kept his social life private so she wouldn't know what was going on. "I can't be thinking about a relationship right now because of soccer. Lucy doesn't want to be entangled by any guy while she's taking care of Connor."

His mom studied him. "So when you go back to Phoenix..."

"It's over."

"And when you come back?"

"You and Dad can visit me," Ryland said. "I've worked too hard to get out of Wicksburg."

"You ran away."

"I left to play soccer."

His mother took a deep breath then exhaled slowly. "You're an adult and capable of making your own decisions, but please, honey, think about what you may be giving up if you leave town, leave Lucy, and never look back."

He picked up the container of meat and placed it in the refrigerator. "You're way off base here, Mom."

"Maybe I am, but one of these days you're going to realize soccer isn't the only thing in the world. I'd like for you to have a life outside the game in place when that happens."

"You just want me back in Wicksburg raising a bunch of kids."

"I want you to be happy."

"I am happy." So what if a lot of his happiness right now had to do with Lucy? Their dating was only for the short-term. They both agreed. His mother was wrong. This was for the best. "I know what I'm doing. I know what I want."

And that didn't include Wicksburg or…Lucy.

Later that evening, after everyone had left, Lucy sat with Ryland on his parents' patio. Mr. James was showing Connor his big-screen TV while Mrs. James gave Cupcake a bath after the dog jumped into a garbage can.

Ryland leaned back in his chair. "The boys enjoyed themselves."

"Their parents, too." Lucy had thrown herself into playing soccer. A way to put a game face on, perhaps?

"Cheryl showed me an article from a U.K. tabloid tonight." Lucy held up the display screen of her smartphone. "It's about…us."

Heaven help her, but she liked saying the word "us." Ryland had to see how good they were together.

He took the phone and used his finger to scroll through the words. "This happens all the time. Don't let it bother you."

He sounded so nonchalant about the whole thing. "You don't mind that total strangers halfway across the globe are reading about us?"

"It's not about minding." As Ryland laced his fingers with hers, tingles shot up her arm. "Football is almost like a religion in other countries. Fans follow their favorite players' every move. If someone tweets that a star player is at the supermarket buying groceries, hundreds of people might show up in minutes. This article is no different than others they've published about me and other players."

"But you don't play over there anymore."

"I did," he said. "I could go back someday."

So far away. Lucy felt a pang in her heart. She didn't want him to leave. Not to Phoenix. Not anywhere.

She took a deep breath to calm her nerves. "The article makes it read like we're seriously dating, practically engaged."

"But we're not."

Ryland sounded so certain. No hesitation. No regret.

Lucy searched his face for a sign that he'd had a change of heart like her, but she saw nothing. Absolutely nothing to suggest he felt or wanted…more.

That frustrated her. She wanted him to be her boyfriend. The guy should want her to be his girlfriend.

Ryland put his arm around her. "This can be hard to deal with when you're not used to it. But it's how the game is played. You have to ignore it."

Lucy didn't want to ignore it. She wanted the article to be true. She wanted to be a WAG. Ryland's WAG. Not only his girlfriend, she realized with a start. But his…wife.

Mrs. Ryland James.

Lucy suppressed a groan. This was bad. Horrible. Tragic.

No promises. No guarantees. No sex.

"Hey, don't be sad." Ryland caressed her face with his hand. "It's just a stupid article full of gossip and lies. Nothing to worry about."

His words were like jabs with a pitchfork to Lucy's heart. The more he downplayed the article, the more it bothered her. And hurt.

Irritation burned. At Ryland. At herself.

Forget about telling him how she felt. She wasn't going to give him the satisfaction of knowing how much she cared about him when he didn't or wouldn't admit how he felt about her.

Annoyed at the situation and at him, she raised her chin.

"I'm not worried. I just wanted to make sure this wouldn't damage the Ryland James brand."

The next day, Ryland took Cupcake on a walk around the neighborhood without the boot per his doctor's orders. He'd chosen this time because he knew Lucy had a call with a client and wouldn't see him.

He didn't know what was going on with her. She'd given off mixed signals last night. Her good-night kiss suggested she was into him. But her attitude about the tabloid article made him think she might be getting tired of him and unsettled by that side of his fame.

Ryland didn't know what her reaction to his getting the boot off would be.

The little gray dog ran ahead, pulling against the leash.

"Are you ready for me to go back to Phoenix, Cupcake?"

The dog ignored him and sniffed a bush.

"I'm not." He had to leave, but what he and Lucy had together was going to be hard to give up. More time with Lucy would be nice. More than nice. Too bad he couldn't go there or anywhere on the other side of nice. "But I'm not going to have a choice."

His cell phone rang. He pulled it from his pocket and glanced at the touch screen. Blake. About time. Ryland had left him a message last night.

"Did you plant the story about me and Lucy?" he asked.

"Hello to you, too." Blake sounded amused. "Yes, I'm doing well. Thanks for asking."

Ryland watched Cupcake sniff a patch of yellow and pink flowers. "Was it you?"

"No," Blake admitted. "That's not to say I didn't have a suggestion for the person who did."

Ryland knew it. The PR firm had to be involved. But Blake would never give him firm details. At least he hadn't in the past when something like this occurred. "Why?"

"Your future with Fuego isn't a sure thing," he said. "A serious girlfriend will help your image. Bad Boy Ryland James getting serious with a hometown girl. It sends the message you're maturing and getting out of the party scene."

Ryland pulled Cupcake away from a rose bush with thorns. "You're reaching for something that isn't there."

"I spoke with both your coach and Fuego's owner," Blake said. "Settling down is the best thing you can do right now."

"You're sounding a lot like my mom."

"Your mom's a smart woman."

Ryland looked around to see if anyone was on the street. Empty. "Lucy and I aren't serious."

"A big, sparkling diamond engagement ring from Tiffany & Co. will change all that."

He felt a flash of something, almost a little thrill at the thought of proposing to Lucy. Must be a new form of nausea. "Yeah, right. I'll catch a flight to Chicago tonight and go buy one."

"Indianapolis is closer," Blake said. "They have a store there according to their website."

"You're joking, right? Otherwise you've lost your mind."

"You said you wanted to play in the MLS," he said. "I'm making that happen for you."

"By lying."

"It's called stretching the truth," Blake said. "Let people see you buy an engagement ring. They can make their own assumptions."

"Lucy would never go for something like this."

"She'll be thrilled. Anyone who looks at those photographs can tell she's as crazy about you as you are about her."

"Crazy, maybe. But not in…" Ryland couldn't bring himself to say the word. "I like her." A lot. More than he'd ever thought possible. "But that doesn't mean I'm ready to get…serious."

Okay, so he'd thought about summer break and time off when he could be with Lucy and Connor. And Manny, the fat cat, too.

But Ryland had realized doing anything more than thinking about the future was stupid. He needed to focus, to prove himself, to play…

"Her life is in Wicksburg. At least as long as she's taking care of Connor," Ryland said. "My life is in Phoenix."

"You don't sound so excited about that anymore."

"I am." Wasn't he? Of course, he was. All this was messing with his head. "But Lucy can't spend the next year or so with us traveling back and forth between here and there, to see each other."

"You can afford it."

"Blake."

"Just playing devil's advocate."

"Be my advocate. That's what I pay you for."

"What do you want?"

Lucy. No, that wasn't possible. "I want to play again. Not the way I played last season with the Fuego, but the way I played over in the Premier League. When it…mattered to me. Working with the kids and Lucy reminded me how much I love the game. And how much I miss it."

"You don't sound the same as you did a month ago." Emotion filled Blake's voice. "For the first time in two years, it sounds like the real Ryland James is back."

"Damn straight, I am." But he couldn't get too excited. Thinking about leaving Lucy left a football-size hole in his chest.

But what could Ryland do? He had a team to play for, a job to do. His goal had always been to escape Wicksburg, not move back and marry a hometown girl.

Whoa. Where had that come from? Marriage had always been a four-letter word to him.

"The team's training staff is itching to work with you," Blake said. "They've been concerned about your training and conditioning."

"They'll be pleasantly surprised."

"Exactly what I hoped you'd say." Blake sounded like he was smiling. "My assistant can make your travel arrangements to Phoenix when you're ready."

Ryland's stomach knotted. He should be ready to leave now

after weeks in Wicksburg, but Phoenix didn't hold the same appeal for some reason. "I see the orthopedist this afternoon."

"I hope we hear good news."

We. The only "we" that had come to matter to Ryland was him and Lucy. Uh, Lucy and the Defeeters, that is. They were a package. Emotion tightened his throat. "I'll let you know."

Face it. What could he do? No matter how wonderful Lucy might be, Ryland wasn't picket-fence material, even if he could now understand the appeal of a committed, monogamous relationship. Marriage wasn't a goal of his. He had a career to salvage. The longer he stuck around playing at having a relationship, the deeper things would get and he might end up hurting Lucy.

Ryland knew what he had to do. Get the hell out of Wicksburg. And get out fast before he did any more damage than he'd already done.

CHAPTER TWELVE

OUT on the field Wednesday afternoon, Lucy glanced at her watch. Fifteen minutes until the end of today's practice. Strange. Ryland had yet to show up or call. She glanced at the parking lot, but didn't see his father's blue truck.

Even though he'd annoyed her on Monday night, she still wanted to see him. She hoped nothing was wrong. He'd bowed out of dinner last night. After Connor went to bed, she'd used the time to paint.

Marco passed the ball to Tyler. Connor, playing defense, stole the ball and kicked it out of bounds.

Lucy blew the whistle. "Push-ups for the entire team if the ball goes out again."

The boys groaned.

She scooped up the ball and tossed it onto the field. Play continued.

"You're doing great, coach."

Her toes curled at the sound of Ryland's voice. She glanced over her shoulder. He walked toward her in a T-shirt and shorts and…

She stared in shock at the tennis shoe on his right foot. "Your boot. It's gone."

"I no longer need it."

"That's great." And then she realized what that meant. With his foot healed, he would return to Phoenix. Her heart sank, but she kept a smile on her face. Pride kept her from showing how much he'd gotten to her. "I'm happy for you."

"Thanks." He stared at her with a strange look in his eyes. "I want to talk to the boys."

Her muscles tensed. Lucy had a feeling this might not be his usual end-of-practice pep talk. She blew the whistle.

The boys stopped playing and looked her way. Smiles erupted on their faces when they saw Ryland.

He motioned to them. "Everyone gather around."

The boys sat on the grass in front of Ryland. So did Lucy.

"Sorry I was late for practice, but I like what I saw out there," Ryland said. "Keep talking to each other, passing the ball and listening to your coach."

He winked at Lucy.

Her tight shoulder muscles relaxed a little.

"I appreciate how hard you're working. I know the drills we do can be boring, but they work. If you do them enough times at practice, you won't have to think about doing the moves in a game. It'll just happen."

"I can't wait until Saturday's match," Connor said.

"Me, either," Jacob agreed.

The other boys nodded.

Ryland dragged his hand through his hair. "I know you guys are going to play hard on Saturday. But I won't be there. My foot's better. It's time for me to return to my team."

Frowns met his words. Sighs, too. The disappointment on the boys' faces was clear. The kids talked over one another. A few were visibly shaken by the news.

Tears stung Lucy's eyes. She blinked them away. She needed to be strong for Connor and the team. "Let Ryland finish."

The boys quieted.

"I'm sorry I won't be able to be with you during those last two games," he said. "But Coach Lucy will do a great job."

She cleared her dry throat. "Why don't we thank Ryland for all his help with the team?"

The boys shouted the Defeeters' cheer, but the words lacked the same enthusiasm shown on game day. Their hearts weren't in it.

Lucy didn't blame them. Her heart was having a tough time,

too. She couldn't believe Ryland hadn't told her about leaving before he'd told the boys. He could have called if he hadn't had time. Even sent a text. But then she remembered the all-too-familiar words.

No promises. No guarantees.

Lucy couldn't be angry with him. Disappointed, yes. But Ryland hadn't played her. He hadn't lied. She'd known all along he was leaving. So did the boys and their parents. She just wasn't ready for the reality of it.

But this couldn't be goodbye. Even if he wasn't willing to admit it, they'd had too much fun, gotten to know each other too well for their dating to simply end. Of that, she was certain. They would stay in contact and see each other…somehow.

While Ryland said goodbye to each boy personally, she gathered up the equipment. As they finished, the boys ran off the field toward their parents.

Finally it was Connor's turn. He threw himself against Ryland and held on tight.

Her nephew's distress clogged Lucy's throat with emotion. She hoped this didn't put him back into a funk. He'd been handling his parents' deployment much better recently. Ryland might have been part of their lives for only a short time, but Connor had already gotten attached.

As Ryland spoke to her nephew, Connor wiped his eyes. This was one more difficult goodbye for the nine-year-old. But it wouldn't be a forever kind of goodbye. Ryland wouldn't do that to the kid, to his bud.

Someone touched Lucy's arm.

"Marco is in the car pouting. He told me Ryland is leaving," Suzy said. "I take it you didn't know."

"I knew he would be leaving. I just didn't know when," Lucy admitted.

"Cheryl showed me that article. His leaving won't change anything between you. You'll see each other. Every chance you can get."

Lucy nodded, hoping that was true.

"I'm going to take Marco to the pizza parlor for dinner. I'll take Connor with us," Suzy said. "You need some alone time with Ryland."

Yes, Lucy did. "I'll meet you there."

"If not, you can pick Connor up at my house."

She appreciated Suzy's thoughtfulness. "Thanks so much."

Suzy winked. "Don't do anything I wouldn't do."

Lucy could imagine what Suzy would want to do. If only she were that brave…

All Lucy could think about was how much she would miss Ryland, his company and his kisses. The memories would have to suffice until they saw each other again.

Ryland finished talking with Connor and sent him over to Lucy. She hugged her nephew and explained the plans for the evening.

Connor nodded, but the sadness in his eyes made her think he was simply going through the motions. Still, he hadn't said no. Being with Marco and having pizza, soda and video games might help Connor feel better.

Lucy watched Suzy walk off the field with an arm around Connor.

"He's upset," Ryland said, sounding almost surprised.

"He's had to say goodbye to his parents and now you," Lucy explained. "That's a lot for a nine-year-old boy to deal with."

"He'll rally."

Eventually. "So when are you leaving?"

"Tonight."

The air whooshed from her lungs. "That soon?"

"You knew I'd be leaving."

"Yes, I did." She kept her voice steady. Even though she was trembling inside, getting emotional would be bad. "But I thought I'd find out before everyone else."

She expected an apology or to hear him say this wasn't really goodbye because they would see each other soon.

"I have to go."

No apology. Okay. "You want to go."

A muscle twitched at his jaw. "Yeah, I do. I'm a soccer player. I want to play."

"I was thinking Connor and I could come and watch you play against the Rage when you come to Indianapolis."

"That would be—" Ryland dragged his hand through his hair "—not a good idea."

His words startled her. "Connor wants to see you play. So do I."

"I'm going to be busy."

"Too busy to say hello to us?"

"I need to focus on my career," Ryland said, his voice void of emotion. "I don't want a long-distance relationship or a girlfriend. I thought we were clear—"

"You can't tell me the time we spent together didn't mean anything to you." Hurt, raw and jagged, may have been ripping through her, but anger sounded in her voice. Lucy didn't care. She'd fallen in love with Ryland. She believed with her whole heart that he had feelings for her, too. "Or all those kisses."

"You know I like you," he said.

"Like." A far cry from love.

"Nothing more is possible."

Lucy stared down her nose. "Maybe not for you."

His gaze narrowed. "You said you weren't ready for a relationship or a boyfriend."

"I wasn't, but you showed me how good things could be. You opened me up to the possibility."

"I…" He stared at the grass. "I'm sorry, but I don't think something more between us would work out."

"It would." Her eyes didn't waver even though he wasn't looking at her. "I think you know it, too."

His gaze jerked up.

"You've admitted we're good together," she added.

"Chemistry."

"It's not just physical."

"We were never that physical."

"Sex is the easy part. Everything else is a lot harder."

"If we can't even manage the sex part, then we're not going to be able to handle anything else."

Ryland might like her. He might even care for her. But he

would downplay whatever he felt because it would be too hard for him to deal with. Distancing himself rather than admitting how he felt would be much easier. He liked being a famous footballer. Soccer was safe. What he'd found here in Wicksburg with her wasn't.

Lucy took a deep breath. "You're scared."

"I'm not scared of you," he denied.

"You're scared of yourself and your feelings because there might be something more important in your life than soccer."

"That's crazy."

"No, it's not." Sympathy washed over her. "I've felt the same way myself. Not wanting to take any risks so I wouldn't get hurt."

He shook his head. "Did you take some headers with the boys during practice?"

Lucy wasn't about to be distracted. She pursed her lips. "I know you. Better than you realize. I'm not deluding myself. I'm finally being honest with you. But it's too late."

"I know you're upset. I have time before my flight. I can drive you home."

"No." The force of the word stunned her as much as Ryland. She almost backed down, but realized she couldn't. Dragging this out any longer wouldn't be good for either one of them. It was obvious he was pushing her away. Ryland wasn't ready to step onto the pitch and take the kickoff from her. She'd thought he was different, but he wasn't. Not really.

If he couldn't be honest with himself, how could he ever be honest with her? Bottom line, he couldn't. Even though her heart was splintering into tiny pieces, she needed to let him go.

"It's time we said goodbye." She would make this easy on him. Lucy took a deep breath. "Thank you your help with the team and Connor. You've taught me a lot. More than I expected to learn. Good luck. I hope you have a great career and a very nice life."

His nostrils flared. "That's it?"

That was all he wanted to hear from her. He wasn't about to

say what she needed to hear. That he…cared. And even though she was positive he did, he couldn't say it.

Her heart pounded in her throat. Her lower lip quivered.

Hold it together. She didn't want him to see her break down. "Yeah, that's it."

Time to get out of here. Lucy gripped the equipment bag. She forced her feet to move across the field, but it wasn't easy. Her tennis shoes felt more like cement blocks. Each step took concentration. She wasn't sure she would make it all the way to her car.

Her insides trembled. Her hands shook. She thought nothing could match the heartache and betrayal of her husband and best friend. But the way she felt about Ryland…

I really do love him.

A sob wracked through her. Tears blurred her vision. She gripped the equipment bag until her knuckles turned white and her fingernails dug into her palms.

"Lucy," he called after her.

She forced her feet to keep walking.

Even though Lucy was tempted, she didn't look back. She couldn't. Not with the tears streaming down her face. And not when Ryland wasn't ready to admit the truth.

Saturday evening in Phoenix, Ryland stood next to the wall of floor-to-ceiling windows in his condominium. He rested his arm against the glass and stared at the city lights.

What a day.

He'd gotten an assist as an eighty-fourth minute substitute. He hadn't expected any playing time his first game back, but was happy contributing to the 2–1 win. Mr. McElroy had greeted Ryland with a handshake when he came off the pitch. Coach Fritz had said to expect more playing time during a friendly scheduled for Wednesday and next Saturday's game.

Ryland James was back in a big way. Blake agreed. His teammates, however, were more subdued about Ryland's return. A few handshakes, some glares.

He didn't blame them. He was captain of the team and had

missed the start of the season because he'd goofed off and injured himself. Really bad form. Irresponsible. Like much of his behavior last season and the one before that. At practice, he'd apologized, but it would take time to build that sense of camaraderie. He was okay with that.

On the coffee table behind him, his cell phone beeped and vibrated with each voice message and text that arrived. People, including the bevy of beauties he'd left behind, were more than happy to welcome him home with invitations to join them tonight at various clubs and parties, but he didn't feel like going out and being social. Not when that scene meant nothing to him now.

He kept thinking about Lucy and Connor and the rest of the boys. The Defeeters had played a match today. Ryland wondered how they did. He hoped they'd played well.

A part of him was tempted to call and find out. But appeasing his curiosity might only hurt Lucy more. She'd been angry with him. Hurting her hadn't been his intent, but he'd done it anyway and felt like a jerk.

Ryland missed Lucy, longed to see her, hear her voice, touch her, kiss her. But he needed to leave her alone. He needed to respect her decision to say goodbye the way she had. Respect her.

Aaron had warned her not to see him. Rightfully so. She deserved more than Ryland could give her. Not that he'd offered her anything. But he'd thought she was okay with that. Instead, she'd gotten upset at him. Told him he was scared.

Yeah, right.

All he'd tried to do was be honest with her. That had worked out real well.

Regret poked at Ryland. Maybe he could have done things better. Told her about his leaving differently. Said more… He shook it off.

What was he supposed to do? Give Lucy an engagement ring as Blake had suggested? Pretend he felt more for her than he did? She deserved better than that.

His cell phone rang. The ringtone told him it was his mother. "Hey, Mom. Did you watch the game?"

"No, we lost power."

Her voice sounded shaky. His shoulders tensed. "Is everything okay?"

"A tornado touched down near the elementary school. Your father and I are okay, so is the house, but we don't know the extent of the damage elsewhere," she said, her voice tight. "A tornado watch is still in effect. We're in the basement with Cupcake."

"Stay there. Keep me posted." Concern over Lucy and Connor overshadowed Ryland's relief at his parents being safe. A ball-size knot formed in his gut. "I love you, but I need to make a call right now."

"Lucy?"

"Yes."

"Let us know if she needs anything or a place to stay."

A potent mix of adrenaline and fear pulsed through him. He hit Lucy's cell-phone number on his contact list. Aaron's house was nowhere near the elementary school, but Ryland couldn't stop worrying. The Wicksburg soccer league played homes games at the elementary and middle schools. If the tornado touched down during match time…

There would have been sirens. No one would have been out at that point. Still he paced in front of the windows.

The phone rang.

Tornado warnings were all too common in the Midwest, especially in springtime. More than once he'd found himself in the bathroom of their apartment building in the tub with a mattress over him. But the twisters had always touched down on farmland, never in town.

On the fourth ring, Lucy's voice mail picked up. "I can't talk right now, but leave a message and I'll call you back."

The sound of her sweet voice twisted his insides. His chest hurt so badly he could barely breathe. He should be in Wicksburg, not here in Phoenix.

"Beep."

Ryland opened his mouth to speak, but no words came out. Not that he had a clue what he wanted to say if he could talk. He disconnected from the call.

Maybe she didn't have her cell phone with her. If she were at home…

He called the landline at Aaron's house. The phone rang. Again and again.

Ryland's frustration built so did his fear. He clenched his hand. Why wasn't she answering? Where could she be?

"Hello?" a young voice answered.

He clutched the back of the couch. His fingers dug into the buttery leather. "Connor?"

"Ryland." The relief in the boy's voice reached across the distance and squeezed Ryland's heart like a vise grip. "I knew you wouldn't forget about us."

"Never." The word came from somewhere deep inside him, spoken with a voice he didn't recognize. "My mom called me about the tornado."

"Aunt Lucy and I got inside the closet in the basement with pillows, a couple flashlights and the phone. It's one of those old dial ones." His voice trembled. "I have my DS, too."

"Extra playing time for you," Ryland teased, but his words fell flat. "Can I talk to your aunt?"

"She's looking for Manny."

The fat cat always tried to escape whenever the door opened. But if he'd gotten out today… "Where is he?"

"I don't know. Aunt Lucy moved the car into the garage and thinks he could have slipped out because she was in a hurry," Connor said. "We couldn't find him after the warning sounded. The siren might have scared him."

Sounded like Manny wasn't the only one frightened by the noise. Poor kid. "Your aunt will find him."

The alternative, for both Lucy and Manny, was unacceptable. Ryland glanced at the clock. If he caught a red-eye to Chicago and drove… But he had a team meeting tomorrow. And would Lucy want him to show up uninvited in the morning?

"Aunt Lucy said she would be back soon," Connor said finally. "She waited until the siren stopped to go outside. She didn't want to leave me alone if it wasn't safe."

Lucy would never put her nephew at risk, but Ryland didn't like the thought of her outside in that kind of weather with a tornado watch still in effect.

Silence filled the line.

"You hanging in there, bud?" he asked.

"Yeah," Connor said. "But the flashlight died. It's kind of dark."

Ryland grimaced. "See if your DS gives off some light."

"That helps a little."

Being thousands of miles away sucked. "I wish I were there."

"Me, too. But even if you were, you still wouldn't get to see our last game next Saturday," Connor said.

"Why not?"

"The field was destroyed so the season is over with. No more soccer until fall. If then."

"Because of the tornado?" Ryland asked.

"Yeah. Marco's mom called earlier," Connor explained. "My school is gone. The fields. The middle school. Some of the houses around there, too."

Gone. Stunned, Ryland tried to picture it. He couldn't. "Are Marco and his family, okay?"

"Yeah, but a tree landed on their car. Marco's dad is mad."

"Cars can be replaced." People couldn't.

Lucy.

Ryland wanted her in the basement with Connor, not out looking for Manny.

Damn. He hated not being able to do anything to help. Not that Lucy would want *his* help. Still... He gripped the phone.

Images of his weeks in Wicksburg flashed through his mind like a slideshow. Lucy handing him a container of cookies, teaching her how to do the warm-up routine and drills, watching her coach during the first match, drinking slushies with the team after games, kissing her.

You said you weren't ready for a relationship or a boyfriend.

I wasn't, but you showed me how good things could be.

Things had been good. Great. If he could go back and do over his last day in Wicksburg…

But soccer had been the only thing on his mind. That and getting the hell out of town, running away as his mom had accused him of doing before.

A lump formed in his throat and burned like a flame.

"It's probably a good thing we can't play the last game." Connor's voice forced Ryland to focus on the present. "We got beat six–nothing today. Aunt Lucy said we were going through the motions and our hearts weren't in the game."

That was how Ryland had spent the last two years. He'd gotten tired of having to prove himself over and over again. He'd lost his hunger, his drive and his edge. He'd acted out without realizing it or the reasons behind his actions—anger, unhappiness and pressure. But he hadn't figured out how self-destructive his behavior had become until he'd returned to Wicksburg. Lucy and the boys had been his inspiration and let him rediscover the joy of the game. He'd connected with them in a way he hadn't since leaving town as a teenager.

And Lucy…

She showed him it wasn't about proving things to others, but to himself.

"The Strikers would have killed us anyway," Connor continued talking about the game that wouldn't be. He sounded more like himself, less scared. "Ten–nothing or worse."

Ryland may have gotten his soccer career back on track here, but he still had things to take care of in Wicksburg. He wasn't about to drop the ball again. "No way. The entire team has improved since that first match. The Strikers won by three goals. You need to play that game if only to prove you can challenge them."

"There's no field to play on."

"Come on." Ryland couldn't let those boys down after all they'd given him. He pictured each of their faces. In a short time, he'd learned their strengths and discovered their weaknesses. Secrets were hard to keep when you were nine and ten. He'd watched their skills improve, but also saw other changes like limbs lengthening and faces thinning. "That's not the Defeeter attitude."

"It was a big tornado."

And a big loss with the game today. Ryland took responsibility for that. The way he'd left, as if he could ride into town and then just leave again without anyone noticing or being affected was selfish and stupid. "No worries, bud. I'll figure something out."

"Really?"

"Really." Ryland didn't hesitate. He would find the team a place to play next Saturday. "Is your aunt back?"

"No, but I don't know how to use call-waiting. I should get off the phone in case she needs to talk to me."

"Smart thinking. Tell your aunt to call me when she finds Manny." Ryland checked the time again. "I'll let you know where you're going to play against the Strikers."

"I wish you could be there if we get to play."

"So do I." A weight pressed down on Ryland. "There's no place I'd rather be than with you and the team and your aunt Lucy."

But it wasn't possible. Ryland had an away match next Saturday. He was supposed to get playing time. But he needed to be in Wicksburg with Lucy and the boys.

Just remember, actions speak louder than words.

Blake's words echoed through Ryland's mind. He straightened. He'd been so blind. What he wanted—needed—was right there in front of him. Not here in Phoenix, but in Wicksburg. He just hadn't wanted to see it.

But now…

Time to stop talking about what he wanted and make it happen.

For the boys.

And most importantly, with Lucy.

CHAPTER THIRTEEN

LUCY's arms, scratched and sore after digging through tree limbs and debris to reach a howling Manny, struggled to carry the squirming, wet cat with a flashlight in her hand down to the basement. The warning siren remained silent, but they would sleep downstairs to be on the safe side. "You need to go on a diet, cat."

"Aunt Lucy?" Connor called from the closet. "Did you find Manny?"

"I found him." She opened the door, happy to see her nephew safe, dry and warm. "Why is it so dark in there?"

"The flashlight stopped working."

Yet Connor had stayed as she asked, even in the pitch-black when he had to be scared. Her heart swelled with pride and love for her nephew. Aaron and Dana were raising a great kid. "Sorry about that. The batteries must have been low."

"It's okay." He held up his glowing DS console. "I had a little light."

Manny pawed trying to get away from her. The cat looked like a drowned rat with his wet fur plastered against his body. "I think someone wants to see you."

Connor reached for the cat. "Where was he?"

"In the bushes across the street. I have a feeling he's had quite an adventure." Enough to last eight lives given the winds and flying debris the cat must have experienced. "I doubt he'll be so quick to dash outside again."

Connor cuddled Manny, who settled against her nephew's

chest as if that were his rightful and only place of rest. At least until a better spot came along. "Oh, Ryland called."

Lucy's heart jolted. She hadn't expected to hear from him again. "When?"

"A little while ago." Connor rubbed his chin against the cat. Manny purred like a V-8 engine. "He wants you to call him back. He was worried about you finding Manny."

Lucy whipped out her cell phone. Service had been spotty due to the storm, but three bars appeared. She went to press Ryland's number.

Wait. Her finger hovered over the screen. Calling him back would be stupid. Okay, it was nice he was concerned enough to call and want to know about Manny. But this went beyond what was happening in Wicksburg today.

Lucy had been thinking about him constantly since he left town. She missed him terribly. She needed to get him off her mind and out of her heart. But she wouldn't ignore his request completely. That would be rude.

Lucy typed in a text message and hit Send. Now she could go back to trying to forget about him.

Early Monday morning, Ryland stood in the reception area of the Phoenix Fuego headquarters. He'd spent much of yesterday trying to figure how to help those affected by the tornado in Wicksburg. Money was easy to donate. But he wanted to do something for the team and Lucy.

Waiting, he reread the text she'd sent him.

Manny wet & hungry but fine.

Ryland had wanted to hear her voice to know she was okay. He'd received a six-word text, instead. Probably more than he deserved.

The attractive, young personal assistant, who was always cheering on the team during games, motioned to the door to her right. "Mr. McElroy will see you now."

"Thanks." Ryland entered the owner's office. The plush furnishings didn't surprise him. All the photos of children everywhere did. "I appreciate you seeing me on such short notice."

Mr. McElroy shook his hand. "You said it was important."

"Yes."

He pointed to a leather chair. "Have a seat."

Ryland sat. "A tornado rolled through my hometown on Saturday night."

"I heard about that on the news. No casualties."

"No, but homes, two schools and several soccer fields in town were destroyed," Ryland said. "The Defeeters, a U-9 Boys rec. team I worked with while I was home, has their final game of the season this Saturday, but nowhere to play. I want to find them, and all the teams affected by the tornado, fields so they can finish out their spring season. I'd also like to be on the sideline with the Defeeters when they play."

Mr. McElroy studied him. "This sounds important to you."

"Yes," Ryland said. "I'm who I am today because of the start I got in that soccer league. I owe them and the Defeeters."

Not to mention Lucy. He wanted a second chance with her. A do over like young players sometimes received from refs when they made a bad throw-in or didn't quite get the ball over the line during kickoffs.

"That's thoughtful, but haven't you forgotten about the match against the Rage on Saturday night?"

Mr. McElroy's words echoed Blake's, but Ryland continued undeterred. "The Rage plays in Indianapolis. The stadium is a couple hours from Wicksburg. I know a way I can be at both games, but I'm going to need some help to pull it off. Your help, Mr. McElroy, and the owner of the Rage."

A tense silence enveloped the office. Ryland sat patiently waiting for the opportunity to say more.

"You've been nothing but a thorn in my side since I bought this team." Mr. McElroy leaned forward and rested his elbows on the desk. "Why should I help you?"

"Because it's the right thing to do."

"Right for the kids affected by the tornado?"

"And for us. Those kids are the future of soccer, both players and fans." Ryland spoke from his heart. The way Lucy would have wanted him to. "I know you don't want me on the team. I wasn't okay with that before. I am now. I don't care what team I'm on as long as I can play. But until the transfer window opens so you can loan me out across the pond, you need me as much as I need you."

Mr. McElroy's eyes widened. No doubt the truth had surprised him. "What kind of help are you talking about?"

Ryland explained his plan. "This is not only good for the players and the local soccer league, but it's also a smart PR move for the Fuego and Rage."

"Not smart. Brilliant. You can't buy that kind of publicity." Mr. McElroy studied him. "You're not the same player who left the club in March. What happened while you were away?"

"That U-9 team of boys taught me a few things about soccer I'd forgotten, and I met a girl who made me realize I'm more than just a footballer."

Smiling, Mr. McElroy leaned back in his chair. "You have my full support. I'll call the owner of the Rage this morning. Tell my assistant what you need to pull this off."

Satisfaction and relief loosened the knot in Ryland's gut. He stood. "Thank you, sir."

"I hope it all works out the way you planned," Mr. McElroy said.

"So do I."

Ryland had no doubt the soccer part would work, but he wasn't as confident about his plans for Lucy. He couldn't imagine his life without her.

She'd been right. Ryland had been scared. He still was. He just hoped it wasn't too late.

On Saturday, Lucy entered the training facility of the Indianapolis Rage. The MLS team had offered the use of their outdoor field for the final game of the Defeeters' spring soccer season against the Strikers.

Parents and players from both teams looked around in awe.

The training field resembled a ministadium complete with lights, two benches and bleachers.

Lucy couldn't believe they were here.

When the soccer league president had offered the Defeeters an all-expenses-paid trip to Indianapolis to play their final game of the season, she thought Ryland was behind it because Fuego was playing the Rage that same day. But then she learned all youth soccer teams without fields to finish the spring season had been invited.

She hadn't known whether to feel relieved or disappointed.

Pathetic. No matter how hard she tried to push Ryland out of her mind and heart, he was still there. She wondered how long he would remain there—days, weeks, months…

Stop thinking about him.

Connor ran onto the field, his feet encased in bright yellow soccer shoes. The other kids followed, jumping and laughing, as if the damage back home was nothing more than a bad dream.

"This is just what we all needed after the tornado." Suzy took a picture of the boys standing on the center mark of the field. "A weekend getaway and a chance to end the soccer season in style."

"The hotel is so nice." Cheryl's house had been damaged by the tornado. They were staying with Dalton's father, who had traveled with them for today's game. Maybe something good would come from all of this and they could work out their differences before the separation led to a divorce. "I can't wait for tonight. I've never been to a professional soccer game before."

Tickets to the Rage vs. Fuego match had been provided to each family. Much to the delight of the boys, who couldn't wait to see Ryland play. Connor was beside himself with excitement, positive his favorite player would be in the game for the entire ninety minutes.

Lucy hoped not. Watching Ryland play for only few minutes would be difficult let alone the entire match. Hearing his name mentioned hurt. Connor talked constantly about Ryland. That made it hard to forget him.

Thing would get better. Eventually. She'd been in this same

place before with Jeff. Except with Ryland the hurt cut deeper. Her marriage had never been a true partnership, but she'd felt that way with Ryland, in spite of the short time they'd been together.

She shook off the thought. The match will be a nice way to cap off the day.

The boys screamed, the noise deafening. Only one thing—one person—could elicit that kind of response.

Her throat tightened.

Ryland was here.

Emotions churned inside her.

"That man gets hotter each time I see him." Cheryl whistled. "But who are all his buddies?"

"Yowza," Suzy said. "If it gets any hotter in here, I think I'm going to need to fan myself."

"Am I a bad mom if I'm jealous of a bunch of eight- and nine-year-olds?" Debbie asked.

"I hope not, because I feel the same way," Cheryl replied.

Lucy kept her back turned so she wouldn't be tempted to look at Ryland. But the women had piqued her curiosity. "What are you talking about?"

"Turn around." Cheryl winked. "Trust me, you won't be disappointed."

Reluctantly, Lucy turned. She stared in disbelief. Nearly a dozen professional soccer players with killer bodies and smiling faces worked with the Defeeters and the Strikers, helping the boys warm-up and giving them pointers.

One Fuego player, however, stood out from all the others.

Ryland.

His dark hair was neatly combed, his face clean shaven. He looked handsome in his Fuego uniform—blue, orange and white with red flames. But it was the man, not the athlete, who had stolen her heart. A weight pressed down on her chest, squeezing out what air remained in her lungs.

Suzy sent her a sympathetic smile. "This is a dream come true for the boys."

Cheryl nodded. "I think I've died and gone to heaven myself."

Lucy had gone straight to hell. Hurt splintered her already-aching heart. She struggled to breathe. She didn't even attempt to speak.

Everyone around her smiled and laughed. She wanted to cry. If only he could see how good the two of them would be together…

"Look at all the photographers and news crews," Suzy said.

Cheryl combed through her hair and pinched her cheeks. "No wonder the league had us sign those photo releases."

The media descended on the field, but their presence didn't distract the professional players from the kids. The boys, however, mugged for the cameras.

As the warm-up period drew to an end, the referee called over the Strikers. That was Lucy's cue to get ready. She had player cards to show the ref and her clipboard with the starting lineup and substitution schedule so each boy would play an equal amount of time.

"We're taping the game." Debbie motioned to the bleachers where her husband adjusted a tripod. "For Aaron and Dana."

"Thanks," Lucy said.

The referee called the Defeeters over.

Nerves threatened to get the best of Lucy. But in spite of all the hoopla and media, this was still a rec. soccer game. She had no reason to interact with Ryland and wouldn't.

With her resolve in place, Lucy lined up the boys for the ref. Ryland stood near the Defeeters' bench.

Her heart rate careened out of control.

Oh, no. He was planning to be there during the match.

The ref excused the Defeeters. As she walked to the bench, she looked everywhere, but at Ryland. Maybe if she didn't catch his eye or say—

"It's good to see you, Lucy," he said.

Darn. She cleared her dry throat. "The boys are so happy you're here."

"This is the only place I want to be."

The referee blew his whistle, saving her from having to speak with him.

The game was fast-paced with lots of action and scoring. At halftime with the score Defeeters two and Strikers three, Ryland talked to the boys about the game. With two minutes remaining in regulation time, Connor stole the ball from a defender and broke away up the left sideline. He crossed the ball in front of the goal. Dalton kicked the ball into the corner of the net.

Tie score!

The parents screamed. The boys gave each other high fives.

The Strikers pulled their goalie. A risky move, but they wanted an extra player in the game. The offense hit hard after the kickoff, took a shot on goal, but missed.

Defeeters' turn. Marco took the ball. His pass to Dalton was stolen. The Strikers' forward headed down the field, but Connor sprinted to steal the ball. He kicked the ball down the line to Dalton, who passed it to Marco. The goal was right in front of him. All he had to do was shoot at the empty goal.

"Shoot," Ryland yelled. So did everyone else.

The referee blew his whistle. The game was over.

The Defeeters had tied the Strikers.

"Great job, coach," Ryland said to her. "You've come a long way.

But she had so much further to go, especially when it came to getting over him. She didn't smile or look at him. "Thanks."

"You boys played a great game," Ryland said to the excited boys gathered around him. "The best all season."

Lucy knew they would rather hear from him than her. She didn't mind that one bit.

Connor beamed. "You said we could challenge them. We did."

Ryland messed up the kid's hair. "You did more than that, bud."

The two teams lined up with the coaches at the end, followed by the professional players, and shook hands. Ryland and the other players passed out T-shirts to both teams, posed for pictures and signed autographs. Talk about a dream come true. And there was still the match to attend tonight.

She gathered up the balls and equipment. "Come on, Connor. We can go back to the hotel for a swim before the game."

Connor looked at Ryland then back at her.

Lucy's heart lodged in her throat. She knew that conspiratorial look of his.

"I'm riding back to the hotel with Marco and his family," Connor said.

"I told the boys we could stop for an after-game treat on the way back to the hotel," Suzy said.

"Slushies, slushies," the boys chanted.

Those had become the new Defeeter tradition. Thanks to Ryland. But he wasn't offering to take the team out today.

Lucy remembered. He had to prepare for the match against the Rage tonight.

She thought about offering to drive the boys herself, but from the look on Connor's face, he had his heart set on going with Marco. She couldn't ruin this magical day for him on the off chance Ryland might try to talk to her.

Time to act like an adult rather than a brokenhearted teenager. She raised her chin. "Sounds like fun. I'll meet you back at the hotel."

As the boys headed out, she followed them, eager to escape before Ryland—

"Lucy."

She kept walking, eyeing the exit.

"Please wait," Ryland said.

She stopped. Not because she wanted to talk to him, but because he'd helped her with the team. Five minutes. That was all the time he could have.

Ryland caught up to her. "You've been working hard with the boys."

"It's them, not me." She glanced back at the field. "I don't know what your part in making this happen was, but thank you. It meant a lot to the boys on both teams." She tried to sound nonchalant, but wasn't sure she was succeeding.

"I didn't do this only for them."

Her pulse accelerated.

"I'm sorry." His words came out in a rush. "The way I left was selfish. I was only thinking about myself. Not the boys. Definitely not you. I never meant to hurt anyone, but I did. I hope you can forgive me."

The sincerity in his eyes and voice tugged at her heart. She had to keep her heart immune. She had to get away from him. "You're forgiven."

His relief was palpable. "Thank you. You don't know what that means to me."

She didn't want to know. Just being this close to him was enough to make her want to bolt. The scent of him surrounded her. She wanted to bottle some up to take home with her. *Not a good idea.* "I need to get back to the hotel. Connor…"

Ryland took a step closer to her. "He's stopping for a snack on the way back."

Lucy stepped back. "I still should—"

"Stay."

The one word was a plea and a promise, full of anxiety and anticipation. She tried not to let that matter, but it wasn't easy. "Why?"

"There's more I want to say to you."

She glanced around the stadium. Everyone seemed to have left. "Make it quick."

He took a deep breath. "Soccer has been the only thing in my life for so long. I defined myself as a footballer. Playing made me feel worthy. But I lost the love for the game. The past couple of years, I made some bad decisions. I had no idea why I was acting out so badly until I got to Wicksburg. I realized how unhappy I'd been trying to keep proving myself with a new league, team and fans. Nothing satisfied me anymore. Working with the boys helped me discover what was missing. Soccer isn't only about scoring goals. I'd forgotten the value of teamwork. You made me realize I don't want soccer to be the only thing in my life. I want—I need—more than that. I need you, Lucy."

The wind whooshed from her lungs. She couldn't believe what he was saying.

"I know how important honesty is to you," he continued. "When I got to Phoenix, I realized you were right. I was scared. A coward. I wasn't being honest about my feelings. Not to you or myself. You mean so much to me. I'm finally able to admit it."

"I'm…touched. Really. But even if you're serious—"

"I am serious, Lucy." He took her hand in his. "More serious than I've ever been in my entire life. I was trapped by the expectations of others, the pressure, but you set me free. I'm more than just a soccer player. I don't want to lose you."

They way he looked at her, his gaze caressing her skin like a touch, brought tears to her eyes. She blinked them away. She couldn't lose sight of the truth.

Lucy took a deep breath. "We live in different worlds, different states. It would never work."

"I want to make it work."

"You know what happened with Jeff."

He nodded.

"Look at you," she said. "You're hot, wealthy, a superstar. Women want you. They fantasize about you. That's hard for me to handle."

"I know you've had some tough times in your life. We can't wash away everything that's happened before, but we can't dwell on it, either," he said. "Trust doesn't just happen. I can tell you all the right words you want to hear. That I'm not like Jeff. That I won't cheat. But what it really takes is a leap of faith. Are you willing to take that leap with me?"

Her heart screamed the answer it wanted her to say. Could she leap when her heart had been broken after spending only a few weeks with him? How could she not when Ryland was everything she'd dreamed about?

"When I was sick, people lied to me. The doctors, my parents, even Aaron. Maybe not outright lies, but untruths about the treatments, how I would feel and what I could do. I hated having to rely on people who couldn't be honest with me."

"So that's where your independent streak came from."

She nodded. "And then Jeff came along. He was honest with me, sometimes brutally so, but I liked that better than the alternative. I fell hard and fast only to find out he was nothing more than a lying, cheating jerk." She took a deep breath so she could keep going. "You've taught me so much and not only about soccer. Because of you I've learned I can accept help without feeling like a burden to someone. I've also learned I can forgive and trust again. I would love to take that leap with you. But I'm not sure I'm ready yet."

"I don't care how long it takes," he said. "I'll wait until you're ready."

"You're serious."

"Very." He kissed each of her fingers, sending pleasurable shivers up her arm. "I love you."

The air rushed from her lungs. She tried to speak, to question him, but couldn't.

Sincerity shone in his eyes. "I tried to pretend I didn't love you, but I'm no good at pretending when it comes to you."

Joy exploded inside her. She could tell they weren't just words. He meant them. Maybe taking the leap wouldn't be so hard. "I love you, too."

"That's the first step to taking the leap."

"Maybe the first two steps." Lucy kissed Ryland, a kiss full of hope and love and possibility. None of her dreams had come true so far, but maybe some…could.

Ryland pulled her against him. She went willingly, wrapping her arms around him. Her hand hit something tucked into the waistband of his shorts. It fell to the ground. She backed away.

A small blue box tied with a white ribbon lay on its side. She recognized the packaging from ads and the movies. The box was from Tiffany & Co.

Her mouth gaped. She closed it. He really was serious.

His cheeks reddened. "If I told you that's where I keep my lucky penny, I'm guessing you won't believe me."

Shock rendered her speechless.

"It's nothing." He took a breath. "Okay, I'll be honest. It's something, but it can wait. You're not ready right now."

She placed her hand on his. "Maybe I'm more ready than I realized."

As he handed her the box, hope filled his eyes. "This is for you. Today. A year from now. Whenever you're ready."

Lucy untied the ribbon and removed the top of the box. Inside was a midnight blue, almost black, suede ring box. Her hand trembled so much she couldn't get the smaller box out. She looked up at him.

"Allow me." Ryland pulled out the ring box and opened it. A Tiffany-cut diamond engagement ring sparkled against the dark navy fabric. The words Tiffany & Co. were embossed in gold foil on the lid. "Nothing matters except being with you. I love you. I want to marry you, Lucy, if you'll have me."

She couldn't believe this was happening. She forced herself to breathe. All her girlhood fantasies didn't compare to the reality of this moment. Ryland James had asked her to marry him. He'd been honest to himself and to her. He was fully committed to making it work. Lucy's heart and her mind agreed on the answer. Make the leap? She had no doubt at all. "Yes."

He placed the ring on her finger. A perfect fit, the way they were a perfect fit together. "There's no rush."

"No, there isn't." The love shining in his eyes matched her own. "Aaron and Dana won't be home until next year."

"It might take me that long to convince your brother I'm good enough for you."

"Probably," Lucy teased. "But with Connor in your corner, it might take only six months."

"Very funny."

She stared at the ring. A feeling of peace coursed through her. "So this officially makes me a WAG."

Ryland brushed his lips across hers. "A *G* who will eventually become a *W*. But you're already an *M*."

"An *M?*" Lucy asked.

"Mine."

"I'll always be your *M*. As long as you're mine, too."

"Always," he said. "I think I may have always been yours without even realizing it."

"If you're trying to score…"

"No need. I already won." Ryland pulled her against him and kissed her again. "I love you, Lucy."

A warm glow flowed through her, making her heart sigh. "I love you."

* * * * *

MILLS & BOON®

Why shop at millsandboon.co.uk?

Each year, thousands of romance readers find their perfect read at millsandboon.co.uk. That's because we're passionate about bringing you the very best romantic fiction. Here are some of the advantages of shopping at www.millsandboon.co.uk:

* **Get new books first**—you'll be able to buy your favourite books one month before they hit the shops
* **Get exclusive discounts**—you'll also be able to buy our specially created monthly collections, with up to 50% off the RRP
* **Find your favourite authors**—latest news, interviews and new releases for all your favourite authors and series on our website, plus ideas for what to try next
* **Join in**—once you've bought your favourite books, don't forget to register with us to rate, review and join in the discussions

Visit **www.millsandboon.co.uk**
for all this and more today!

MILLS_WEB

MILLS & BOON®

Why not subscribe?

Never miss a title and save money too!

Here's what's available to you if you join the exclusive **Mills & Boon® Book Club** today:

- *Titles up to a month ahead of the shops*
- *Amazing discounts*
- *Free P&P*
- *Earn Bonus Book points that can be redeemed against other titles and gifts*
- *Choose from monthly or pre-paid plans*

Still want more?

Well, if you join today, we'll even give you ***50% OFF your first parcel!***

So visit **www.millsandboon.co.uk/subs** to be a part of this exclusive Book Club!

SUBS_2015

MILLS & BOON®

Helen Bianchin v Regency Collection!

40% off both collections!

Discover our Helen Bianchin v Regency Collection, a blend of sexy and regal romances. Don't miss this great offer - buy one collection to get a free book but buy both collections to receive 40% off! This fabulous 10 book collection features stories from some of our talented writers.

Visit **www.millsandboon.co.uk** to order yours!

0316_MB520

MILLS & BOON®
By Request

RELIVE THE ROMANCE WITH THE BEST OF THE BEST

A sneak peek at next month's titles...

In stores from 7th April 2016:

- **His Most Exquisite Conquest** – Elizabeth Power, Cathy Williams & Robyn Donald
- **Stop The Wedding!** – Lori Wilde

In stores from 21st April 2016:

- **Bedded by the Boss** – Jennifer Lewis, Yvonne Lindsay & Joan Hohl
- **Love Story Next Door!** – Rebecca Winters, Barbara Wallace & Soraya Lane

Available at WHSmith, Tesco, Asda, Eason, Amazon and Apple

Just can't wait?
Buy our books online a month before they hit the shops!
visit www.millsandboon.co.uk

These books are also available in eBook format!

0416/05